Rarity

from the

Hollow

by

Robert Eggleton

Rarity *from the* Hollow

Third edition published by
Robert Eggleton

Previous editions published by
Dog Horn Publishing
doghornpublishing.com

Typesetting & cover design by
Adam Lowe

Design work and assets generously donated by
Dog Horn Publishing
in support of children's welfare.

ISBN 978-1-387-80439-9

Cozy in Cardboard

Inside her first clubhouse, Lacy Dawn glanced over fifth grade spelling words for tomorrow's quiz at school. She already knew all the words in the textbook and most others in any human language.

Nothing's more important than an education.

The clubhouse was a cardboard box in the front yard that her grandmother's new refrigerator had occupied until an hour before. Her father brought it home for her to play in.

The nicest thing he's ever done.

Faith lay beside her with a hand over the words and split fingers to cheat as they were called off. She lived in the next house up the hollow. Every other Wednesday for the last two months, the supervised child psychologist came to their school, pulled her out of class, and evaluated suspected learning disabilities. Lacy Dawn underlined a word with a fingernail.

All she needs is a little motivation.

Before they had crawled in, Lacy Dawn tapped the upper corner of the box with a flashlight and proclaimed, "The place of all things possible—especially you passing the fifth grade so we'll be together in the sixth."

Please concentrate, Faith. Try this one.

"Armadillo."

"A, R, M ... A ... D, I, L...d...O," Faith demonstrated her intellect.

"That's weak. This is a bonus word so you'll get extra points. Come on."

Lacy Dawn nodded and looked for a new word.

I'll trick her by going out of order—a word she can't turn into another punch line.

"Don't talk about it and the image will go away. Let's get back to studying," Lacy Dawn said.

My mommy don't like sex. It's just her job and she told me so.

Faith turned her open spelling book over and rolled onto her side. Lacy Dawn did the same and snuggled her back against the paper wall. Face to face—a foot of smoothness between—they took a break. The outside was outside.

At their parents' insistence each wore play clothing—unisex hand-me-downs that didn't fit as well as school clothing. They'd been careful not to get muddy before crawling into the box. They'd not played in the creek and both were cleaner than on the usual evening. The clubhouse floor remained an open invitation to anybody who had the opportunity to consider relief from daily stressors.

"How'd you get so smart, Lacy Dawn? Your parents are dumb asses just like mine."

"You ain't no dumb ass and you're going to pass the fifth grade."

"Big deal I'm still fat and ugly," Faith said.

"I'm doing the best I can. I figure by the time I turn eleven I can fix that too. For now, just concentrate on passing and don't become special education. I need you. You're my best friend."

"Ain't no other girls our age close in the hollow. That's the only reason you like me. Watch out. There's a pincher bug crawling in."

Lacy sat almost upright because there was not quite enough headroom in the refrigerator box. She scooted the bug out the opening. The clubhouse door faced downhill—the best choice since nothing natural was flat in the hollow. If it had sloped uphill, too much blood in the brain would have been detrimental to studying spelling or any other higher calling like changing Faith's future. Faith watched the bug attempt re-entry, picked it up, and threw it a yard away into the grass. It didn't get hurt. Lacy smiled her approval. The new clubhouse was a sacred place where nothing was supposed to hurt.

"Daddy said I can use the tarp whenever he finishes the overhaul on the car in the driveway. That way, our clubhouse will last a long time," Lacy Dawn said.

"Chewy, chewy tootsie roll. Everything in the hollow rots, especially the people. You know that."

"We ain't rotten," Lacy gestured with open palms. "There are a lot of good things here—like all the beautiful flowers. Just focus on your spelling and I'll fix everything else. This time I want a 100% and a good letter to your mommy."

"She won't read it," Faith said.

4

"Yes she will. She loves you and it'll make her feel good. Besides, she has to or the teacher will call Welfare. Your daddy would be investigated—unless you do decide to become special education. That's how parents get out of it. The kid lets them off the hook by deciding to become a SPED. Then there ain't nothing Welfare can do about it because the kid is the problem and not the parents."

"I ain't got no problems," Faith said.

"Then pass this spelling test."

"I thought if I messed up long enough, eventually somebody would help me out. I just need a place to live where people don't argue all the time. That ain't much."

"Maybe you are a SPED. There's always an argument in a family. Pass the test you retard." Lacy opened her spelling book.

Faith flipped her book over too, rolled onto her stomach and looked at the spelling words. Lacy Dawn handed her the flashlight because it was getting dark and grinned when Faith's lips started moving as she memorized. Faith noticed and clamped her lips shut between thumb and index finger.

This is boring. I learned all these words last year.

"Don't use up the batteries or Daddy will know I took it," Lacy Dawn said.

"Alright—I'll pass the quiz, but just 'cause you told me to. This is a gamble and you'd better come through if it backfires. Ain't nothing wrong with being a SPED. The work is easier and the teacher lets you do puzzles."

"You're my best friend," Lacy said and closed the book.

They rolled back on their sides to enjoy the smoothness. The cricket chorus echoed throughout the hollow and the frogs peeped. An ant attempted entry but changed its direction before either rescued it. Unnoticed, Lacy Dawn's father threw the tarp over the box and slid in the trouble light. It was still on and hot. The bulb burned Lacy Dawn's calf. *He didn't mean to hurt me— the second nicest thing he's ever done.*

"Test?" Lacy announced with the better light, and called off, "Poverty."

"I love you," Faith responded.

"Me too, but spell the word."

"P is for poor. O is for oranges from the Salvation Army Christmas basket. V is for varicose veins that Mommy has from getting pregnant every year. E is for everybody messes up sometimes—sorry. R is for I'm always right about everything except when you tell me I'm wrong—like now. T is for it's too late for me to pass no matter what we do and Y is for you know it too."

"Faith, it's almost dark! Go home before your mommy worries," Lacy Dawn's mother yelled from the front porch and stepped back into the house to finish supper. The engine of the VW in the driveway cranked but wouldn't start. It turned slower as its battery died, too.

Faith slid out of the box with her spelling book in-hand. She farted from the effort. A clean breeze away, she squished a mosquito that had landed on her elbow and watched Lacy Dawn hold her breath as she scooted out of the clubhouse, pinching her nose with fingers of one hand, holding the trouble light with the other, and pushing her spelling book forward with her knees. The moon was almost full. There would be plenty of light to watch Faith walk up the gravel road. Outside the clubhouse, they stood face to face and ready to hug. It lasted a lightning bug statement until adult intrusion.

"Give it back. This thing won't start." Lacy Dawn's father grabbed the trouble light out of her hand and walked away.

"All we ever have is beans for supper. Sorry about the fart."

"Don't complain. Complaining is like sitting in a rocking chair. You can get lots of motion but you ain't going anywhere," Lacy Dawn said.

"Why didn't you tell me that last year?" Faith asked. "I've wasted a lot of time."

"I just now figured it out. Sorry."

"Some savior you are. I put my whole life in your hands. I'll pass tomorrow's spelling quiz and everything. But you, my best friend who's supposed to fix the world just now tell me that complaining won't work and will probably get me switched."

"You're complaining again."

"Oh yeah," Faith said.

"Before you go home, I need to tell you something."

6

To avoid Lacy's father working in the driveway, Faith slid down the bank to the dirt road. Her butt became too muddy to re-enter the clubhouse regardless of need. Lacy Dawn stayed in the yard, pulled the tarp taut over the cardboard, and waited for Faith to respond.

"I don't need no more encouragement. I'll pass the spelling quiz tomorrow just for you, but I may miss armadillo for fun. Our teacher deserves it," Faith said.

"That joke's too childish. She won't laugh. Make 100%. That's what I want."

"Okay. See you tomorrow." Faith took a step up the road.

"Wait. I want to tell you something. I've got another best friend. That's how I got so smart. He teaches me stuff."

"A boy? You've got a boyfriend?"

"Not exactly," Lacy Dawn put a finger over her lips to silence Faith. Her father was hooking up a battery charger. She slid down the bank, too.

He probably couldn't hear us, but why take the chance.

A minute later, hand in hand, they walked the road toward Faith's house.

"Did you let him see your panties?" Faith asked.

"No. I ain't got no good pair. Besides, he don't like me that way. He's like a friend who's a teacher, not a boyfriend. I just wanted you to know that I get extra help learning stuff."

"Where's he live?"

Lacy pointed to the sky with her free hand.

"Jesus is everybody's friend," Faith said.

"It ain't Jesus, you moron," Lacy Dawn turned around to walk home. "His name's DotCom and...." Her mother watched from the middle of the road until both children were safe.

Recess

Faith got 100% on her spelling quiz the next day, plus the entire bonus points possible. But, she had added a footnote for the word armadillo: "...also spelled armadildo and available at...."

After she graded the tests, the teacher dialed the phone in the classroom that everyone had been told was for emergency use only and held the receiver away from her ear. The classroom was a former teacher's lounge on the second story of the school building and the only one with a telephone. It had been converted after subsequent floods had caused mold to grow in several classrooms on the first floor. The recorded message of the Department of Health and Human Resources was heard by the first six rows back. She hung up on the answering machine before a human picked up. Therefore, no other official found out that a ten-year-old was suspected of knowing where to buy a sex toy. The teacher left the classroom. After returning, she got her purse out of the second desk drawer down on the left and put a folded piece of paper inside. Lacy Dawn frowned at Faith. *That was a copy of your spelling quiz.*

The teacher got up, walked between rows in her classroom, and announced student scores as she passed out the graded quizzes. When she got to Faith, she patted her on the back and yelled, "A+." "Thank you," she whispered. The other kids clapped because it was the first time that Faith had ever passed anything. Recess was next.

"Don't lean on the fence or you'll get rust stains on your school clothes," Faith said to Lacy Dawn.

"I'm so proud of you. A hundred percent just like you told me you'd get."

"Then why do I feel so pissed off? When I did bad, at least I had somebody else to blame. Now I ain't got nobody to hurt because all the kids clapped. It sucks."

"You're complaining again," Lacy said.

Designated to be consolidated, the school received little maintenance except to reduce liability. The playground had a chain link fence with vines growing through the diagonals, squeaky swings so loud that everyone on recess had to holler, and two teeter-totters with splinters that targeted fresh butt. Only one improvement had been added during the last three years of consolidation controversy. Pieces of shredded car tires were put under the monkey bars to cushion falls.

During recess, the teachers smoked cigarettes behind the corner of the brick school building. It was a designated smoking spot so that students wouldn't be exposed to bad influence. Consequently, the playground was without adult supervision.

"Why do you want to feel angry so often?" Lacy Dawn asked Faith.

"Why not?"

"It messes up your digestion and gives you the farts."

"I like to fart—silent and deadly."

"I've noticed," Lacy Dawn moved toward the gang hanging out under the monkey bars. They were older kids who lived on the hard road and who had parents that had been employed before the coal mine shut down. They still thought they had money.

"My dad got a call about a job in Cleveland. What do you think, Lacy Dawn? Your mommy was born there. Is it cool? Will I meet Eminem?" the tallest kid asked.

"Does your daddy still hit your mommy when he gets drunk?" Lacy Dawn asked.

"Sometimes, but what's that got to do with Cleveland?"

"Everything."

The tall kid grabbed the monkey bars and went to its end. His tip-toes touched the shredded tires. It was easier because the ground was several inches higher than before the shreds had been laid. Nobody acknowledged the achievement and all awaited his response.

"When we get to Cleveland, I'll stand up to him. I promise."

"You'd better or she'll know," Faith pointed at Lacy Dawn.

"I know," the tall kid sat on the rung that had broken off his front tooth two grades before.

"Why'd you tell him that?" Lacy whispered in Faith's ear. "I ain't got that kind of magic yet and you know it. I can only see inside people when they're right in front of me. Cleveland's a long way off and, besides, Eminem's from Detroit."

9

Faith shrugged.

"My mom and dad don't ever hit me. Sometimes, I wish they would. I do stuff so they will, but it don't ever work," the next tallest kid in line for therapy disclosed.

"Parents use different styles of redirection. Yours use guilt." Lacy Dawn said.

"Yeah, I cut myself once. See. It helped a little, but I would really appreciate a switch every now and then."

"Don't fetish. Relax, you're a good kid and your parents want switched, too. It's not your daddy's fault that the mine shut down. He feels guilty about not being a good provider and gets rid of it by giving it to you," Lacy Dawn kissed the scar on the kid's arm above the bottom of his shirt sleeve.

The crowd went, "Oooh..." when the scar seemed to fade.

"You're a good doctor, Lacy Dawn."

"Next," a kid who lay on top of the monkey bars above the gang said.

"Give me your shit. But, don't you ever say anything bad about Faith ever again. I'll vex you into eternity. You've been giving her a hard time since the first grade, Ronny. It ain't fair."

"Sorry. I'm just so sad all the time. I take it out on anybody that will react and she's an easy target — fat and ugly."

"Next year, she'll be hot. You'll regret every mean thing you ever said to her."

Faith moved into position to punch his exposed belly.

"I already regret everything," Ronny said.

"Your parents thought if they taught you how to predict consequences of your behavior you would exercise self-control. You learned it too good and now you go over and over every little detail. Before you do something mean, just take a few slow, deep breaths and you won't hit anybody anymore. Then, you will have less regret. When you stop being mean, I'll help you fix your depression. But, if you ever say one mean thing about Faith again, I'll let her kick your ass like it's never been before."

"My mommy don't do nothing but watch soaps," a girl in the second said.

"Mine too," three smaller children gathered for wisdom.

Cigarette smoke formed a cloud that floated from around the corner of the building. Only one female teacher still had a husband and he had been jailed for manufacturing meth after their house caught on fire. It was another tidbit of conversation during an extra-long recess disallowed by the State Board of Education. Recess was the most productive part of the school day because of Lacy Dawn's magic way of helping others.

"I wish I had a husband," the only male teacher employed by the school yelled. It was loud enough for the kids to hear above the squeaky swings.

"There goes Mr. I'm Gay again," a boy said.

"He's so boring," another said. The crowd nodded.

"I wish I could fix my own family," Lacy Dawn whispered to Faith.

"It's a kid's job to help her parents and any kid who don't ain't much of a kid and maybe don't even deserve to live!" Faith yelled louder than Mr. I'm Gay. It was her daily speech to classmates.

The school bell rang to return to the classrooms. Another fifteen minutes was left before compliance was expected. Several kids gathered tighter around the monkey bars to try to get attention from Lacy Dawn. The healthier ones played more or less organized dodge and kick ball games in opposite corners of the playground.

Like the center on a football team's front line, Faith tried to look mean by grimacing and folding her arms. It was a body-guard-like role so the others used her as an avenue to Lacy Dawn by lining up. A first grader pulled down her shorts to show a blue bruise on her butt. Faith rolled her eyes and turned away. A fourth grader opened his mouth and pointed inside but Faith didn't look. A girl in the fifth who sat beside her in class pointed to her crotch. Tears streamed. Faith winced for a moment but screened her out by turning her head. *Not today, Britney. Lacy Dawn only has so much magic at any given time. She needs to recharge. Everybody has issues and tissues. You can be first tomorrow.*

A fight broke out in the far corner of the playground. The games stopped and the kids rushed for the better entertainment.

Lacy Dawn and Faith followed to get a good place to watch. The teachers saw the action and either returned to the building or gathered behind the crowd to bet on the winner.

"She called my mommy a ho," a second grader with a bloody nose accused a sixth grader and swung air.

"But she is. My daddy told me. I didn't mean to make you mad," – the sixth grader tried to maintain a distance by stepping back – "I'm sorry. I don't even know what it means."

"A ho is a person who has a lot of indiscriminant sex," the smartest girl in school except for Lacy Dawn said to show off. She put on her headphones and walked toward the school to prepare for the next spelling bee, which would include the word "indiscriminate."

Faith picked up the dodge ball and beaned her in the back of the head.

Roundabend

"Around the bend, roundabend, roundabend, roundabend, roundabendroundabendroundabend...," Lacy chanted in just the right way to make it happen. She walked out the back door, floated across the porch, and glided up the dirt path toward DotCom's ship. A year older, her magic had matured.

From under the porch, the family mutt watched the girl pass the trash pile and the barrel used for burning. Her father's truck door slammed. The sound echoed off the hillsides. She stopped at the edge of the Woods and leaned on one of the three big trees that kept watch over the path to Roundabend. *I hope Daddy's leaving.*

"If you won't shoot him, at least get us the hell out of this hollow," Lacy Dawn said to the maple tree as if it were her mother.

"When we got married, your father promised to teach me how to drive just as soon as I was old enough," the maple tree quoted in reply.

Lacy hugged the tree. *That's just the way Mommy always says it.*

She crouched in a shadow to watch down the hillside. Ragweed waved, bees buzzed, and birds flew, but the pick-up truck stayed put in the gravel driveway beside the house. *Daddy's tricked me before.*

"Yesterday, I was so stupid," she said to the walnut tree a few yards uphill. "I stood right there in plain sight on the path—easy pickings."

"No shit," the walnut tree said loud enough to be heard by the entire Woods.

"The switch hurt bad. I ain't got no thick bark like you."

"It's getting thicker," the tree complimented.

"I hope so." she said.

"After you got switched, Lacy Dawn, your father dragged you home and threw you to the ground by the back porch," Walnut began the session.

"You think I don't remember last night?" she asked.

"Your mother had locked herself inside the truck cab so he

broke out all of its windows with a lug wrench. She begged him to stop while you watched. What's a lug?"

"Stop! Daddy, PLEASE stop it! Switch me again. Here! I'm right here!" Lacy relived the incident with her eyes squeezed shut. *I've got to save Mommy, again and again—in real life, in my dreams, should have yesterday, and right here and now. If I'd distracted him last night, maybe she could have run away. If he kills me, maybe they will put him in jail and she'll be safe.*

"Asshole!" Lacy Dawn's mother yelled at the truck from the kitchen through an open window. She turned up the radio to cover Lacy Dawn's screams from the hillside. *I'm the mommy.*

From the path, Lacy Dawn listened. From the kitchen, Jenny also listened as the truck's engine cranked but didn't start. Its door opened and pieces of glass fell from the cab floor. Lacy Dawn's father walked to the front of the truck, kicked the grill, and lifted the hood.

"He grabbed your mother's right ankle and pulled her out of the truck," the walnut tree continued the session.

"It 'bout knocked her out, probably didn't even hurt that bad when she got switched," Lacy Dawn said.

"You counted the strikes out loud so he wouldn't lose track," the tree maintained focus on the incident.

"Ten, but he didn't stop like he was supposed to. Eleven!" she screamed. *Why didn't you help her, DotCom?*

Lacy Dawn slumped on the walnut tree and wiped sweat from her brow. Her long, stringy brown hair stuck to her face. At her grandmother's insistence, it had never been cut. Now ten years old, it snagged on anything, including Walnut's bark. She used the bottom half of her hand-me-down Bratz tee shirt to dry her face, and she worked her hair loose from the bark snags. *Daddy didn't hear me or he'd be getting a switch. I hope he leaves.*

"Walnuts always remember but never warn," she said to the oak tree on the other side of the path.

"It was just a switch," the oak tree said.

Lacy Dawn sat, rubbed a scar on her ankle and looked down the hillside again. The truck was still there with its hood up. Her mother turned on the back porch light. It was a bare bulb in a white porcelain fixture that dangled by its wires. A loose piece of dirty yellow vinyl siding flapped in a wind stronger than a moment before and a loose piece of roof tin banged. Otherwise, the scene had not changed.

"It was sixteen strikes," the oak tree said.

Lacy Dawn winced. *That's the most switches he ever made me watch.*

"It was just another lesson from Mama—like how to string beans or can tomatoes," she bit a tangle from her hair and cleaned a thumbnail with a little stick. *I should've waited until Daddy was gone to leave the house.*

Lacy Dawn took in and exhaled a slow deep breath. It was a relaxation exercise taught during gym class at school by the woman from the mental health place. Moonlight turned the tree leaves olive.

"After Mommy got switched, Brownie came out from under the back porch and licked my face. That's when he got his too. Daddy tricked us when he slammed the truck door like he was leaving," Lacy Dawn said to the maple tree and moved to the other side of the path to slump on the oak tree. Its bark was less rough so her hair didn't snag, but its roots were above the surface and there was no soft spot to sit on. *I hope Daddy never gets a good muffler on that truck.*

"Fifty dollars is a lot of money," she said to the oak tree.

"They doubled the price for a legal vehicle inspection from $7.50 to $15."

"How do you know? You're a tree."

"What's a dollar?" Oak asked.

"It's made of paper and you can buy things with it," Lacy Dawn said.

"Eat shit," the oak tree said. *I wish her the best of all nutrients.*

"Thanks. You guys have been a big help."

As long as Daddy can buy an inspection sticker from his friend at the junkyard, he'll never spend good money for a muffler and I'll always hear it when he goes up the hill. That's what I'll listen for—the bad muffler and not the door slam. It's much safer. This was a good session.

Lacy stood, turned around, and faced up the hill toward Roundabend. Trees, brush, rock, and weeds shared the moonlight. Once wide enough for a tractor, the now neglected footpath curved out of sight. The top meadows had turned to hay, but when that was not harvested, it turned to weed.

"What should I do? Go home or go visit DotCom's ship?" she asked the entire Woods.

"Ask your dead girlfriend. She hangs out around here all the time," every tree within range chorused.

Faith had been murdered by her father during a rage the year before. He had used a switch so fat that it could've hit home runs at the World Series. Faith's mother had watched without intervention. Afterward, her father changed underwear because what he'd worn during the incident was soiled.

"It's a kid's job to help her parents and any kid who don't ain't much of a kid and maybe don't even deserve to live," the walnut tree quoted Faith.

Lacy Dawn hugged Walnut. *That sounds just like her. She said the exact same thing every recess at school for three years.*

"I told you a hundred times you tree. Stop quoting me or I'll get inside you," Faith said from within a boulder beside the path.

"Shut up. You're still on restriction, you eavesdropper," Lacy Dawn said.

"For what?" Faith asked.

"You hit that girl on the head with a dodge ball on purpose. It made her cry."

"Shelly's a bitch. I'm glad she lost the spelling bee."

"You hate everybody," Lacy Dawn said.

"So?"

"So you're on restriction, that's what."

"But that happened before Daddy killed me," Faith pleaded.

"You're still on restriction."

"When my mommy got beat up, I helped my daddy too. It was a big part of my job," Faith said. "It's your job too and don't ever forget it or you'll be sorry or worse."

"I'm trying not to hate him," Lacy Dawn peered around the oak tree. The hood was still open on the pick-up. Her father was standing on the bumper and leaning over halfway into the engine compartment. Moths circled around his trouble light.

"But, you never told me how to help my parents," she said to the boulder.

It didn't answer. Faith had moved on to occupy another inanimate. Lacy Dawn did the relaxation exercise she'd learned at school. *Faith learned how to help parents from her older brother. He quit and made it her turn. But I ain't got no brother to teach me how.*

"You'd better help them good or I'll beat you up," the walnut tree quoted Faith's brother.

Lacy Dawn massaged her butt and sat back down. *Maybe I should ask Faith's brother? No, he'd want too much.*

"I'm too young to barter with a man," she said to the walnut tree. *I hope I'll always be too young.*

"Nothing's free, Lacy Dawn," the oak tree said.

"Eat shit," she said.

"No problem," the tree agreed.

Lacy Dawn looked down the path. A dog face shined in the moonlight. It was on the ground between two loose pieces of porch underpinning. "Tie a Yellow Ribbon Round the Old Oak Tree" blared from the radio in the kitchen and seeped into everything within proximity.

"One time, Faith's brother stole my Frisbee. He wouldn't give it back until Daddy hollered at him," Lacy Dawn said.

"I've never heard this story," the walnut tree said.

"He gave it back right away when Daddy yelled at him." *Nobody messes with my daddy.*

"Tell me how to help my parents. That's what I told Faith's brother after I got a good grip on my Frisbee," she said.

Oak listened and waited to evaluate her performance.

"He said to eat shit. No problem, I said back just like you taught me."

"Good job. I didn't see it. If you'd been in range, I would've had Walnut launch a nut at his ugly shaved head. I supervise the ammunition supply for such noble purposes," the oak tree said.

"It'll take more than a walnut to protect my mommy." *If I sense danger, I've got to go home to help.*

"I wish I had a mommy to protect," the maple tree said.

"Me too, me too, me too, me too, me too…" the entire Woods reacted. It included wishes by some trees Lacy Dawn had never

17

met, much less hugged.

Dew had made her clothes and everything else moist. She wiped off the small twigs that stuck to her palms on the fronts of her cutoffs—the only clean spots left. *I hope I can visit DotCom tonight. Maybe he can teach me how to heal my parents. Besides, I need to feel safe at least for a minute.*

"DotCom's name sounds like a third grade internet class," Lacy Dawn said to the oak tree.

"He taught you how to help your mother stop bleeding, who to call if she was unconscious, what determined whether or not to fix supper, and when to study your spelling even if you didn't need to in order to calm things down," the tree said. "What's an internet?"

"You can bandage dysfunctional family dynamics by doing homework or washing dishes as if everything is functional," the walnut tree quoted DotCom.

"Don't piss me off, Walnut."

"You can impact a family crisis, Honey, by engaging in healthful routine," the maple tree continued to quote. "DotCom sure talks funny."

"And he goes on and on to explain. Sometimes a lesson plan about my family problems lasts for days," Lacy said. *DotCom don't understand humans but I sure do love him anyway.*

She stood up, straightened, and pushed her back against the oak tree to measure her height. She was an inch taller since the last measure but was still three inches short from the "I'm Five Feet Tall" gash she'd made in the bark.

"Just act like you want your daddy's goodnight kiss and everything will be okay," the walnut tree said. "Do you want to role play a kiss?"

"It's a symbolic gesture of male dominance," the oak tree said.

"He mainly wants me and mommy to kiss his ass." *I hate the kiss way more after studying the human psychology lessons that DotCom plugged me into last week.*

She looked down the hillside again. A butt crack appeared when her father leaned further into the engine compartment. Brownie snuck from underneath the back porch and slipped through a slit in the bottom half of the kitchen's screen door. His tail was between his legs. *Daddy, just go away, far way, and never come back.*

"Night, Honey," the walnut tree imitated her father.

"Night, Daddy," Lacy Dawn pulled the butcher knife from her belt and jabbed it into the tree. "It bent. Damn, it's stuck. I didn't mean to hurt you, Walnut."

"It's okay. Your father will think you still carry it," the tree said.

"I love you, Faith. I love you, DotCom. I love you, Walnut. I love you, Maple. I love you, Oak," Lacy Dawn took a muddy step down the path toward her house, stopped, and picked the safest route home. *I've got lots of best friends — a whole woods full.*

"Thanks for the present. I need a little iron," Walnut said.

"I love you more because I'm bigger," Faith said from everywhere.

"Alright, you're off restriction," Lacy Dawn said.

The Magic of the Schoolgirl

There was no safe route home. She stopped to further consider. "If Daddy don't leave soon, I'd better sneak back home on my hands and knees through the weeds. I've got school tomorrow," Lacy Dawn said to the oak tree. "I can hide behind the barn until he's gone." *DotCom said he was training me for a real important job. I need the work, but school has to come first.*

The truck engine raced, idled, and raced. Clinks and clunks of metal tools placed hard on fenders interrupted nature's song. The trouble light went out, came back on, and then went out. Twenty seconds later it came back on. *Shit. He's working on it some more. This could last all night.*

"He shut the hood, Honey," the maple tree said.

"Now, he'll test drive it up and down the hollow," Lacy Dawn said.

She walked to the other side of the path and sat down with her back on the walnut tree. Headlights came on and she moved a leg to get a tighter shield. Weed tops were illuminated and gravel crunched when the truck backed out of the driveway. *Maybe I can still visit DotCom for a few minutes. It's not that late.*

"School is serious business," she said.

On school days, rain or shine, fair or deep snow, Lacy Dawn glided up the path to Roundabend to catch the bus at the top of the hill. She had perfect attendance.

"I've never even been late to catch the bus."

"So?" Faith moved to inhabit a closer rock.

"You learn a lot more from DotCom than you'll ever learn in that school," the oak tree said.

"That ain't it you hardwood. If I don't do good in school, my mommy will think she did a bad job raising me up. It ain't no good report card if it has absences on it. Even if I already know all the stuff they teach at school, it's still top priority. I told you that a million times. I'll wait a few more minutes, but if Daddy don't leave for good soon, I'm going home. I've got school tomorrow."

She adjusted her weight to the left. An almost full moon

20

dominated the 60 watts from the back porch. The truck headlights became distant and faded. *My butt's numb again.*

"Mr. Kiser don't talk to any of the kids on the school bus," the maple tree said.

"How'd you know that?" Lacy Dawn asked.

"You told us this story before. What's a bus?"

"He says hello and goodbye. The only other time he says anything is when a kid messes up," the walnut tree said. "What's a messes?"

"Straighten up or I'll call your mom. I don't want to lose my job," the oak tree quoted. "What's a job?"

"The kids know to be good when he says that stuff. It's hard it to find work. They'd all get switched for a week if he got fired," Lacy answered. *I'm going to buy Mommy a brand new washing machine when DotCom hires me.*

Headlights passed the house and went down the hollow. The cross on top of the church made its statement. The rumble of the exhaust was overcome by the radio in the kitchen: "Wild thing, you make my heart sing…."

"When my dog got rabies, Daddy shot him," Faith said. "It's not fair that dogs get killed just because they get sick."

"What's that got to do with school?" Lacy Dawn asked.

"Nothing, except I told everybody at school about it."

"That 'coon was on my limb just before it went after her dog," the walnut tree said.

"I saw it," the oak said.

"I saw it, too," the maple said. "It was sad. Let's talk about it."

"Okay, we'll talk about Faith's dog," Lacy Dawn agreed.

"I don't want to talk about him," Faith said. "It'll make me cry. Besides you guys, he's the only one who ever really loved me."

The headlights passed the house and went up the gravel road out of the hollow. Crunch and rumble diminished until the frog peeps took back over. Van Morrison sang "Brown Eyed Girl" in the background.

"I'm going home. It's getting late," Lacy Dawn said.

"Sorry it didn't work out," the maple tree said.

"Don't blame yourself because he worked on his truck

tonight," the walnut said.

Lacy Dawn got up, stretched, and massaged her butt. The back of her cutoffs became more stained than the front. Her mother's silhouetted face stared out of the kitchen window at darkness speckled with lightning bugs.

"I'll walk home. Mommy likes to see muddy shoes. She don't understand when they ain't. Besides, it's a sin to waste good magic," Lacy said. *DotCom taught me that there's a finite amount of everything in the universe.*

"Wait. Your father made a left towards Tom's place," the oak tree said.

She wiggled the butcher knife in Walnut, pulled, and fell backward to the ground without the knife. *It's stuck good.*

"Your father slammed the truck door twice in Tom's driveway," the walnut tree said. Lacy Dawn nodded. *I've got a few minutes before bedtime.*

"Roundabend, roundabend, roundabend..." she chanted, elevated above the ground's surface, and glided toward DotCom's ship. *Daddy might be trying a new trick.*

"He used to be a good man, used to be a good man, used to be good..." Lacy Dawn chanted, reversed direction, and sped back down the path toward her house. She stopped the exercise and her feet hit the ground.

"Girlfriend, I'm soooo jealous," the maple tree said.

"You don't know whether you're coming or going," Faith said. "Where'd you get those good words?"

"In the first grade, DotCom told me to make up a phrase to use in an emergency in case I needed to go home quick. I didn't have to think about it. 'He used to be a good man' are words that helped Mommy and Grandma a lot of times. DotCom made them stronger and I practiced until they worked real good."

"Why didn't you tell me about him until after I got killed?"

"I tried to. I told you I got extra help learning stuff when we had our clubhouse. You said he was Jesus and I got pissed off. He's a lot more powerful than Jesus." *Daddy burned my clubhouse.*

The relationship between Lacy Dawn and DotCom was slow to develop. He was prohibited from leaving his ship if there was any risk of discovery. It was always a possibility. And, until preschool, she was under her mother's strict supervision most of the time. The two had communicated through the broken radio in her bedroom. Both learned a lot. Once Lacy Dawn was allowed to go into the Woods to play alone with Brownie, the relationship blossomed. She visited DotCom's ship every day where plug-in lessons on all subjects were required.

"Your mother can transcend pain by surrealistic dissociation," the walnut tree quoted DotCom. "Sorry, I don't know what that means."

Lacy Dawn yawned. *I've got to go home.*

She scratched a mosquito bite on her calf, another on her already skinned right knee, and pressed her thumb to a switch cut on her shin that had started bleeding again. She peed beside the path, told her friends to be quiet, and listened for the truck.

"There's a big difference between a pretend and a real-life escape from a dangerous situation," Lacy Dawn said after it was okay to talk again.

"Correct," the oak tree said. *How would escape feel?*

"My mommy never says the words you used," Faith said.

"Maybe that's why you're dead. My mommy's told me that Daddy used to be a good man for as long as I can remember. She whispers it to me every time we're alone."

"My daddy ain't no good," Faith said.

"It still helps. I say the magic words everyplace. There could be danger anyplace." *I should be asleep by now.*

"I'm already dead. Your timing sucks," Faith left the conversation.

"My bad. Anyway, this visit to DotCom is different," Lacy Dawn said to the maple tree. "I couldn't wait to be sure that Daddy wouldn't catch me when I left the house." *If Maple don't understand, nobody will.*

"Go with your feelings, Honey Child."

Lacy Dawn hugged the tree again. *There has to be a lot more magic in the words than I know about.*

"I want a family where everybody loves each other...nobody gets hit.... a new couch... a television that gets more than two channels... Brownie comes out to play even when Daddy's home...so I don't care about the truck's muffler... Mommy learns how to drive and goes to nursing school like she always wanted to... Daddy stops smoking so much pot, finds a job and still gets his VA check... Brownie gets a rabies shot so I don't have to worry all the time about him getting into a fight with a 'coon... a real Barbie instead of a fake one... a pretty ashtray in the living room instead of that beer can ... Mommy gets her teeth fixed...and, Daddy never blames me again for all the family's problems."

"That's a lot of magic for just words," the walnut tree said.

Lacy Dawn nodded agreement, sat down, leaned back, and waited to make sure that her father wasn't trying a new trick to catch her. She had left the house while he was home and without his permission. *I deserve to be disciplined.*

Gnats circled in front of her face. She freed an ant from her elbow, took off her tennis shoes, wrung the sweat out of her socks, and put them back on. *But, I'm too exhausted to volunteer to be switched tonight unless he can't sleep and goes after Mommy.*

"My magic words came from Grandma," Lacy Dawn said.

"I wish I knew my grandma," the maple tree said.

"Me too, me too, me too..." echoed through the Woods until the attention span of the softwoods forgot the topic.

"Mommy got the words from her mommy who got them from her mommy. They've been around for a long time before that. I found out in Head Start when I went to Grandma's funeral. I heard my aunts talk about what Grandma used to say every time she had a chance and to anybody who would listen."

"He's a good person on the inside, honest," the walnut tree said.

"How'd you know that?" Lacy Dawn asked.

"You've told us this story before."

"Mommy changed the words to fit Daddy. He's bad inside and out." *Grandma always believed the best about everybody and so does DotCom.*

"Your grandmother was wrong most of the time about humans," the maple tree said. "So is DotCom."

"Maybe, but that's when I first believed in the words and their magic power. I believe in them even if Grandma is dead and wrong."

"It's been five minutes and no truck sound," the oak tree said. *Daddy's bound to be gone for the evening. But, I'd better walk up the path real slow so I can listen for his truck just in case.*

"See you guys in a few," Lacy Dawn stepped over the sewer pipe which had fed the creek from the house that burned down before she could remember. She stepped on a sandy bank where she used to play. Brownie barked once. It was an encouragement from the edge of the shorter weeds they called the back yard. It got darker.

"Good boy," she yelled down the path.

Brownie waited in the yard and would stay until the pickup came down the hill toward the house. Then, he'd start barking nonstop, loud and often. It was his warning of a menace returning. Every now and then, Brownie was too busy to warn.

"I love you," she yelled. *I know about the ham hock Mommy used in the beans for supper.*

Brownie barked one more time. *I love you too, but I'm just a dog.*

"One time, Daddy came home right after leaving," Lacy Dawn said to a softwood beside the path on her way Roundabend to DotCom's ship.

"And?" the tree asked.

"Brownie saved me, kind of. Except, when Daddy got home he went straight to bed and cried himself to sleep." *I didn't need to hide that night but why take the chance?*

"What were you saying?" the softwood asked.

"The vicinity is under surveillance. It is monitored. I have installed an implant to assist Brownie's function as an early warning system. The optimal system for this application is one that supplements Brownie's protective tendencies and skills. It will be most effective when Brownie is fully trained. Using him as a warning system will blend into the natural environment," an oak tree quoted DotCom.

Lacy reflected: *You sound just like your cousin, Oak.*

Almost at DotCom's ship, the path was narrower. The moonlight was more obscured by denser forest and the bank to the creek was much steeper. The porch light from her house was no longer visible, but "I've Got You, Babe" by Sonny and Cher could be heard if she listened closely.

"All systems are go," Lacy Dawn said. It was a phrase borrowed from fifth grade science class. *I hope my return home don't meet the same fate as Challenger.*

Lacy Dawn visited with DotCom. She got home before her father and for twenty seconds watched her mother pretend to be asleep. The evening cooled down. She fed Brownie and placed the leftovers in the refrigerator. *Daddy loves pinto beans and cornbread.*

In the bathroom, Lacy Dawn washed with a rag. It was a piece of last year's Pooh top. She brushed her teeth and went back into her parent's bedroom to project love to her mother by soft touch. *It's been a beautiful evening. We didn't get switched.*

A kiss-on-the-side-of-the-head later, she pulled a quilt over her mother's shoulders and left the bedroom. She unscrewed the bulb to turn off the living room light. Bugs had invaded through the screen-less open windows. *Why'd I think there'd be something special about a visit with DotCom tonight? It wasn't worth the risk of slipping out the back door while Daddy was still home. He didn't teach me nothing about fixing my parents. Maybe I should ask Faith's brother.*

Lacy Dawn went into her own bedroom, took off her clothes, and threw them into the too-dirty-to-wear-again pile. She put on her extra-large Hulk Hogan tee shirt that she had been lucky enough to find at Goodwill and lay down. *I'll dream about a new couch in the living room. No more dreams about being too late to help Mommy stop the bleeding.*

"One of these days, I'm going to ask how you got such a stupid name, DotCom," she said to the surveillance camera and fell asleep.

The End of Perfect School Attendance

Despite the same bad dream, Lacy Dawn slept well. The next morning, she was up early, got 100% on a math test at school, and nobody got beat up. *The world's a better place.*

That evening, her father came home late, went straight to bed, and cried himself to sleep. It took two hours, kept her awake long past bedtime, and the next morning she didn't wake up on time for school. It was the first time since Head Start that she'd missed.

At 9:00 a.m., her parents were still asleep. She tiptoed to the back porch and lay down to talk to her dog. "What would DotCom do if he was me?" she asked Brownie through a crack in the floor boards. "I bet he's never missed one day of work in his whole life, and that's a real long time." *He's taught me so much—plugged me into libraries. I've learned a lot but I don't know how to deal with this. Maybe....*

DotCom had taught her logic so she made up an excuse: *How could I be expected to get up on time to catch the bus after I spent the entire night hiding under my bed? My daddy was acting so weird....*

She got up, tiptoed into the living room, and punched a hole in the wall with her fist. Although it looked like other holes made by her father, it was lower. She rubbed her knuckles, found the old NAPA calendar that she'd taken down the week before and turned the page to find her father's favorite picture. She hung a 1966 Dodge truck over the new hole on a nail that was already in the right place. She gave it the finger. *I've been through a lot worse than last night and still made it to school.*

DotCom had taught her advanced mathematics. She went to her bedroom, got out a textbook she'd bought at Goodwill, and did a college calculus problem that no sixth grader or even her teacher could have done. Five minutes later, she closed the book. *If I'm so smart, why couldn't I figure out how to make it to school today?*

DotCom had taught her about the power of love so she returned to the back porch and tried to love Brownie.

"Pfllt," he farted and wouldn't come out from under the porch.

Brownie knows I should be in school.

DotCom had taught her about how work is healthy and that people are happier when busy on things they think are important. *I'll clean house for Mommy.*

She walked through the house and looked for a project: two bedrooms, a living room, a kitchen, and a tiny bathroom attached to the creek side of the kitchen. Her bedroom was also used for storage. Cardboard boxes were stacked to the ceiling. She didn't bother to look for a project there. Her parents' bedroom was occupied so she skipped it too. She blew off the dust on top of wood stove in the living room, replaced the beer can used as an ashtray with an empty one, and rubbed her finger across the mantle but found no project there, either.

In the kitchen, she emptied the mop bucket into the back yard, set it back in the corner beside the sack of potatoes, and looked around. Except to straighten a school picture held onto the refrigerator with a magnet, there was no project there. Clean cups and glasses were in the dish drainer, but there was no more room in the cabinets to put them away. She tightened the assortment of stuff that was always on the kitchen table—spices and canned goods that wouldn't fit under the sink. She looked in the bathroom where everything shined. *Ain't nothing dirty. Mommy would be scared if the house wasn't clean.*

DotCom had taught her about human mental disorders and how disease can cause violence. She went to the living room, moved an extra fuel pump for the truck that was sitting on top of a cardboard box, and got out the psychiatric manual that Dwayne had stolen from the public library—DSM IV. After finding the right page, she tiptoed into her parents' bedroom.

"A psychological reaction occurring after a stressing event that is characterized by depression, anxiety, flashbacks, recurrent nightmares, and avoidance of reminders of the event," she read to her mother about post-traumatic stress disorders. Jenny was still asleep. Lacy Dawn tiptoed back out. *There ain't no answers in this book.*

Lacy Dawn went back to bed. *Maybe DotCom can help me get over this shit.*

After Lacy Dawn heard noises, she got out of bed. Jenny, her mother, was sitting on the commode in the bathroom with a washrag held on her right eye. Another rag cooled in the sink.

"Can't you see I'm using it?" Jenny reached for the toilet paper.

Jenny's panties were up and not in the right place to pee. She blew her nose on the toilet paper and waved her daughter to leave. The motion drew the attention of a yellow jacket which defended its nest in the crack of the corner of the bathroom wall. The block had settled after the bathroom had been added to the house and created the perfect habitat for nests of this and that.

"Go peel some potatoes, Lacy Dawn, right now," Jenny said. *God, I wish this bathroom had a door.*

Lacy Dawn backed out of the doorway into the kitchen. After a moment, Jenny came in, opened the dented refrigerator door, got out four brown eggs, washed them again, and hugged Lacy Dawn. They started lunch. *Mommy's smart. She's not book smart, but maybe she can help me feel better about missing school today.*

"Hell, I was pregnant with you before the middle of the eighth grade. It's not so bad missing one day of school. Just make up for it tomorrow by doing great."

"I will."

"I know you will. Your dad used to do so good in school—he graduated and everything. He was good looking, smart, popular, and on the basketball team. I was in crazy love. He was all I could think about. Everybody thought he would be a big success one day. He was sane. You know all this stuff because I've told you a zillion times."

"I still like to hear about it—especially the part about when he tried to kiss you the first time and you wouldn't let him." *That's what I'm going to do to when DotCom tries to kiss me one of these days.*

Jenny reached up and pulled another piece of loose latex from a ceiling board. Lacy Dawn held open the plastic Kroger garbage bag already full of potato peels and took it to the burn pile. They washed their hands under the faucet drip that caused the electric bill to be high because the water pump ran so much.

"It's all on account of that Gulf War," Jenny said.

29

"I know, Mommy."

"Last night, it was an accident. I'm for real. He was asleep and didn't realize that he'd hit me. Honest, Honey. I rubbed his shoulder because I thought that maybe it'd help him stop crying. He rolled over on his side and his elbow hit my eye. He didn't mean to this time. It was my fault. I touched him without asking first."

"I know, Mommy." *DotCom don't sleep so he'll never hit me by mistake.*

Lacy Dawn scooped more potato peels and egg shells into a new Kroger bag that she'd gotten from the metal sink base. She tried to turn on the faucet to wash her hands, gave up, and washed them again under the drip. *I wish I could tell you about DotCom. He knows a lot more than us about the types of chemicals used in human wars.*

DotCom had drawn maps on his monitors, provided details, and answered as many questions as she could think of to ask about the Gulf War. It was a lot of questions. Despite several months of studies, every now and then Lacy Dawn would think of a new question to ask about her father's military experience. *DotCom is going to help us fix Daddy.*

Coffee had brewed. Jenny got a cup and sat down. Lacy Dawn stroked her mother's hair. *I've studied amyotrophic lateral sclerosis. I don't understand it yet. One thing I know for sure is that when Daddy's speech slurs, that's why he wants to kill the world.*

"Not now. You might get hair in lunch. Don't forget to wipe down the counter top before you slice the potatoes. I wish we could afford a new one," Jenny said.

"I do, too. This counter's gross."

The counter top was covered with left-over linoleum pieces that used to match the floor. The heads of the tacks that held it down had rusted but the flowers on it were much brighter because they had not been walked on. Lacy Dawn wiped. *I know more about post-traumatic stress disorder. I've got it too. Like DotCom said, I'll turn it into an advantage when it's time.*

Lacy Dawn threw away the envelope for her father's VA disability check that had been left on the counter and got the cutting board off the wall. It was a wobbly square that he wouldn't let them burn because it was made in ninth grade shop class. She tried to whistle Jefferson Airplane's "Volunteers to America." *$1,724.58 a month ain't enough for what he went through.*

Jenny left the kitchen to check on her husband. Lacy Dawn sliced potatoes, cut bacon from the slab they'd been given by a neighbor who raised pigs for slaughter, peeled onion, and cooked. Aroma filled the space. She gave up on the tune. *I'm depressed. I hope DotCom can help. I wish he could smell.*

"He's breathing," Jenny yelled from the bedroom.

"That's a good sign," Lacy Dawn said. *War is bad.*

DotCom and Lacy Dawn had discussed how this or that · politician thought this or that war was either good or bad. It was part of her Earth World History plug-in lessons and included how some people made money off war and others paid. Despite her best efforts to start an argument about war, DotCom like Switzerland, always maintained neutrality on the topic.

"It's not fair if you don't pick a side," she said to the skillet of potatoes.

"Just turn them when they brown, Honey. I'll be there in a minute."

"Okay, Mommy." *Nothing's fair in love or war. I hate it when DotCom says that.*

"Put in a little more bacon grease if you need to."

"Okay, Mommy." *I'd better turn down the burner to reduce my moral anger. I get so emotional and he always stays so calm. I guess it's in his programming.*

She flipped the potatoes. *Since he won't take a side, I'll never win an argument about war anyway.*

"Nothing's fair in love and war," she said to the skillet, turned to the open kitchen window and yelled loud enough for the maple tree to hear, "He loves me!"

"Are you okay?" Jenny asked from the bedroom.

"I'm just playing with Brownie." *It's his way of telling me he loves me. Just like war, our love ain't fair either. One of these days, I'm going to tell him that I love him back.*

Lacy Dawn flipped the potatoes again and started the bacon.

Almost immediately, it competed with the redolence of frying onions. She grinned for a moment. *Sometimes love ain't enough. There's got to be something practical or magical that DotCom taught me that'll make me feel better about missing school today.*

Most of her plug-in lessons were presented by DotCom because Lacy Dawn kept asking one question: "Why?" He would plug her in to the next lesson plan. A tiny port had been installed on her spine below her shirt collar. She could reach it when she stretched. It was the exact same color as her skin.

"Why is blood red?" she asked the bacon.

"Because God made it that color," Jenny answered from the bedroom.

Lacy gave Heaven the finger. *That ain't why. It's because of the iron in it. DotCom told me so and he would never lie about bacon or anything else.*

She checked to see if the potatoes were browning and flipped the bacon. *DotCom knows everything about everything. But, sometimes he's like the psychiatric manual that Daddy stole. Knowing everything doesn't mean that a person has a true answer to an actual question. He's been doing the same thing since I was five—telling me why even when I don't ask.*

She flipped the bacon again. *Like Oak said, I don't learn nothing at that school. DotCom is my true education. I just hope I didn't mess it all up by missing school today. He's bound to be disappointed in me.*

"Is Daddy okay?" Lacy Dawn asked. *How about the how part? Sometimes, DotCom's answers take so long that I have to go home before he gets to the how part. When he gets to the how part, sometimes there're so many that I can't sort them all out.*

"He'd never lie to me!" Lacy yelled through the open window to the maple tree.

"Never trust a man," Jenny smacked her on the butt. "Dwayne's alive. I gave up on getting him out of bed to eat lunch."

They ate and did the dishes. Jenny washed. Lacy Dawn dried and stacked. Every now and then there was a whimper from the bedroom.

"Go outside and play with Brownie. I want to check on your dad again."

Lacy bolted out the back door.

"C'mon Brownie, let's go Roundabend to ask DotCom why I missed school today." Brownie came out from under the back porch. Brownie concluded: *I heard the whimpers too. It's safe.*

Brownie looked like a beagle with floppy ears and squat body, brown and tan, but often acted like his daddy—a German shepherd a foot taller who guarded the next farm down. The shepherd had been caught in the act with Brownie's mother, who was killed by truck tire because of her compulsion to chase them. Brownie's name came from when he stole a brownie instead of a wiener from Lacy Dawn's plate that she'd put on the back porch floor during a cook-out. He was still a puppy. Lacy Dawn got switched for it. Brownie was rewarded with the rest of that wiener and Lacy Dawn's next one, too.

"Roundabend, roundabend, roundabend...," she whizzed by one tree after another without acknowledgement. Brownie trotted up the hill. Less than a minute later, she sat in front of her monitor. She sobbed, wailed, screamed, cried, blew her nose and wiped snot on her forearm.

"I feel like such a failure. Always making it to school no matter what was the only thing that ever made me feel good about myself. Now, it's gone."

DotCom took a screw out of his mouse.

"And, I don't want any more psychological bull crap either. If you ever remind me about what my IQ is again, I swear I'll unplug your monitor for a week. I ain't kidding. And don't tell me that I already know all the stuff they're teaching in the sixth grade, the tenth grade, college or anything like that. It's not the stuff. It's the perseverance—the determination—the will—that's what counts. I messed up. All I want you to tell me is why. I haven't asked you why for a long time but this is killing me. I never want to feel this way ever again."

Her head down, Lacy Dawn sank lower in her chair, sobbed, and waited. There was no answer from DotCom. She looked up at her monitor and watched data flash on the screen. Data also flashed on the screens of DotCom's monitor and the ten others

33

hung around the ship.

"Well?" she said.

DotCom swiveled his chair and stood.

"I don't know." He sat back down. "My analyses found that you are the strongest human known by my people to have existed in this planet's history. We have a detailed marketing directory which spans centuries by your calendar. Personal, socioeconomic, social, cultural, psychological, physical, health, environmental, and political factors were included. I found no correlates that could explain why you missed school today. As a friend—maybe you just overslept."

"I love you, DotCom," she said.

He stood up again. *She has never said that to me before.*

"I love you too, Lacy Dawn." She noticed: *His voice quivered. It's never done that before.*

"Give me a hug bye-bye. I've got to get home to wash clothes because I ain't got no real clean jeans. I sure don't want to miss school tomorrow and I want to look perfect." *He ain't like other boys.*

She extended her arms. *Daddy would be pissed if he found out that I let a naked older boy like DotCom hug on me.*

She took a step toward him. *DotCom don't say nasty things to be cute. He don't tease or try to touch my butt and never laughs at the loudest fart in class. Besides, he ain't got no private parts—not even a little bump. He'll be a perfect boyfriend for when I grow up.*

They hugged goodbye and she left his ship. Outside, Brownie had treed a 'coon and ignored her command to leave. He ran around the tree and barked until Lacy Dawn said, "Good dog."

"That guy sure is smart. I feel a lot better," Lacy said to Brownie and chanted. Her feet elevated off the ground and Brownie chased her down the path. She beat him home by five minutes. Inside her house, she got Brownie some fresh water and table scraps. He dragged the scraps under the porch. Her father was still in bed, and supper, untouched, was on the stove. There was an occasional whimper. Jenny pretended to be asleep on the couch. Lacy Dawn ate and put the leftovers in the refrigerator. *There won't be no goodnight kiss tonight. Cool for a day that started out as the worst of my life. Failure feels worse than being hurt by others. It hurts more than being switched. But, it turned out okay. DotCom said he didn't know the answer to a question. I never thought I'd ever hear him say that.*

"Since DotCom don't know everything, I've got a little room to mess up every now and then. Nobody's perfect," she said to Brownie through a crack in the back porch floor boards. He came out and rolled on his back. She rubbed his belly. *No more mistakes—straight As in school—and I'm going to fix this family too.*

Lacy pulled the extension cord out the back door and plugged in the washer on the porch. She picked out school clothes that Jenny had left in the tub, wrung them, hung them on the line to dry overnight, unplugged the washer, and went to bed. *A nice house that is warm in the winter even if we run out of firewood. Daddy has a job and Mommy drives the truck.*

It was her best dream ever.

Please Don't Call Child Protective Services

It was the second week in June but it had been midsummer hot in the hollow since May. School ended so the children could work the gardens. Lacy Dawn didn't miss another day of school and got all A's on her report card. Dwayne, Lacy Dawn's father, never tried to get a job and Jenny never learned to drive the truck.

"Next month, we'll put a down payment on that new couch, Honey." Dwayne walked through the front door.

"Told you so," Jenny whispered and dried another plate. Lacy Dawn put one in the rinse water. Brownie gave the skillet on the kitchen floor a last lick and returned to his station under the back porch.

"I thought it was my turn to not get something," Lacy Dawn whispered back. "Thanks for letting me spend the night with Grandma tonight," she said out loud. *He bought something he didn't need for the truck.*

Lacy turned to face the doorway between the kitchen and living room.

"All the other kids have seen the Harry Potter movies."

"He switches harder when he feels guilty," Jenny whispered.

"Sorry for being stupid. It's a lie anyway. They all know about Harry Potter but almost nobody has seen one."

"I know you want stuff like other kids. I'm doing the best I can. I went to Tom's house to borrow his drill." Dwayne walked into the kitchen, sneaked a cucumber slice from under a paper towel, and winked at Lacy Dawn.

She put another plate in the rinse water. *Don't feed his emotions—not even positive ones—or he might get explosive.*

"Get out of the kitchen until supper's ready or that'll be all you get," Jenny said. "Don't forget, Lacy Dawn's spending the night at your mother's."

Dwayne went into the living room and opened a cardboard box. It contained new fog lights for his truck's front bumper. Lacy Dawn delivered his supper plate to the couch cushion beside him while he continued to read tiny-print instructions. She moved a beer can ashtray on the orange crate table and sat on the living room linoleum. Jenny ate in the kitchen with her GED study guide that she kept hidden behind a gallon jug of gasoline mixed with oil for the chain saw.

"Can I watch TV? Channel three was coming in good last night."

Dwayne's supper plate slipped off the cushion. Fried cabbage and a piece of cornbread spilled onto the floor. He stood up and squashed it with a foot.

"Roundabend, roundabend, roundabend…," Lacy Dawn started her chant and stopped. She had almost dodged the chrome bracket which was deflected by her forearm. It hit her on the right temple. She pressed the wound with her thumb to curb the flow of blood that had already streamed to her elbow and which dripped into a pool on the linoleum. *Lower my blood pressure like DotCom taught me. Soon, we'll be together for a whole night, the first time ever. Just be cool and don't blow it.*

"They left out the bolt! If you get blood on that bracket, Lacy Dawn, you know what you'll get."

Jenny finished a math problem, put the GED study guide in its place behind the gas can, and waited at the kitchen table. She put a paper towel over her plate and shooed away the flies.

"God, please protect me… protect my Lacy Dawn… she's my baby… help him find the bolt… help the pick-up start the first time, every time he tries… thank you, Jesus …thank you, Jesus…," Jenny prayed.

Lacy Dawn moved from the living room into the kitchen where she stroked her mother's hair and turned the other kitchen chair away from the table to scratch a rust spot on the chrome of its back rest. *Mommy changed her prayer. She added a part to resolve a specific problem. This time, Daddy was mad about the missing bolt, so that was put in. It's an adjustable prayer. Cool.*

Lacy pulled a gray hair and gave her father the Italian gesture for, "up yours." She'd learned it from her World History studies Roundabend. They hugged and smiled. Blood dripped onto the kitchen linoleum. *Mommy also added a new part to the prayer about the truck always starting.*

Dwayne had tried to leave one time after he switched Jenny for something or another last winter, but the truck wouldn't start.

So, he came back to switch her some more until it would. It worked and he left.

She pulled another gray hair from her mother's head and looked for more. Once blond and beautiful, Jenny's hair had prematurely grayed. It was seldom brushed and now looked like Jerry Garcia's before he died. Lacy Dawn stroked it into a pony tail, let go, and it returned to its natural look.

"I'd take a switching if he'd leave."

"Me too," Jenny said.

Over the years, Lacy Dawn had listened to her mother try many different ways to make the prayer more effective. The current prayer was a monotone interspersed with speaking in tongues between phrases.

"I'll save up my money from picking beans to buy you some Clairol." *Mommy must have learned how to speak in tongues at the church down the hollow. I like it. It goes good with the cricket chorus.*

Lacy Dawn walked to the back porch, pressed her wound, and listened. Blood dripped onto the floor boards. There were other stains. Blood soaked into the wood, but had wiped up good on the worn linoleum. *I ain't going Roundabend unless I know it's cool here. That prayer never works. There just ain't nothing powerful in it. DotCom will rescue me if I need it and will understand if I can't make it for the overnight.*

"It's cool," she said to the surveillance camera that covered the back porch.

"Even if I do find a bolt to fit, Lacy Dawn, you know we'll blow a fuse if the TV is on when I drill a hole in the bumper."

She nodded agreement. *I'm so stupid.*

"Learn how to think, girl, if you want to make it in this world." Dwayne searched on his knees for the bracket he'd thrown.

Jenny got out her GED study guide and erased an answer. Lacy Dawn stepped off the back porch and waited for things to calm down. Ten minutes later: *He's got lots of bolts in jars in the shed. He'll find one and put on his fog lights. Mommy will be as unsafe as always and I'll know if she ain't. I'm going Roundabend.*

"I'm going to Grandma's if it's okay." Lacy Dawn stepped back onto the porch and peered through the kitchen window.

"Just don't come back too late in the morning. She ain't got no phone and I'll worry," Jenny said. "Did it stop bleeding? Here, put this on it." Jenny handed her a rag soaked in peroxide.

Lacy was half-way Roundabend when Dwayne found the fog light bracket under a chair. It was the second time she'd decided to take a big risk in the last few weeks. She hadn't asked his permission to leave the house, so she stopped on the path and listened to make sure he wasn't coming after her. *Maybe I shouldn't go? No, he's into fog lights and won't even know I'm gone. One of these days, he won't be able to hurt me or Mommy no more. I'll be too powerful for him.*

"That wound's not bad," an oak tree said.

"It ain't nothing," she agreed.

"You have to first learn how to protect yourself, then we'll work on how to fix your family," the tree misquoted DotCom.

She stuck her tongue out at the tree and sat down in the middle of the path. *DotCom will see this cut. It's sure to scar and he hates scars. I'm still going to pressure him to teach me about helping my parents. I have to fix my family before the same thing happens to me that happened to Faith.* A dirt clod hit the back of her head. She fingered it from her hair.

"Get your ass back down here and take your medicine!" Dwayne yelled.

She got up and ran the path. A rock missed her head. Jenny screamed. Lacy Dawn elevated and rocketed beyond a stone's throw. *I'd sense it if Mommy was in real danger.*

"You fucking asshole!" Jenny yelled.

Lacy stopped, hid behind, and hugged a new tree friend. A minute later, she sneaked back down the path, one tree to the next. She waited some more. *Door slam...gravel sound under tires...and muffler rumble up the hill. He's gone.*

"Mommy's not hurt—at least not bad," she said to a multiflora Rosa bush. *I ain't the strongest human ever. I'm a kid out past my bedtime and alone in the woods.*

Safe House

Five minutes later on the way Roundabend: "Maybe I should chant again and switch to autopilot?" Lacy Dawn asked a hickory tree when she heard a rustle beside the path.

"Perhaps, it's a skunk," the tree answered.

She stopped. *One bite and I'm a goner. I'll have to take big rabies shots in the stomach.*

"Maybe I should just go home before Daddy gets back?" she asked Faith.

"Do whatever it takes to save our planet, your parents, and start with you first."

"You never said nothing about start with me first before now, Faith."

"My bad."

The skunk scurried down the bank toward the creek. Lacy Dawn used her index finger to rub the teeth that showed when she smiled, tried to pull the wrinkles out of her shirt, and, at dusk, looked to make sure that her fingernails were clean.

"What if the boys find out that I spent the night with him?" she asked. *I ain't even thirteen yet. All the other boys will want me to spend the night with them too.*

"You're a total dip shit," Faith said. "How could anybody find out?"

Lacy padded her training bra with leaves and took them out. She double checked her fingernails and wiped off lip-gloss—the first time she'd stolen from her mother. She used a fancy handkerchief that had been a Christmas present from her grandmother, unused until now. It was the only appropriate accessory she had for the most important occasion of her life—spending the first night alone with her man. *She's right. Nobody will find out. I just need to make sure I get back home before Daddy wakes up in the morning.*

"There's your old house," she said to Faith. "Tom must be home because the lights are on."

Tom and his wife bought the farm after Faith's father went to prison for murder. Faith's family had moved because her mother couldn't pay the rent since the house didn't meet standards for

Section Eight subsidy under Housing and Urban Development guidelines. Despite being from a big city, Tom was a good neighbor and Dwayne's best friend—he fit in the hollow. Lacy Dawn approached the garden that Tom took great effort to conceal. It had been tilled, and tiny plants had sprouted in rows—the only piece of worked soil near the path to Roundabend.

"I wish I still lived there," Faith said.

"At least you're close by."

"You can't get rid of me that easy, Lacy Dawn. Don't even try. Watch out for the alarm wires."

"Mommy told me we'd be blown up if I went into that garden," Lacy Dawn said. "But, when Brownie chased a cat into it, all that happened was the horns of the old cars in the yard blew. I didn't even get switched."

"I did," Faith said. "I had to miss school for a week so our teacher wouldn't see the cuts and bruises and call Welfare."

Lacy winced. *I remember. You got it good.*

They passed the secret garden. Lacy Dawn walked the path to Roundabend so that Faith could keep up. Faith inhabited one piece of wood or rock after another and was quicker at it than when she had first learned how. But, actual occupancy of an object was a slower process than walking past it.

"Careful. We're not allowed to talk about the garden," Faith said.

"Sorry. I should've asked Daddy to save you sometimes. He's good at that stuff because he loves to control things."

"You sure are slow," Faith said. "You must be scared to spend the night alone with that man. Don't worry. It don't hurt that much the first time. It didn't when my daddy did me."

Lacy Dawn winced and quickened her pace. Faith kept up.

"I'll be in the seventh," Lacy said.

"Asshole, I flunked. I'm still in the fifth. I guess I'll always be in the fifth," Faith said from within a fallen cedar that Lacy Dawn sat on.

"First you moved, then you flunked, and then you got yourself killed," Lacy accused.

"Eat shit. I didn't do it on purpose. I just messed up."

41

"I tried to talk DotCom into helping you but he said he couldn't."

"Some boyfriend you got."

Lacy got up, brushed off, and looked at the back of her shorts. It was her best pair. She walked around the fallen tree rather than risk another stain by going over it. "There's Devil's Tabletop."

Faith didn't respond.

Lacy walked up then down the path. *Hope her feelings ain't hurt. I should've said something more when she told me about what her daddy did to her. I hope the teenagers that party on Devil's Tabletop don't stagger onto my path and discover DotCom's cave tonight.* She waited for two minutes. The sun was almost down and the mosquitoes launched. The dab of her mother's cologne on her neck acted like a magnet. *DotCom said nobody could find him. If Faith can't, nobody can.*

"Sorry. I had to go pee," Faith said.

"It's fun to think about the first time I met him in person."

"If you get romantic, I swear I'll puke even if I can't."

"Here, hide in here, the Cave told me," Lacy Dawn reminisced.

"What cave?"

"Never mind what cave. You and me, we were in the first grade. One day on the way home from the bus stop your brother said he was going to pull down my panties."

"That sounds like Tommy. He loves teasing little kids," Faith said.

"I wasn't no little kid. Anyway, the Cave told me that it would be safe inside."

"There ain't no cave Roundabend."

"Watch me walk inside." Lacy pointed at a rock outcropping on the side of the hill to their left. Like all other exposed and settled rock in the hollow, vine roots had attached to the surface. It was bare, gray, and jagged in the middle. "See you tomorrow," she said. *I'm safe. Nothing in the world can even think of hurting me. It's like a bubble bath on TV, a cuddled baby, the direct deposit of a VA check, or a home-grown tomato on the plate. This is the only safe place in the world.*

"Your boyfriend's a pervert!" Faith screamed from inside a log near the rock outcropping.

The wireless surveillance system had picked it up. DotCom had covered the entire vicinity. Everything said and done was monitored.

"I wish," Lacy Dawn teased.

She had been invited into the safety of DotCom's home when she was six and had been going back ever since. It was a place that nobody else knew existed. He'd lived there much longer than Earth's recorded history. She tried to pull the wrinkles out of her shirt. *He's lived here a lot longer than I've lived in my house.*

"A pervert...," Faith repeated until she quit. *It's too late to help. It don't take men very long.*

"I love you, Faith," Lacy Dawn said into the microphone that had never been used except to communicate with Brownie when he stayed outside to hunt while she visited.

DotCom's cave was a place that didn't need trees, bushes, or car horns to hide and protect it like Tom's garden. It was a place that was always warm in the winter and cool in the summer without people taking turns sitting in front of the window fan. And, nobody got switched. Lacy Dawn pushed down an ugly mosquito bite bump on her neck. *That's the best part—no switches. Even if I do something real bad, like spilling Big K pop on the floor, DotCom will never hurt me.*

"It's me," Lacy Dawn approached the ship. *I'm the only person who visits DotCom. Who else would it be?*

Grandmother had taught her good manners. Anytime someone goes into another person's house, the visitor is supposed to yell, "It's me." "Ain't you got no manners?" would be the criticism of any grandmother in the hollow if the visitor failed to announce herself. A grandmother would be insulted if someone came into a house and didn't. Then one grandmother would tell all the other grandmothers and her reputation would be shit. Lacy Dawn waited by the microphone with a finger on the speak button. *I've got good manners.*

She had learned all the manners that she could from her grandmother and picked up a few more at school. She always minded her manners when she visited DotCom and he minded his, too.

"It's me," Faith said from within the rock outcropping. She couldn't penetrate any further. DotCom's defense held.

"You're just jealous cause you ain't got no boyfriend," Lacy Dawn said into the microphone. *I've got to be more careful. She's super sensitive now that she's dead.*

Faith hadn't been very good at helping parents. The truth was in the newspaper that Dwayne had stolen from the library and brought home. It was a big blow to Faith's ego.

"I hate you," Faith called. She otherwise failed to penetrate the rock outcropping.

Lacy Dawn waited. *Only bad people knock on doors: the Welfare Woman, extension agents, deputies, and repossession men who take back cars and tractors. They always knock on doors. I wouldn't knock on DotCom's door if a cave had a door. It'd be bad manners.*

"You'd better get out of there quick," Faith tried again.

"Watch your manners."

"Sorry," Faith said to give up.

Lacy Dawn walked toward the ship. *His ship ain't like any I've seen in TV movies. It ain't got flashing lights, attached projectiles, or moving compartments. There's no insignia. It don't even have a decent paint job.*

Inside the cave, DotCom's ship was a shiny metal oblong with one window and one door. It looked like a huge, squished, silver football. *It might look better in flight. I'm sure it could fly if there was an emergency, but I hope it always stays put.*

The ship's door slid open. Lacy Dawn tried to pull the wrinkles out of her shirt again, rubbed her teeth again with an index finger, adjusted her training bra, and slowly approached the entrance. *What can I do to show him how glad I am that he's here?*

She'd tried to help out around the ship, but nothing ever seemed to get dirty or messed up. There were no chores to volunteer for and nothing seemed to make him happier because he was always happy when she was there. She pushed the peroxide rag against the newest wound and threw it against the

44

cave wall. *Since DotCom don't eat, the best beans and cornbread won't work. I can't think of a good present.* He had thanked her for the presents she'd given: drawings, some clothes, and a school picture that she'd framed in light blue construction paper.

"There's only one thing a man really wants," Faith said into the surveillance system through a remote sensor. Without any wiring to occupy, she had no better success gaining entrance than when she'd tried through the rock outcropping.

Lacy nodded agreement. *She's right. My presents ain't even as good as giving a person something really needed like fixing the toaster or an unopened pack of cigarettes.* Lacy Dawn climbed on-board and sank into her living room recliner. *I'm safe at last, safe at last.*

"Put some antiseptic on your temple and ankle wounds." DotCom said and handed her a small container. He returned to his monitor.

"Thanks for letting me spend the night. I need it." She yawned and sprayed her wound.

"You are welcome," DotCom said.

"I love you," she said.

"I love you too, Lacy Dawn."

He returned to his monitor. DotCom clicked a mouse that needed to be cleaned. Besides Lacy Dawn, it was the only thing that needed attention in his ship. He got out a screw driver. *She has to find some way to show appreciation for my involvement, but I have everything I need, everything.* He straightened her school picture, which was attached to his monitor. *Everything....*

DotCom shut his body down to discharge and recharge. The main server was guaranteed by his Makers for centuries. He was never turned off.

Constipation

"The sound of beautiful music," the disc jockey said the next morning on the channel that DotCom had tuned in for her. The recliner vibrations decreased in intensity.

"Morning, DotCom."

"Your parents are each at forty percent awakened. Your father did not urinate after Earth twenty-one hundred hours and this could skew my calculations. I estimate final alpha at twenty-two minutes."

"You sound like a worried boyfriend. Are you afraid of getting caught for sleeping over with Daddy's little girl? Shame on you since you never even saw my panties. Why don't you just tell me in regular words how long we have before I need to go home?"

"Your father did not urinate after nine o'clock. I do not know. It is beyond my capabilities to measure his bladder capacity. I am sorry."

"Did you teach my parents anything last night, DotCom?"

He shook his head no. It was a motion that he had learned from her, an Earth nonverbal that fit the circumstance. He pointed a thumb up, turned it down, and shrugged. *Assertion of priorities is a management plug-in she has just completed. A few hours ago, she committed to a safe place to spend the night. Now, she asserts priority projects. The training was effective. Knowledge is so much more powerful than magic.*

"I researched suspected chemical imbalances in your father's hypothalamus. I estimate natural regeneration at fifty-four percent. These data are based on remote magnetic imagery. It is an ancient and flawed technology. To give you anything definitive, I will need a direct connect."

"I know," she said. *Brownie will dig the ditch line for the computer cable from the ship to the house. He's a good dog.*

"Once the fiber optic cable has been laid, you must plug each of your parents into the base for at least two hours per Earth day."

She nodded agreement and gave him a thumbs-up. It reinforced his training on Earth gestures.

I hate it when he uses all those fancy words. "That ain't much progress, is it?" she asked.

"No."

Lacy Dawn stood up. *Daddy's treatments will be long-term. At least there's a plan. It's more than what the VA hospital came up with the last time he checked himself in.*

"Once base line data are available, initial diagnoses will take two Earth weeks. My findings must be verified by an independent laboratory."

She stretched. *Brownie's the only one who can help. If somebody sees me with a shovel digging a trench Roundabend, it'll be impossible to explain.*

"Brownie's a hard worker," she said.

"He is becoming more competent."

She sat back down. *Dogs dig up stuff all the time. Nobody will think nothing about it unless someone notices how he's digging such a straight, nine inch deep trench from Roundabend to the house.*

"Show me one more time about making the cable connections," Lacy said.

"Connecting two fiber optic cables requires precise alignment of the mated fiber cores. This is required so that the light is coupled from one cable across a junction to the other cable. First, wipe off any dirt or moisture on the cable. Then, put the two ends in the fusion splicer. Press this button. This light will come on when it is finished. It should take no more than twenty seconds. I will have everything ready. All you will need to do is wipe, place, and press the button."

"I can hide that little machine in my panties." *I've said that ten times.*

"Yes."

"Even if they're quite stinky?"

He turned away. *I should not have made that comment last night.*

"Show me the twist connections one more time," she said. *I love him so much.*

DotCom got materials out of a cabinet on the wall. His ship had three white cabinets that she couldn't open. He could touch a door anyplace and as if by magic it would open. Like the ones in the kitchen at home, his cabinets were filled with stuff. Under the cabinets, there was a counter where he worked on things. And, like in her kitchen, under the counter there was storage with lots more stuff. The setup was cleaner than the one in her kitchen at home. There were no rusty tack heads. Tools were hung between the cabinets and the counter on the curved ship wall. It was like the peg board in the barn behind the house, but she couldn't pull off the tools no matter how hard she tried.

He leaned toward her and said, "Place the sleeve over the splice and twist the nuts like this on each end until they are snug. At this point, you have already obtained perfect cable alignment with a precise gap between the fibers. The sleeves are waterproofing. It is an extra precaution to fit this particular application. Do not twist the nuts too hard. You might crush the fiber." It was the tenth time that she'd been shown how to make the twist connections.

"You're sure all this is needed to fix my family?"

"Yes. I am prohibited from using a wireless connection for this application because it would be detectable. Further, wireless is not an acceptable method of medical diagnoses. Data could be lost or contaminated. Use for diagnostic purpose is prohibited by medical standards on every evolved planet."

"Okeydokey. I'll have Brownie dig and lay the cable in twenty-foot sections. Since he can't splice, I'll wear a dress, squat, and look like a little girl peeing in the woods while I make the connections." *Peeing in the woods is an everyday thing in the hollow.*

"You are the boss," he said.

"I want this to happen as soon as possible."

The Management Training had internalized. She walked to her toilet and sat down without pulling the curtain. It was a privacy that she'd insisted on during installation. He'd designed the commode based on research on the Lowe's website. Lacy grunted.*No other butt has ever touched this seat.*

"You just want to watch," she'd argued, and DotCom expended resources to install a curtain around the bathroom in the ship.

He watched Lacy Dawn sit on the commode. Something about the curtain had stimulated their mutual interests. Otherwise, the curtain had been a waste of resources.

Lacy wiped several times, very slowly. She had hoped that her excretions might be used to help fuel the ship. While her primary motivation was modesty, the first installation of a bathroom by an android was a hard sell. DotCom, at the time, didn't comprehend human motivations. Poop and pee for fuel sounded like a better justification for the curtain. *If he can use my shit, it's more than I can.*

She later learned that the ship's fuel was coal. Her personal contributions wouldn't be enough to count regardless of how much. She had listened but did not understand when DotCom detailed how coal had more potential energy, if converted and directed, than any other source known within the universe. It would be a valuable export if Earth ever earned a place in the universal marketplace. She had not skipped home that day. *I've lost my motivation to excrete. Everybody respects a mother lode.*

"Did you enhance my mommy's REM last night?" Lacy Dawn moved to the sink to wash her face and brush her teeth. The sink didn't look anything like she'd seen at the hardware store or in a Lowe's catalogue. It was about the same size as a large can of peaches from the grocery store and had suction tubes instead of a drain.

"Use level four on the toothbrush, Lacy Dawn. Pay particular attention to your molars. Do not forget your fluoride tablets."

She swallowed and hung her washrag on the rack. A light came on to decontaminate it. *There's not much he can do to help my parents until the cable is laid. It's hard to fix anything by remote control.*

"Fix Daddy first," she gargled. *Daddy's a higher priority than Mommy. Faith's right.*

"Yes," DotCom said.

Fix my daddy, DotCom, nobody else can help. Parenting education is stupid. Counseling? He'll kill me and Mommy before he lets that work. Jail is temporary and foster care will make it way worse. Even if Daddy makes big bucks from selling pot, gets free inspection stickers, and buys fog lights with all the right parts, he'll still be sick.

"You're my champion," she spat.

"Guinevere."

Lacy brushed her hair over the sink. She winced with each stroke that touched the knot caused by last night's dirt clod. The incident went down the vacuum tube as if the sink had a drain. She moved away from the sink and the suction went off. A minute later, with tennis shoes on, she faced DotCom.

"Are you in there?" she asked his body.

He was dressed in Traditional Appalachian Goodwill apparel. It was a Christmas gift from her last year. His form sat slumped in a swivel chair before a monitor in the living room of the ship. After a moment's delay, he raised an expressionless face, with the jaw protruding from a head that was small by contemporary standards. She waited. *He looks so weird when he comes back to his body. It's like a rapid replay of human evolution every time he returns from the guts of his ship.*

Thirty seconds later, facial muscles changed the shape of his face. His posture straightened and his hair became finer. The color of his skin got lighter and darkened again.

"I want a hug," she said. *He never gets even a little bump of private parts when he goes through the change from being part of the ship to back into his body. That's the best thing.*

"Yes, I am here."

DotCom's eyes brightened, smile warmed, he stood, flexed muscles, and walked to within a foot of her. He stood several inches taller than she did and had a muscular frame that curved slightly to the left until the shorter leg grew straight.

She smiled. *He's the cutest boy in the hollow.*

Lacy Dawn stroked his close-shaven jaw, except he didn't shave to maintain the appearance. DotCom returned the affection with a broad smile that revealed unused and perfect front teeth. *I wish I could learn to pucker. She might kiss me.*

"I'd better get home before my daddy wakes up."

"I cannot be absolutely certain, but there may be approximately seven minutes left until your estimated mandatory departure time. As you consider, remember that I could not measure the content of your father's bladder after he

50

went to bed. I have a video to present to you that will take six minutes. It can wait until later if your think that the risk of delayed departure is too high."

"Does the video have important information for me?" she asked.

"Yes."

"Why didn't you plug me into it last night while I slept?"

"The video is a copy made a little less than three million years ago by market analysts from my planet. It shows the dawn of humanoids on your planet and was originally recorded to justify a proposal to exploit resources—a common practice now outlawed. At the time, under-evolved planets were stripped of anything of value and left to return to rock."

"What's that got to do with me and my family?"

"You are the star performer in the video," DotCom said.

"Bull crap. I'm eleven not three million. Just plug me into it tonight. Let's get to work on running the cable."

"The format is not compatible for a plug-in."

"What's that supposed to mean? I know you'd never lie to me, but sometimes you don't give me straight answers either. Where'd you get that Robby the Robot monotone?"

"Sorry. I tried a different approach to avoid direct questions about the relevancy of my instruction. While being assertive in directing your goals and objectives, please remember that you are the student and not the teacher."

"My bad," she said.

"You must be conscious with all of your natural psychological defense mechanisms engaged in order to receive the information from the video without it causing damage to you," he said.

"Well, I don't have time now. Your answer took so long that I've got to go home before Daddy wakes up. Besides, I'm in the mood to poop. I couldn't do it this morning when I tried. I couldn't do it yesterday either. I almost never get to see a movie. But my Grandma always told me that before you go to the movies use the bathroom first. I'll watch the video tonight. Let's get forty feet of cable run today."

"I love you, Lacy Dawn." *I wish I could pucker.*

She did not give him a hug good-bye.

Lacy Dawn Goes to the Movies

"Pay attention to the video, Lacy Dawn," DotCom said later that evening.

"I am." *His ship's about the same size as my school bus. Bright curtains on the picture window might work. He's got the best view because his chair's right in front of it, but there ain't nothing to look at anyway since we're inside a mountain. A purple throw rug in the middle of the floor would look good.*

Lacy Dawn glanced at the scene on her monitor. *My chair's just like his. Maybe a plaid cushion on one would provide a little contrast. I can't do anything to brighten up our keyboards and monitors. I wonder if those extra monitors on the walls are necessary. They're always on and he never pays any attention to their reports.*

She turned her head to look around the ship.

"Focus," DotCom said.

Lacy glanced at the video. *Those extra orange recliners bolted to the floor with seat belts and fold up trays look like shit. The old quilt I brought for Brownie to lie down on looks good. All in all, it's a pretty nice living room. It's better than the one at my house....*

"I'm going to hang a curtain on the picture window and bring a nice ashtray from the next time I go to Goodwill," Lacy Dawn said.

"Pay attention to your monitor, please."

"You remember the first time we met?" she asked. "Your voice sounded different."

"I transmitted through the clock-radio in your bedroom," DotCom stopped the staff training video.

"I thought you were a commercial. That's what you sounded like. Then, I realized it was impossible because only the clock part worked. The radio was broken. I got super scared. It was worse than when Daddy goes Roundabend to get a new switch." *He likes new switches the best.*

"Finish the diversions so you can get back to your studies."

"If I study hard, can I fix up your living room?"

"Do you need a little more Ritalin?"

"Go away," she said. It was an imitation from the first time they'd met. *Daddy knew that radio don't work. That's why he gave it to me.*

She shut her eyes.

"When we first met, I was hid under my bed behind that trunk full of stuff that I was told to never ever get into."

"It is on permanent record that Dwayne stored magazines with pictures of nude human females inside the trunk. Please resume your studies, Lacy Dawn."

With her eyes still shut, she nodded her head no. *I liked the trunk. Behind it was a good hiding place.*

She pulled the comforter she'd brought from home over her shoulders.

"I am your shepherd. You shall not want. I will lead you on the path to safety. Fear no evil for I am with you. I will comfort you. Come dwell in my house forever," DotCom replayed his first communication to Lacy Dawn.

"You just scared the shit out of me, again," she said.

I've heard someone say something like that before.

"I want a commitment that you will resume your studies if I replay the scene," he compromised.

"I cross my heart. I feel romantic. Besides, I don't see how any computer cable will get laid if I watch movies all day."

"I am your shepherd…," the audio began.

She closed her eyes again. *I know my part in this scene.*

"I ignored you and hoped you'd go away," she remembered.

Dwayne's footstep sounds got closer and closer in quadraphonic. She squished up in the ship's swivel chair, covered her eyes with her hands, and relived the scene. *He knows where I'm hiding. This is some realistic shit.*

"Say something I can understand," she said in role.

"Get inside the trunk, Lacy Dawn. It is empty. Your mother found the magazines and burned them last night when your father wasn't home. He has not found out about it and will not look inside. You will be safe there until he leaves."

"Thank you," Lacy Dawn said in perfect timing to the video. *I hope we'll be friends forever.*

"That was fun. Let's replay another scene."

"You have a contract," DotCom restarted the training video.

"But this movie is boring. I want a cartoon."

Planet Earth revolved on the monitor. Continents were distinguished with black outlines as if someone had taken a magic marker to a globe. The land surfaces were too bright a green and the water surfaces were too bright a blue.

"Maybe this will help." DotCom increased the volume of the ocean sounds.

"I'm gonna fall asleep."

The ship's lights dimmed.

She watched as bright red equator, brown latitudinal, and white longitudinal lines appeared. Zero meridian was the brightest. Words or numbers appeared then disappeared at the bottom of the screen.

"It gets more exciting, Lacy Dawn. Please pay attention."

"What's all that stuff at the bottom of the screen?"

"It means nothing now. When the video was produced, data were included to describe the quantity of Earth's available resources for the marketplace. The report covered minerals, organic chemicals, gases, water, wood, fuels, and food. Those data describe the types of food that might be marketable to connoisseurs."

"But that don't even look like Earth. I did your geography plug-in and I know what the planet I live on looks like."

"I hope you tease. Earth continents have since shifted."

"Oh, yeah, I was just kidding."

The Earth on the screen stopped. All the lines except the Equator and the line for ten degrees west longitude faded. A green circle appeared at the juncture.

"Hey, that looks like Africa," Lacy said.

At last, a little action.

"Where else would you expect?"

"It sure looks different than the map we put in last year's social studies project."

She looked at the clock that she had insisted be put on the wall

54

as her fashion statement. It was an old-fashioned one with a second hand. Five minutes of the eight-minute video had passed.

"This ain't going to be no big box office hit like Harry Potter. I wish you'd played that instead." *Brownie probably finished digging forty feet by now. It's almost six.*

"Dude, I've got to go check in with Mommy. It's past time for supper."*This movie is borrrrring.*

"I was late for lunch once because I didn't want to leave. I know better now."

"I remember," DotCom said.

"Mommy got Daddy's favorite switch for the week. She held it above her shoulder and tried to strike me. After dropping the switch, she broke down and cried all that afternoon until she went to bed to cry some more."

"Your mother felt guilty," DotCom said.

"Daddy said it happened because Mommy didn't know the name of the switch. He names all of them and calls it with each strike. That switch's name was Sissy." *Mommy burned Sissy.*

"The past is the past, Lacy Dawn. Please prepare for the future."

Five minutes and thirty-five seconds had passed. She had watched the second hand—occasionally glancing at the monitor.

"Finally, there's a little action in this movie."

The focus zoomed toward a green circle. It became a blur of green. Jungle sounds filled the ship, dense vegetation filled the screen, and, a zoom again—it looked like something on a microscope slide during a biology class.

"What the heck is that?" she asked.

"It's a recording error. Please watch the video."

An image of a square piece of land surrounded by water appeared. Lines on the screen intersected at the center of the land mass. The recorder zoomed to a group of hairy bipeds. One animal tilled the ground with its tusk. Irrigation ditches watered a garden and small animals played with smaller animals. A large pyramid-shaped structure appeared on the monitor's top edge.

"This is pretty cool," Lacy Dawn said.

"Photosynthesis occurred on Earth 3.4 billion years ago. It thereby permitted ocean animals to evolve 600 million years

55

ago. Plants conquered land 400 million years ago. This led to vertebrates on land 380 million years ago. It all occurred on your planet before our technicians had invented field recording equipment...."

"You said ago too many times. Just be quiet. This movie's getting good now and I don't need the chatter."

The angle changed. The camera operator was walking on the ground. The pyramid got closer with each step. There were several close-up shots of beings. She focused. *Are those animals or people?*

"It's you!" Lacy screamed.

It was an accidental close up of a crotch. There were no genitals. DotCom did not confirm or deny her exclamation. The camera continued to move toward the pyramid: females with hairy breasts exposed, young eating berries, and larger, more erect males chasing a deer-like animal. They caught it and ripped it apart on the spot. The entrance of the triangular structure could be seen in the background.

"This movie is cool," she said.

The pyramid was made of wooden poles tied with vines and covered with large leaves. The exterior surface no longer appeared smooth as it had from a distance. The glow of a fire could be seen but there was no smoke. Individuals and small groups entered and exited the structure. One group looked like the hunters that Lacy Dawn had just watched. They carried meat and animal parts into the pyramid.

"Daddy got an eight-point buck last year. He sold the head to Harold for ten dollars. We still have some of it in the freezer." *They were butchering it to bring home. Cool. That's the way it's supposed to be.*

Inside the pyramid, small groups sat together. Humanoids came and went. There were several floors connected by pole ladders and all spaces were occupied. It was very noisy. The space teemed with grunts and groans.

"Turn the volume down a little. That vine's still alive. It's been trained to wrap around the joints just like Mommy's pole beans. They're ready to pick."

"Correct," DotCom said.

"And it don't just grow on the outside. It grows on the inside too. That pyramid is one huge green bean casserole."

"Correct."

People were gathered around a rectangular box that glowed orange in the center of a dirt floor. The tallest people stood the closest to the box. One person was at least a foot taller than all the others.

"That box looks like my old clubhouse – the one that Grandma gave me when she got a new refrigerator. It glowed when Daddy let me put the trouble light inside." *Daddy didn't mean to burn me with the trouble light. DotCom hates the scar.*

The next scene was a close-up of the box. Between males with hairy legs and butts and other private parts—big private parts—Lacy Dawn saw a smooth surface. Every possible angle was recorded. Data flashed at the bottom of the screen. On top of the box, pieces of meat cooked beside large green beans. Water steamed and spit over the mess.

"It's a cook stove. But, that's impossible. There ain't no fire or smoke and it can't be no electric stove like Mommy wants. There's no electric back then. This is a made up story. It has to be."

"The stove was a trade from my planet," DotCom said.

"For what?" she asked.

"You," he said. *Sometimes employees will bait their bosses for over-reaction. The employee will then request favors not consistent with organizational objectives as a make-up for the boss's loss of control. Lacy Dawn is more organically intelligent than ever measured and is capable of manipulating outcomes to her naïve advantage. I need to provide two seconds for processing between her outbursts and my responses.*

The next scene introduced a very small biped that held out a large bean leaf toward a much larger biped standing by the stove. Larger kicked Smaller to the ground. Smaller got up. Blood ran from her nose. She went back to Larger, extended the leaf, and was again kicked to the ground. It looked like a much harder kick than the first. Smaller got up again and re-extended the empty leaf. Larger slammed his fist down on the top of Smaller's head. She fell.

"That had to hurt bad," Lacy Dawn said

"You should know, Lacy Dawn," DotCom failed to implement delayed processing despite programming to do so.

"Duh," she said. *She's down for the count.*

Smaller got up, wobbled to Larger, and extended her leaf with unsteady arms. Larger ignored Smaller until she tapped him on the calf with her foot. Larger showed Smaller his sharp teeth, turned to the stove, and picked up two handfuls of meat and beans. He placed the food on the leaf extended by Smaller. Smaller nodded to Larger and stumbled backward away from the stove.

"Big Mac time," Lacy Dawn said.

The camera followed Smaller. She staggered and dodged her way to a small group of bipeds that squatted several yards from the stove. Smaller handed the leaf, now rolled around the food, to an adult female. The adult distributed pieces to others in the group.

"The smaller is you," DotCom said.

The picture faded.

"That's not me. It's a monkey."

"If you call her a monkey again, I will plug you in to the same biology course that you completed two years ago."

"Okay, so she looks like a chimpanzee. Big deal. It's still not me."

"Yes. It is you."

"Now I get it. You mean that humans evolved from that type of primate over millions of years. I liked the movie after all. Thanks. Do you have any more movies that I can watch? Movies are a lot more fun than plug-in lessons."

Lacy Dawn got up from her chair. *It's time for supper before Mommy worries.*

"No, Lacy Dawn, you do not get it. And, yes, I have more movies as you call them. The video was of you. It was not a video about the evolution of your species. The Marketing Department on my planet traded the cook stove that you saw on the video for you. After you received an initial plug-in, for millions of years the Department has tracked your purest genetic contributions to your species. It monitored without interference

58

or intervention. Here you are today. The same Lacy Dawn now as then. Except, of course, you have a few insignificant different physical characteristics. You have a little more knowledge and have continued to get stronger."

"If my grandma would have heard you say what you just did, you'd get switched for sure. You'd have to go to church for a whole month. I don't mean just Sunday school. The whole thing right down to the part where you have to give God a quarter of the money you made for picking beans. You'd be in big trouble because everybody knows that God made me and not your Marketing Department."

One Moment, Please

After she left, DotCom paced. *Lacy Dawn did not react as anticipated.*

He contacted his Supervisor to report. His email was forwarded to the Manager of the Mall, Mr. Prump. He was the highest authority on Shptiludrp—DotCom's home planet. Mr. Prump was the highest authority in the universe.

Five minutes later, DotCom received his performance evaluation. He got perfect scores on risk-taking, work ethic, and commitment to corporate interests. However, the narrative conclusion of the evaluation instructed DotCom to deactivate and to return home by autopilot if he did not finalize a contract within three Earth months. He paced some more. *This is the first time-line measured by Earth clock after thousands of equivalent years spent on project programming.*

The summary statement had been a direct threat to his existence: "…monitor all activities. Deactivate DotCom if at any time there appears to be a risk of psychological harm to our product. Replace him with an exact duplicate. The maximum transition period for return to full operations is two Earth days."

DotCom returned to the keyboard. "Yes, sir," he typed and said to one of the now activated surveillance cameras in his ship. Processing began.

"What's next on the big screen?" Lacy asked. She was back from supper and ready for the next movie.

DotCom scanned for viruses. *If I were a human, I would go to bed and whimper.*

"How about a re-creation of the big bang that created your planet?" he asked.

"Cool, I like action movies."

The video began. Lacy Dawn squirmed in her chair.*This movie ain't about stars and planets and stuff like that.*

A steady beat of drums increased in tempo and became a reverberating bass note. A group of bipeds with long, sharp teeth invaded a village of bipeds with short and stubby teeth. Long Teeth chased a deer which ran into the Stubby Teeth's village. It escaped because the two groups got into a fight.

"Daddy lost a deer last year because Harold said he shot it first. They got in a big argument and it got loose. It's sad. It walked around hurt and everything until Daddy found it and put a bullet in its head."

The video scenes were bloody.

I'm used to blood.

Long Teeth raped the village females. *Daddy rapes Mommy every now and then. Mommy says it's all her fault because she don't give it up like a good wife.*

"Uh, DotCom."

He looked at the screen, put an index finger to his lips, a learned human gesture, and stopped the video.

"Sorry, wrong CD," he whispered. *I hope the monitoring of my performance missed the error.*

"I love you, DotCom."

He got up to look for a different video.

"I learned something from you today, DotCom," she said. *Someone else is listening.*

"I learned that evolution doesn't result from the good guys or bad guys winning the gene pool game. There are many other factors. A tall mom and a short dad don't always have a medium-tall kid. Each parent has dominant and recessive genes that can combine in a number of ways. I learned that a horrible event can have a positive long term result. It's like when the meat-eaters raped the female vegetarians. It was a very bad thing that made very good babies who reproduced and advanced the species. That's what happened to my cousin last year. She told everybody about it, but had the most beautiful baby girl who is the pride and joy of the family. You're so smart and have helped me so much. I'd do anything you asked me to. I know you'd never ask me to do anything that would have a bad final outcome."

DotCom was summoned by a beep to his monitor. *My performance evaluation has been revised.*

"Management has reached the conclusion that intensive monitoring would be an inexcusable waste of resources. Your immediate supervisor has been ordered to take a week's vacation without pay," the e-mail read.

"Thank you," DotCom said to Lacy Dawn.

"For what, Dude? What's the next movie?"

"If you do not mind, I need to rest a circuit or two."

"Okay, I need to go pee in the woods so Brownie can bury the two sections of cable he laid this morning."

DotCom watched her leave.

Beautiful.

"I was a love child," Lacy Dawn said to him the next morning. "My mommy told me so."

"Do you still have those disturbing videos on replay, Lacy Dawn?"

"I guess so. It's so mean. I can understand switches and beating people up. I can understand not buying someone medicine. I remember when Grandpa wouldn't buy Grandma her heart pills and she died."

"I apologize for showing you the wrong video," he said.

"I don't understand how someone can turn an act of love into an act of hate. It don't seem human. Sorry."

"Quite a few human psychology theorists have earned good wages with that issue. Lots of human psychotherapists have made ends meet also. If you want, I can build a lesson plan on the subject and plug you into it this evening."

"Naw, rape is just one more pain in the butt called life. Excuse the pun. It's not a subject worth a plug-in. It's the images and not the psychology that freaks me out. I know the remedy—let's get to work."

"You are the boss."

"I want to lay sixty feet of cable tomorrow. Brownie dug a forty-foot ditch line before we went home for supper and seemed fine. He had fun. I decided to walk off sixty feet before I put his bone down to mark where to stop."

"I can put the connectors on the ends of one piece instead of on three twenty-foot sections," he said. "I do need a few minutes to talk with you sometime today. I know you have to pick beans for Tom before it gets dark. However, I need your help with something important."

She scratched a mosquito bite. *He said he needed me.*

"I don't think Brownie can handle that much cable in his jaw and get it to lie in the ditch line without kinking out. Let's stick with the twenty feet sections. That worked good today. Do you have a water bowl? I forgot to bring Brownie's when I went Roundabend and you know how...."

Her eyes widened.

"He used to be a good man, used to be a good man, used to be good...."

Three minutes later, Lacy Dawn stood on the back porch. She was keen to hear a whisper. The yells could be heard half-way Roundabend. She peeked through the kitchen window. Her mother was on the floor with her back propped against the gasoline can that hid her GED study guide. Jenny's nose bled.

"WHAT THE HELL . . . GIVES YOU THE RIGHT . . . TO THINK . . . that you can THROW AWAY . . . something that is MINE?" her father screamed.

Jenny adjusted her position. So did Lacy Dawn to get a better view through the window.

"Where's my SWITCH?" Dwayne left the kitchen.

Lacy Dawn felt for her knife. *I hope Mommy runs for it.*

Jenny moved the gasoline can to cover a corner of her study guide that stuck up. Dwayne had put the can in the kitchen two winters ago after he cut firewood. At the time, snow on the path to the shed had been deep. Jenny didn't complain about the can in the kitchen because it turned into her best place to hide her GED book. It was convenient and the mice stayed away because of the smell. When her GED book was hid behind the refrigerator, it lost a corner to the nibbles. She repositioned her bra so that everything was contained. *If it's okay with him, I'll take it right here with my arms over my face. God, I wish I'd worn long pants today. If he finds that book he might kill me. Maybe that'd be better. I can't handle anymore anyway. Welfare would take Lacy Dawn and put her in a group home. She'd have friends and stuff to do and decent clothes. That's more than she's got now. Who am I kidding? I'll never get my GED or learn to drive. I'd be better off dead. She'd be better off. I ain't no kind of decent mom anyway.*

Jenny pulled out her GED study guide. Lacy Dawn burst into the kitchen and, at the same time, Dwayne appeared in the

63

opposite doorway from the living room. Lacy Dawn and Dwayne stood face to face.

"She didn't throw away those magazines, Dwayne. I burnt them all!" Lacy Dawn looked him in the eyes. *I've never called him Dwayne before.*

"Well, here's my switch, little girl, and you can kiss your white ass goodbye because it's gonna be red in a minute."

"I told Grandma that you had pictures of naked little girls my age kissing old men like you."

"Well, your grandma's dead and gone now and it don't make no difference."

Dwayne grinned at Jenny and resumed eye contact with Lacy Dawn. Jenny did not move. The GED study guide was in the open. Lacy Dawn straightened her posture.

"Not that grandma. The other one, your mom. I tore out a page and showed her. She said the Devil must've made you have those pictures with naked girls way too young for you to look at. She told me to burn them to help save your soul before it was too late and you ended up in Hell."

Dwayne raised the switch to waist level. Lacy Dawn took a step forward.

"I was sick of them being in the trunk under my bed anyway. I did what Grandma told me to and now they're gone."

"That was my Playboy collection from high school. I bought them when I used to work at the Amoco station before I joined the Army."

Dwayne lowered the switch and leaned against the door frame. Jenny sat up straighter and slid her GED study guide back behind the gas can. Lacy Dawn maintained eye contact. *He's starting to lose it. Where's my new butcher knife?*

Dwayne looked to the side and muttered something that she did not understand. He raised the switch and then lowered it.

"But, Mom knew I had them when I was in high school and never said nothing. Hell, those girls were older than me back then. I bet they're all wrinkled now, with tits pointing straight to the ground, false teeth, and fat asses."

Dwayne muttered again. Lacy Dawn maintained eye contact. *I must have hit a nerve. He always mutters when he's thinking too hard.*

"Anyway, you're both still getting switched even if Mom told you to do it. But, I won't make it too bad. She wouldn't like it."

He paused. The point of the switch lowered to the floor. *Damn. I can't think of a new name.*

"Tammy, bammy, bo mammy..." Dwayne sang.

"If you even touch me or Mommy with that thing, I'll tell everybody about Tom's garden. I'll tell Grandma, the mail man, my teacher after school starts, and the food stamp woman when she comes next week for our home visit. I'll tell Tom that I'm gonna tell the men working on the road at the top of the hill. I'll tell all your friends when they come by after the harvest. And, I'll call that judge who put you in jail for a day for drunk driving if Grandpa will let me use the phone. I swear I'll tell everybody."

"Oh shit," Dwayne said. *I knew this day would come—ever since she brought me those DARE to Keep Kids off Drugs stickers to cover up the rust holes on my truck....*

"Lacy Dawn, drugs are bad. I don't take drugs and hope you never will either."

"Cut the crap, Dwayne. This ain't about drugs. The only thing this is about is if you even think about switching me or Mommy, that garden has had it—period."

"But smoking pot is not the same as taking drugs," he let go of the switch. Thirty seconds later, Lacy Dawn picked it up and hung it in its proper place on her parents' bedroom wall.

"I love you, Daddy," she said on the way back to the kitchen.

Dwayne went out the back door and walked to his pick-up. The truck door slammed. It started, gravel crushed, and the muffler rumbled. He floored it up the hollow road. *Things will be forever different.*

Lacy sat down on a kitchen chair, did her deep breathing exercise, smelled an underarm and said, "Yuck." *Things will be forever the same unless DotCom can help me change them.*

Jenny got off the floor, sat on the other chair, scooted it closer beside her daughter, put an arm around her, and kissed the side of Lacy Dawn's head.

The muffler rumbled to nonexistence.

"Asshole," they screamed out the open kitchen window at the exact same time without cue.

"He used to be a good man," Jenny giggled and hugged.

But, I'm Too Young to Marry You

For the next few weeks, everything was different yet the same. The incident during which Lacy Dawn had stood up to Dwayne was never discussed. The GED study guide was still safe behind the gasoline can in the kitchen. Occasional switching continued just like before, but was now open to victim objection and debate. Dwayne had been put in his place, but his place remained authoritative and the symptoms of his mental illness were getting worse. After at least one daily explosive episode during which he destroyed something, he cried himself to sleep every night.

"Have you seen Brownie's water bowl?" Lacy Dawn asked Jenny from the back porch.

"Your dad shot it up for practice yesterday. It's close to hunting season and he's had nothing but squirrel gravy on his brain all week. I'll get you another one."

Through the kitchen window, Jenny handed her an empty plastic container that had contained margarine when purchased. It was the one that Lacy Dawn used as a cereal bowl every morning and the only bowl left in the cabinet. When it was filled from the pump, Brownie lapped his water and trotted to work. The ditch line for the computer cable was almost to the edge of the back yard and soon Brownie's digging would be in plain sight. Lacy Dawn surveyed. *I've got to come up with a plan. We need to be careful or we'll get caught. Plus, the ground is going to freeze soon and it'll be too hard for Brownie to dig.*

"Hey Mom, can I plant a few rows of greens in the back yard? I've never had my own garden before and now's a good time to plant mustard or creasy or collards." *Grandma told me to plant greens after the other vegetables were harvested.*

"I don't see why not. There's a lot of seed in the cellar." *Ever since she stood up to Dwayne, I can't say no to nothing. I used to say no sometimes just for practice. It made me feel like a good mother. Now I feel like an even bigger piece of shit. I've never been able to stand up to Dwayne. She did. I'm sure glad she ain't a teenager yet. No is usually the best word to say to a teen.*

"I'll look and see what seed we've got," Lacy said. *I need a no sometimes too, Mommy. But, now is not the right time.*

Over the summer, Lacy Dawn had spent countless hours peeing in the Woods to make dozens of fiber optic cable connections. The project was forty feet from completion. She gripped the handrail for support and descended into the cellar. *Work the gardens, pick up more cable, make the connections, work the gardens, and pick up more cable.... Soon we'll have quality time together, DotCom. I know I've been neglecting you and my studies. But, you'll see that it was worth it-- a good daddy and a good mommy who feels like one.*

"Do you think Daddy will mind if I plant these greens?" Lacy Dawn held up a zip-lock baggie filled with seed.

"I don't think so. Besides, you can handle him." *I haven't been able to control Dwayne ever since he came back to the hollow from the Army. Now, Lacy Dawn can get to him with a look. She's a better woman than me.*

Lacy Dawn went inside the house and hugged her mother. *Hold on a little longer, Mommy.*

"Can I get started on my garden right now?" Lacy Dawn requested permission from an authority that had resigned.

"You know what's funny, Lacy Dawn? I burned those Playboys years ago and he just now found out. Before I got pregnant with you, he used to tell me I looked like a magazine lady and it drove him crazy. I liked it. He stopped so I burned his Playboys."

"Is this mustard or collard? I can't read grandma's cursive."

A truck pulled into the yard. Jenny looked out the window. "It's your uncle James. Be nice, Sugar."

Lacy Dawn nodded agreement and went to the front porch. *He only visits this time of year, and every time he's got a new girlfriend pregnant.*

"Hey, James," Lacy said. *What a shit head, but he may have good money.*

"Is your daddy home, Lucy Ann?" James asked through the driver's side window.

She waved for him to get out of the truck. James had visited every season for as long as Lacy Dawn could remember. To the extent that a family member could be trusted if busted, he was okay. She sat on the front porch floor to begin negotiations. *A customer is a customer and the customer is always right.*

"Daddy will be right back," she said and stared at the tiller in the back of his pick-up. "I bet you two will be glad if you wait for him," she winked.

"I guess we'll visit for a spell. I promised her mama that I'd bring back a present if she let Debby ride around with me," James pointed at his new girlfriend waiting in the truck.

"Does that thing run?" Lacy Dawn pointed at the tiller.

"I don't own no junk. Why?"

"If you till a stretch for me, I'll let you sample this year's crop. I want to plant some greens."

"How old are you?" he asked.

"I'm sixteen and old enough to smoke pot." *He knows I'm not or he'd ask me to go for a ride with him. I ain't ever getting in that truck. Grandma said that girls get pregnant by its seat covers.*

"Since you're old enough and I'm just hanging out anyway, where do you want tilled? But ,if my girlfriend bitches, I've got to go. I ain't taking no chance on losing her."

"Invite her into the kitchen for a glass of ice cold Kool-Aid."

"Good idea. You sure are smart for sixteen. I was a dumb ass at your age. I guess I'm still a dumb ass," James said.

The girlfriend got out of the truck and waddled up the front steps. Lacy Dawn got her seated in the kitchen, found her father's stash because it wasn't hid, and picked the best bud available. She put it in Dwayne's corncob pipe, walked to the back porch, told him where to till, and handed the pipe to James. He toked and tilled, toked and tilled, toked and tilled until the job was done. Lacy Dawn watched from the back porch.

Lacy followed the girlfriend up the steps. *It was last year's pot but James won't know.*

"Thanks for the garden spot," she later said to James. *He sweats like a pig.*

"Have a beer," she handed him the only one left. It was a little warm because she'd gotten it out five minutes before.

James loaded the tiller onto his truck. Dwayne pulled in and carried a garbage bag full of plant tops into the kitchen. A short time later, James and his girlfriend left with smiles on their faces.

"Good job, Lacy Dawn. I needed the gas money," Dwayne said.

"Thanks. Is it okay if I plant some greens in the back yard?"

"Sure," he separated leaves from buds and put the leaves into plastic Kroger's bags that Lacy Dawn would later take to the burn pile. Lacy Dawn held one colander after another in which Dwayne carefully placed the buds to dry. The stacks of colanders were placed on top of the stacks of cardboard boxes in Lacy Dawn's bedroom. "We're a good team and I'm so sorry I ain't a better daddy." *Where's my corncob pipe. It's almost always lost.*

Dwayne got high on marijuana that wouldn't stay lit because it was not dry, ate four bologna sandwiches, went to bed and cried. Lacy Dawn and Brownie installed the last of the fiber optic cable from the ship to the house and planted greens to disguise their work. The next day, they visited DotCom.

"Install the two-way splitter for the cable," he demonstrated. "Take the drill home to punch a hole through your parents' bedroom floor."

"I don't need the drill. There's already a gap more than an inch wide between the wall and the floor that I can slip the cable through. Are you sure you'll get good diagnoses if I use this splitter?" *I don't know if I can do this. I ain't no doctor. What if I mess up? What if the medicine don't knock them out and they wake up right in the middle? What if I don't cut in the right place and they end up paralyzed? What if the glue don't stick and the cable ports just fall out?*

"Do you want to watch the video on the procedure again?" he asked.

"I've already watched the video a dozen times."

"Do you want to practice on me again?"

"I've practiced enough. It's now or never," she said.

"Relax, Lacy Dawn. The only component that could fail, given your education, equipment, materials, and supplies, would be if your father drinks alcohol tonight. Alcohol ingestion would interfere with the initial programming. It would be correctable as

70

long as he did not discover the port before the desensitization programming is completed."

"And if he drinks beer tonight?"

"Wait until tomorrow night."

"Okay, I've got it and I'm sorry. It's like when I gave Brownie his first shots. I've never done anything like this before and don't want to mess up."

"Before you go, Lacy Dawn, do you remember at the beginning of the summer when I told you that I needed your consultation on a project? I still do and I'm almost out of time."

"What are you talking about? Are you just trying to see my panties like a regular boy? Well, even if I had my very best pair on, the answer to that is the same as always—NO!"

"No, err, is that how regular boys are expected to behave? I do not know. That is not what I am talking about."

"Well make up your mind."

Lacy Dawn pointed her nose up, gave a little twist of her not-yet-fully-developed-butt, and the hearts on her panties flashed.

"I want you to help me move," DotCom said.

"Move where? That's what Faith did. She moved. Then she flunked and now she's dead," she hyperventilated. "Why do you want to move anyway?"

Tears dripped onto her keyboard. Her monitor went black—a programmed response to excessive moisture.

"I have a job to do," he said.

"Job, job, job, job, job..." she cried. "So many people have taken the Hillbilly Highway out of this hollow that there's almost nobody left. They all went to Charlotte, wherever that is. Or, to Cleveland, wherever that is. Everybody's moved to other places to take jobs and now you too."

"I'll be back soon."

"Sure, that's what you say now. Grandma and Grandpa took that highway once. Grandpa went to TV school in Cleveland. That's where Mommy was born. I don't think you ought to go because Grandma said it's full of big potholes. What if you fall into one? You might get hurt and not be able to make it back home. Grandma said they were lucky to make it back home alive."

"I'll be careful."

"And what about your job right here? You told me that you'd help me fix my family. Just because Daddy don't switch me as much, that don't mean the job's finished. He's destroyed almost everything in the house that ain't his."

"My, ahh, my supervisor gave me a timeline for a project and, ahh, by Earth time tomorrow is the deadline. And, ahh, I, ahh, just a moment please.... I want you to consider the option of going with me, Lacy Dawn."

DotCom turned his back to her and wiped his first tear ever with the back of his wrist. He licked at his second with his tongue, but it escaped and hit the ship's floor. She noticed and wilted into her recliner.

"What? No way. I promised my mommy that I'd never move in with a man unless we're married. Besides, I'm too young. I'm just going in the seventh unless they double promote me. My cousin got married in the sixth, but she'd flunked a grade so she was old enough anyway. Besides, she was pregnant and had to. My mommy told me to never let a man think he was single with benefits. I'm sure it means you. My mommy would kill me if I even mentioned such a thing. You must have gone crazy!"

DotCom faced Lacy Dawn, made momentary eye contact, and dropped his head. His monitor went black. The other monitors continued to report whatever was important to know for a director of marketing. Tears dripped to the ship's floor.

"I agree that you are not ready. I will come back if I can."

She wiped her keyboard with a hand, dried the shift key with her shirt, stood, and turned her back on him. Tears formed little pools on the ship's floor. *How could he do this to me?*

"Don't forget. Plug each of your parents in for two hours each night and brush your teeth," DotCom slumped into his swivel chair. "Even though I will not be here, when you are ready, the diagnostic and preliminary treatment programs will be operational. I have installed the equipment in the cave and it is set to cure your parents."

Lacy left the ship, stepped from the cave entrance, and reached back to touch where the entrance used to be. *Hard as a rock cause that's what it is, a rock.*

72

"He used to be a good man…," she chanted and glided down the path.

"Roundabend, roundabend, roundabend…," she chanted and elevated to face what used to be the cave entrance.

"It's me," Lacy Dawn announced.

It didn't work.

Nothing was there except a hillside. She walked home. *What's life worth without a best friend? The weeds are growing over the trench. Pretty soon, nobody will be able to tell that there's a computer cable laid beside the path. Brownie's such a good dog.*

"How could he do this to me?" Lacy Dawn asked the Woods.

"It'll be alright, Lacy Dawn," the maple tree said.

"But, he up and left me and I didn't even see it coming."

"He'll be back for you someday," the tree consoled.

Lacy Dawn collapsed on the path. The maple tree had nothing to say after her last lie. Neither did anyone else. The Woods became silent—even the creek stopped its gurgling. She died for a few. *Good thing James showed up with that tiller. I wish DotCom knew how long my parents' treatments will take.* Lacy got up, made it to the back yard, passed her garden, went inside the house, fed Brownie, went to bed, and got up after her parents were asleep to plug them in as she had been instructed by DotCom. *This is easy.*

The two-week diagnostic period was a complete success. The green light on the little rectangles attached to each cable end came on just like DotCom said they would if everything was okay. Treatments began. She didn't get switched for another month. Her collards had come up, were a big success, and nobody would ever suspect that the hope for her family was a cable beneath them. Lacy had tried to smile in different situations. *Mommy and Daddy are a lot better.*

A week later, grief hit worse. On her way again to see if DotCom was back home, Lacy Dawn collapsed, got into a fetal position behind the oak tree, and bawled. Brownie ran up the path. Instead of licking her face, he snuggled. He howled in unison with her bawl. She didn't go home for lunch. She bawled. She didn't pick the last of Tom's beans like she was supposed to. She bawled. She didn't go shopping with her mother that evening even though her clothing voucher from welfare had come in yesterday's mail. She bawled. Brownie howled.

"I'm too young to get married," she sobbed to Brownie.

"Let's go home, sugar," Jenny whispered and combed leaves from Lacy Dawn's hair with her fingers. *Don't ask what's wrong. It's none of my business. Don't fuss at her for missing work and shopping. That's child abuse.*

Jenny supported her daughter as she tried to walk down the path—directed her away from the sinkhole and around the broken glass pile. Neither said anything. Brownie followed and howled. When they got home, Lacy Dawn went into her bedroom, crawled under her bed, and went to sleep.

"What's wrong with that damned dog?" Dwayne asked later.

Brownie howled from under the back porch.

Sixty Percent of All Job Opportunities Are Never Advertised

"Lacy Dawn, get up now!" Jenny yelled and added for a second time, "School starts tomorrow. You'd better get in the habit."

She rolled over in bed. *Thank God. I'm soooo bored.*

Awake for hours, she'd pretended to be asleep and listened to her parents go about their morning without argument. *They're healthier every day.*

"I was too young," she said to Brownie who lay on the floor.

Every morning, she debated with herself about whether or not she should have gone with DotCom. He'd been gone three hundred and seventy-six days. Each day was represented by a small cut on her abdomen where nobody would notice unless she ever went swimming again. She'd made sure that the single-edge razor blade was well-hidden. *He didn't give me the name of the place so I couldn't even brag about going there to the other kids at school. I was right to turn him down.*

"I'm not ready to get married."

Brownie didn't move an inch.

Lacy almost said: *A lot of girls marry when they're fourteen cause they're pregnant.*

"Twelve's too young to get pregnant," she said to Brownie who was eight and credited with three litters. He made momentary eye contact and went back to sleep.

I don't want to be one of those kinds of girls. If he ever comes home, I'll wait until I'm old enough and then I'll say yes, yes, yes, yes…. When we get married….

She rolled over again and faced the wall. *Five more minutes and I'll get up. My wedding will be beautiful. It will have….*

A car pulled into the driveway and its door slammed twice. She grimaced. *Damn, I'd better get up. It's somebody with a good muffler.*

When friends visited in the hollow, they intentionally left cigarettes on the dash so there was always one or more door slam followed by one more single slam at least ten seconds later—even if they didn't smoke or have any cigarettes to share. It was an audible notification that a friend, as opposed to a stranger, was approaching the house. Any other pattern of shutting car doors was cause for procedural safeguards, such as to pretend that nobody's was home.

Lacy stretched. *At least I don't have to get the shotgun.*

"Rise and shine," Jenny said after the follow-up car door slam.

"Okay, Mommy."

Lacy Dawn sat up, combed her hair with her fingers, rubbed the stuff out of her eyes, and acted like she'd been playing with her fake Barbie for hours. Her bedroom had a rollaway bed, flower wallpaper that had peeled up to a curl in every convenient location, a dresser with the same laminate problem, and stuff that she didn't own piled along the walls. She smiled to the extent appropriate.

"It's me," Tom announced as he walked through the front door.

Tom nodded to Lacy Dawn from the living room. She waited for her father to give her the Look. Dwayne was shaving in the bathroom. He had trained her to wait for his signal to respond. He did. She got up and shut the front door behind Tom. *Except in the winter, it's the host's job to shut the door.*

"What's up, man?" Dwayne greeted him and peered around the bathroom door frame with a BIC razor in his hand.

"Nothing much," Tom responded.

"Sit down. Have some coffee. I'll be right out."

"Cool."

Tom sat on the living room couch that Jenny wanted replaced. He read an old newspaper. It had an article about a kid who was killed by her father. The couch had no springs, smelled like dog—not Brownie—and had frayed corners. It would have been the ugliest in the world if new.

"Johnny Cash died?" Tom asked.

"You want some coffee?" Lacy Dawn asked. "We have a biscuit left over from breakfast," she lied like she was supposed to. They had not yet eaten. After she brought Tom his coffee, she stayed in the kitchen with Jenny. They listened as Tom offered Dwayne a job—a routine transaction. Lacy Dawn kissed her mother. *Daddy will take anything that pays unreported income.*

76

"I'm not talking about paying you in smoke," Tom said.

Dwayne roofed, plowed, brush hogged, and would do anything but steal. A good worker for temporary jobs that lasted no more than a month, he flipped out on long-term ones. He would get fired, punish the world, get depressed, and stay in bed for days—one job after another.

Lacy Dawn stroked her mother's head and pulled out another gray hair. *Everybody hates thieves.*

"Just keep an eye on things and call me if anything comes up," Tom said.

"What if I get busted? It's almost harvest time," Dwayne said.

"Don't be so paranoid. I've got an invitation to the Keys for a couple of weeks. I can't pass on that. Just call me if you see anybody messing around my place. You're the only one I trust for the job and I'll pay you good."

Lacy Dawn pulled out two more gray hairs. *Tom's rich.*

"A hundred and fifty a day," he said.

Dwayne was skilled. He identified and listed all the factors that had a bearing on how much he should be paid. Tom assigned each component a dollar value. It was a game with strict rules. Dwayne couldn't list something that wasn't true and Tom couldn't pay more than the job was worth. It would have insulted Dwayne.

"I do need the gas money. School's about to start and Lacy Dawn does need clothes. She's growing like a weed," Dwayne said loud enough for all to hear.

Lacy Dawn smiled. *Maybe he'll buy me a Harry Potter lunch box. No, I want a brand new training bra—not that hand-me-down piece of shit. I ain't got much yet, but I'm working on it.*

Dwayne went into the kitchen and refilled their coffee cups. He raised his eyebrows at the women. Neither of them commented. *There ain't no risk. Nobody in the hollow who's had any upbringing would mess with Tom's place. He's my friend. Back-to-the-Land Carpetbaggers are fair game and don't last long, but Tom's earned respect. He employs neighbors and goes to church on Sundays.*

"I'll need something up front," Dwayne offered a fresh cup of coffee.

"Hell, you can have it all up front," Tom said.

"No. I'd just spend it on something I don't need, like another accessory for my truck."

Lacy Dawn smiled bigger. *He's healthier by the minute. Thank you, DotCom.*

Lacy Dawn hugged Jenny who hugged her back harder. Both were misty eyed.

"Give me a quarter now and I'll wait for the rest."

"Yes sir," Tom paid in cash.

In recent years, gasoline prices had drained commuter pocket books and folks lost their jobs because they couldn't afford to get to work. After the bottom fell out of the shallow natural gas well market, Tom was the first employer to come back to the hollow. Nobody wanted to see him leave, not even teenagers who'd lost their ethical sensibilities. Not even law enforcement which would ignore the garden if reported. Dwayne counted the money. *This job will be easy.*

In the kitchen, Lacy nodded agreement.

"I bet Tom will give me a real job when I get older," she said to Jenny.

"I bet so too. He trusts you. You're not like the other kids."

Lacy frowned. *Now that DotCom's gone, I wish I was like the other kids. Maybe when I go to college....*

Dwayne stuffed the up-front money in his shirt pocket. Lacy Dawn and Jenny stayed in the kitchen and nibbled. They had heard Tom increase his offer to the most that Dwayne could accept—two hundred dollars a day. It was a done deal. Dwayne had recounted it aloud and Lacy Dawn had kept up. *It's chit chat time now.*

The aroma of early harvest filled the house. Living room murmurs, man talk, and familiar old rock and roll sent Brownie into the kitchen. Jenny put the skillet on the floor and went back to nibbling.

"Dwayne, I know you can handle it. Give it a try. I can fix it so VA doesn't know anything until you're sure it's right for you."

Lacy Dawn stopped her bacon crunch. *Tom ain't talking about watching the garden while he's on vacation. This is something different.*

"I don't know. It'd be a lot of responsibility. I've never been a manager and I don't think I'd like living in a big city."

"Wheeling ain't a big city. I've got a laundry and an auto parts store there, too. You could run either one. I'll make sure you get trained. Or, I've got some property that I rent in Pittsburgh. You could collect the rents and do maintenance. Sure would take a big load off of me if you'd help me out. I've got a few pizza shops here and there if you are interested in running one or even managing the whole kit and caboodle."

Lacy stepped out the back door to go Roundabend. She walked the hillside path, ignored her friends despite their beckons, and didn't ask Brownie to accompany her. *What if DotCom comes back home to get me and I ain't here?*

"What do you all think?" Dwayne asked from the living room. *They've been listening.*

Jenny sloshed a gulp of water around in her mouth, rubbed her front teeth with her index finger, wiped her chin with a forearm, and walked into the living room. *This is first time he's asked for my opinion in years. I don't want to blow it.*

In front of Tom, Jenny combed her hair with fingers, crossed her arms to cover up, and made eye contact. *I wish I'd put on a bra this morning.*

"I'd have to think about it, Tom," she said. "This is the first thing I've heard about moving out of the hollow for a job. Dwayne and I've talked about it before—when we were young. Life is unfair. Still, it's not healthy to be mad all the time like happens in the city. Dwayne's gotten a better handle on his anger and the idea of employment in the last few months. I think he deserves a shot at a job, but moving to a big city is something else. You're a nice man and a good neighbor, Tom."

"I wasn't always either. I used to be mad all the time. I hurt people when I didn't want to for no good reason. Just before he died, my father taught me how to stop my anger. I used to hate my dad. He was rich. All he cared about was making more money. He was always involved in some kind of deal and never had time for me. I was pissed off about it for years."

Jenny sat down on the couch beside Dwayne, and stayed out

of Tom's direct line of vision.

"Go on, I love these kinds of stories," she said.

"The day after my dad's first heart attack, he called me into his hospital room for a talk. He told me that he wanted to make a deal. I thought it might be his last and final so I went along. He said that he'd show me love every day for the rest of his life and I would inherit everything if I'd just get rid of the chip on my shoulder. At first, I had to pretend that the chip wasn't there. I smiled, laughed, and didn't cuss or put people down. You know—stuff like that."

"Don't stop," Jenny said. *I bet Dwayne hopes he'll stop.*

"After a while, I wasn't mad anymore and couldn't figure out why I'd been mad for all those years. I guess sometimes a person becomes what he pretends to be. I pretended that I had a good reason to be mad and I was. Then, I pretended that I wasn't mad and somehow it went away. It's weird, huh?"

"What happened with your dad?" Jenny asked.

"He lived for about six months, never acted like he loved me anymore, and conducted business until the day he died. But, since I wasn't mad at the world any more, I could see that my father had always loved me. I got the better end of the deal."

"Thanks for sharing the story, Tom," she said. "I agree that a person's beliefs can have a big influence in life. Our self-esteem is in the shitter. It's like when you hated yourself for hating your father."

Jenny pointed at herself and then at Dwayne.

"I know we're interested in your job offer, but there's a lot to think about. Lacy Dawn has to be involved in the decision," Jenny scooted to the edge of the couch and twisted to face Tom. Dwayne and Tom stared at her nipples for a moment and glanced away. Jenny moved back out of sight. Dwayne continued to keep quiet.

"We ain't got much to look forward to around here—the next raise in food stamps or VA benefits," Jenny continued. "That's about it. We'll talk about your job offer while you're on vacation. If Dwayne wants to give it a try, we'll work out something. I just hate for the whole family to move. Lacy Dawn is doing too good in school to chance it." Jenny stood. *Tom will come up with a job that lets Dwayne come home on weekends.*

"I'll think on it too." Tom got up to leave, blinded and baffled.

"Have a good time," Dwayne and Jenny said at the same time.

"And, don't get busted," Dwayne said.

Dwayne followed Tom onto the front porch. Nothing plumb or level, the porch invited friends and discouraged others. Dwayne leaned on a banister that also leaned and watched Tom get in his vehicle. *Man, if I go to work...I might be able to afford a new truck too.*

"You've got my cell number?" Tom asked out the window of his new Ford Expedition. "And you've got the phone I loaned you?"

"Know it by heart. Don't worry about nothing."

New DARE stickers rolled up the hill out of the hollow almost without a sound. Every opportunity, Lacy Dawn always got more—DARE stickers were in high demand in the hollow for all the right and wrong reasons.

Mom, I'd like to Introduce You to My Fiancé

Crack! The gunshot echoed through the hollow well past hunting season.

"Lacy Dawn is Roundabend. I'd better go check on her," Jenny rushed out the back door. *Who could that be this time of year?*

Dwayne felt for the cell phone in his shirt pocket. *If Bill let his boys target shoot on Tom's bottom again, I'll make him pay for those cows losing weight. It scares them half to death—all the whooping and hollering.*

He left the house and walked the dirt road toward Tom's bottom. The County had stopped the gravel at the bottom of the hill. It was the last place that the school bus would deliver kids. Dwayne crossed the road to walk around a puddle. *At least it ain't near Tom's garden.*

A fourth shot cracked.

Tom had bought three abandoned farms—each adjoined by at least one common line. The hidden garden was Roundabend. The cattle bottom was a quarter mile away. Dwayne checked the load on his revolver. *Next time, I'm going to ask for more money to keep an eye on this shit.*

Crack! Crack!

Dwayne identified the target just like in the military. *Right there in the bottom where I thought, but it ain't Bill's boys. It's his daughter.*

Crack!

Dwayne hid behind a bush and watched the girl. *What the hell am I supposed to do now?*

He was prepared to haul the boys' asses to their daddy and demand restitution, to confront any adult trespasser on Tom's property in any way necessary, but he had no game plan for a six-year-old girl shooting at her Barbie. *What did Barbie ever do to that little girl?*

Dwayne called Information to get Bill's number and stayed out of sight.

"Bill, this is Dwayne."

"No it ain't. Dwayne ain't got no phone."

"Tom loaned me his cell."

"Oh. Well, what do you want? I'm busy changing engines in Little Albert's Bronco and he expects it done today. I want paid before he drinks up all his paycheck. He ain't getting it back unless I get paid. What's your number? I might need a witness to say he deserved a round of buckshot in his ass," Bill coughed.

The phone slipped out of Bill's hand and fell to the floor. There were grease smears on all interior corners of his kitchen. A tub of GoJo mechanic's hand-cleaner sat on the counter beside his wife's canned tomatoes. Motor grease dripped from its push-down spout and had formed a large, shiny black spot on the floor.

"You still there?" Bill picked up the phone.

"Yes."

"Sorry about that. I've got so much slick on my hands that I can't hold onto nothing. My wife is going to kill me when she sees what a mess I've made of this new phone. I told her not to pick white."

"Your daughter is down here on Tom's bottom shooting the shit out of her Barbie."

"Bull. She ain't got no Barbie. Oh, it must be her cousin's who went back to Tennessee. They visited last week. We looked all over the place for that damn thing before they left. My Crystal Ann has one of them fake ones."

"I can't tell what kind of doll it is. All I know is that she's scared the hell out of Tom's cattle. I want it taken care of now," Dwayne said.

"I'll send my boys down to get her. It'll never happen again."

In five minutes, three boys arrived to get their little sister. They all had shaved heads, wore camouflage tee shirts, and carried rifles. Kid Rock sang from the rigged four-wheelers.

"I don't want that!" the girl screamed when one of the boys picked up the Barbie doll.

"We do," the biggest boy said. "It'll make great target practice."

"Not on this bottom," Dwayne stepped into the open.

"No sir," the three boys said at the same time. Dwayne exhaled. *That's that.*

83

Dwayne walked home to begin the rest of his rounds. Jenny had not returned from Roundabend. He pumped a large metal cup full of water from the well and poured it over his head. The water was from the original hand-dug well that animals kept drowning in and which was not safe to drink according to the State Health Department. Unlike the drilled well that fed the kitchen sink faucet, the hand-pump still worked over a century after its installation. He left to begin his work.

Jenny walked up the hill to Roundabend. She called Lacy Dawn's name every few yards. Her muddy tennis shoes slipped and slid. *I hear her voice. Why won't she answer me?*

"Sounds like she's talking to someone," Jenny said to the Woods.

Nobody responded. The trees weren't supposed to since Jenny was no longer a child. Her former best friends had made no long-term commitment beyond childhood victimization. They had not agreed to help her deal with domestic violence in adulthood. She hugged the closest tree. *I will always love you guys.*

Jenny quickened her pace, stopped, and listened for human voices. A few yards later, she stopped again. *Now it sounds like she's behind me instead of in front.*

Jenny looked to the left of the path. *There ain't no cave Roundabend, but there it is.*

She walked toward the entrance. The voices grew louder and she looked inside. Lacy Dawn sat on a bright orange recliner— tears streamed down her face. Jenny ran to her daughter through a cave that didn't exit and into a blue light that did.

"All right, you mother fuckers!"

"Mom!" Lacy Dawn yelled. "You didn't say, 'It's me' like you're supposed to."

DotCom sat naked in a lotus position on the floor in front of the recliner. Jenny covered Lacy Dawn with her body and glared at him.

"Grrrrr," emanated from Jenny. It was a sound similar to the one that Brownie made the entire time the food stamp woman was at their house. It was a sound that filled the atmosphere with hate. No one moved. The ship's door slid shut.

"Mommmmmy, I can't breathe. Get up."

"You make one move you sonofabitch and I'll tear your heart out," Jenny repositioned to take her weight off Lacy Dawn. *Stay between them.*

"Mommy, he's my friend. More than my friend, we're going to get married when I'm old enough. He's my boyfriend—what you call it—my fiancé."

"You been messin' with my little girl you pervert!" Jenny readied to pounce.

"MOM! Take a chill pill! He ain't been messing with me. He's a good person or whatever. Anyway, he's not a pervert. You need to just calm down and get off me."

Jenny stood up. DotCom stood up. Jenny's jaw dropped. *He ain't got no private parts, not even a little bump.*

"DotCom, I'd like to introduce you to my mommy, Mrs. Jenny Hickman. Mommy, I'd like to introduce you to my fiancé, DotCom."

Jenny sat down on the recliner. Her face was less than a foot from DotCom's crotch and she stared straight at it. It was smooth, hairless, and odor free.

"Mrs. Hickman, I apologize for any inconvenience that this misunderstanding has caused. It is very nice to meet you after having heard so much. You arrived earlier than expected. I did not have time to properly prepare and receive. Again, I apologize." *I will need much more training if I'm ever assigned to a more formal setting than a cave, such as to the United Nations.*

"Come on, Mommy. Give him a hug or something."

Jenny's left eye twitched.

DotCom put on clothing that Lacy Dawn had bought him at Goodwill. It hung a little loose until he modified his body. Lacy Dawn hugged her mother.

"I don't know if I can cope with a regular job or not—maybe," Dwayne said while on his inspection of Tom's property. "What if I try and it makes me sick again? It might be better if Jenny and Lacy Dawn stay here while I give it a try. But, they helped me get well and I might need them there. It ain't going to be Wheeling, no sir. That's too big and too far. Tom better come up with something else or I'm staying right here in the hollow."

"Dwayne!" Jenny said into Lacy Dawn's face with rotten teeth bad breath so terrible that Lacy Dawn couldn't back up fast enough.

"He can't hear you, Mommy. Daddy's talking out loud to himself. He's over at Tom's on his rounds. He does that sometimes when he's alone. We can hear him, but he can't hear us," she pinched her nose.

"What if Tom moves out of the hollow? Then I'd miss out on a good deal—that's what. It's now or never," Dwayne said.

"How come we can hear him talk?" Jenny asked.

"I installed a tiny audio transmitter under the skin at the top of his spine," Lacy Dawn answered.

"A what?"

"It's a teeny thing about as big as the head of your knitting needle that lets us hear him when he talks."

"That's impossible."

"I have to cope now, for Lacy Dawn's sake," Dwayne kept talking. "She needs a chance. She's smart—smarter than me and her mom put together. She could go to a real school. But, what if I lose my VA checks and then mess up...?"

"I guess it's not impossible," Jenny said. "But, it's a terrible thing to do. It's something that this bad man put you up to. It's an invasion of privacy. You probably have one of those things in me too. It's reading my mind. I bet this pervert even listens when Dwayne and I have sex."

"Mommy, you make so much noise that everybody in the hollow hears when Daddy does you. DotCom don't listen. He ain't even got no private parts. But, if he wanted to, all he'd have to do would be to open up a window—if his ship had a window that would open."

DotCom jiggled his mouse. Lacy Dawn stared him down. He stopped and waited for the next cue. It never came.

"Besides, the transmitter was part of Daddy's treatment. There're a lot of other things that he did to help fix Daddy. DotCom is like a doctor. You can see that Daddy has gotten better every day. And no, there ain't no transmitter in you. He figured you out like a good doctor and the only things wrong are

86

a lack of opportunity and rotten teeth that poison your body. You don't need no transmitter. He just gave you a few shots of ego boost. I don't know what medicine that is, but I trust him. You ain't complained since the shots started—not even with an upset stomach."

"He's a doctor?" Jenny asked.

"What's your problem anyway?" Lacy Dawn asked. "I know. You're prejudiced. You told me that people have much more in common than they do that's different—even if someone is a different color or religion, or from a different state than us. You told me to try to become friends because sometimes that person may need a good friend. Now, here you are acting like a butt hole about my boyfriend. You're prejudiced because he's different than us."

"Honey, he's not even a person—that's about as different as a boyfriend can get," Jenny said.

"So?" *Mommy's right. Maybe I need a different argument.*

A fast clicking sound, a blur of motion, and a familiar smell assaulted them.

"What's that?" Jenny asked.

She moved to protect her daughter from whatever threat loomed. Brownie, who had been granted 27 / 7 access to the ship, bounded over the orange recliner, knocked DotCom to the floor, licked DotCom's face, and rubbed his head on Jenny's leg. He then jumped onto the recliner and lay down. His tail wagged throughout. Jenny sat down on the recliner beside Brownie and looked at Lacy Dawn.

"But, you were crying when I first came in. That thing was hurting you." Jenny shook her finger at DotCom to emphasize a different argument against him.

"Mommy, I'm so happy that I couldn't help but cry. My man just came home from an out-of-state job. I didn't talk to him for a whole year. Before he left, he told me that he wasn't even sure if he'd be able to come home. I still don't know what happened while he was gone. We ain't had no chance to talk. All I know is that he's home and I'm sooooo happy."

"Your man came home from an out-of-state job?" Jenny patted Brownie on his head, some more and some more…. *It's unusual for a man to promise to come back home and ever be seen again. Brownie likes him and that's a good sign. Maybe she's right about him helping Dwayne. Something sure did and it wasn't me. It is a nice living room. They've been together for a while and I ain't seen a mark on her. That's unusual too. He ain't got no private parts and that's another good thing. Hell, if I get in the middle, she'd just run off with him anyway. I'd better play it smart. I don't want to lose my baby.*

"What about his stupid name?" Jenny asked.

"I've got a stupid name, too. All the kids at school call me hick because my last name is Hickman."

"My name was given to me by my manager a very long time ago. It represents a respected tradition—the persistent marketing of that which is not necessarily the most needed. I spam...," DotCom said.

They both glared at him.

"Dwayne is sure to be home. I don't want him to worry. Let's go," Jenny said.

"Okay, Mommy."

"I love you, DotCom," Lacy Dawn stepped out the ship's door, which had slid open. Brownie and Jenny were right behind her.

"I love you too," DotCom said.

Lacy Dawn and Jenny held hands and walked down the path toward home. The trees didn't smile—at least not so Jenny would notice. On the other hand, no living thing obstructed, intruded, or interfered with the rite.

Jenny sang to the Woods, "My little girl's going to marry a doctor when she grows up, marry a doctor when she grows up, when she grows up. My little girl's going to marry a doctor when she grows up, marry a doctor when she grows up, when she grows up...."

Shop Until You Drop

"I'll give the pizza job that Tom offered a try," Dwayne said to Jenny two weeks later and who told Lacy Dawn. Tom had been influenced to come up with an offer that did not involve relocating the family. He had returned from vacation in the Keys and Dwayne agreed to accept employment with the blessings of his family. Dwayne would become the district manager for eight of Tom's small town pizza shops—a main office location close enough to the hollow.

"I'll come home every weekend," Dwayne promised to himself more so than to anybody else. "Call me if you need me," he hoped.

Tom gave Dwayne a company car and cell phone, a negotiated salary twice that of the district manager he replaced, and a job that paid in cash for the first six months. Except for living expenses from the drawer before bank deposits, Dwayne's salary would be paid biweekly to Jenny. Family and friends had gathered for the departure.

"Tom said he'd help out if you need anything," Dwayne said.

"I'll always wear a bra if Tom comes around," Jenny promised.

"I'll never miss another day of school," Lacy Dawn said.

"I'll let you pat me on the head goodbye," Brownie wanted to say.

Reverend Casto was there and agreed to have the congregation pray for Dwayne's success every Sunday in exchange for a small offering. Harold was there and agreed to have his boys drop off firewood to Jenny during the winter for ten dollars a load. Dwayne fidgeted with the car keys. Church members and a few other neighbors watched. They were ready to run if Dwayne became explosive. He started the car. *It's all set. Everybody agrees.*

Dwayne got out and hugged Lacy Dawn, Jenny, and a few neighbors goodbye one last time while the car warmed up. He patted Brownie on the head. Metallica blared from the car stereo. He drove off in his company car with a good muffler and brand new DARE stickers on the front and rear bumpers. It went up the hollow road.

Less than an hour later, Lacy Dawn, Jenny, and Brownie went out-of-state. DotCom, of course, drove for the trip. Jenny had written a note to the school teacher—Lacy Dawn had the pinkeye and would be out-of-school for at least a week. Out-of-school was an understatement. Out-of-state was an understatement. According to DotCom, no other human had visited where they were going.

"It will be more enjoyable than Disneyland," DotCom said.

"Let's rest up before we go shopping," Jenny flipped the lever to recline. *I've shopped at a Mall once.*

Lacy Dawn shut her eyes. *I'm too excited to sleep.*

Brownie curled up beside the captain's chair and helped DotCom watch his monitor.

"Good dog."

Jenny snored. DotCom patted Brownie's head rhythmically. *I'm relieved that Lacy Dawn does not snore. It is an offensive human sound caused by a defective atmospheric exchange design. I hope to learn to sleep and must carry out a program modification to never make that noise.*

Dwayne's treatments were down to weekend nights to fit into his new work schedule. He no longer stuttered and twitched. He didn't put a new hole in the living room wall when he got his VA check; the most recent deer he killed only had one bullet instead of a million to dig out; and, he had replaced the kitchen faucet with one of the good ones that had been in the shed for so long. Lacy Dawn was confident in his treatment plan. She opened her eyes, looked at the monitors that reported nothing meaningful to her, and closed them again. *I wish I could sleep. Daddy's new job has to be stress city. I'm glad we didn't tell him about us going to the Mall. He couldn't have handled it. Hope I can. Everybody's noticed the big difference in him—a lot of progress, but he might have had a setback if we would have told him about....*

"We're almost there," DotCom announced.

Lacy Dawn and Jenny, awake from her pretend sleep and manufactured snore, looked out the ship's picture window. A bright white ball got brighter as the ship got closer.

"It's almost like trying to look at the sun," Lacy Dawn squinted.

"Yes, the planet consumes a lot of energy in order to keep the Mall open at all times."

Other ships of various shapes and sizes could be seen— silhouettes with detail as angles changed. Traffic appeared heavier the closer they got to the planet. Smaller ships became visible. Large ships appeared much larger and all approached a traffic jam.

"Those ships wait for a dock to load or unload. We have a VIP pass and will not be required to circle the planet once I work into the flow of traffic."

"What's a VIP pass?" Lacy Dawn asked.

"It is special permission to dock. We are permitted to arrive without a long search and decontamination procedure required for other visitors. A VIP pass is only granted to Very Important Persons. You are important, Lacy Dawn, and not just because I love you."

"I think you're important too," Jenny said to Lacy Dawn. *I've never felt important.*

DotCom flew his ship into ever tighter circles until it was in the inner-most lane. The light from the picture window was blinding. Jenny covered her eyes with her hands. Lacy Dawn tried to ignore her behavior. It was just like the last time they'd gone to a Mall.

"Shptiludrp is the largest Shopping Mall in the universe," DotCom grinned. He was ignored by his passengers. With an escort, check-in at the hotel went smoothly. Their room was fancy—a bathroom with a door and carpeting throughout. The lamps worked and it had real ashtrays. The temperature was perfect. There were two beds, a closet, and dressers with drawers that didn't stick. Nothing was broken, chipped, warped, torn, stained, moldy, or smelly in the room except for Brownie who had come with them.

"Sure ain't very homey, is it?" Lacy Dawn asked.

She unpacked her other pair of jeans and fresh shirt. Jenny hadn't brought anything. The next morning, DotCom gave them an overview of the Mall and tried to send them on their way.

"You're sure it's safe to go out there all by ourselves?" Jenny asked. "I've been to a Mall once. He ain't ever been to one," she pointed at Brownie.

"There has not been a crime committed on this planet for centuries. Management is stringent when reviewing applications to shop. You have received language interpretation devices. Coordinates are marked by corner posts. The posts can verbally respond to questions about directions and a host is stationed every fifty Earth feet in any direction to help shoppers with anything. Pick up your hotel's homing card on your way out. You two will be fine. I have a meeting to attend and must not be late. I will check back with you later. Enjoy the experience."

"Let's go shopping!" Lacy Dawn whooped.

Nothing could have prepared them for what they found when they left the hotel. Beings were everywhere for as far as they could see. There was not a human in sight. Shoppers walked on two, three, four, five, six or more legs, rolled as if they demonstrated somersaults, or levitated above the floor. Everyone rushed to the next shop or to get into a checkout line. They grabbed, examined, and carried merchandise with as much variety in the numbers of arms and hands or other appendages as they had methods of locomotion.

"Wow," Jenny stalled.

Some people looked like animals dressed in clothes. Others were naked. There were people with feathers, short or long fur, scales, and shiny skin that looked like metal. They were different colors and multi-colored. Some were two feet taller than Dwayne. Others were as short as Brownie. People who looked very different from each other had conversations in long check-out lines as if they were best friends.

"Let's get on one of those moving beltways, Mommy."

"Okay."

Jenny allowed herself to be led by the hand. They got on a beltway and didn't get off until exhausted. Having toured only a small portion of the Mall—hundreds of side-by-side storefronts in row after row—they had gotten a good sample for day one.

"Home, James, and don't spare the horses," Jenny said to the beltway. *That's from eighth grade world history class.*

"Yes, darling," Lacy Dawn said. *I know about Queen Victoria.*

"Brownie must be ready for some bacon by now," Lacy Dawn said.

Brownie had been left in the hotel room where he'd paced in circles for hours. But, he didn't poop regardless of how appropriate to the circumstances. The room had no aroma—it was too sterile to justify a good load.

Day two was the real thing. Even though they didn't spend any money, they window-shopped until they dropped. Brownie tagged along with them and fell asleep on the beltway on their way back to the hotel. On day three, they spent some of DotCom's money. Afterward, despite being tired, they were energized by the experience of buying. Brownie stayed awake almost all the way back to the hotel. He had achieved his home smell on a far-away planet and led them back without electronic directions.

"I wish cartoons or something good was on this TV," Lacy Dawn complained back in the hotel room.

Jenny shaved her legs over the bathtub. They had slept for a few Earth hours—maybe more—and Jenny had awakened eager to shop. *I've lost track of time, not that it ever meant that much in the hollow.*

"That's not a TV to watch shows on, honey," Jenny said and smiled in the mirror at her new teeth. "DotCom told me it shows a different shop on each channel in case we get too tired to shop at the Mall—we can shop by remote control."

"Boring," Lacy Dawn said.

"DotCom said that if you want a TV to watch cartoons on we can buy one. And, if I want a TV to watch soaps on we can buy one of those too. But, I've already bought new teeth. You bought that computer thing. Brownie bought twenty pounds of rawhide chews. That's enough."

"It's called a laptop, Mommy. Wait until the kids at school see it. They will flip out to the max."

"Where'd you pick up that language?"

"These girls I met at the Mall. I think they were girls."

"What did they look like?" Jenny asked.

"There were three. They had bright feathers on their heads

instead of hair. It was all different colors. They had shiny shirts, big boobies with no bras, short tails with lots of different colors like their hair, and snouts like Brownie's except with gold rings. They were a little shorter than me and more human than most of the other shoppers. They were nice."

"Where was I?" Jenny asked. *I hope I wasn't a bad mommy.*

"Getting your teeth fixed."

By Earth time, this was their fourth morning on Shptiludrp. Jenny's watch didn't work — not that it ever did before — and so Lacy Dawn gauged time passage by her sleep pattern that had gotten her to the school bus on-time, every time since Head Start. She typed a thank you note to DotCom and deleted it. *We've learned a lot: how to travel the fast and slow beltways, how to order food we like part of the time, how to negotiate the price of an item and not buy it, and how to communicate with people who ain't human.*

"I think it's time to go home," Jenny said through the microphone of her language conversion device.

Lacy Dawn's headset lay on the bed. She got a stereo effect of parental guidance. "It was fun," Lacy Dawn tried for the same effect. *Damn, I forgot to push the "On" button.*

"What?" Jenny said and unhooked her headset and bra. *That feels better.*

"DotCom was great," she said.

He had checked in several times a day, located them regardless of which crowded direction they had wandered in, and had paid for anything they wanted. The Mall was crowded. Somehow, he was always near from somewhere. Jenny bounced her breasts. *Everybody must know DotCom. Sometimes sales clerks ignored their other customers to try and sell us stuff.*

"It was a lot more fun than a hay ride," Lacy Dawn agreed. *My first time going out-of-state.*

"Now I can brag about traveling for real," Jenny said. "Plus, we went a lot farther than Cleveland like my parents."

"You weren't lying to nobody when you said you'd been out-of-state, even if you were just a baby and can't remember nothing."

"One thing bugs me," Jenny said. "Of all the places DotCom

94

could've picked, why Shptiludrp? Why not Hollywood or to see Elvis' house, someplace like that?"

"Yeah, shopping is more work than picking beans."

The next morning, they were on their way back to the hollow. Lacy Dawn played with her new laptop. Jenny smiled at anything that would reflect her new teeth and Brownie chewed his rawhide. The ship's window revealed a blur without definition or interest to the passengers. Brownie had been chewing his tartar control pet treats nonstop for two days so nobody could tell if his teeth were whiter, as well.

"I don't know what to tell Dwayne about my new teeth. I guess I'll tell him that Mr. Kiser let me ride the school bus to the Greyhound stop. Then, I went to that new free dental clinic they opened up near the state capitol. It sounds fishy. What do you think, DotCom?"

"It stinks," he said.

I made a pun.

"Can you think of something better to tell him about these pearly whites?"

"You could blacken part of your new teeth. If you do a few less each weekend, after several weeks your teeth would all be pearly white as you call them. This would give him the impression that you had made several visits to the free clinic to have your teeth repaired or replaced. Such a gradual change may seem less suspicious to him," he said.

"You're talking like a shit salesman with a sample in his mouth. I'm going to get the first good kiss I've had in years. Unless he's lost his touch, Dwayne's a great kisser."

She puckered for practice.

"After I had Lacy Dawn, my teeth went straight to hell. I brushed them twice a day until it hurt too much. My mom said it was because the baby stole all my calcium. Is that possible?"

"Did you take prenatal vitamins?" DotCom asked.

"Anyway, after the side of my front tooth rotted off, I couldn't pay Dwayne for a kiss. When he sees these, I bet I'll feel like a teenager again. This time I ain't going to be so self-conscious. I ain't worried about getting pregnant and I ain't going to wear no bra or panties either."

"I would like to learn how to become a great kisser," he said.

"Well, you ain't practicing on her. I ain't gonna let some hot little bitch steal my man!" Lacy Dawn said in an accent that neither had heard before.

Brownie stopped chewing.

"Sorry. I was practicing. It's on the CD that the girls at the Mall gave me. It's called, "101 Phrases to Help You Survive or Get You Killed in the Ghetto." I'm checking it out on my laptop. Mommy, what's a ghetto?"

Lacy Dawn put her headphones back on and shut her eyes. The volume was so loud that the CD could be heard by all. Brownie covered his ears with his paws and tried to sleep.*Chewing rawhide is more work than digging.*

Jenny looked at DotCom. He concentrated on his autopilot reports. The reports had always been needless but he performed as dutifully trained. Jenny smiled with her new teeth and crossed her legs. DotCom didn't notice. She tried it again. Lacy Dawn was engrossed in the CD she'd gotten from the girls at the mall. *This is the first time we've ever been alone together.*

"I want to ask you a question, DotCom," she said to capture his attention. *I shouldn't get in the middle but I can't help it.*

"Where did you get that stupid name?"

"I direct the universe's spam."

"Spam? I like Spam. If you chop it into small pieces, it mixes good with collards, macaroni and cheese, or baked beans. Wait a minute. What do you mean you direct Spam?" *I shouldn't have asked. It's way too personal.*

"We will hit Earth's atmosphere in six hours and twelve minutes."

"That's nice. I think I'll take a nap," she said. *It'd be wrong for him to tell me without Lacy Dawn's permission. I might as well let him practice his kisses on me or not wear a bra for Tom on purpose. I ain't no slut.*

They didn't talk for the rest of the trip home. Upon arrival, DotCom docked his ship inside the cave. Jenny, Lacy Dawn and Brownie left to return home. Lacy Dawn looked back at him over her shoulder.

"Be cool, fool," Lacy Dawn flipped him the bird and giggled.

"I love you, Lacy Dawn."

She ran back and gave him a kiss beside the lips. He frowned.

I forgot to pucker.

I Want a Full Report

Lacy Dawn slept late the next morning. *My teacher thinks I've still got pinkeye. Today will be an excused absence.*

She patted Brownie's head, picked up her laptop, and went to the bathroom. *Daddy will be home in a few hours. I've got to find a good place to hide this.*

A few minutes later, she flushed, shut down, took off her headphones, and carried the laptop into the kitchen. *It'll be hard enough to explain Mommy's new teeth. If Daddy sees this..., he sure ain't ready for the truth about the universe.*

Lacy Dawn set the laptop on top of an iron skillet on the stove. It still contained last week's grease, which had been left during the rush to leave for out-of-state.

"Why didn't you wake me up, Mommy?"

Jenny smiled at her new teeth in the dresser mirror.

"I just got up myself." *This is some deep shit if Dwayne don't believe me about the dental clinic.*

"Where can I hide this thing so Daddy won't see it?" Lacy Dawn pointed at the laptop.

Without comment, Jenny went into the bathroom and smiled big at the next mirror. Lacy Dawn picked up her laptop, went into the living room, and sat on the couch with it on her lap.

"I know. I'll hide it in the old shitter," she yelled. *It's close—just past the edge of the backyard. The roof is pretty new and nobody's been in it since Daddy plumbed the house.*

She typed and deleted another thank you note to DotCom that she had no way to print or send anyway. *But, the outhouse is bound to be full of snakes.*

Jenny tried pink lipstick—rubbed it off—and put on bright red. Lacy Dawn got a plastic bag from under the kitchen sink and put the laptop inside. She then put it inside a burlap seed bag that her mother had meant to turn into a window curtain. *Wrapped and safe.*

"Here, Brownie," Lacy Dawn said and walked out the back door. *He's been bitten so many times by copperheads that they won't bother him no more.*

Brownie went in the outhouse, chomped five snakes in half,

shook one loose from his snout, and sat down. A few small stragglers slithered away. He barked. *That was fun.*

Lacy Dawn scooted snake parts out the door with her foot and sat her package on the toilet bench. She put a Sears catalogue on top of it. *That's that. I already feel withdrawal symptoms.*

"Love you bunches," she said to the package, latched the door, and returned to the house.

Brownie stayed by the outhouse, killed another snake in the weeds, shook it in the air, and hunted for more. The swaying tops of the taller weeds gave away the snakes' locations.

"I'm going Roundabend to talk with DotCom, okay? I'll be back before Daddy gets home to give him a big hug and kiss right when he gets out of the car."

Still in the bathroom, Jenny watched herself brush her teeth.

Lacy Dawn chanted, glided, and arrived in DotCom's living room. He was busy with routine maintenance, but stopped when he heard, "It's me." They sat in their respective recliners.

"I want another kiss," DotCom said. "I have practiced. I watched three James Bond movies and I hung this mirror to use to measure my pucker," he pointed to a small mirror glued to his monitor.

"Not until you give me a full report," Lacy Dawn said.

"You require a report about what?"

"A report about what happened in your meetings, silly. First, you scare me half to death by leaving and saying you might not be able to come back. You're gone forever. I'd just about given up on ever getting married. After you do come home, you take us out-of-state but spend almost all your time in meetings, meetings, and more meetings. I want to know what the hell is going on with my man on the business side of things and before I give up one more kiss."

DotCom peeled the mirror off his monitor.

"Don't get me wrong. I'll marry you for love. I don't care whether you've got a penny. But, I do believe that a future wife should be told more about your work—like what happens at important meetings. We're a team. Your business is my business. My business is your business."

He slumped.

"Last year, my teacher went on and on about the importance of open communications in a marriage. That's all she taught us except for giving us homework. She told us the reason she ended up divorced was because her marriage didn't have enough communication. All the kids knew her husband had run off with a waitress from the restaurant in the state park. Still, what she said was right. I want to know everything about everything—and right now."

"You want to know everything right now?" he slumped further.

"Just tell me what happened in the meetings and I'll give you a kiss," she said.

"Yes. My previous Supervisor required that I obtain your signature on a contract referred to as an offer of employment. The deadline was three months from the assignment. I was not able to perform because you were not ready. I thought that I might be deactivated because I missed the deadline. Instead, my former Supervisor was fired. I have a new Supervisor who concluded that I am doing a good job. She said that the project is too important to rush. While you and your mother were shopping, I met with her to report our progress. That is all. Can I have the kiss now?"

"Yes."

She planted a big smacker on his cheek and sat back down. Three seconds later, he closed his eyes and puckered.

"Want another?" Lacy asked.

DotCom's face went blank.

"What is this job offer?" she continued ten seconds later.

He refocused and made eye contact.

"Your job is to save the universe, of course. Did I not tell you that when you watched the videos? It is your destiny. Your personal evolution has been monitored for many generations for the sole purpose of identifying when you will be ready to sign the contract." *I said more than required. It was an error in judgment caused by the promise of a kiss.*

She gave him another — a good one on the other cheek, and left to greet her father. *What the shit? Save the universe?*

100

Paid by the Hour

When Lacy Dawn got home from Roundabend, the company car was parked in the yard. Inside the house, a quilt was over her parents' bedroom door. It was a first-time barricade that hadn't been there when she'd left to visit DotCom.

"The new teeth must be a big hit," she whispered to Brownie. *They deserve a little privacy.*

Instead of starting supper, she went to the outhouse to get her laptop. No snakes were inside. She spread the burlap bag on the ground, pushed down the weeds, and sat on it where she couldn't be seen from a window. *I wish I had the internet.*

She found nothing preloaded on her laptop about saving the universe. After repacking and storing it, she left to talk with her best friends in the Woods. *He won't get any more kisses until I figure this out. It's my own fault he got so excited. Boys are easy.*

"Park it if you don't know how to drive," she said to the maple tree.

"What's a park and why are you talking so funny?" it asked.

Lacy smiled at her best friends. *I'm too young to be kissing on a boy like I did—even if he ain't human.*

"It's an idiom. Oh, never mind," she explained.

DotCom got no more sugars after Lacy Dawn's talk with her best friends. The next weekend, she was there when her father got out of the company car. The previous weekend, her parents had spent almost the entire time alone in their bedroom. She was determined to visit with him at least long enough for a hug. *This weekend might be even worse. Mommy just took another bath.*

Jenny had brushed her teeth so many times that Lacy Dawn gave up trying to count. Every time that she encountered a reflective surface, such as her stainless steel skillet, she smiled and admired.

"I'm so jealous," Lacy Dawn gritted into the breeze before her father got out of the car.

Dwayne gave Lacy Dawn a quick kiss and gazed at Jenny.

"Maybe I should've gotten new teeth instead of a laptop," she whispered to Brownie who didn't even get a pat on the head from Dwayne.

Jenny leaned on the porch banister. She wore a print dress with no slip and stood at the correct angle as rehearsed. The setting sun showed through at the perfect place. The breeze gently whipped her hair. She smiled, gazed into the distance, and waited.

Lacy Dawn gave up on getting any attention from her father and decided to practice for the next spitting contest at school. Brownie identified the distances of the wet spots on the grass by pointing his nose and giving an official bark for each goober glob. A tear hit the flat rock walkway to the house steps Lacy had designated as the starting line for the contest, a competition that no longer included another person now that Faith was dead. *Mommy's a beautiful woman. She's way too much competition.*

With his arm around her waist, Dwayne escorted Jenny inside the house. Lacy Dawn and Brownie left to go Roundabend to visit DotCom. *I wonder what's in the big box on top of the car. It's probably something for Mommy.*

On arrival at the ship, Lacy Dawn plugged her cord into the top of her spine without assistance or preface and with no hello kiss or hug. "DotCom, what's the next lesson to learn?" she asked after her first plug-in on Universal Economics. *Mommy's been a real bitch since she got new teeth.*

"Yes," he said as he installed the next Economics disk.

"I've been thinking about the job you offered me," she said.

"And?"

DotCom had responded as if he had been born in the hollow. Lacy Dawn was becoming more diversified by education. He was becoming more colloquial by experience. DotCom looked up from his monitor and directly at Lacy Dawn for the first time that afternoon. *This could be a step toward her signature on the contract.*

"I'm still too young to get married. But, if my daddy comes along to help me check out the job, I can go with you. He would be like a whatchamacallit—a chaperone. What do you think?" *It's one way of getting a little time alone with Daddy.*

"You are the boss," he said.

She plugged herself back into the network, completed her next economics plug-in lesson, and left the ship to go home. DotCom did not get a hug goodbye. She walked the path home. *For the first time in my life, I've got a father worth love. I need my fair share of attention and I'm going to get it.*

"And just where have you been, Little Miss?" Jenny asked with a grin when Lacy Dawn walked through the back door. She didn't respond to her mother. Instead, she refilled Brownie's water bowl from the barrel under the downspout, scooted out a few dead flies with the side of her hand, and slid the bowl back under the porch. *What's wrong with me? They're healthy and now I feel left out. Maybe I need some mental health treatments too.*

Without a word, Lacy passed Jenny in the kitchen, went into the living room, and flopped on the couch. After a few deep breaths with her eyes closed, she got up to give her mother an apologetic hug. *Something's different around here. There's a door on the bathroom, their bedroom, and one on my bedroom. It wasn't a present for Mommy on top of the car. It was a home improvement project.*

She went back into the kitchen and smiled big at Jenny, who was waiting for it. *I've got privacy when I use the bathroom. And, there's a door on my bedroom. I don't do anything private in there—not yet—but it's sure cool.*

"Open, shut, open, shut, open, shut..." Lacy Dawn said to Brownie with a door knob in her hand. *This feels good.*

Brownie whimpered. She patted his head.

Lacy noticed a gizmo. *My new bedroom door's got a lock.*

She tried it.

"Open, shut, open, open, open.... Shit, I've locked myself out," she went into the backyard, climbed through her bedroom window, and unlocked her brand new lock on her brand new bedroom door from the inside.

For the next two months, Dwayne came home every weekend. Home improvement projects continued despite the time he spent courting Jenny within their renewed romantic relationship. Lacy Dawn festered with issues. *I can't get rid of this feeling. DotCom told me that it's my job to save the universe. Maybe I should give him a good kiss or let him see my panties. Maybe I should tell Daddy that I feel neglected. I hate to put off something until tomorrow that can be taken care of today. But, Christmas is almost here. For once, I've saved enough money to buy them nice presents at Goodwill....*

She got a piece of paper and pencil and started a shopping list. *I'll buy DotCom a jock strap. When he puts something in it—like an orange—it'll look like he's got private parts when he wears pants.*

She had learned about jock straps on the school bus when an eighth grader pulled one over the head of a boy in her class. Everybody laughed until Mr. Kiser got mad. He stopped the bus, made the eighth grader explain what a jock strap does, and why his was so small. The eighth grader had to apologize on one knee to the sixth grader for acting like such a moron. It took twenty minutes.

The next weekend, they went Christmas shopping. Lacy Dawn couldn't find a jock strap at Goodwill. There was a big pile of men's underwear on a table. Each pair had at least one hole and the stain—except for a pair of boxers with a Scooby Doo print that was perfect. She put them in her buggy. *I ain't going to ask no sales clerk if they have a jock strap. But, you'll look hot in these, DotCom.*

She picked out a diamond necklace for Jenny and bought a pair of Reeboks for Dwayne that was almost the right size. *At least the tennis shoes ain't fake.*

"Come on. Let's go get your mom's present," Dwayne whispered. He looked over his shoulder at Jenny, who was busy shopping.

"Are we going to leave Mommy?"

"You know your mom. When she finishes here, she'll go to the Dollar Store. She has a lot of money and I told her there's more where that came from."

"I know. I got your VA check out of the mailbox yesterday," Lacy Dawn said.

"I need to get that sucker cut off before I get into trouble. Anyway, let's slip out the door while she's not looking," Dwayne ducked behind a shelf.

They left. Dwayne parked in front of the furniture store and got his work phone out of his shirt pocket. The store had a vacant second story with white paint peeling off of lap siding and a crooked sign. It could have been another second-hand shop except everything inside was new.

"Depending on how long it takes Lacy Dawn to pick one out, I should be there in about a half-hour to forty-five minutes," Dwayne said into the phone.

"I'll be parked in your yard," Tom answered. "After we haul the old one to the burn pile, let's roll up a fatty to celebrate."

"I wouldn't talk like that on cell," Dwayne said.

"Right," Tom agreed.

Lacy Dawn looked at the store's window display. Under bare fluorescents, everything was dingy except the merchandise that sat on a hardwood floor which had lost its shine decades before. The contrast made the furniture more exciting. She browsed. *Pick out a couch for Mommy…not an almost new one…a brand new. I've never been in a furniture store that sells new stuff. I feel nauseated.*

"That's the one," she pointed.

Lacy Dawn's decision took less than thirty seconds. It was a couch that looked like the picture on a page that her mother had torn out of a furniture catalog. It was the one that they would own when they got rich. Dwayne haggled over the price for twenty minutes and declined less expensive couches. He settled on a twenty-five percent discount.

"Old habits die hard," Lacy Dawn apologized to Couch for the delay. "You're worth more and we need to hurry." *Tom might pass out in his SUV before we get home.*

Dwayne and an employee of the furniture store loaded the new couch on the pick-up. A sheet of plastic was tied over it for protection. On the hard road, he drove the exact speed limit home—45 m.p.h. Since Dwayne was still without a driver's license because of the DUI, it was his best option. Back home, Tom opened his door and a thick cloud of smoke billowed out. The old couch was already in the front yard. The new couch sat in its place in ten minutes. They all looked at it. Lacy Dawn cried. *It's the best Christmas present ever.*

Dwayne and Tom carried the old couch to the burn pile behind the house. It was the only spot in the back yard not covered by frosted weeds. Lacy Dawn said goodbye to the old couch and waited in Tom's warm SUV. "I'm too high to go shopping," she said to her eyes in the rear-view mirror, put out the roach that Tom had left burning in the ash tray, and opened the window. The guys came back and she got out.

"Merry Christmas." Tom kissed the top of Lacy Dawn's head, got in his SUV, relit the roach, and pulled out of the yard. Moody Blues bounced off the hillsides until the window was closed.

Lacy and Dwayne got in the company car to return to town and to find Jenny. She relaxed by the time they hit the hard road. *I'm too high not to go shopping.*

"Daddy, a friend of mine offered me a job and I'm trying to decide whether or not to take it."

"You've already got a good job at Tom's place."

"I know. This is a big time job."

"It's a bad decision to go to work for a friend, but it worked out good for me with Tom. It's a matter of distinguishing between objective and subjective."

"I think I know what those words mean. I learned how to spell them in school." *Be careful. My education might scare him. I'm so high.*

"Well...objective...," he began.

"I just don't know how to apply the appropriate analytical concepts to this highly personal situation," she said. *Oh, shit, shit, shit.*

Dwayne raised an eyebrow.

"Do you remember when I overhauled the motor of that red VW bus for Harold? After I got it put together, I couldn't get it to start. I tried everything and was ready to tear the engine back down. I was so mad I couldn't think straight and so was Harold. He needed his bus back real bad. He was my friend and I felt awful. I was subjective. My friendship with Harold, while it increased my determination, messed up my thinking about the solution for the problem."

"I remember the bus," Lacy Dawn said.

They passed the road sign that meant halfway back to town.

"Well, you know Tom don't know nothing about engines. He came over to help me lift the motor back out. After we had the bus jacked up, Tom asked me if I'd checked the gas. I got even madder. Just to show him, I turned on the ignition but the needle on the gas gauge didn't move. What had happened was that the stick I pushed into the gas line to plug it up while the engine was out didn't fit good. All the gas leaked out while I overhauled the engine."

They were in town.

"So?" she asked.

"Tom was objective and guessed right. I felt stupid but was sure glad to get the bus back to Harold. Subjective means to be so involved in something that the odds of figuring out any problems are decreased. I was subjective because I was pissed off at the VW and worried that I'd let Harold down. I couldn't think right. Tom was objective because he was there just to help lift the engine back out. That was all. He wasn't pissed off and thought clearly. He was objective about the problem and figured it out."

"I understand. I'm too subjective about this job offer and need your help to decide if it's a good one or not."

They parked in front of the Dollar Store.

"First thing, if you're in doubt about an offer, make sure right up front that you'll get paid by the hour. If you get paid by the job, there'll be bad vibes on both sides. You'll think you got ripped off and so will your friend. That can mess up your relationships for a long time. You know how people talk."

He turned off the ignition key.

Dwayne jumped out. Lacy Dawn stayed put and turned the ignition key and radio back on. She found a station with country music and rolled down the window. *Get paid by the hour. I've never thought about getting paid for saving the universe....*

Jenny shopped.

107

The Devil's in the Details

"Ring, ring, ring...." Lacy Dawn awakened on Christmas morning. *I must be getting tinnitus.*

She put a pillow over her exposed ear. Tinnitus was one of several human medical conditions that she had studied at DotCom's ship. Although a little muffled, the ringing did not stop. On her dresser was something that had never been in her house, much less in her bedroom—a telephone. She climbed down the three rungs of the ladder that Dwayne had screwed to the side of her loft bed, a replacement for the roll-away when floor space had run out, and answered the telephone.

"Hello?" she said as if under her grandmother's strict supervision.

"Lacy Dawn, this is Tom. I'm getting the hell out of this hollow until it thaws—back to the Keys. I suppose your dad is still in bed with your mom. I don't blame him. Do you remember Jerry Lee Lewis? Never mind. It was a stoned comment."

She caressed the smooth, shiny red plastic base which sat on her dresser with her other hand. It stayed there.

"Anyway," Tom continued, "your dad has made me so much money that I want to give him a good Christmas present. Tell him he can have a month off with pay if he has somebody that he can assign as an acting manager. He's trained his staff. I'm sure he has options. Anyway, I'm out of here. I'll see you when I get back. And, Lacy Dawn, if I was fifteen I sure would ask to sit beside you at next year's Hayride during the Walnut Festival. Sorry. I'm stoned. I'll talk with you when I get back. How'd your mom like the new couch? Bye."

"Goodbye."

She wiped the boogers from her eyes, pinched herself, and climbed back into bed. A few minutes later, the telephone rang again.

"It's me again," Tom said before she said hello. "I just wanted to let you know that the ISP people said you'd be hooked up on Monday. Sorry, they don't run cable down the hollow. At least you'll be online by dialup. I wish that WiFi worked down here.

Tell your dad to call me if he gets up in the next hour. I'll be on my way to the airport. If he gets up later, tell him to call me late tonight. I want to tell him where I hid another of his Christmas presents."

"I got you a present too, Tom. I'm sure Daddy did too."

"Okay. I'll be over in a few. But don't wake your dad. He needs all the rest he can get since your mom got so fabulous." Lacy Dawn nodded agreement. *ISP! I can't wait to tell my teacher.*

Lacy Dawn wrapped Tom's present in newspaper comics that she had gotten from her grandmother. She taped a used bow on top, put on her coat, and waited on the porch. Tom arrived and opened it.

"Holy shit, Lacy Dawn, a box full of science fiction and fantasy novels: Piers Anthony, Kurt Vonnegut, Arthur C. Clarke, and some I haven't heard of. This is perfect timing. I'll read them while I'm at the Keys. Thanks."

He kissed her on top of the head and ran to his car.

"They only cost a dime a book."

Lacy Dawn went inside and waited by the Christmas tree. An hour later, Dwayne and Jenny came through their bedroom door. As her parents emptied their first cups of coffee, she told them about Tom's call, the month off with pay, and how Tom liked the novels she'd given him. Dwayne kissed Jenny's hand, cheek, neck, closed eyes, and shoulder, but avoided her lips. *I know better than to get started there. I won't be able to stop.*

"I don't know nothing about ISPs and computers," he said. You'll have to pick out a computer tomorrow when we go to the big city," Dwayne said during a kiss break for air. "Tom told me to get you one."

"I've already got a laptop," she blurted. Jenny gave her the evil eye.

Without reaction, Dwayne returned to kisses.

"Stop. We ain't even passed out gifts," Jenny demanded. She opened her next present—another very sheer nightgown similar to the first two. Lacy Dawn went to the bathroom and returned a minute later because her parents waited to open more presents. Jenny also got new underwear that she hid from view and a new skirt. Composed, Lacy Dawn held up the skirt, frowned, and then smiled at her mother. "It's cute," she said. *I just hope I don't get a Barbie.*

Dwayne got smacked when he kissed the back of Jenny's neck.

"Anyway, here's the rest of the shit that I got," he said. "I don't even know what most of it is."

He handed Lacy Dawn packages of store-wrapped presents. She got Microsoft Office, Computer Chess, an encyclopedia CD, a mathematics tutorial that she didn't need, a game she had never heard of, and a CD of the greatest hits of Metallica that was a present to her from her father to himself. And, she got a pair of speakers to go with the computer that Dwayne wanted her to pick out. She went to the outhouse and brought back her laptop.

"Ain't gonna waste my hate on you…," Metallica played.

Dwayne strummed air guitar. They passed out more presents. He sang along. *I should've got Lacy Dawn their newest CD. I wonder where she got that CD player.*

Jenny spread a sheet over the new couch to protect it. It was the first time that she'd let anyone sit on it and she'd be extra careful for its lifetime—forever. She then tried on one dainty thing after another. Dwayne admired. Lacy Dawn looked at her presents and pretended to ignore her mother's behavior, but focused every few seconds on Jenny's exhibition. *She's good. I bet that'll work on DotCom. He's so easy.*

Lacy Dawn gave Dwayne the tie and tennis shoes she bought him at Goodwill. Jenny gave him underwear, socks, a belt, and two dress shirts with button-down collars. The socks were black instead of white. Dwayne kissed Lacy Dawn's cheek. She grinned. *He didn't say nothing smarty pants about the tie.*

Lacy Dawn gave Jenny the diamond necklace, a picture frame, and six romance novels. Jenny put on the necklace and started reading on the spot until she noticed the reflection of her new teeth in the picture frame glass and kissed Dwayne on the lips. He held up both palms to hold her off.

Jenny gave Lacy Dawn a hope chest with a baby quilt inside that had been made by her grandmother.

"Oh, Mommy, I'm going to cry."

She put them under her bed. *After we get married, DotCom and I will adopt a baby.*

"I don't know what I'm going to do with a whole month off work," Dwayne said after the presents were passed out. He winked at Jenny, who smiled.

"I've got an idea," Lacy Dawn said.

"Check out your job offer?" Dwayne motioned Jenny toward their bedroom. She went.

"I could use your help, Daddy..."

"You ain't getting nothing if you don't agree to help," Jenny said from the bedroom. It was loud enough to be heard in the living room. From around the door frame, she showed off her butt in the first pair of brand-new panties since they'd gotten married.

"Okay, okay," Dwayne got up and skipped into their bedroom.

Lacy Dawn went Roundabend to wish DotCom a Merry Christmas. They exchanged presents. He tried on his new outfit, which fit since he could adjust his body size and shape. She made him download a Scooby Doo cartoon so as to understand the underwear she'd given him, and then she became engrossed with her present—Ms. Pac-Man.

"That game is older than you are," he said. "It was an appropriate gift since, with respect to humans, only females can save or destroy a world."

"Daddy agreed to help me check out your job offer," she said as she continued to play.

"I'll notify my Supervisor." He sent an email.

"All arrangements will be in place. Please tell me when."

"Shit. I'm sorry. Hold up a minute. After this screen, I'm turning this thing off before I become so addicted that I can't ever turn it off." *Double damn. I missed the points from that fruit.*

Lacy Dawn went home to a huge meal. The centerpiece was a turkey that Dwayne had shot on the ridge. That evening, they visited several relatives where they were required to sample more food. Dwayne gave the adults the traditional gift that they'd come to expect on Christmas—homegrown buds. Since he also drank a few beers, Jenny drove them home.

The day after Christmas, Lacy Dawn took Dwayne to Roundabend. Afterward, he spent hours looking for his old medication. It had been trashed by Jenny with much celebration a couple of months before. Instead, Dwayne settled down on the new couch with the cigar box full of his Christmas present from Tom.

"It's not possible that the guy I met is an android who lives up the hollow. I need some new kind of medication," Dwayne said to the cigar box.

After a week during which he made several visits to the cave, Dwayne started to accept that the world—the universe—was bigger than he formerly conceived. It took reassurance from Jenny, her new teeth and panties, and a high performance carburetor from DotCom. *That truck's never run so good. Even Harold's amazed. DotCom must be real 'cause there ain't no mechanic born on this Earth that's better than me.*

Dwayne took another hit. *Ain't nobody going to rip off my little girl.*

He took another hit. *I need details, a contract, health insurance, and worker's compensation coverage.*

He took another hit. *Mostly, I need more proof that I ain't crazy.*

He didn't get it. Nobody ever does.

"I might be crazy, but I've got to do what's right for my daughter," he said to the cigar box an hour later.

Jenny heard. She came into the living room and kissed him on the forehead. Dwayne got up and hugged her—too long and too tight to be sexual. It was more like a goodbye hug to a visitor by a patient involuntarily committed to a mental health facility—a hug intended to squeeze out and steal some sanity because nothing else had worked. Dwayne let go and sank back onto the couch.

I bet I wake up still sick, hated, and ashamed.

He took another hit. *Like the manager of a rock star, I'll negotiate a killer deal.*

Dwayne listed Findings of Fact and Conclusions of Reality on his Manager Legal Pad—a concrete and undeniably yellow, lined pad of paper. *I'd never spend good money on a legal pad. I got it from somewhere—so my job must be real.*

"Breakfast's ready," Jenny yelled.

Dwayne took the legal pad to the kitchen with him. It lay on his lap as he ate. Two grease drips later, he finished the first breakfast that he'd eaten at the kitchen table since Lacy Dawn had outgrown her highchair. *There are grease spots on this pad. It's got to be real, I'm real, and so is DotCom.*

"The Devil's in the details," Dwayne yelled an hour later from the living room. Lacy Dawn and Jenny were washing dishes. They smiled at each other. Jenny smacked her on the butt.

Jenny shut her eyes and nodded her head. *He's committed to the project, Honey. It'll be a father–daughter outing. I'll stay home to give you two some time alone together.*

For the first time ever, Lacy Dawn smacked her mother on the butt right back. They gave each other a high five.

"He loves me," Lacy Dawn yelled out the open kitchen window to the maple tree. *Daddy will go to Shptiludrp to represent my interests, negotiate, and chaperone.*

"I'm so sorry," Lacy Dawn whispered to Jenny.

"It's okay. Sometimes, I get jealous of you too."

They went into the living room to be with Dwayne.

"Give me a hit," Jenny said for the first time since before they had gotten married.

"Me too," Lacy Dawn said. *I know he won't.*

"Ain't you been paying attention to your DARE classes in school?" Dwayne pinched a butt cheek.

"That's spoken for if you don't mind," she answered.

"Well, go up and tell your boyfriend that we're ready whenever."

"He ain't my boyfriend. He's my fiancé for when I'm old enough."

"Whatever. Your mom and I have to talk."

Jenny took one hit.

"Do you remember Grandpa's '69 Chrysler?" she asked. "It had the best back seat I've ever...."

"And how many back seats do you know that well?" he asked.

After Lacy Dawn came back home from Roundabend,

113

Dwayne called for a family meeting. He looked serious.

"There's one more piece of info that I need. What's up with his stupid name?"

"I asked him once and he said something about Spam. I don't know what he meant," Jenny answered.

"I like Spam and eggs okay, but not really," Dwayne said.

"You like Spam in all kinds of stuff I fix."

"Not really."

"Me either, Mommy," Lacy Dawn agreed.

"The Devil's in the details," Jenny said. *I hope to never touch another food stamp card.*

Lacy Dawn went into her bedroom to surf the internet with her door closed and earphones on — one spam after another. Twenty minutes later, she could still hear her parents having sex. *Thank God. He's okay.*

The Scope of Work

Dwayne slept for three thousand, two hundred and eight light years. Upon arrival on Shptiludrp, he followed DotCom and Lacy Dawn to the hotel and slept some more.

"I wish there was at least one channel for kids on this TV," Lacy Dawn said as she clicked through channels the next morning. Management of their hotel provided free TV reception to all rooms. After an uneventful trip across the universe and a good night's sleep, however, there was nothing very interesting on the tube. *I'd settle for one with Daffy Duck, but I'd give a dollar to watch Eliza Thornberry sell language conversion devices.* "I'm worried that we ain't going to figure out what needs to be done and DotCom will be disappointed. Hurry up, Daddy, I've got to pee."

"Hold your horses and don't worry so much. We just got here," he said.

Whenever she was depressed, worried, had a cold, or was lonely on a Saturday morning, Lacy Dawn glided past Roundabend to watch cartoons at her grandmother's house. Grandma had a satellite dish because she loved soaps and the company it drew. Lacy Dawn crossed her legs. *It feels like it should be a Saturday morning at Grandma's house.*

Dwayne flushed. Lacy Dawn re-crossed her legs and surfed channels. *At least this one shows shoppers instead of more stuff for sale.*

"Some of the shoppers look like they could be cartoons," she yelled.

"Shame on you, Lacy Dawn." He flushed a second time. *I thought our commode was weak.*

She flipped through more channels. *I guess I'm racist.*

"Daddy! There's a kid on TV who looks like Deborah from school. Come and look — hurry, hurry!"

Dwayne switched on the monitor in the bathroom and continued to shave. He'd been prepared for the trip by a plug-in on cultural diversity and three videos in which nobody looked Earth-like. But, on the TV, he saw people who could have been shopping in any 7-11 across the street from any elementary school in America.

"Do you see Deborah?" Lacy Dawn asked and pushed her father out of the bathroom.

"Sorry, I don't remember what Deborah looks like."

"This ain't the same channel." She sat on the commode adapter that the hotel staff had placed for human-like people, flipped from one channel to the next, and looked for scenes of shoppers instead of merchandise. On several channels, at least a few Earth-like people could be seen.

"Hurry up, Daddy. Let's go meet some of those people," she urged, flushed, pulled up her panties and jeans.

Ten minutes later, they headed toward the shop where she'd seen Deborah. The shop's numerical identifier was on its advertisement. They asked a street pole for the exact location, "Shop 10056787, by your measure, is two hundred and twelve shops on the right, straight ahead."

The pole estimated arrival time at two Earth minutes by the quickest route, the fast beltway. The database to which it was networked was updated each time a shopper with a new language or measurement system was approved to visit. Lacy pushed the beltway's Load button and they got on. She plugged her language conversion device into a port and watched shop address numbers increase. One shopper after another delayed their arrival by pushing the beltway's stop button to hop off. Three minutes later, standing on the walkway, she looked to the left and right for the shop. *That stupid pole missed our estimated arrival time by a whole minute.*

"There it is," Dwayne pointed.

Lacy Dawn crossed her fingers, rushed toward a shop, and walked through the entrance. The shop specialized in pipes. It looked like a tobacco or head shop. Pipes of every imaginable shape and size and with various numbers of stems were displayed. There was a black curtain that sectioned the shop into front and back. Some patrons went behind the black curtain.

"This is my kind of place," Dwayne said after he caught up with her.

She began searching the front section and he went straight to the back. Two minutes later, they got together and shook their heads. *No humans here.*

"I can't wait to tell Tom that getting high is a universal phenomenon," he said.

She pushed him out and toward the next shop.

"What am I thinking? I can't tell Tom nothing."

"She's not here. Let's look in the other shops." Lacy Dawn exited the second shop that Dwayne had almost entered. She gave him The Look. *Hurry, hurry.* She ran to the next shop entrance, looked in, and ran to the next and the next.

Dwayne followed but didn't try to keep up. *She won't allow herself to become separated from me.*

It had happened once at Kmart when Lacy Dawn was five. "If you have lost your child, please come to the service desk," a loud page had told the entire store. "You must provide proper identification to claim this child," another clerk said, held her hand tight, and wouldn't let go. Dwayne didn't have his driver's license because of the DUI. They had to use their electric bill for an ID. The clerk held onto Lacy Dawn's hand until after he had made a long notation on a pad at the service desk. Tears streamed down Lacy Dawn's cheeks for the duration.

"Stay up, Daddy, please." *I'll never get lost again while shopping. I'll never lose my kid when I grow up and shop at Kmart. I'll always carry an electric bill in my purse. But, if he don't hustle it up, I'll sure kick his ass.*

Dwayne quickened his pace and then waited in front of the next shop. *She must have scored.*

Five minutes later, he walked through the shop entrance and found himself surrounded by what appeared to be grade school-age children. He went back outside. Lacy Dawn also exited the shop.

"It's a school field trip. They don't just look like kids. They are kids, sort of. They're nice."

"What do you mean sort of?" Dwayne asked.

"The best I can figure out, they're all older than you but they're still kids. The tall ones are teachers and parents who volunteered to help supervise the field trip. I couldn't get anybody to say if he or she was a boy or a girl. It looked like a girl that I talked to last but it wasn't the Deborah I saw on TV. I can't pronounce the name of where they are from. A lot of schools send classes here for some kind of history lesson. They're going to have a test and everything."

"Far out," Dwayne said. *We can scope out the job by talking with these kids. Nobody will ever know.*

"What?" Lacy Dawn asked.

"Except for no ears, they do look human. I'm sure you're right that they're nice and they don't look interested in shopping. Maybe we can ask them some questions. Everybody else has looked too busy. What do you think?"

"It can't hurt."

Dwayne filled her in on his plan and they went into the shop.

"Why is the Mall important to history?" Lacy Dawn asked the first kid they encountered.

"Is this a pop quiz?"

"No. I was just wondering about it. This is the first time I've shopped here."

"I hate shopping," the kid said. "I never get to watch cartoons."

"Me either," Lacy Dawn said. *Establish a bond.*

"Okay. The Mall is the center of the economic universe. It was built on the oldest known habitable planet and is managed by life forms that are no longer carbon-based. There's a series of mid-level management classes that all kids are required to attend. We have to recite what each administration accomplished within single-sentence bullet points in order to pass the essay. There has always been the same Manager of the Mall, Mr. Prump, since the beginning. He is the big boss of the universe and will live forever. All the other bosses on all the other planets answer to him. Did I pass the pop quiz?" the kid waited.

"Yes," Lacy Dawn answered. But the kid made eye contact with Dwayne so she jabbed him in the ribs.

"B+," Dwayne said.

"Thank you," the kid moved into the center of the group and yelled, "Next."

"One more and let's get the hell out of here before we're noticed," Dwayne whispered.

Lacy Dawn engaged the next kid with a touch on its shoulder.

"I'm ready," the second kid said without delay.

"Are there any big problems here at the Mall that need to be fixed in order for it to continue to fulfill its mission?" Lacy Dawn asked.

Dwayne had whispered the revised question into her ear. Students closed around to hear an answer to a question that had never been asked on a field trip.

"No. The Mall is self-contained and perfectly maintained. It is managed without flaw, never closed, environmentally healthy for and designed to accommodate visitors from any planet in the universe. It is profitable, easy to get to, and always has the best buys and the newest merchandise available."

The second kid continued to list wonderful things about the Mall. When he was finished, the kid looked into Dwayne's eyes.

"A+" Dwayne said. *I'm afraid to grade him lower.*

The kid skipped into the center of the group. The adults clapped. Lacy Dawn smiled. *We made his day.*

Lacy and Dwayne left the shop and returned to the hotel. Dwayne went to bed in his clothes and was snoring a minute later. DotCom arrived shortly thereafter.

"Where have you been?" Lacy Dawn yawned. It made her sound like she had a speech impediment. *DotCom forgot to say, "it's me" when he came in. It's the first time he's ever used bad manners since I met him. Something must be wrong.*

"Meetings."

When Lacy Dawn told him about the incident at the hotel room, DotCom taught her a Mall Law: "If a student gets an A+ on a pop quiz, the shopkeeper is required to offer a fifty percent discount on all purchases to anybody on the field trip—teachers and volunteers included." DotCom had read a proviso from the School Field Trip Manual on his screen, which he had helped write Earth centuries before. "The student's picture is also hung on an interior school wall for eternity," he summarized so he didn't have to click Next for the exact phraseology.

"Man, everybody here is manic—rush, rush, rush," Dwayne got up to pee. *I shouldn't have gone to bed. If she starts in on him about bad manners, I'm next.*

He hadn't been asleep, but in a zone that emphasized its sounds for effect.

"Shoppers try to avoid wasting time. One reason why is that vehicles are assessed a fee for each period docked."

"What've you been doing in meetings when you're supposed to be showing us the job? We've got to decide whether we can do it or not," Lacy Dawn said.

"My attendance was mandatory."

"Daddy has stuff to do around the house before he goes back to work. I can't afford to miss any more school. I've already had pinkeye once. What's so important about meetings?"

"Reprogramming," the android answered.

"Do we still have a deal in the making?" Dwayne asked, back from the bathroom.

"Yes."

"What does reprogramming mean?" she asked. *This sounds serious.*

"I have a maintenance schedule. Files are backed up or deleted during a review program written by my Supervisor. There has been no modification of files pertaining to our business relationship. In human terms, I have been cleaned-up to original programs that were installed before our relationship contaminated them with viruses then unknown to my makers. I am now protected from future similar infections, such as caused by human emotions—respect, love, ancillary duty, or affection."

"Give me a kiss," a tear swelled in Lacy Dawn's eye.

"What?" he didn't try to pucker and was expressionless.

"At least you're still my best friend—right? You'll be my best friend even if we ain't still engaged and even if we don't get married, right?"

Her tears dripped like the kitchen faucet did before Dwayne replaced it.

"No," the android answered.

"Eat shit! Eat shit! Eat shit you mother! This deal is history you ass wipe. Take me home right now. Don't you even look in my direction—ever? And give me back those clothes I bought you with my bean money...."

The android took off its Christmas presents and she stomped

them. She ran out of steam five minutes later, sat on the edge of her bed, and refused to let deep breathing exercises engage. *Best friends never last. Faith turned inanimate and now DotCom has too.*

Dwayne went into the bathroom to sniff a small roach that was too small to hold with his fingers, but which helped him think when it burned between match sticks. *I've never heard her almost say the F word before. My baby's in pain. She's lost her man. I should wash her mouth out with soap, but that's too stupid.*

He returned and faced DotCom.

"Sounds like the scope of work is over our heads," Dwayne said. "Report the finding to your supervisor."

In less than an Earth hour they were on their way home.

Going on Thirteen (And Never Been Kissed)

Back from Shptiludrp, Dwayne chopped enough firewood for the week and returned to work. When home on weekends, he never mentioned the shopping trip on which nothing was purchased and nothing was achieved. Home improvement projects continued with less enthusiasm.

Lacy Dawn returned to school, maintained her reputation as the most perfect student ever to come out of the hollow, and cried each night about her lost love. She found her old single-edge razor blade. It was rusty.

Jenny spent her time studying the driver's education manual that Dwayne had gotten her for Christmas free from the Department of Motor Vehicles. The NAPA calendar on the kitchen wall—the one that was current—had two dates circled: the first of the five-part GED test that she was scheduled to take and the other for when she planned to take the test for her learner's permit. Otherwise, the calendar did not have notes to remind them of significant events. There was nothing on it about saving the universe.

Two months and sixty cuts after returning home, Lacy Dawn went up the path to talk to her best friends about the disadvantages of true love.

"All things considered," Lacy Dawn said to the walnut tree, "everything in my life's much better than before I met him—even if DotCom don't love me anymore."

"Eat shit," the oak tree said because the Walnut wouldn't talk about it and the maple just seeped. It was a short session.

Afterward, Lacy Dawn no longer went Roundabend to visit because the real DotCom wasn't there and the trees had no advice to offer. However, one evening in May, she had no choice. Her sixth grade final essay on literature was due and her laptop had locked up. She couldn't do anything with it. DotCom was the only person in the hollow who had seen a laptop, much less fixed one.

"Roundabend, roundabend, roundabend…," she chanted.

It still worked.

"It's me," she announced, walked through the ship's entrance, and presented her laptop to him. DotCom looked up from his monitor.

"You are behind on your plug-in lessons," DotCom said.

"Can you fix this?" she continued to hold it forward with both hands.

"Yes, for a price," he answered.

"I know you don't want to see my panties and I ain't got no bean money left." *I'm going to flunk sixth grade Literature, what an embarrassment.*

"I have been instructed to offer you anything within my capability. In exchange, please listen to one statement from Management. Then, you must process it for one Earth minute."

"Okay," she agreed. The android clicked his mouse:

"Files concerning your relationship with DotCom were not deleted, merely inactivated. Analyses of all data predicted maximum outcome by reprogramming DotCom to eliminate your emotional dependence. To date, you have failed to negotiate a purchase of the basic information needed to define my job offer. You were to consider the offer with the assistance of your father. Management analysis of the situation found that you had an irrational expectation that the information that you needed would be provided for free. Or, that you expected DotCom to negotiate the purchase of the information on your behalf. Your personal relationship with DotCom appeared detrimental to the mission. It is possible to restore DotCom's files if you can demonstrate to the satisfaction of Management that the above analyses were flawed."

"Haven't you ever loved?" she reacted and held back. *Wait. A deal is a deal. One minute of silence and I'll blow that asshole away.*

Her forehead beaded with sweat.

"You stupid shit. Haven't you ever been in love? You either give me back my man or I'll steal Tom's dynamite that he stole from the mines and blow this cave to bits. I ain't kidding. You ain't experienced nothing until you've experienced a woman's anger. I'm almost thirteen and that's close enough. You are warned. It's the last warning you'll get until tomorrow evening and then it's war."

She took the repaired laptop from the fake DotCom, put it in its canvas case, and left. *It's getting late and I still have to finish my essay.*

Despite her panic to complete her homework, she walked, rather than glided, home from Roundabend. The path was covered with fallen leaves. She crunched them hard step by step by step. *A taste of vengeance might be a good idea.*

"Brownie, go get one stick of dynamite out of Tom's shed."

He did. She had him put it back.

At home, Lacy Dawn was almost finished with her Literature essay when the telephone rang. Multiplying like rabbits, phones were now in all four rooms of the house. Their rings would have been loud enough for a neighbor to hear, if they had a neighbor. She clicked Save and answered the one in the living room because her phone was under a pile of draft essays. *Next Christmas, I'm asking for a printer so I don't have to handwrite my homework.*

"Hello," she answered. *Pretend it's perfect timing.*

There was no response for ten seconds.

"Lacy Dawn, this is Mr. Prump, Manager of the Mall. I decided to handle your customer satisfaction complaint personally. As you know, we take all complaints very seriously. You are one of our most valued customers. How can I help?"

She gave the bottom of the handset the finger and rubbed it up and down on the plastic for emphasis. *I bet he uses that line on hundreds of other customers.*

After five seconds to collect her emotions, she said, "You soured our deal when you turned my fiancé into a robot. I want my man back and not a reprogrammed idiot look-a-like."

There was a minute delay.

"I see."

"I don't think you're capable of understanding or you wouldn't have authorized such a huge mistake. You sent that moron to me like I wouldn't notice the difference."

There was no response for two minutes.

"Let me call you back. I have to process the possibility of error. It will take five Earth minutes."

Lacy Dawn hung up the phone, returned to her room, and

finished her essay. She was ready for bed except for brushing her teeth. An hour later the phone rang again.

"Hello."

"Still up?" Dwayne asked. He was on the road heading back to work.

"Yeah, I just finished my homework. I'm waiting for Mommy to get out of the tub so I can brush my teeth."

"I've never known you to be so shy."

"Since she got the bubble bath, I like to give her a little privacy."

"For what?"

"Let me put it like this. Not too long after she gets in the tub, she starts calling your name. Then, she starts calling Jesus' name. Sometimes, she's in bubbles all evening. I try not to listen but you know these walls."

Lacy Dawn knew about masturbation. All the girls at school were doing it. Except for talking about boys, masturbation was the only other thing that they talked about during recess even though most of them couldn't even spell clitoris.

"Hold on a minute and you'll hear her for yourself," she said. *I'm not going to try masturbation. Once you start, you can't stop. Life is too busy for addiction. Plus, DotCom didn't have no private parts except for a little bump that showed up before I lost him. I wouldn't have nobody's name to call out anyway.*

"Never mind. When you get a chance, tell her that I'm going to be home a day early this week. I can take her to test for her learner's permit. Plus, I've got a present for you."

"It's not my birthday, Daddy."

"No big deal. It's a printer that we replaced in the company. It works fine. Tom told me to turn over all of the computer equipment for tax purposes. I gave everything to a nonprofit that fixes computers for kids. I figured you're a kid too. Plus, I got an extra receipt for this one too. See you when I get home."

Lacy reminded herself: *My daddy is smart. He didn't ask me about DotCom and didn't even beat around the bush trying to pry. There ain't too many women smart enough to keep their mouths shut when lover's break up. Maybe men are smarter about some things.*

Ten seconds later the phone rang again.

"Hello."

"Hey, girl," Tom said. "You must've been talking with your boyfriend because it's been busy. I guess you two made up. Your dad told me you had a falling out. Break up, make up. Anyway, I called to ask you to do me a favor. I'm still in New York messing around. Tomorrow or the day after, I should get a package from Amsterdam too big to fit in my mailbox. The mailman will lean it on the post. That's what he did last time. Would you put it in my shed before it gets rained on?"

"No problemmo," she said. *That trashed my theory about men being smarter.*

"Thanks. See you soon. It's party time."

She hung up the telephone and it rang.

"Lacy Dawn, it's me, Mr. Prump. Please state your terms of employment. My analysts could find no logical flaw in reprogramming DotCom. As a former carbon-base, however, I have concluded that a flaw must exist or you would be on the job."

She covered the mouth piece and yelled, "Mommy, get out of the bathroom! I have to pee and brush my teeth."

"Here's the deal, dude. I want my man back just like he was before. I love him and he loves me. He's finally grown up and there ain't no other. He's unique. Whether this generation or the next or the next for a million years, I won't take a job at the Mall without my man by my side. I'll remember—forever and ever. It's over if you don't come through. You'll have to start with a new genetic spawn. You're in a big pickle and I recommend that fix it now. That means, in human terms, you can take this job and shove it if you don't give me back my DotCom."

"Let me clarify," Mr. Prump said. "You want all of DotCom's files restored to the point of your last arrival at the Mall. When that is performed, you will reconsider your resignation."

"I want my man back—the one that you stole from me. I want him back in body, mind, spirit and soul—all of him."

"Our warranty on his body, if the original is returned, is limited. We have no ability to endow bodies with spirits or souls if such exist."

"What do you mean by warranty?"

"The body that you know will last for between one thousand to two thousand more years. It depends on environmental conditions. If the body malfunctions while under warranty, it will be repaired or replaced."

"Good enough."

"I will have it delivered within twenty-four Earth hours, complete with all former programs and memory banks."

"I will know the difference. My man almost knows how to pucker, and is growing private parts. Plus, he loves me in so many ways I can't describe. If you try to trick me, I'll know and you'll be sorry."

"I will not try to trick you, Lacy Dawn. I am having a hard time remembering love. It has been so long—thousands of years."

"Give me back my man and you'll learn." *Shit, he's the most powerful being in the universe and I'm treating him with disrespect.*

"I hope to re-learn."

Mr. Prump had been beaten in negotiations for the first time in eons. Lacy Dawn hung up the phone and went to bed without brushing her teeth. An hour later, she got up and peed in the back yard because her mother was still in the tub of bubbles and calling out names.

Re-Scoping the Scope of Work

Mr. Prump restored DotCom as agreed. Lacy Dawn reconsidered the job offer as agreed. A week of emotional adjustment later, things were back to non-normal in the hollow.

The real DotCom had been returned to Lacy Dawn and she'd laid down the law to him for the next trip. No more meetings. No shopping for fun. This trip would be strictly the business of the job and its terms. DotCom was back—the one who would face deactivation to protect his love and who begged for a goodnight kiss.

On Shptiludrp, DotCom gave them as much of a tour as a full day would allow. The tour was not of the shops, but of the inner workings. They visited storage areas, docks, staff lounges, repair and maintenance areas, and employee training and conference centers. It was the real Shptiludrp hidden from shoppers—the Employees Only parts of the planet. They stood in front of a vending machine.

"You have clearances to see any place you want," DotCom said. *Every word is monitored.*

That night, Dwayne ordered a six pack of Budweiser. He received a close match and was on his fifth beer. It was a good buzz.

"All right, buddy, give it up. Where the hell did you get your name?"

Lacy Dawn stopped playing Ms. Pac-Man, looked up, and waited for the answer. *Since Daddy asked the question.*

"I am Spam. I have already explained that to Jenny."

"That's what she told me but I don't get it," Dwayne said.

"Spam?" Lacy Dawn asked. *It ain't Spam with eggs for breakfast. It's those advertisements I get on my laptop, like the one that asks if I want to grow my member three to four inches longer. My teacher called it spam and said there ain't nothing I can do to prevent it. I'm such a dumb ass.*

"I get it, now," Lacy Dawn said. "You use e-mail at work, Daddy. Spam is like the ad that asks if you want to grow your member longer."

Dwayne opened his last beer and took a sip.

"What a rip-off. I spent $59.95 on a bottle of those pills. After I took 'em, your mom said I was the same as always—perfect." *Am I drunk? What the hell am I doing talking with my daughter about my dick?*

"Anyway, spam is when somebody sends you an e-mail to sell you something that you never asked about," Lacy Dawn said.

"Are you trying to sell us something, DotCom?" Dwayne asked.

DotCom stalled. *He is intoxicated.*

"I am one of a series of units manufactured on Shptiludrp. The series was given the title of Corporate Director. Several thousand years ago, the name of the line was changed to the Director of Development series. The individual units were named Director for short."

Dwayne leaned back on the headrest and shut his eyes.

"As planets became computer literate, the name for the series to which I belong was changed to DotCom. The new name signaled revised marketing strategies."

Dwayne snored.

Lacy Dawn got up and jabbed DotCom in the side. He tried to ignore her by clicking another icon that opened another screen, but it was her permanent school record and an obvious mistake. She jabbed him again. *Don't quit now.*

"So, everybody that works on Shptiludrp is a robot?" she asked.

"No. Top management is carbon-based with add-on components to increase efficiency. All shopkeepers are carbon based with plug-in training. Some sales clerks have received plug-in treatments similar to treatments that your mother and father received from me. The official philosophy of the Mall has always been to work with carbon as a means to stay in touch with its customers' needs."

"There are a lot of DotComs out there?" She pointed around the hotel room.

"There have been hundreds of Directors manufactured over the years. All had a form identical to mine. The form was selected by Management based on marketing research. My form has been involved in the least recorded interplanetary conflict and the fewest wars."

"You're about to experience a conflict if you don't answer the question."

"Originally, Directors traveled among planets to promote development. My form had the greatest potential for success since they were least likely to stir up old biases. However, today, marketing is conducted by electronic networks. Directors were deactivated and the materials recycled."

"Just tell me how many others look like you," she demanded.

"None," he complied.

"Cool beans."

"Let me elaborate. There are six other deactivated units that are almost identical in storage. I can spam the universe in less than an Earth hour. This includes the rotation of Hot Items for Sale each Earth week. Given technological advances, there is no need to activate more than one DotCom at any given time. The other units remain as replacements for the eventuality that I wear out."

"What do you mean almost identical? What's the difference?"

"I do not understand and cannot explain. I have started to grow human-like genitals. I have searched my files, drives, and plug-ins but have not found a reference to such a growth program. In the history of my series, there is no penis precedent."

"Oh, my God, let me see it!"

"Not until we are married."

"Well, I bet it's cute." *Pink is my favorite color.*

"Those other units have to be recycled," Lacy Dawn said. "This universe is only big enough for one DotCom. Tomorrow, I want you to contact Mr. Prump—not your Supervisor. Tell him that as a condition of reconsidering the employment offer I demand that the other units be recycled. Tell him that I also demand that no other unit shall be made in your likeness. I want it in writing by tomorrow afternoon."

"I hope that you do not get me fired," DotCom said.

"If there was any risk of that, you wouldn't be here now. I already told your boss about the bump of private parts. Besides him, who else on Shptiludrp knows?" she asked.

"You told Mr. Prump that I'm growing a penis?"

"Not in so many words," she answered. "I was pissed off. It just came out. Sorry. He must be cool with it or he wouldn't have sent you back to me. Maybe he didn't know what I meant. I don't know. But, let's not tell anybody else for now. C'mon, let's go to bed."

"First, I have work to do. I need to analyze the changes that have occurred in my body so as to forecast future physical ramifications. I also need to style your demand to Mr. Prump so as to increase the odds of favorable reception. And, I do not think it would be moral to spend the night with you in bed before we are married—not feeling the way I have begun to feel and with my growth of private parts."

She frowned. *Sounds like something Grandma would say if she'd learned big words.*

"Linda Lou is in the sixth," Lacy Dawn began an argument. "She told everybody—not the boys—that it's okay to sleep with your man before you're married if you're engaged. That came from her mom, an authority who has been married five times."

"We are engaged, but this is going to be a very long engagement," he said.

"But, I'm almost thirteen."

"Thirteen human years is much too young to get married."

"Whew, am I glad you said that. I love you, DotCom."

She went to bed and pulled the blanket over her shoulders.

"I love you too, Lacy Dawn."

"I was just wondering. What are you trying to sell me, DotCom?"

"Your destiny. Please fall asleep. I have work to do."

The Advocate

"Man, I feel like shit," Dwayne said the next morning. He took a swig of what was left of last night's sixth beer and stumbled into the bathroom. The commode flushed several times. Lacy Dawn grimaced.

He barfed his guts out. "He'll be okay," she said. "Last night was the first time he's gotten really drunk in a long time."

"I have considered why people do such things to themselves," DotCom said.

"It's human celebration and tragedy," she continued to defend.

"It's not just a human behavior. With limited subcultural exception, what your father did last night falls into the category of a universal phenomenon. He recognized it on the last shopping trip."

"All over the universe, people get high?"

"Or the equivalent," he answered.

"And have hangovers?"

Dwayne came out of the bathroom. He rubbed the facial stubble on his cheeks, massaged his eyeballs, and lay back down on his bed.

"Not so loud, sugar. Man, six Buds never did me in like this before. You bought some ass-kicking beer, DotCom."

"Back to what we were talking about before Daddy woke up. You told me that if we want information to scope out my job offer on Shptiludrp we have to buy it from others?"

DotCom pointed at his monitor and read a section from the official Personnel Policies and Procedures Manual:

IV.1 Prohibition Against Posting Job Descriptions.

It is the policy of Management that job descriptions for all personnel vacancies on Shptiludrp shall be secured through confidential and individualized negotiation between applicants and potential employers.

IV.1.a After a public posting of a vacancy, the potential employer shall assess the value of the information requested by the applicant and charge a reasonable fee for the information based on each assessment.

IV.1.b Prior to the release of any part of a job description, the applicant shall sign a confidentiality agreement (Appendix F) . . .

"Nothing is free on Shptiludrp?" Dwayne rubbed his temples.

"That is correct. However, you are not a typical job applicant, Lacy Dawn. You are a Recruit. Your father is your consultant and therefore covered by the same policy. I have never met or represented a Recruit before. It cost me my job. Nothing is free on Shptiludrp."

"You got fired?" Dwayne sat up in bed.

"No. I have been reassigned to the role of an Advocate. I am no longer the Director of Marketing and, therefore, no longer in charge of universal spam. Management decided that you have become emotionally committed to the project and that my marketing of the project to you is no longer required for it to progress. However, I found no plug-in training on my new role and very little in personnel policy to instruct me on my new assignment as an Advocate."

"Does this mean that you can change that stupid name?" Dwayne asked.

"Yes," DotCom answered. *I have already considered the same.*

"Fellows, let's get back to the bigger picture. DotCom has been my advocate for years because he's loved me for years. It's not that much of a change, except he don't have to continue to sell me on something that I've already agreed to buy. The big deal is that we don't know enough about my job offer to identify what information would be worth buying to define it. At least for now, let's continue our observations and interactions on the surface. With our new Advocate, I'm sure we'll figure this thing out."

"Hey, Bob, if we're going back out there would you please see if you could negotiate me a couple of aspirins?" Dwayne pointed to what could have been an outside wall. *My head hurts too much to hit a punch line.*

"No problemmo, Mike," DotCom said. *That was my second joke.*

"As your Advocate, I will provide direct assistance to help us accomplish our mission."

Two aspirin and three cups of coffee later, Dwayne was ready to shop. Lacy Dawn drank her first cup with four teaspoons of sugar. DotCom tried a sip to see if he could taste it. *Not yet, but soon.*

Rules of the Game

"C'mon guys. Get it together!" Lacy Dawn yelled and herded them toward the door. "Do you have any money, DotCom, in case we need to buy a piece of information?"

"Whatever they cost," Dwayne said, "Jenny's new teeth were worth it. I'll pay you back someday."

DotCom nodded his head in agreement. She punched them both hard on their upper arms and stomped out the door toward the elevator.

"Focus on the job!" She waited for them to catch up.

"Information can be bartered for. It cannot be legally bought," DotCom said as they waited.

"Shit," Dwayne said. "My head hurts too much for this."

"Just tell us what to do, DotCom. You're our Advocate now," she said.

After exiting the hotel, they got on the slow beltway. DotCom sat his laptop on a handrail. It booted up and he clicked the Shoppers Instruction Manual. Over his shoulders, Lacy Dawn and Dwayne read:

Chapter Three
How to Score Big Points:
Guidelines for the Novice Shopper

"Just tell us what to do," Lacy Dawn repeated.

"Management grants temporary shopper visas very selectively to eligible applicants," DotCom introduced the material on the screen as Dwayne and Lacy Dawn read it. "Many applications are denied because of character defects of the applicants. There is a comprehensive list of character defects appended to the manual. Would you like to review it?"

"I've been there and done that." Dwayne continued to read over DotCom's shoulder.

"In addition to eligibility, suitability to shop is evaluated before a visa is approved. This determination is based on an applicant's personal wealth or game point balance. Credits to continue to shop are scored during shopping trips. It's similar to Earth's video lottery games."

"We ain't here to shop," Lacy Dawn said.

"Earned points can also be traded for the information upon which to define the scope of work for your job offer. Since you have nothing else to trade except my wealth, at this point, I advocate that you both learn the basics of playing The Game. My role is less than fully defined. Dependent upon judicial interpretation if challenged, use of my wealth to purchase information to define your scope of work could be found in violation of a constitutional principle." He outlined a section of the correct chapter of the shoppers' instruction manual on the screen with his finger:

1. Do not talk to others when shopping. It will slow you down.

2. When in line at the checkout and delay is expected, use the time to ally with the shopper waiting immediately in front or behind you. A united front on maximum negotiated purchase price of merchandise will result in bigger discounts by shopkeepers and increase your score.

3. Do not allow yourself to be tricked by a non-player into violating either of the above two procedures. While you are in competition for your survival with everything else in the universe, only a small proportion of shoppers are players at any given time. Remember, all other players want you to lose.

"It's the same old, same old," Dwayne said. "Everybody always wants a high score except in golf and Uno. What's the next rule?"

DotCom clicked on the chapter entitled "Calculation of Final Scores." After its heading was a half-page explanation in much need of clarification:

A final score is calculated based on:

One: the grand total time spent on Shptiludrp from landing to take-off, or an allocated portion thereof for officially registered period play;

Two: negotiated purchase price analyses of discounts received;

Three: market factors affecting supply and demand at the time of the shopping spree;

Four: raw score adjustment in relation to a player's registered assets to obtain greater fairness among classes;

Five: the adjusted score is entered into the universal database and becomes the final score unless grieved within thirty rotations of Shptiludrp;

Plus, the Scoring Council holds the sole authority for resolving grievances and handling complaints, except upon reversal by the Manager of the Mall;

And, a player's final score is updated by average with scores earned during subsequent shopping trips.

After reading about score calculations, Dwayne massaged his temples again. Lacy Dawn did the same. DotCom shut down the laptop, put it back in its carrying case, and faced them.

"Especially since you two are Earth humans, I must emphasize two other important rules of The Game that appear as footnotes in the manual. First, once the game begins, there are no time-outs, recesses, smoke breaks, video replays, or grace periods to sleep, eat, urinate, defecate, or to relax. Secondly, only registered purchases from official shopkeepers networked into the Scoring Council's database are counted."

"That ain't fair," Dwayne said. "The best deals are from bootleggers and shoplifters."

"Thousands of years ago, some terminally ill shoppers were willing to risk a ban from Shptiludrp by profitable off-record trading during shopping trips so as to increase the inheritances passed on to their children...."

"You're digressing again," Lacy Dawn said. *Shit, I used another big word.*

"You're getting a little too big for your britches, Lacy Dawn," Dwayne said. "I've learned a lot about game rules so far. He's already told us that we need to play it so we can get points to trade for information about the job. How are we supposed to play if we don't know the rules? He ain't been digressing. He's our Advocate and would never waste our time." *Maybe the hair of the dog would fix me up.*

"Just tell us what to do," Lacy Dawn said. *Get to the point.*

"Man, the rules here are more complicated than the IRS! I thought that the new tax codes at home were supposed to be simple, but you still need an accountant to figure it out. This is worse."

137

"Lacy and Dwayne, you two need to negotiate the biggest discounts on as much merchandise as possible within the time period provided by Rule. In the final analysis, that is how you will earn the most points on this shopping trip."

"Thank you," Lacy Dawn said. *He got to the bottom line, but why do we want a high score? I'm afraid to get him started on that topic right now. It'll take another hour.*

"While overall time spent on the planet is a typical factor affecting the final score of most shoppers who play The Game, this is because most shoppers want to spend as long a time as permitted on Shptiludrp. A player can also register to compete by periods. It significantly shortens visits. The rules provide for a maximum of three periods allowed per approved visit. A period is the equivalent of three Earth hours. All three periods must be used within the same Earth week."

Lacy Dawn nodded. *Just like always, he's got more than one bottom line. Maybe there's a school somewhere in the universe where I can send him to learn how to become an Advocate.*

"If you two can score very high during a period, the rules permit a trade of that high score with another shopper. It would be a personal transaction that would be registered and which would increase your final score if the information later proved helpful to the mission—saving the universe."

"I used to like to score when I was high," Dwayne said.

"You still do," Lacy Dawn corrected.

Playing the Game

Ten minutes later, DotCom pushed the button and stepped from the slow beltway onto the walkway. Lacy Dawn and Dwayne followed. They wore normal Earth clothing. DotCom was not clothed since he was well known as a naked android and it could draw attention to the party if he had and, possibly, slow down shopping. In public while on Shptiludrp, he had kept the laptop in place to cover his penis at all times.

"That's the main thing I used my geography book for in the eighth grade, too," Dwayne said to DotCom.

The outside of the shops all looked the same. Only by examining the window display could a novice tell what a shop specialized in unless one carried a hand-held video language converter. DotCom's group didn't need one and his laptop was being used for an alternative purpose—to cover his penis and its adolescent erections. He had catalogued every shop on the planet and was familiar with their specializations. Sometimes computers are slower than verbal instruction.

"Your odds will be better in this section than any other on the planet. The merchandise will be more familiar. The shopkeepers will be less astute."

"I trust you, honey."

"So you're gonna help us score big time? Dwayne asked. "Then we can trade points for information. But where's all the money coming from?"

"I will not shop with you. It would likely be prohibited. I am not certain about my limitations as an Advocate. However, I presume that you must score the points by yourselves and I do not recommend asking for clarification. Since I occupy a unique role, a request for clarification could result in a listing of new Rules by Management that do not now exist and which could limit current operations."

"It's your call, Mr. Advocate. You're too sexy for your shirt," Lacy Dawn said. He wasn't wearing one.

"Watch it. I'm your chaperone and have to report to your mom," Dwayne said.

"Since I am no longer required to market to maximize return, I am in a better position to assist you to score. But, I cannot cheat. It could void your score. I have all the money that you could spend in many lifetimes—a salary for hundreds of thousands of Earth years that I have never spent. I have been without needs until now. Subsidized shopping is permitted and encouraged by Rule. A subsidized shopper gets one period free parking."

"So I'm really going to marry a rich doctor?" she asked.

"At this time, it appears so," DotCom said. "The lucrative contract that I signed to become your Advocate had no termination or review date; no clause pertaining to dismissal for lack of performance; and, the "will and pleasure" language authorized you, rather than Management, to dismiss me."

"I would never dismiss you, DotCom — not me, not the next generation of me, not the generation after that, or ever. You are my man forever."

"Would you two cut the shit before it makes me puke again?" Dwayne complained

"He's right. Our clock is ticking," Lacy Dawn said.

"The clock is not ticking as a shopper. It has not yet started. You two are here as a recruit for employment and as her advisor. Any time spent before you begin shopping will not count in your final score calculation. Once you start shopping, the clock will start."

"I thought we were trying for a high score so we could trade it for information about the job offer. Why should we be interested in our final score?" Dwayne asked.

"This is my home planet. I hope to visit it after I marry your daughter. A good score for a period does not guarantee authorization to shop in the future. I want a strong final score."

"That's not fair. What for?" Dwayne complained again.

"Cut the crap you two. Is it your recommendation as an advocate that we score as high as possible for nine straight Earth hours, three periods, and then leave?" she asked.

"Yes. This would eliminate down time that would be factored into your score."

"And, our score will be saved until the next trip?" Lacy Dawn asked.

"Yes."

"Then, we'll come back and use our score off-the-clock to buy information?" She pressed for detailed advice.

"Yes."

"And, if we score high, we might be able to come back for our honeymoon?" She hit pay dirt. *This has to be the real bottom line. It's in the basement. Why didn't he explain this stuff when he was going over all the other rules?*

"Yes," DotCom said. *Apparently, I still have a lot of marketing department in me — start soft and lead them into the hard sell. If our upcoming honeymoon doesn't motivate her to maximum performance, I have not yet fully grasped the concept.*

"Huh?" Dwayne asked.

"What's a honeymoon?" DotCom asked for fun.

"A honeymoon is like a vacation after a couple gets married." Lacy Dawn played along. "It used to be for the first time that they had sex. Go off someplace private and do it for a minute and then wave at anybody who had tracked them—like parents. Things are different now, but it's still called a honeymoon," she answered.

"I want the first time that we have sex to be on our honeymoon," he said in role.

"Me too," she insisted. *I love you so much, DotCom. Stop, stop thinking about it—love, sex, children, and family—none of it is worth shit if I don't perform on this job. You are too anxious. Focus on the job — take a deep breath — you have no guilt or stress of significant cause, focus.*

DotCom turned his back on her. Lacy Dawn pretended not to notice.

DotCom had come up with a theory about his body. Motivated by love, he theorized that unconsciously utilized carbon found in the natural environment was used to build internal biological structures at what a Christian might call a Genesis-like speed. He further theorized that his penis was the primary target because of the drive to reproduce the species. The theory failed because he couldn't define a species. Except—maybe a baby in any species might be helpful in some way. He moved the case an inch to better conceal. *It is too late to stop my evolution into humanity. We have to succeed with this generation of Lacy*

Dawn because if we fail I will not survive to assist the next.

Though she was still skinny and had stringy brown hair, Lacy Dawn's beauty began with a gaze that was increasingly intense. Her pupils were always dilated and her matching green aura had increased to six inches of radiation beyond her flesh. She emanated: *my love.*

"Did you ever see the original *Blind Faith* album cover?" Dwayne asked DotCom.

"Say something, Honey. We're not getting anywhere like this," Lacy Dawn instructed, oblivious to her impact.

"I will provide relevant history about the planet on request if it will cause us to function better on the shopping spree. It is irrelevant to our objectives." He turned to face her.

"Do it," she said, noticing his growing adolescence from an angle. *Yes, PLEASE concentrate on the job.*

She gritted her teeth.

"The option of scoring points by a period was established many centuries ago Earth time," DotCom said. "The practice was an accommodation to the slave industry. Buyers of slaves were unwilling to lose points because of the time spent during unregistered and time-consuming transactions. Even though slavery has always been illegal, by common practice, the slave industry was vibrant until about two thousand years ago. The trading of scores among shoppers permitted wealthy shoppers to spend time negotiating the purchase of slaves. They would then make up for their lost time by buying period points from other shoppers. Today, the trading of scores between shoppers still connotes a possible sale of an intelligent being. By policy, an internal investigation is conducted. However, there has been no documented incident of slave trading on Shptiludrp for hundreds of years."

"Whatever," Dwayne said. *I guess it's all cool. He needs some pants.*

DotCom lost his erection. It was time to start shopping.

"If we score high and then trade our score, won't we end up with a low score that won't qualify us for future shopping trips?" Lacy Dawn asked.

"No. Your score is a permanent record that will exist forever until it is updated by averaging with a more recent score. Nothing else is permitted to increase or decrease it. Similar to your country's civil service system, it is illegal to change a score based on political connections, friendship, physical attractiveness, or any other potential influence, including trades. A trade, similar to your country's copyright law, is permission for another to use your score but the score remains your own."

"Way cool," Dwayne said. "It's like getting something for nothing if you've got it to begin with." *I'm ready to kick ass. DotCom sure explains into much detail. Let's get going.*

At home, Dwayne was respected for his negotiation skills. His unregistered used car business, one car at a time, always made significant profit. It was tax-free and unreported to VA. His skills would serve well on the shopping spree. He remembered: *nine straight hours of negotiation isn't even close to a record setter car sale in the hollow. I can negotiate nonstop for days. I'll skin these shopkeepers.*

"Would it be possible to find two more aspirins before we start?" Dwayne asked.

"Here you go, Daddy." She had anticipated.

Dwayne crunched and swallowed without liquid, took three long, slow, deep breaths as he had learned in the VA yoga class, and shut his eyes for a moment.

"Let's get ready to rumble!" he said.

DotCom issued final recommendations: "In the first shop, take your time to select the items that you will take to the counter to negotiate prices. I will not start the clock until you are next in line at the check-out—a leeway allowed by Rule. It's the only leeway until it is time for us to depart. The more items that you select from the first shop, the better your odds. At checkout, do not rush regardless of how many customers behind you complain. You are there to score points, not to win a popularity contest."

"Got it," Lacy Dawn and Dwayne said at the same time.

"Remember your unique code assigned for this trip: Earth numerals 696969690. Punch it in to seal the purchase. If there is a problem with the code, which I doubt will happen, yell the word 'Fraud'. Ask for and file a written protest on the spot. As your Advocate, I will negotiate another spree beginning at another start time."

"Cool number," Dwayne said.

"Do not let the shopkeepers trick you. It is their job to deliver purchases as coded. If he or she asks for an address, leave for the next shop without response. This will prevent subsequent shopkeepers from asking for one as they are networked. Your purchases will be scored at checkout when you punch in the code. Delivery is inconsequential to your final score."

"Should we take notes?" Dwayne asked.

Lacy Dawn gave him The Look.

"Move briskly but do not run between shops. You do not want to call attention to the fact that you are in the period game option. There are professional period shoppers who might try to obstruct your progress. Therefore, during the next nine hours do not trust, talk, or make eye contact with anybody except me. Please do not be polite or nice. That is one of their oldest tricks. They may also fake disability or disadvantage to slow you down."

"Like when I shopped at the junk yard before I got well?" Dwayne asked. *I give up. I ain't hitting a punch line today. It must be my headache.*

"I will keep time and indicate when to get in your last check-out line before the end of The Game. Do not hesitate. One second late will result in disqualification of that entire purchase. This Rule applies even when every item except the last one has been rung up. The shopkeepers sometime identify period shoppers and slow down checkout to cause a loss. The common belief is that some shopkeepers accept kickbacks from professional period players. There has never been a prosecution. If a shopkeeper is slow, announce that you intend to file a consumer complaint."

"Ready, set, go," Dwayne joked again. *The aspirins have kicked in.*

"I love you, DotCom." Lacy Dawn blew him a kiss. They entered their first shop of the spree. DotCom had picked out the shop. It specialized in leather goods. He pointed. *Humans are familiar with the uses for skins from lower life forms.*

144

"I'm going to puke," Dwayne said loud enough for others to hear.

It was an unintentional but effective strategy. His language conversion device had been on. People left the shop. The ones that stayed gave them more room to work. He pretended to gag. Other shoppers left.

"I'm okay," Dwayne whispered to Lacy Dawn. "Here's what I think we should do. Get a buggy and I'll get one. Let's put two same items in my buggy and the same two in your buggy. After the buggies are full, we'll pick the best time to get in line. I don't want us to get right behind someone who has a lot of stuff. As we check out, I'll negotiate the price on the items in my buggy and you take notes. Oh, do you have a pad and pencil? Make it a pen because the lead might break."

"I'll see if DotCom can get them."

He stood a few feet from the shop entrance, faced a blank wall to conceal his manhood, and typed on the laptop that he almost always carried. It was plugged into one of the numerous ports located on the rail that separated the walkway from the beltways and it sat on one of the fold-up counters designed for the purpose. Nobody else in sight was involved in anything except shopping. She told him about Dwayne's plan. *Daddy came up with a good plan but I don't want to give him the big head until he's earned it.*

"There is an antiques shop nearby where I can get a pad and pen," DotCom agreed. Two minutes later, with them in hand, Lacy Dawn went back into their first shop for their first period of shopping.

"Anyway, after the first buggy is checked out, place your items two by two on the counter in the exact same order as the items from my buggy," Dwayne continued. "Tell me what we were charged the first time and I'll try for a bigger discount. I'll insist on wholesale. We buy in quantity so we can retail at home. What do you think?"

"Implement," she said.

"What?" he asked.

"Cool beans," she corrected.

They selected and organized upcoming purchases in the

buggies. Lacy Dawn checked to make sure the pen worked, wrote numbers on the side of the page with a brief description of each item, but often couldn't identify objects. They got in line, were next in line, and the clock started.

"Fifty percent off or I'm going elsewhere," Dwayne said to the shopkeeper at checkout.

The shopkeeper looked at the long line of expensive objects on the counter. "Agreed," he said.

Dwayne muttered. *The retail mark-up must have been more than 200% of what we paid.*

The shopkeeper scanned the full price of the first object. He pushed it and the second identical object down the counter. An assistant loaded the two objects into a compartment on a conveyor belt which sank through the shop's floor.

"Contract violation!" Dwayne yelled.

"What do you mean, sir?" the shopkeeper asked.

"We agreed on fifty percent discount for each item, not two for one." *Unless each item is registered as a sale, our score will be based on half the purchases at full retail price for each.*

"But what makes the difference, Sir?"

Dwayne scowled.

"Good job, Daddy," Lacy Dawn whispered.

"Sir, I have voided the last purchase. I'm sorry," the shopkeeper motioned for his assistant to hand him back the first object, scanned it twice, and entered the negotiated discount. The first buggy full was checked out.

"Will that be all, sir?"

"No." Dwayne removed the divider used to separate purchases on the counter.

"I want wholesale prices on these," Dwayne said.

"Sir, that is not possible. I would lose money. I have to cover shipping and handling, rent, employee salaries, health insurance…"

"I retail my purchases on my home planet and have all the same costs."

"Okay, you're a good customer," the shopkeeper whispered. "Here's what I'll offer. I'll give you a fifty-five percent discount on the rest of your purchases for today." *I hope nobody else hears this offer.*

"Sixty-five percent," Dwayne countered.

They settled on sixty percent. With her language converter plugged into the register's port, Lacy Dawn checked the display as each object was scanned. She compared it to her notes. On the last set of objects she jabbed Dwayne in the ribs.

"I think you made a data entry error on that—that—whatever it is," Dwayne pointed to the objects which had been placed on the conveyor belt.

"Let me double check," the clerk said. "Sir, I am so sorry. Since I inconvenienced you, I'll take seventy percent off the retail price on those bustles."

"Fine," Dwayne said. *There's no time to be mad.*

"I need your signature to finalize the transaction," the storekeeper smiled.

Dwayne moved out of the way. Lacy Dawn punched in the number that DotCom had given her and pressed her thumb on the scanner face. Several shops later, four of the nine hours of the shopping competition had passed without them taking a break. The rest followed the same strategy. DotCom rushed them cup after cup of coffee. When necessary, they peed in a bucket.

"Are you sure this is cool?" Dwayne said as he peed. The shops were side by side. There were no alleys or cubby holes to hide in.*I'm glad that I don't need to shit. I don't want a fine for indecent exposure like I got when I couldn't hold it anymore and crapped on the Kmart parking lot while Jenny was shopping.*

Afterward, one shop to another, Lacy Dawn picked merchandise starting with the on-sale items. At checkout, Dwayne battled with shopkeepers over final prices. By the tenth shop, Dwayne's reputation preceded them. By the twelfth, the sales clerk gave them an immediate seventy-five percent discount. *I don't want to deal with Dwayne.*

"Yes sir," the shopkeeper repeated throughout checkout, regardless of Dwayne's demands.

At number 976,581, the shopkeeper announced a 90% off blue light special and the store lights turned blue. DotCom motioned for them to leave. Despite their surprise, Lacy Dawn and

Dwayne immediately obeyed.

"There is no competitive advantage to a discount given to all customers," DotCom explained on their way to the next shop.

The last shop was easy pickings. Its customers had run to the shop next door—to the blue light special. With no other customers, the sales clerk accepted any offer including free samples on request to test in Earth's marketplace. Dwayne made sure the free samples were scanned and with zero recorded into the database.

"Come again," the clerk said, cut power and closed shop after they left. *They cleaned me out. I need to restock shelves.*

Nine hours and fifteen minutes after the start of the shopping spree, Earth time, the team was on its way home. DotCom had on pants. Lacy Dawn and Dwayne, exhausted, pulled the levers on the side of the ship's recliners to maximum recline.

"Perhaps you are too effective as an Advocate," Mr. Prump said into the earphones worn by DotCom, who navigated out of the congestion of Shptiludrp.

"It's in the contract." DotCom squeezed his crotch to reinforce an erection which was caused by no recognizable stimulus. *So this is what accomplishment feels like.*

Yard Sale in the Hollow

"What the heck is a bustle anyway?" Dwayne asked the next morning. They were back on Earth and he had experienced a fun night with an energetic Jenny.

"I'll look it up on the internet," Lacy Dawn went into her bedroom.

Jenny shrugged. The answer took one minute.

"It's to make a woman's butt look bigger."

"Your mom sure doesn't need that."

Jenny pouted, smiled, and punched the air. Lacy Dawn giggled.

"We need to get all that stuff unloaded and into the barn. I've got to go back to work in a couple hours," he said.

Lacy gave a thumbs up. *Daddy sure sounds like management material.*

"Next weekend or the next, let's have a yard sale," Lacy Dawn said.

"I can put up signs all over the hollow now that I've got my learner's permit," Jenny agreed.

"You couldn't even get that old truck started, much less drive it," Dwayne said.

"Bull crap," Jenny headed out the back door with keys in hand. For ten minutes, they listened to the loud muffler as she drove up and down, up and down, up and down the hollow. She came back to cold eggs and jingled the keys before she hung them back on the nail in the door frame.

"All right, I was teasing anyway," Dwayne said. "Just don't get busted when you hang the signs for the yard sale. A licensed driver is supposed to be in the vehicle with you when you drive with a learner's permit. I'll come home early Friday. Be ready to take your driver's test in the company car. It has a legal inspection sticker. Why don't you try it out just to get used to it a little?" He tossed her the car keys, went in the living room, rolled a fatty, and called Tom. Lacy Dawn went to the front porch to watch her mom pull out of the driveway. Jenny floored it. Gravel from the driveway hit the side of the house.

"So, you don't mind if she takes her driver's test in the

company car?" Dwayne asked Tom on the telephone.

"Dude, you're super cool, don't worry. You don't need my permission about anything. I thought we had an understanding. You run the shit and I count the profits."

"Maybe I'm paranoid. For the first time since high school, my life is going in the right direction. I just don't want to piss you off." *I shouldn't have called Tom.*

"Dwayne, chill. You're a permanent player like a rock. I've been thinking about how to sell you the shops for cheap as a birthday present to Lacy Dawn."

"Cool. But, the real reason I called is that I've got a lot of stuff to move into the barn and wanted to know if I could borrow your four-wheeler and trailer for a couple of hours." *Good cover. I've come to my senses after a few hits.*

"Sure, if I can get it back from Harold. He borrowed it last week. I'll call him. What kind of shit do you have to move?"

"It's stuff for a yard sale. You might get off. Come over and look at it. It's very unusual."

"What kind of stuff?"

"All kinds—I got it from this dude. He laid it on me. There are a lot of collector's items—not good for a yard sale in the hollow—no baby clothes or toys, but there could be a dollar or two in it. If I can sell it, at least it'll be out of my barn."

"Call you back in a minute," Tom said.

"Thanks."

Five minutes later, Tom reported. "The four-wheeler will be there in a little bit, but someone will need to drive Harold's boy back home."

Dwayne told Lacy Dawn. She went Roundabend to tell DotCom that it was almost time to unload their cargo. Jenny drove Harold's boy home in the company car. Harold's boy told his mom and it caused an argument about women drivers. When Harold called to complain, Dwayne told Harold to eat shit. The Hickman family members gave each other high fives and walked Roundabend to move the stuff to the barn.

"DotCom volunteered to take pictures of the merchandise and to help create a website to advertise on the internet," Lacy Dawn said.

"Does that man of yours know how to work?" Dwayne asked. *I've never seen him lift a finger.*

"Sorry I'm late," DotCom said five minutes later.

The cargo bay was a standard add-on accessory. It had been dropped outside of the cave as the ship landed on return from Shptiludrp. To open it, DotCom had left his body to demagnetize the connections. As usual, he had gone inside his ship to make sure that there would be no loss of energy. He'd gotten stuck trying to get out and back into his body.

"The more I become human, the more I lose my ability to leave my body and become part of the ship," he whispered in Lacy Dawn's ear. *This is the first time I've gotten stuck.*

"About time you showed up, dude," Dwayne said. *I'm too hot and sweaty to come up with a better insult.*

DotCom picked up a loaded pallet and placed it on the trailer. Its tires squashed from the weight. All human eyes widened and mouths gaped.

"I recommend that you three fill the barn and then drive the tractor back. I will load it until the cargo bay is empty. I need to dismantle the cargo bay and store it in the cave before someone sees it."

"That's one strong mother," Dwayne said.

Lacy Dawn gave DotCom a peck on the cheek. *I'm so proud of him.*

Within an hour, enough merchandise to stock a Dollar General had been loaded into the barn. Dwayne drove the four-wheeler to Tom's barn and walked home. *Maybe the tough-man contest would pay off. There's got to be some way to make money off DotCom.*

"That boy's a good worker," Dwayne said to Jenny after he got home. The comment elevated DotCom's status. It was the highest compliment that he could have given anybody. Lacy Dawn heard it said a second time when Dwayne was in the bathtub—he often talked out loud when bathing. Positive comments had become a part of family life never exhibited before DotCom's interventions. Dwayne was cleaning up to return to work. He shaved. *Next weekend, I'll put in a tub / shower combo.*

Beginning Monday evening, DotCom tutored Lacy Dawn in website design. She learned presentation of images, marketing, and customer service. By Thursday, they agreed that two more days would be too short a time to plan a yard sale. She e-mailed her father.

"I've got a home improvement project for Saturday anyway," Dwayne replied. "I don't care about the full barn since my new job ain't farming."

"Maybe we should put off the yard sale until Labor Day weekend. I'll have an extra day off from school," Lacy Dawn sent.

"The next step is display," DotCom said. "Emphasize great attributes. The setting is important to the final price that a customer will pay. Establish a designated spot for each item to show it off—as a singular like no other. After the singular is sold and the customer has moved on, a duplicate, if available, should be placed in the same spot. The purchaser of the former should not become aware of the duplicate."

"We don't have any tables or cases or anything to display stuff on," she said.

"In this setting, tables and cases would be inappropriate."

"What are we supposed to use — logs?"

"That is a very good idea, Lacy Dawn. Logs sitting vertically with one or two items on the top of each would be nice. Mood lighting for the evening would be appropriate. Your Earth's Beethoven in the background interspersed with thirty seconds of Pink Floyd at irregular intervals would add to the atmosphere. You will need to arrange parking and a shuttle service from the parking area to your yard. I recommend that silent bids be taken for each item and with bid openings every five minutes."

"I thought we were just having a yard sale."

"You must design the Woodstock of all yard sales if you want this merchandise to move. Local residents will not be able to identify the objects or purposes. Your buyers must be those who want objects that are difficult to define, rare, and of questionable origin and purpose. You will need to market to reach this audience."

"You're right, but maybe we ought to work on the real job

instead of all this yard sale stuff. Besides, school started and I ain't even had time to go shopping for a new notebook, new underwear, or nothing."

"The opportunity to design an effective yard sale presents most valuable learning content consistent with the values upon which Shptiludrp was founded."

"School's important too."

"The job is your destiny. However, your credibility at this generational juncture and as a candidate for the position could be jeopardized if you fail to exploit this opportunity."

"Okay. This is just much more involved than I ever thought it'd be. Let's place the logs. I'll call Tom to see if he'd mind if customers park in his bottom. He has a hay wagon that the fire department borrowed a couple of years ago for the 4th of July parade in Spencer. Maybe we can use it to transport the customers from the parking lot to the yard sale."

That evening, DotCom placed logs to use as display tables. On the sloped lawn on both sides of the house, he pushed them down so hard that they stuck like nails. Lacy Dawn supervised. *I've got to be careful. I don't want nobody to see DotCom.*

"Good," she said to the level.

DotCom was in open sight. He was dressed for chopping firewood, but any stranger in the hollow was big news. Plus, he cut the logs with a laser. It was quicker than a chain saw with a new chain and brighter than the beam from Dwayne's halogen from AutoZone. Paranoid, she looked up and down, up and down the hollow road nonstop. *If somebody sees him....*

A pickup came down the dirt road.

"Hide!" Lacy screamed.

The adults waved and the six boys in the bed whistled. "I've got a big log I bet you'd like," a boy said as the truck passed, followed by something bound to have been nasty but that she didn't understand. The truck stopped several yards farther on. Mr. Johnson got out and switched all the boys. He didn't know who had said what, but they were all due.

"Are you crazy? That's Dwayne's girl!" he yelled at the boys.

Lacy Dawn gave the boys the finger, hung the level on its nail on the porch, and put the weed eater and gas can in the shed.

Mommy don't need the can in the kitchen any more to hide her GED study guide.

She looked at their display area: fifty-six upright logs of various diameters, four tables made of thin trunks, and six tripods made of small trees with nails to hang objects. She smiled at DotCom.

Another pickup came down the hollow road. Harold stopped.

"Your daddy's getting an early start on his firewood ain't he, girl?" Harold slobbered from the driver's side.

"We're gonna have a yard sale. I'm trying to make enough money to go to Washington, D.C., with the school trip. They want a truck load of money to let you go."

"I figured your baby clothes and toys would have been long gone by now. You're 'bout grown. Did your mommy save them hoping for another baby?" Harold yelled so loudly that if they had a neighbor it would start gossip.

"Get your ass on up the road, Harold, before I call your wife. I can smell the liquor from here," Jenny yelled back from the porch.

It almost worked. Harold tried to leave but the motor on his pickup quit because he had let the clutch out too quickly. Jenny had scared him. He staggered to the front of the truck and opened the hood after putting another dent in it with his fist.

"I need a jump start." Harold rubbed his knuckles.

"Give him a jump, Lacy Dawn. I'm frying 'taters."

Jenny went into the living room, threw Lacy Dawn the truck keys, and peeked out the window. Nobody trusted Harold unless under close supervision. Lacy Dawn rolled Dwayne's truck down the hill, pop-started the clutch, and pulled beside Harold's. He took care of the rest and was gone a minute later. Lacy Dawn waved goodbye. *Harold's the nosiest person in the hollow—the biggest mouth. Everybody will know about the yard sale by tomorrow night, but I can't think of anything we've got that anybody would pay ten cents for. We have to advertise on the internet.*

"Let's call it a night," she said to DotCom, who had hidden behind the house for the duration of the Harold's visit. It was almost dark. She sat on an upright log and peed toward another directly in front, but came up way short. When she was much younger—three years ago—she had beaten a boy in a distance pee contest. She frowned at the dry bark on the target. *I still have to eat and get ready for bed.*

"Kiss goodnight?" DotCom asked.

"Sure," she pecked him on the cheek. Too late, DotCom puckered his lips and closed his eyes. Lacy Dawn laughed. *He's like a seventh grader.*

The next week was busy. Dwayne installed a tub / shower combination, Jenny got her driver's license, and Lacy Dawn got a job promotion. Harold had told everybody that there was going to be a yard sale and that Lacy Dawn had given him a jump-start.

"I hope she don't get caught," Harold had said to everybody. "She's been driving Dwayne's truck all over the place."

Tom heard about it, including reports that she'd gone into town to run errands for Jenny. Afterward, he promoted her to the position of Tractor Driver of the Farm at a much higher wage.

"Tom put Lacy Dawn in charge of his entire operations," Harold told everybody the next day.

She had never driven a tractor. Dwayne gave her instructions and brought a tractor home for hands-on experience. Up and down, up and down, up and down the hollow she went. Every boy was jealous because she had landed the job they all wanted. Harold's oldest boy fumed and fired his shotgun at anything he wouldn't get in trouble for shooting up. *She ain't even thirteen yet.*

"I love this shower," Lacy Dawn said after her tractor practice.

"I love bubble baths," Jenny said.

"We know," Dwayne and Lacy Dawn said at the same time.

Harold's oldest son, Darrell, had the tractor driver job before Lacy Dawn, but had gotten over losing it by the time she sat on the tractor seat at the job site. He flicked a booger at the tractor and it stuck on the shiny red metal that covered the engine—his last protest.

"My plow lines were always curvy anyway," he said.

"You shouldn't get high before going to work," she admonished.

155

"Next season, I'll have my driver's license. I'll take Tom's produce to the Farmer's Market." *I'll sell bud from the booth at the same time.*

"I'm the man with the plan. My dad said he don't want to know nothing about it."

"Just don't get Tom busted." *Tom has to be told.*

"For what?"

She picked and flicked a boogger at the tractor. It didn't show. Darrell didn't comment on her lack of aptitude. Lacy Dawn picked again but her nose was clean—too little, too late. *Oops.*

"I'm so glad this is the last Saturday for us to work," she said.

Darrell unhooked the trailer from the tractor. They'd used it to load and haul greens from the garden. Lacy Dawn turned off the ignition and they closed the barn door for their season. Harold would clean, package, and label the greens as 100% organic despite the Miracle Grow that had been used as fertilizer. Then, he would begin to sell them at the Farmer's Market on Monday for twice his competitors' prices.

The stuff from Shptiludrp had been in the barn for a month. It was way past the original date for a yard sale. Day after day of working in the sun, Lacy Dawn decided that there was merit to a career in merchandising. She floated Roundabend by chant to talk with DotCom. *I'm too tired to walk.*

"What's the next step in the yard sale?" She sank into her recliner.

"We have received over one thousand random hits. But we need a list of search terms that lead surfers to our site, a better title, and an automated e-mail reply that draws in customers instead of turning them off."

"Do I have to do all the work?" Lacy Dawn slumped.

"Technically, yes," he answered.

She closed her eyes. *I'm so tired.*

"Let me work on a name first." She chose what she thought would be the easiest assignment and yawned.

"That's acceptable. But, if you click right here," DotCom pointed to an icon on his desktop, "a list of related search terms will be automatically generated and attached." He pointed to a different icon.

"Ain't that cheating?"

"There is an original proviso in the Rules that can be broadly interpreted to authorize substantive assistance by an Advocate."

"You're slick as a whistle, boyfriend."

He smiled.

"You can select among three recommended automatic e-mail responses to hits on our website if you click here." *Click and click. Click and click.*

Most of the preparation work for the yard sale was done, but it still needed a good name. "I'm too tired to think," she said.

"Kiss goodnight? Please," he begged.

"Sure," she got up and approached.

DotCom tricked her and almost got a kiss on the lips by puckering, then turning his head a little at the proper moment to achieve a more direct hit. She smacked him on the butt—a non-sensitized area of his body that didn't register as anything. She smiled. *He's getting smarter about kisses. It was a pretty good pucker. I'm sorry it missed. I'm in the seventh and never been kissed.*

For days afterward, while she plowed mulch into Tom's fields after school, Lacy Dawn thought about possible website names. Nothing struck her fancy until she settled on Unique Universal Sales, Rarity from the Hollow. *Cool enough beans.*

After she gave him the name for the website, DotCom performed technical applications, added graphics, placed a picture of upright logs with merchandise as a background, and added hundreds of pictures. A link to get a detailed county map to the hollow was added at Lacy Dawn's suggestion.

"All we need now is a date," DotCom said two evenings later.

Lacy Dawn sank into the recliner. *School, mulch, school, mulch... I'm so tired and I still have to shower, do homework, and get ready for bed.*

"It's time to go home," she said. *Mulch is almost finished. At least I don't have to work this Saturday.*

"We missed Labor Day. Let's have the yard sale on Columbus Day weekend. I'll have an extra day off school. That'll give way more than two weeks' notice. Our website might draw folks who need to plan ahead for an extra day off, too."

"Smart plan," he said. "I'll announce the exclusive date on the main page and modify our hit description and eBay account."

"I'll tell Mommy and Daddy."

The weekend arrived. Despite Lacy Dawn's exhaustion from the continuing hard work in the fields, great care had gone into planning the yard sale. It began as scheduled. She watched the crowd gather and pace on the front porch. *There's been a giant oversight. Since he don't pee or poop, nobody can blame DotCom. But, everybody needs to use it BAD.*

"Tom, it's an emergency. Please pick up," Dwayne spoke to an answering machine. He had recognized the same planning error.

"Sorry. I was on my front porch looking at the traffic jam," Tom giggled. "When I moved here, I thought it was back to the Earth—some peace and quiet away from the hustle and bustle of the city." He continued to giggle.

"We need some port-a-potties. We need lots of them and quick! Can you help?"

"For a cut," Tom answered.

"Fine, whatever, just hurry."

"I'll need to fly them in with helicopters to the top of Roundabend. There's no way to truck anything in through this traffic jam. You'll need to have someone place them here and there using the four-wheeler and trailer. Do you want me to call Harold and have one of his boys walk down?"

"Yes," Dwayne said.

A half-hour later, choppers with port-a-potties dangling from them filled the sky. The potties were lowered on ropes at various spots. Several had to be turned upright by customers waiting in lines that formed before they had hit ground. At one location, a woman who had been first in line smacked a man who had gotten in front of her. She rushed in. He peed on its door in protest. Elsewhere, long lines formed, dwindled, and customers browsed the items on display at the yard sale in the hollow. Lacy Dawn, Jenny, and Dwayne answered customer questions. Dwayne's cell phone rang.

"Dude, you owe me one. It's a good thing I own a port-a-potty business that's a little down. Except for a construction strike, all my units would have been on-site. I want ten percent of gross for whatever you're doing."

"Shit," Dwayne coughed and puffed his corncob pipe.

"Exactly," Tom coughed and puffed.

"Come on over. Maybe we can trade," Dwayne said.

"Be there in a minute. I was coming anyway to see what all this is about."

Twenty minutes later, Tom arrived. Lacy Dawn and Jenny were running between displays to gather written bids on merchandise. Dwayne was picking up, dropping, and picking up the paper bids that didn't float off the porch. He was announcing names through the amplifier that DotCom had set up. The yard sale was short staffed and had fallen apart.

"David James—item number 107," Dwayne said, grabbed the money and put it in an already full cigar box.

DotCom showed up unannounced to help. He wore traditional Appalachian garb. Lacy Dawn had no time to object to the risk.

"Appropriate," she said. *It's worth it. Everything's falling apart. Besides, the customers look like they're from further away than DotCom.*

"Add some flesh to your cheeks. Grow eyebrows," Lacy Dawn told him. He went inside the house and returned, hung a large monitor from a porch rafter, typed in names on his laptop after Dwayne's announcements, and deleted them as the objects were picked up. Tom pitched in. He handed the purchased items to high bidders and stashed their money in a barrel Harold's boy had gotten from the shed.

"I don't know what it is, but it's very cool," another customer said to Tom.

"Use the four-wheeler to move the stuff from the barn to the display areas a little at a time. Keep the displays neat and full and don't let anybody see our stash," Dwayne told Harold's boy. The instruction was consistent with DotCom's marketing plan. Darrell nodded and got to work. With proper instruction, he strived to achieve. That was why Tom had hired him in the first place. Darrell rushed between the barn and the display areas. He blew off the dust that had gotten on merchandise in storage and despite his lack of recognition of the items, placed them properly on the tops of logs and tables. *This is a better job than setting up port-a-potties.*

The yard sale smoothed out. Lacy Dawn sat down on the ground—the first time she'd sat in three hours—and got back up. *I forgot the music.*

She ran into the house and pushed the Play button. *Crap, the light show.*

It was brighter than a laser beam in the eye at a Pink Floyd concert. Streaks of different colors streamed across the displays as the sun set. At dusk, familiar smoke from unfamiliar sources filled the hollow to augment. Dwayne and Tom laughed. *The yard sale has grown up into a party.*

The sale continued. At 5:00 A.M., the last customer bought the last item. Lacy Dawn turned off the music and DotCom turned off the lights. People were passed out in their cars in Tom's bottom and in vehicles blocking the road. Two cars needed to be pulled out of the creek. But, the yard sale was over.

"Thank God," Tom said.

"Let's crash," Dwayne said.

They went to bed. Tom slept on the new couch. It was the first sleep-over on the couch that Jenny had permitted. DotCom sat in the dilapidated living room chair, closed his eyes, and pretended to sleep. *I want to remain a part of the situation for as long as possible. I feel so human.*

That afternoon, Tom was the first human awake. He made sure that everybody else was up soon thereafter. He opened the bedroom doors to let Brownie inside, lit a roach, and stared at DotCom. Brownie was persistent. Everybody was in line for the bathroom within ten minutes.

"How much do you figure you made—you back stabber son-of-a-bitch?" Tom confronted.

"What do you mean?" Dwayne asked.

"You had a good thing going on and didn't cut me in on it until the last minute and only then because you were desperate. I would have never played that shit to you, Dwayne. What's up?"

"Chill, Tom. I had almost nothing to do with this going down. It was Lacy Dawn's thing. I thought it was going to be a yard sale—not Lollapalooza."

160

"It's true, Tom. Me and Bucky set this up," she pointed at DotCom who was still pretending to be asleep on the chair. Everything about the chair was frazzled. Despite its prominence in a dingy living room, nobody ever sat in it because everyone knew it had cooties.

"It was advertised on the internet. I had no idea that so many people would show," Lacy Dawn said. Jenny put on the bacon. *Maybe this will calm things down. The aroma always helps.*

DotCom got up and went into the kitchen. *I have never seen bacon fry.*

"I am going to take a shower," DotCom said two minutes later to Jenny. *Bacon is boring.*

Jenny flipped it. *I've never thought about DotCom's personal hygiene, but a water shower?*

Dwayne saw the closed bathroom door, heard the shower, and went to the back yard for his second whiz. Jenny looked out the kitchen window and changed angles for a better view. *Cheap thrills are fun.*

Dwayne had his back to the house, so Jenny couldn't watch him pee. He was joined by Tom who had already peed twice, but after another cup of coffee was ready again. They talked and peed. Two minutes later, Jenny looked out the window again. *I might get lucky.*

Lacy Dawn sat on a kitchen chair, crossed her legs hard, and waited. *Heck with this!*

Without a word to the men who were still outside, she walked up the path toward Roundabend far enough not to be seen and squatted. *I've peed on the path lots of times to lay the cable.*

They all returned to the kitchen. DotCom was still in the bathroom. Lacy Dawn looked at her mother and shrugged. The guys went into the living room to talk business.

"I've never known him to shower. What could he be doing in there?" Jenny asked Lacy Dawn.

Inside the bathroom, inside the shower, DotCom stared at his penis. It was still small but no longer just a bump. When he touched it, it got BIGGER, so he didn't stop. An hour later, he tried to quit. *It won't grow if I just touch it. The process to become more human-like can't be rushed. It takes time to incorporate carbon into internal systems, but this was fun.*

DotCom got out of the shower and looked at the commode. *Hmm.*

"Your man's slow in The Head," Tom yelled from the living room.

"Maybe, but he's fast in the head," Lacy Dawn defended at the same volume.

During the yard sale, DotCom had eaten two cookies. It was the first time that he had ever eaten. One got stuck because he had forgotten to chew. He turned the second one to powder because his salivary glands were not yet fully functional. Still staring at the commode, he pushed the lever to flush. The guys were in the kitchen stealing bacon and listening. DotCom flushed again and resolved to complete the task. *What goes in must come out.*

He sat on the commode. A few seconds later, with his head between his knees, he watched a very small round brown ball plop into the water. He stood up, picked the ball out of the water, squished it a little, smelled it, dropped it back into the commode, and flushed. *I wish I had put it in my shirt pocket. There will be more where that came from.*

Before DotCom had taken two steps out of the bathroom door, Lacy Dawn intervened. She pushed him back into the bathroom.

"Put on your pants," she scolded.

"I wouldn't count on any grandkids!" Tom grinned and picked up a can of soup off the table. He read its label for a second and sat it down. Then he coughed to cover a laugh and went into the living room. Dwayne looked at Lacy Dawn. *He's got a penis and not just a bump like the last time I saw it?*

She smiled. *I saw it on Shptiludrp. It's still small but impressive. I hope it stays that way.*

DotCom came out of the bathroom. He was dressed. Lacy Dawn grabbed his hand and they went into the living room holding hands. Dwayne and Jenny followed.

"Tom, I'd like for you to meet my boyfriend, Bucky. Bucky, this is Tom."

They shook hands.

"Lacy Dawn, I would like to speak to you in private,"

DotCom said immediately afterward. He didn't realize that Tom might be insulted by the too-quick introduction without the normal follow-through with meaningless chatter.

They went onto the front porch.

"I pooped," he said.

"Did you wash your hands afterward?"

"No, I forgot."

"Well, don't tell Tom. You just shook his hand. Go wash up right now. Never forget again or, if I find out, you will be in big trouble, young man."

They returned to the living room. DotCom went into and came out of the bathroom.

"So how much money did we make?" Tom asked.

"I don't know, but I'll get it and we can all count." Lacy Dawn went into her bedroom and dragged back the barrel full of money. It was too heavy for her to lift. The uppermost layers of loose bills fell off and floated to the floor in different directions.

"There's more that wouldn't fit." She returned to the bedroom several times and returned with handfuls of money. She scooted what had fallen from the barrel toward the center of the living room floor with her foot. Dwayne dumped the money out of the barrel into a pile that became two feet high.

"I need to finish up breakfast. You guys count it," Jenny said.

Brownie ran through the torn back porch screen door, passed up the bacon grease in the skillet on the floor of the kitchen, and rolled on top of the pile of money. It scattered all over the living room. Brownie then jumped on DotCom's lap and licked his face.

"That's one strange dude," Tom whispered to Dwayne. "He must be super cool though or Brownie wouldn't make up with him like that." *That dog's never paid me any attention.*

"He's not from around here. Please don't tell anybody about him. He's kinda hiding out for a few," Dwayne said.

"No problemmo," Tom said.

The group sorted bills—hundreds in one pile, fifties in another, twenties in another and made piles for tens, fives, and ones. DotCom got into the act and everybody else sat back for a minute to watch. His hands moved faster than the others could keep up with. Each took a pile and moved it to a corner to count. Jenny brought pens and paper and took a stack of ones into the kitchen to count. DotCom worked at a disadvantage because Brownie still wanted to play. But, he finished well before the others. Afterward, each called out her or his total.

"$754,582," DotCom said one second later. Tom double checked and ten minutes later agreed with the grand total.

"While only Management is authorized to announce official net profit, I estimate it at approximately $627,000 American, Earth, after deducting what you paid for the items on Shptiludrp and the travel costs to get them here," DotCom said.

There was a pause.

"I've got to get my VA check cut off before I get busted."

Everybody laughed, including DotCom.

"Lacy Dawn, you have four hours of Earth time left to finalize your yard sale and to establish eligibility to keep the net profit. It is a simple step and a requirement that you must figure out without my direct assistance."

"What about that policy on Advocacy you found?"

The phone rang and Lacy Dawn went to her bedroom to answer it.

"Hello."

"Honey, I'm so sorry I didn't make it to your yard sale. I came down with a bad case of the gout," Grandma said. "I want you to know that if I'm still alive when your class goes to the nation's capital, I'll make sure you go with them. I don't know a kid from the hollow who's ever made that trip, but you will. So, don't worry about nothing."

"Thank you, Grandma."

"Bye, and don't worry and have your dad pick me up a can of Bugler tobacco. I'm almost out."

Lacy Dawn hung up the phone and sat on her bed. *I need some help. Even if DotCom can't help, I've got Tom who's a great businessman and administrator; and Daddy, a great manager; and, Mommy's always supportive.*

She returned to the living room, turned around, and went back to her bedroom. *Wait a minute, what about objective and subjective? They're looking at all that money. The yard sale took a lot of hard work. They're too subjective to think straight. If I was a shopper of rarity from the hollow, what would I expect next?*

Five minutes later, she came out of her bedroom again with a big smile.

"Tom, what if you sold so many pizzas during homecoming weekend that you ran out of ingredients? What would you do?" she asked.

"I'd put up a sign that read 'Sold Out' and send the employees home so I wouldn't have to pay them for standing around."

"That's what I need to do, except on the internet," Lacy said.

"Correct," DotCom said. "I can now further instruct you because you analyzed the situation and elicited the correct response. You have three hours and thirty-two minutes left to complete a five-minute operation that I recommend you do now. The home page of your website requires modification to ensure future customer satisfaction."

"He sure does talk funny," Tom whispered.

"Shh," Lacy Dawn, Jenny, and Dwayne shushed at the same time.

Brownie stopped playing. Lacy Dawn patted him on the head. *Future customer satisfaction-- that has to be a hint.*

"I'm sorry. We have temporarily sold out of stock. Please check back often for more Rarity from the Hollow," Lacy Dawn announced.

"That's perfect. Do it," DotCom said.

"Can't she, at least, eat breakfast first?" Jenny asked.

Lacy Dawn ignored her mother and went in the bedroom to modify the website. Five minutes later, they ate breakfast one-half million dollars richer than when they had eaten breakfast the morning before the yard sale. DotCom ate almost a whole piece of bacon and nibbled from a biscuit.

"He don't eat much," Tom whispered to Jenny.

After breakfast, Dwayne called for a business meeting. Jenny and Lacy Dawn stopped washing dishes and came into the living room. The money, in bundles tied with knitting yarn, was piled on top of the stack of old magazines in the corner of the living room.

"Okay, DotCom, I mean Bucky, here's your $225,000 to cover your initial costs," Dwayne counted out bundles and scooted the money on the floor toward him. Brownie bounced around and tried to play with Dwayne and the money.

"Let us know if it turns out to be more," Dwayne said.

"I am required to recover my investment," DotCom reached for and embraced the bundles.

"Now that I have recovered my investment, a fact that will be included in my next weekly report to Management, the money is hereby returned to business interests authorized by the Board. This will also be so reported and is legal." He tried to push the money back toward the piles but Brownie busted a bundle and scattered it all over the living room. Lacy Dawn gathered it.

"Okay, Tom, what were your costs for the shitters?"

"Let me think for a minute." He retrieved the piece of paper and pen that he had used to count his pile of money. After a few scribbles, he scratched out his figures and looked around the living room. *What a dump. Nobody deserves to live like this.*

"Three copters traveled fifty miles here and fifty miles back totaling three hundred miles for delivery. It will cost twice as much for pick-up because now the shitters are full and heavy. The copters can't haul them all in one trip. Plus, there is an extra ten miles per trip to dump them."

"Why don't we dump them ourselves in your compost pile?" Dwayne asked.

"I don't want the Health Department and whoever else down here nosing around," Jenny said. "I wouldn't be surprised if I turn on the news this evening and see our yard sale covered."

"I agree, Daddy. What if we decide to do this again but the Health people get wise and try to stop us the next time?"

"Besides," Jenny continued. "There's already enough shit in this hollow."

"Alright, you guys. I tried to pinch a penny. Old habits die hard."

"The best I can figure out without enough sleep and with no consultation," Tom said, "I need about $6400 in gas money to break even on the copters."

"What about your staff costs?" Dwayne asked.

"They were just sitting around. This gave them something to do. A vendor challenged the award of a big construction contract with State Purchasing last Friday. My boys couldn't deliver the shitters for that project because of the work stoppage. I can't lay them off. Copter pilots are too hard to find." *Dwayne will never find out the true costs.*

"Cool beans," DotCom said.

Tom folded the money, stuck it in his shirt pocket, and phoned to get the shitter removal process started. All evidence of the yard sale would be gone before civil servants reported for work on Monday.

"Now, we need to figure out wages for Tom and Bucky," Dwayne said.

"I'm insulted," Tom said.

"I am also insulted," DotCom agreed a few seconds slow, just like his pucker.

"I'm sorry," Dwayne said. "Sometimes a relative gets paid for work for another relative. I thought that maybe you guys expected to get paid for the yard sale."

"Eat shit, Dwayne," DotCom said.

Everyone smiled except Brownie, who was still trying to get him to play.

"What are we going to do with all this money?" Lacy Dawn asked.

"First, we will stash $10,000 and claim that we grossed $20,000—just in case the IRS decides to take an interest," Dwayne said. "We should be okay since it was all cash sales with no transactions to trace. After that, honey, it's your money."

"No it's not. It's family money."

"But, if you start to spend, especially on big ticket items, you'll draw attention to yourself," Dwayne continued. "We could end up in a position of being required to explain where the money came from. That's how a lot of drug dealers end up busted. They buy stuff but have no way to explain how they earned the money."

"That's right. Listen to your daddy." Tom got up to go home, looked at the piles of money, and lay down to roll with Brownie.

Dwayne joined him. The bills scattered. They piled them a foot high to use as pillows. Jenny and Lacy Dawn laughed. DotCom sat without expression but with an erection in the cootie chair.

"I'm going to buy a used but nice SUV for Mommy; a new TV; a Barbie and not even take her out of the box since I'm almost grown anyway; a cushion for the tractor seat because it's so hard; some real ashtrays; a brand new outfit for DotCom—not Goodwill clothes; a muffler for your truck, Daddy; a pound of bacon every week for Brownie for as long as he lives; a book of stamps so I can write Faith even if she is dead; a new mattress—one that ain't been peed on; a trunk full of dirty magazines; a flea collar and shampoo; three brand new training bras; new toothbrushes for everybody I know; a used automatic washing machine from that man in town that works on them so Mommy won't have to use that old wringer anymore; every Metallica CD ever recorded; a bottle of Greased Lightning so Mommy don't have to rub so hard; a new car battery for Harold so he never gets stuck in front of our house ever again; a copy of High Times for Tom—with a thank-you card stuck in the middle; some brand name deodorant for DotCom because he's beginning to need it; an alarm clock so Mommy won't have to wake me up; gas for Mommy to go to math class at the adult education place so she can pass her GED; a pizza from a pizza shop for everybody and maybe even give a tip; a new outhouse so that maybe we can talk grandma into visiting; every shot that a real vet has for Brownie; and flowers with no name on the card for my last year's teacher so she will think that there's a man someplace who likes her. Am I broke yet?"

"No," Dwayne answered. Tom got up and left.

"Goodbye kisses?" DotCom asked. She gave him a giant one, almost on the lips.

"Do us a favor, Bucky, take this money with you," Dwayne said.

"He's right," Jenny agreed, "we have no good place to stash it. Our windows don't even lock. Nobody can get into your ship. I'll get some plastic grocery bags. It'll be safer there."

"For a storage fee," DotCom said. *I have become more human. I made a bad punch line.*

"You've been paid all you're going to get, young man," Lacy said.

"Congratulations on a most successful yard sale. Although I need to file my report for an official evaluation, I'm sure you scored a lot of points."

"Don't forget your manners!" Lacy yelled a minute later to DotCom as he walked up the path like a human. DotCom had no actual magic, but he would have been a close second in a race with Lacy Dawn if he exerted himself, even with the ten double plastic Kroger bags filled with bundles of money. Lacy Dawn watched until he turned the bend. *Once a person starts shitting, it won't stop no matter how hard the person tries. He's got to remember to wash his hands afterward. It's a basic duty.*

Dwayne got out his construction square and tape measure to plan more home improvement projects that would not draw too much attention to the fact that they were rich. None of the walls were square and the front of the house and bathroom had settled. The small creek of the hollow drew and drained everything over time. *Level the house or better; build a foundation to replace the corner stones; vinyl windows; new tin for the roof; a forced air furnace ....*

Jenny went to the back porch and sat on the oak rocker that her grandfather had made for her grandmother as a wedding present. She rocked in silence with an "I told you so" smile that had been absent since junior high. *Ever since I was a little girl, I knew I'd marry a rich man. Now it's true. I wish Mom was still alive.*

"Don't take no shit, girl," she said to Rocker. "That's what Mom said when she handed me the pistol." *Now, that gun has rusted away in the outhouse hole. It didn't work anyway or Mom would have used it. She'd sure be proud now.*

"I think I'll get a red SUV. Dwayne will want to get the best buy no matter what color, but I know how to control him now. Bye, Rocker."

It didn't answer like it used to. It no longer needed to console. Likely relieved, the rocker had spent many hours as an advisor to its owners and deserved a break. Jenny got up, went into the kitchen, washed dishes, changed into a sheer nightgown and took off her panties. *I hope he hasn't let money get the better of his senses.*

Lacy searched on the internet for the best soundproofing available. She re-read her own website ten times, logged off, plugged in the charger, and went to the back porch.

"Hey, Rocker. Are you bored and lonely too?"

"No," it objected to the needless intrusion. Lacy Dawn didn't press. *It seems the more you get, the more you need.*

She rocked and waited.

"Happy Birthday, Lacy Dawn," Rocker eventually creaked at midnight.

"Sometimes, I want to be just like any other kid. I feel like I've missed my whole childhood with all this responsibility stuff. Maybe it's not supposed to be a kid's job to fix her parents or the universe. Sure, I've done okay at it so far, but what about me? I'm supposed to be almost grown but I've been grown since I was five. So what if I've got the best looking boyfriend in the hollow—he ain't even human and he's like a child. He doesn't even really know me, not the real me. And, now that he's healed, Daddy don't hardly pay no attention to me. All he thinks about is sex with Mommy and home improvements. A switching might feel good. At least it'd be some kind of feeling. I'm numb. And, Mommy's so much in love with him again that I can't save her anymore. She'd object. I'm fired. And, big deal that I've got the best job in the hollow on Tom's farm. Harold could do it if he didn't get drunk so much. Maybe I should get drunk."

The next day she got a cake with a "1" and a "3" candle on it, presents, and funny cards. Tom told her that Dwayne was now a business owner and not just a manager. They each ate more pizza than anyone should. Lacy Dawn burped. *What's wrong with me? Maybe I'm bipolar, too. I wish I was pregnant instead of destined to save the universe.*

She hugged Tom and DotCom goodbye, kissed her mother and father, went into her bedroom, locked the door, crawled under the bed, and went to sleep. It was only one-half hour into a birthday party expected to last a couple. Nobody asked her why she left the party. Instead, they all got high.

Not Entry Level

Dwayne had just finished the installation of the trim around the last of the new windows when the telephone rang. Lacy Dawn and Jenny were shopping—a common occurrence now that Jenny had an SUV and money to spend. He climbed down the step ladder and made it to the phone before the new answering machine picked up.

"Hello."

"Dwayne, this is DotCom, I mean Bucky. Is Lacy Dawn available? I received your cumulative scores from the shopping trip and yard sale."

"Bucky, Dude, that was months ago. What took so long?"

"The scores were tied up in litigation. A Complainant alleged that I had provided too much direct assistance for the scores to be eligible for entry into the permanent record. I had to submit copies of my back-up tapes to the Scoring Council. I just now received the findings."

"Well, they ain't home. They went shopping again. Call back in a few."

"Dwayne, you and Lacy Dawn have the highest period score ever placed on permanent record and the equivalent of an A- for the yard sale."

"Cool, but it's not like beating Miami in football. Did we win a prize or something? I'll tell them when they get back. See you later."

"It's much more important to your planet than you realize."

"Hold on a minute and I'll get ready."

He went to retrieve his most accessible stash because there was no such thing as a short explanation by DotCom and he needed a little help sustaining interest. The cigar box was never too far away and it always contained the cream of the crop. Since he was fourteen, he had never actually been out of marijuana. But, as an adult, he had sometimes been inconvenienced and needed to go to one of several hiding places on the 74 acres they owned. He never kept more than twenty grams in the house—a misdemeanor at most. He found the cigar box under the couch. *This is going to take a while.*

"How did you call us anyway?" Dwayne lit his corncob pipe. "You ain't got no phone."

"Cell."

"Okay, shoot," Dwayne puffed.

"Shoppers have priority life status over other life forms, including protected classes, commercial plants, and animals. You two are now official shoppers from Earth and the first shoppers from a planet formerly ranked very low because it had never shopped."

"I'm used to ranking low."

"Children, shopper trainees, and retired shoppers who averaged a minimum life score are protected classes. It depends on the law of the particular planet. All other life forms except shoppers and protected classes are designated as expendable. However, an expendable designation does not require termination on most planets since people die of natural causes or accidents."

"That's reassuring."

"Planetary governments are not required to offer support services to expendable life forms, but some do. For example, some governments provide food or shelter. It is a planetary policy outside of universal Law."

"You can't buy toilet paper with food stamps either."

"Centuries ago, Mr. Prump required the governments of all planets on which shoppers live to submit annual extermination schedules. Habitable planets which had not achieved shopper status were logged as potential sites to relocate the more advanced species. These schedules were filed and are maintained in the event that an ecological imbalance would be declared by Management."

"I know about feeling imbalanced. I also know about feeling embarrassed for using food stamps. The card that Welfare gives now is better. Maybe you should recommend it to your boss. If it works on some of those other planets, you might get a raise."

"I'll consider your suggestion. In any case, employment is open on most planets. Some intelligent but expendable life forms claim a positive adjustment to their status. They have clubs, unions, and religions on many planets. Nevertheless, attainment of priority life status is the goal of every intelligent person born on all known planets, except for persons who, like insects, live in a microcosm."

"What would've happened if we'd ended up with a bad score?"

"You and everybody that you know—all people of your planet—would have been designated as expendable."

"I'm already considered expendable by most people."

"Earth has not submitted a list of protected life forms or an official ecological balance statement."

"You just don't want to lose your girlfriend."

"You are perceptive, Dwayne. However, it is more." *A tear? So this is how sorrow feels.*

"Earth has been protected from exploitation for thousands of years despite abundant resources that could have been easily marketed. Along with a few hundred other underdeveloped planets, Earth was protected because Mr. Prump found that it was a potential future site to market goods. More recent surveys have verified Earth's potential."

"Hold on another minute."

Dwayne got a pipe cleaner, ran it through, and tried to rub off the black smudge on his index finger with his pant leg. The smudge resisted but the pipe drew fine.

"Okay," Dwayne said.

"As examples you would most recognize, the science of antibiotics was traded by Management for some of Earth's ozone layer. What Americans call a White Supremacist Group bought Acquired Immune Deficiency Syndrome adapted to humans. It paid Shptiludrp twelve volunteer subjects to use for medical study. What Americans would call a fanatical religious group purchased a kilogram of mind-altering hypnotic drugs in exchange for forty tons of Earth sand. These were not large transactions. Nevertheless, they did demonstrate Earth's potential to trade." *I need to control my emotions.*

"Holy shit!" Dwayne said. "You mean that AIDS was bought from…."

"Yes, human shit is marketable."

173

The conversation stopped for a moment. Dwayne puffed. The kitchen was full of smoke. He turned on the new exhaust fan over the stove and smiled as attractive streams formed shapes on their way to the shroud.

"Excuse me. I have identified an unanticipated reaction of my developing emotional structures."

"Call me back in a few when you get it together, Bucky."

A few minutes later, Lacy Dawn came in the house with something held behind her back, and smiled. "Close your eyes and hold out your hands," she said to Dwayne. She gave him a used Metallica CD that she'd bought at the pawn shop. Jenny followed, draped in a sheer dress over her jeans that she bought from a store named Second Time Around. It cost four dollars. *I'll get my money's worth out of this.*

"My engine knocked on the hill just before the exit," Jenny said. Dwayne looked through the dress and frowned. *Business before pleasure.*

"Give me your keys and I'll check it out," he said. *Man, what a dress. I can't wait.*

She tossed the keys and winked.

"Oh, DotCom called and said that we scored good on the shopping trip and yard sale. He said some stuff about how important it was to our planet. I didn't quite get it but he's supposed to call back when he stops crying."

"He called? He's crying?" Lacy Dawn asked.

"He has a cell," Dwayne left to check out the car. *I'm glad I didn't pay more attention to DotCom's rant. The universe is too big to think about. It gives me a headache.*

The telephone rang. Lacy Dawn answered and DotCom started repeating the message he had given to Dwayne in the exact same words. She put the corn cob pipe inside the cigar box, stretched the telephone cord to put the box back under the couch, and listened without comment.

Next week, I'm going to buy one of those phones that doesn't need a cord.

"In summary, Earth has lost its status as an underdeveloped planet. Further protection must be earned within the point system. The odds are that someone will eventually beat your

174

high score for the period game. An A- for the yard sale is strong but there is a statute of limitations. However, do not worry. Earth is in a much stronger position now and is no longer subject to the whim of Management. There has been pressure to revise policies to open up exploitation of underdeveloped planets. Earth is no longer available if such is sanctioned in the future."

"Cool," Lacy Dawn said.

Dwayne returned from the test drive. Jenny modeled her new dress without her jeans underneath. He turned his head away and felt the putty around a newly installed window to see if it had dried in order to delay his urgency.

"Where and what kind of gas have you been buying?"

"Regular, but I want extra," she cooed.

"Try Go Mart high test. It's a low octane knock that you heard coming up the hill." *The hell with auto mechanics. She ain't got on no panties on.*

Dwayne and Jenny went into their bedroom.

"The parameters have changed for the job offer," DotCom said again when Lacy Dawn didn't respond the first time.

"Sorry, I was distracted. I love you, DotCom. Let's talk about this in person. I'll be up in a minute." *I hope I won't be that noisy when I grow up. Or, maybe I don't.*

Five minutes later, face to face, DotCom began the same full report for a third time. Almost at the point in the report where parameters had changed for the job offer, he stopped and fiddled with his mouse. Nothing new appeared on his monitor's screen. *I do not want to cry in front of her. I am too young and inexperienced to handle her emotions.*

"I've already heard the report. What does it mean to our marriage?" she asked.

"Minor modification to the plan is required," he said several seconds later. *I feel like hugging, laughing, crying, hugging, laughing, crying, kissing, hugging, and kissing, kissing, kissing. Maybe I need to take a break or a Zoloft.*

"What do you mean?" she asked.

He exhaled. A moisture spot appeared on the monitor—his first. He wiped it with his hand. It smeared. He got one of Lacy Dawn's tissues and wiped again. *Humanness is hard but I can*

175

do this. Do not disappoint her.

"The position that you were offered has been upgraded because of your player status and your high score. It is no longer an offer for an entry level position."

She took two steps toward him. He stood up and took three steps back. His back was against the wall of his small ship.

"That's good, right?" she asked.

"You will be in a position to demand compensation and benefits that correspond to a professional consultant, paid in increments regardless of final outcome, and you can negotiate a bonus for full project completion."

"Like no exploitation of Earth, ever?"

"Perhaps, however, based on the litigation outcome heard by the Scoring Council, a professional consultant is prohibited from having an Advocate. My role has changed. Of course, Mr. Prump has the authority to overrule the Scoring Council, but I do not recommend a premature motion."

"Crap. Let me think about it. Tomorrow, we're having a party to end the school year and I need to get to bed. I'm going to Middle School next year, honey. I'm growing up fast. You'd better be ready for it when I am because I'm going to be really ready." *I'm a professional and a consultant.*

Lacy Dawn left the ship and glided home.

A Family Affair

Middle School was more of an adjustment than Lacy Dawn had anticipated. First, she didn't expect so many pimples — not just on her — on everybody. Kids she used to joke with in elementary school were hard to look at in Middle School. She'd spent almost the entire first month just getting used to it. The job offer on Shptiludrp had received no attention. She was in the bathroom getting ready for school.

"Squeeze," she said to the bathroom mirror.

The girls, Lacy Dawn included, were growing larger breasts. All the boys looked and all the girls talked about how big or small they were compared to others.

"Grow," she said to the mirror.

And, instead of one teacher, there were several teachers who taught periods — what a total hassle. She had started carrying a purse just so she would have a place to store a tampon in case the unpredictable occurred.

"Flush," she said to the commode. It floated and spun in circles. She crossed her fingers and flushed again. *Daddy will get pissed about that thing going into the septic tank. But, it's better than when Brownie got one out of the trash can and scattered pieces all over the house.*

The second week of school, a boy asked her to go with him to the first school dance. She told DotCom. His face turned red. "I can practice and be your date," he replied, and downloaded videos until that Friday evening.

"Squeeze," she said to him as Creed's 'Arms Wide Open' played during the dance, and pressed. *That made me dizzy in love. I'd better quit before I can't.*

"I'd like for you to meet my boyfriend. He goes to a different school," she said to classmates at the dance. It was the first of several wonderful evenings: two dances, three parties, a fair, and a formal prom. No longer introverted and insecure, Lacy Dawn had come out of the psychotherapist's closet and was popular just like her daddy when he went to school. DotCom had been introduced and fit in. She blow dried her hair. *I've got it all planned — homecoming queen and king, parking in Mommy's car.... Earth's safe enough for now.*

When dressed, Lacy Dawn glided up the path Roundabend to catch the school bus. She didn't get a spot of mud on her shoes. The next time she gave the job offer on Shptiludrp any thought was winter break. She'd been too busy with school and its functions. On December 17th, 2017, holiday break began. Lacy Dawn had tried to sleep late but couldn't. *That job's got to be figured out. Maybe if DotCom goes to Shptiludrp by himself and gathers more information. No, it has to be me. More important right now — Christmas presents. I'm thirteen and rich.*

Jenny had started as a volunteer for Head Start and was subsequently employed as an aide. She had money to spend. Dwayne had re-established credit all over town and had money to spend. Proprietors of the small town shops that were experiencing hard times greeted them when they came in. Lots of presents were bought. On Christmas Eve, Lacy Dawn decided to move on her job offer.

"C'mon, Daddy, let's go back to Shptiludrp and check it out some more."

"Talk with Bucky. I'll contact my staff and Tom to make sure all the bases are covered while we're gone. What do you think, honey?" he asked Jenny.

"I'd appreciate an email every now and then so I don't worry so much this time."

"Unless we can negotiate high priority service, there's a long delay between send and receive," Lacy Dawn said.

"Anything's better than nothing," Jenny said and looked at Dwayne.

The day after Christmas, they were on their way back to Shptiludrp. Lacy Dawn and Dwayne brought more changes of clothing now that improved family finances allowed. DotCom had washed his outfit in Jenny's wringer washer, a necessity since he had started to sweat. An automatic washer and dryer had been ordered.

"Since I am no longer your Advocate, I can only verify or refute. I cannot provide direct analytical assistance."

"Are we still engaged?" she asked.

"Yes," he said in a manner consistent with the strictest

178

construction of the Opinion by the Scoring Council.

"Good," she said. *This trip is going to be boring.*

"Incoming," DotCom said an hour later in possible violation of the new rule.

Dwayne grabbed Lacy Dawn, unhooked her seat belt, threw her to the ship's floor, and covered her with his body as if shielding her from gunfire. The sudden weight shift in the small ship set off a malfunction alarm that DotCom turned off.

"Get off me, you pervert!" *That'll move his ass quick.*

"Thank God," DotCom said after reading the email. "Mr. Prump has over-ruled the Scoring Council. I am your Advocate again."

Lacy struggled to breathe.

"Sorry, it took me back to the Gulf," Dwayne got up and tried to explain. "There's only a few of us there now, so that makes it feel even more solitary. Sorry. I didn't know you believed in God, Bucky," Dwayne said.

"I guess I've smoked too much carbon," he responded.

"Is that a hint?" Dwayne said and lit one.

"Don't Bogart that joint, my friend," DotCom said.

He had learned contemporary American subculture. Dwayne passed it to DotCom who inhaled like he'd seen on Reefer Madness and passed it back. Lacy Dawn reached out for the joint and was rebuffed by both.

"You can get married now that you're thirteen if you want. I can't say much because I married your mom when she wasn't much older. But, you ain't smoking pot with me until you turn at least sixteen. It's the rules. If you snitch anything before then, I'll know and bust your ass like never before. You'll be grounded for a lifetime—no more school dances or anything."

Their ship hovered for five minutes, was granted VIP status, and docked.

"It is not that I do or do not believe in a god. It is a cool thing to say at particular points in time," DotCom landed.

When they registered at the hotel, they ordered a room with three beds on DotCom's insistence. An hour later they left the room, and remained on the slow beltway all evening to talk in private about their observations of the Mall.

"What's the difference between you being an Advocate and whatever role you had before?" Lacy Dawn asked.

"I'm still researching the technicalities."

Everything that DotCom saw and heard was on permanent record and potentially subject to subpoena regardless of his role. It was in his memory banks. The recruitment and training of Lacy Dawn was high priority and critical to survival of the universe. Management had access to anything on his hard drives at any time.

"I am bound by confidentiality standards as an Advocate. According to law, we can have private discussions. However, that is the strictest construction of an ancient statute and I do not trust Management to comply."

"I agree," Lacy said. "Let's play it safe." *Either his explanations are getting better or I'm more used to them.* "I love you," she mouthed.

A strategy emerged. DotCom would connect to the Management database to research and point out shoppers who would be the most likely to take time out to talk. They were the ones who didn't need high scores in order to maintain their shopper status. Lacy Dawn would try to engage them in conversation and Dwayne would arrive a few moments later to help out.

"I agree with the plan," Dwayne said. *I feel like I'm panhandling.*

Ten shopper conversations later, they met to discuss tentative findings. Twenty-five shoppers had been approached. Most ignored the invitation to talk. Instead, it caused them to rush into the nearest shop, grab merchandise, and get in line at checkout.

"Shoppers seem to know that there's a big problem and that Management has no solution," Lacy Dawn said. "They also seem too paranoid to talk about it."

"Why don't you just tell us what the problem is, DotCom, instead of playing games?" Dwayne asked.

"I will walk with you a mile but I won't carry you an inch," he said.

"Eat shit," Dwayne said. *He sounds too human for my taste at the moment.*

"I'm going shopping." Dwayne walked away.

"C'mon, Bucky. Before Daddy goes, it's obvious that something is up and you know what it is. Why won't you just tell us so Daddy and I can work up an estimate for the job and go home? Holiday break will be over soon. I don't want this job to hang over me. I've got important things to plan—like what to wear when I give the Martin Luther King report that you've got to help me with."

"Leon Sullivan," he answered. *I like the name "Bucky" but I've been DotCom for so long.*

"No, Martin Luther King," she said.

"Leon Sullivan was the answer to your question."

She shrugged. *What the hell does that mean?*

"Let's see, Opportunities Industrialization Council? That's where your Grandma thought about going to school before she got married and wasn't allowed to work. That couldn't be the answer. Nelson Mandela? How folks are treated on Earth? Sullivan's the most famous person from West Virginia? I give up. Can you explain?"

"I thought you'd never ask. The answer to why I cannot define the job for you is the Sullivan Principles."

"Daddy told me that the main principle for us from Dr. Sullivan was to never shoplift from the local grocery. It will just cause the store to raise prices and hurt everybody." *I still feel bad about stealing that hair conditioner from Kroger's for Mommy.*

"That could be a derivation, I suppose. Dr. Sullivan proposed that larger market influences should be utilized to stimulate the creation of opportunities for all beings to participate in a planet's economic systems. Self-help through established opportunity, such as education and fair play, were cornerstones of his universal success as a philosopher. Mr. Prump has a picture of Dr. Sullivan on the wall in his office."

"Dr. Sullivan was known way out here?" Lacy Dawn asked.

"Yes. So far, he has been the most famous person from your planet. To be frank, he has been the only notable person from Earth."

"And, he wouldn't approve if you told me more about the

181

job?"

"A self-analyzed problem definition is an essential ingredient to establish motivation to move on available opportunity."

"Bull crap. That's just another way to stall progress on human rights and has nothing to do with our situation. It's like saying that exploited people have to learn how to read and write first so that they can express their plight in letters to the editor before schools should be built. Dr. Sullivan would've never put up with such logic."

"Your cousin's principles are open to interpretation. I follow clear instruction from Mr. Prump based on his interpretation."

"My cousin? No way. I'm as white as a snowflake in a blizzard."

"His ancestry received the same genetic implant as did your ancestry. There were two of you on Earth—him and you. He has more biological relationship to you than your own mother and father."

"Now you're telling me that my own cousin would object if you help me out?"

"No. I am telling you that I have received very clear instruction from management. Based on interpretation of the Sullivan Principles, you are required to define the problem on your own before you are eligible to bid on the project. I do not agree or disagree with the interpretation. You will have as many opportunities to identify the nature of the project as you choose—this generation, the next, or the next. If at any point I violate the instruction, it will void your opportunity to fulfill your destiny. Mr. Prump could recreate, activate, and assign another DotCom to cultivate the next prospect—a being not from Earth."

Dwayne looked back over his shoulder and went into another shop.

"Some Advocate you are," she said. *This is some personal shit. It's more important than the next school dance. It's my marriage, my reputation, the reputation of my family, Earth — it's bigger than if we beat Ravenswood in football and more important than making all the other girls jealous.*

"If I fail, will I lose you?" she asked.

"No way, Jose," he cupped his crotch. "I will retire to marry you when you are grown by human measure. It would be a waste to revert all of this to original programming." He cupped his crotch again. "I now qualify as a carbon base and can assert free will. Further, you out-maneuvered Mr. Prump in contract negotiations and our relationship is protected by law." He cupped his crotch a third time.

She turned her head. "Let's go find Daddy and see if he found out anything. And another thing, if you start to act like one of those nasty boys at school, grabbing your crotch and all that, I won't marry you until you grow up."

Popularity Pays

Ten Earth minutes later, with DotCom's assistance, Lacy found Dwayne surrounded by beings of various shapes, sizes, and compositions. She got off the slow beltway and was immediately surrounded also.

"Can I have your autograph, Lacy Dawn?" a green blubbery ball with four eyes and five antennae created and extended an appendage from its mass and handed her a small screen that had been inside its body. In her best cursive, Lacy Dawn signed her name with a thin pencil that was attached to something by a cord, dried her hands on her cutoffs, and pushed through the crowd.

Atop a building, two large screens showed different scenes of Lacy Dawn and Dwayne. Their location number flashed at regular intervals. The crowd tightened and became elbow to elbow — except many shoppers surrounding them didn't have elbows.

"We need a strategy!" she hollered.

Dwayne nodded.

Over shoulders and various other body parts, Bucky reached out hands to both and pulled. Dwayne and Lacy Dawn held tight. Bucky edged them away from the crowd and they returned to the slow beltway. The autograph seekers didn't follow. Dwayne sat down on the beltway, crossed his legs, and bowed his head. His sweat dripped onto the beltway surface. Lacy Dawn stood before him with her arms crossed in case her deodorant had failed. DotCom's sweat system had not yet become fully functional, but downwind would have been a better position — if Shptiludrp had wind. He fanned his face with his free hand.

"Shopping with you goes from one extreme to the next, Daddy."

"I got trapped," Dwayne said.

"You used to take me shopping for car parts at junk yards, wasn't allowed to say a thing — not one word. You told me that I had to look a little dirty and very poor, as if we weren't. I wasn't allowed to smile. You told me to look sad and skinny."

"It worked, didn't it?"

"You got famous in the hollow for fixing up old cars. Now, we're superstars here too. The public demands that we make ourselves available and presentable."

"What the heck are you talking about, Lacy Dawn?" Dwayne asked.

"Nothing, I'm just trying to perk you up a little. Did you find out anything?"

"Yeah—one thing—these people will do anything for an autograph. I was shown breasts. I think they were breasts. I was shown other body parts, kissed, patted, and offered what must have been money, drinks, and food. They all wanted autographs. Our high score in The Game must have made us celebrities."

"Why don't they try to get autographs while we're on the beltway?" Lacy Dawn asked.

"It's against the Privacy Act," Bucky said. "That's a universal statute highly regarded by carbon based units. Despite its open and obvious location, the beltway was designated by statute as a private means of transportation. This designation was intended to reduce resistance to the abolishment of personal scooters, ships, and various other means of individual or enclosed transportation. On Shptiludrp, an individual may not be disturbed while on the beltways."

"I'm already disturbed and I got a check to prove it," Dwayne said.

"Violation of the Privacy Act is subject to the death penalty. The only other violation that is as harshly punished is a third offense parking violation."

"Let's go back to the hotel to figure out a way to take advantage of the situation. We need to make sure our popularity pays off," Lacy Dawn said.

"I need to email your mom anyway."

They got off the slow beltway and onto the fast. Eight minutes later, guests in the lobby made a pathway to the elevator without saying a word, although several held out autograph books, pictures, and laptops just in case.

"I'm taking a nap," Lacy Dawn said when they entered their room.

"Me too," DotCom said. *I hope I can sleep for the first time.* He lay on his own bed.

Dwayne went into the bathroom, turned on the vent fan, and stayed there with the laptop on his knees. DotCom closed his eyes with his fingers. Lacy Dawn fell asleep and dreamt about when she gave an Indian artifact to her mother to help prove DotCom's existence. In her dream, Jenny scolded. *You mean that Indians used to go into our mountain and meet with this robot? And, that's why the Indians started building mounds? He told them that it was the best way to preserve a record of their way of life? That's silly, Lacy Dawn. And, you're the next person to meet him after the Indians? The only person who can help him on a secret mission? He needs help all right. I ought to call Welfare on him if I was that kind of person. They'd put him someplace. Or, maybe they'd put me someplace.*

Lacy Dawn smiled in her sleep and picked a different dream. It was a technique that DotCom had taught her to fight off the same old bad dream about being too late to help her mother stop the bleeding. The technique had also come in handy for recreational pursuit.

"I've got it!" She sat up in bed two hours later.

DotCom woke up with the announcement. *Who got what?*

Dwayne was still in the bathroom. The place smelled like hooch before he opened the door. He exhaled directly into the fan but most of the smoke followed him out the door. *That exhaust fan is a piece of trash.*

"Mommy told me in my dream," Lacy Dawn said.

"Faster than this e-mail service," Dwayne said.

"Huh?" Bucky asked.

"Mommy told me that the best use of popularity within a group is to isolate and get commitments from individuals in private. She said that's how all the popular girls in high school get boys to marry them and how all the popular boys get sex even though they don't deserve it. Popularity is an effective tool to use in individual negotiation and that's how group consensus is achieved."

"Bull shit," Dwayne said. "Your mom don't talk nothing like that. You were dreaming."

"And that's how you first got it from Mommy. You were popular in high school and used it on my mommy."

"Ain't nothing wrong with using what you've got to get what you want." *I wish I hadn't gotten so high.*

"I agree," Lacy Dawn said. "We need a solid plan—a strategy to make our popularity pay. I've only been popular at school since the beginning of the year, but one thing I know is that it may not last long. We need to use it before it's gone."

"You sure have grown up. You use big words and everything," Dwayne said.

Dwayne lay down on his bed. Bucky followed suit. He was more disoriented than Dwayne. It was his first sleep.

"That's it, goof balls. We're going home to sort this out. Can you drive, fly, or whatever it's called, Bucky?"

Five minutes later, Bucky was ready to file his departure report with Management. On their way to the ship, the crowds behaved in compliance with the Privacy Act. Fans waved good-bye with one appendage while holding autograph notebooks with another.

"It's a good strategy to tease," Lacy Dawn said. She had learned it from her mother. "It builds for the next time — especially if press coverage of our visit is complimentary. Please clip all the articles for me, Bucky." *Which of his plug-in lessons taught me how to manipulate fans?*

On their trip home, Bucky wiggled in his seat, tapped his foot, and repeatedly crossed and uncrossed his legs. An email reply from Jenny was received. It didn't say much more than to be careful and that she loved all three of them. It seemed to make matters worse for Bucky.

"Is something wrong, Honey?" Lacy Dawn asked.

"From now on, my name is Bucky," he said.

Dwayne approached and waved his daughter to her seat. Dwayne and Bucky talked. Bucky left the commander's seat and Dwayne sat down. He didn't touch anything but watched everything. There were ten digital displays that stayed constant. There were numbers or words that Dwayne couldn't read and a joystick—like one for a video game. He faced the picture window where blurs of light came and went. Two minutes later,

Bucky returned to resume command.

"Did you wash your hands?" Dwayne whispered. Bucky returned to the bathroom. When he came back, Dwayne went to his recliner and Lacy Dawn came to Bucky's side to find out what was going on.

"I love you, Bucky," she whispered in his ear.

"I love you too."

"It pays to be popular," Lacy Dawn said clear and loud so that both males could hear. It was a tone that implied that nobody else in the universe could have made DotCom want to become human and that nobody could satisfy him as a human except for her — when she grew up.

Strategic Planning

After the trip to Shptiludrp, Dwayne and Jenny went back to work. Lacy Dawn went back to school. Bucky spent so much time in the bathroom of his ship that he was no longer available to develop lesson plans. One evening, Lacy Dawn arrived at the ship and plugged herself into a Human Philosophy throughout Earth History lesson. She didn't bother to ask for Bucky's assistance or recommendation. He was in the bathroom admiring the plumbing after his latest bout of onanism. She relaxed to absorb the content of the plug-in while he slowly, indulgently, rinsed his hands. *This sink was a great idea.*

She took notes. *Was Leon Sullivan really the greatest human ever?* she considered.

"I'll be out in a minute," Bucky yelled.

Adolescence! Masturbation seems like a time-consuming hobby and an inefficient use of work time, she thought.

"It's okay. I'm already plugged in." *Timing is everything.* An hour later, she left. *Maybe I should walk the path. It will help me think things through. No, I'll elevate an inch above the ground's surface so my new tennis shoes won't get muddy.*

Otherwise, step by step at a normal pace, she went down the hill. *Tom's an experienced and successful project administrator. I need him on my team for the job....*

The next day, she returned to the ship in the same manner, elevated an inch and step by step up the hill. It was a refined magic that her best tree friends appreciated because it gave them time to say hello. She had been so busy with school and work that visits with them had become rare. And, too soon, the time approached when trees would no longer talk and she would no longer believe they could. Best friends never last.

"If you rush it, you'll blow it," Faith said on their way to Roundabend.

"If I don't do something, nothing will ever happen," Lacy Dawn argued.

"Nothing is better than something bad. Look what happened to me," Faith said. "It started a little at a time—a kiss, a touch, a suck. By the time he actually did me, it wasn't even me. I'd learned how to leave my body until it was over. I guess that's why I'm so good at moving from inside trees to inside rocks now. I've had lots and lots of practice. Now that I'm dead, it's really easy since I ain't got no body to clean up afterward. It never got clean anyway."

"You can get inside me anytime you want, Faith," the maple tree said.

"Don't be such a worry wart. I promise I'll come back from my out-of-town job. Best friends always last."

"Liar, liar, pants on fire," Faith sang from the next tree.

When Lacy Dawn got to the ship, Bucky was in the bathroom—as if he ever left. She hit an interior wall with her fist, but not hard because she knew it wasn't mere sheetrock. She rubbed her knuckles from habit rather than pain. *This is the final straw. Mommy and Daddy act like there ain't no universe outside the hollow, much less one to save, and all DotCom does is play with himself. I've lost control of my team and the team has lost sight of its mission.*

"School's near agricultural break. Please find whatever plug-in will work to keep you out of the bathroom long enough to attend a staff meeting," she yelled and left.

"I'm sorry," Bucky said from the bathroom. It was too late for it to have any possibility of delaying her departure.

When she got home, Lacy Dawn gave notice to her parents that a staff meeting was in order. When they groaned, she gave them The Look and they nodded and smiled. She went into her bedroom.

"Have you resigned from your position as Plow Master?" Tom replied to her email.

"Not," she sent. *The plow is hard work. I don't need the money. But it's wrong to quit a job unless a person has a better one.*

The next day, Lacy Dawn got up bright and early. This year, she had started to plow a month early. Otherwise, Harold's boys would've said that she was just a girl. She allowed them to drive the dump truck filled with manure, but she controlled to the inch where it was put and when. Nobody was permitted to touch one of her tractors at the risk of death. She pointed to the proper place to dump. *All the boys in the hollow know I'm serious.*

"If you don't come back, I'll die!" Faith said that afternoon. She was louder than the tractor and inside the walnut tree that kept watch over the path to Roundabend.

"You're already dead!" Lacy Dawn yelled back at the tree and steered around a stump. She idled to read Tom's instructions for micronutrients in the soil of his secret garden.

"Good job!" Tom yelled.

She didn't hear him but saw the thumbs up. *It looks like he'll be at the staff meeting. Timing is everything. Copper sulfate, a pinch here and there…?*

That evening, the staff meeting began with an agenda that Lacy Dawn had prepared. She had printed enough copies for all. At the top, centered, in a fourteen point bold font was the header, Rarity from the Hollow. Beneath was a numbered list of items to discuss in a twelve point font. It was her first agenda. She read it again. *Good practice for the future.*

"Since there're no old Minutes to approve, I'll move straight to the first item, 'Tell Tom the Truth about the Situation'." She had two video tapes that Bucky had edited to show to Tom. The first started. Dwayne and Jenny recessed to the kitchen to snack and kiss.

"Is this an old *Star Trek* rerun?" Tom asked five minutes into the video.

"It's the real thing, Dude," Dwayne yelled from the kitchen.

"Think about the yard sale, Tom," Jenny said. "Have you ever seen anything like what we sold here in the hollow?"

"What's a bustle, anyway?" Tom asked.

"It is an undergarment that makes a woman's buttocks look bigger," Bucky said.

"There's the shop where the eight bustles we sold came from," Lacy Dawn pointed at the TV screen.

"Seven," Jenny said.

"So that's why we only got an A minus. The books didn't balance by an item. You kept one, Mommy."

"Do you want me to pay for it?"

Tom watched the video. Weird people or animals picked up items and got in line as if they were at the Kroger's grocery. The scene was a place where there were several objects that looked like ones sold at the yard sale. He squinted at the nineteen inch screen. *I wish the twenty-five incher still worked.*

"I still can't believe any of this shit," Tom said.

Both videos had finished.

"Roll up some inspiration," Dwayne said.

"Why don't you get rid of that old console TV since it don't work?" Tom asked. *I don't know what the hell I just watched?*

With the portable TV still on top, Bucky lifted the console with one hand, spun it, and removed the back cover. It worked in two minutes after Lacy Dawn changed cables.

"Fucking A," Tom said and licked the joint.

"Alright, Tom, since you're a hard-sell, we're just going to have to take a little trip around the world a few times," Lacy Dawn said.

"You guys go ahead. Jenny and I need to talk in private," Dwayne said.

Tom slid the joint into his shirt pocket.

Ten minutes later at Roundabend he inhaled hard. "Man, this was a good harvest," he said, and walked through the stone outcropping into Bucky's ship.

"This shit can't be that good."

After take-off, Tom watched the Earth shrink through the picture window. He gripped the armrests.

"Either I need to go back to Detox or this shit is for real."

The ship circled the Earth. Tom's fingernails dug all the way through the vinyl-like cover of the armrest. *This is really, really cool.*

"We'll go back home whenever you are convinced," Lacy Dawn said from the floor of the ship where she played with Brownie on the old quilt.

"Convinced of what? I'm as good as I'll get, but I need some time to digest what the hell has happened."

"Lacy Dawn wants to hire you as a business consultant, Tom," Bucky said. "I would do anything for her smile."

Twenty minutes later, the scene from the ship's window was the blackness inside the cave. Tom swiveled his chair to look around. It looked a little like the shop owned by his friend in

New York who repaired computers — equipment everywhere. But, the tools and parts that hung on the wall above the counter were organized and the counter itself was clear. Everything was attached to something except for the old quilt that Brownie used as a bed.

"Are you ready to go back to the staff meeting?" Lacy Dawn asked.

"I'll try," Tom followed Brownie out of the ship, out of the cave, and reached back to verify that it was solid stone. In the living room, he sat down hard on the couch. Jenny was still with Dwayne in their bedroom. Lacy Dawn sat down gently beside Tom. *Good thing Mommy didn't see him sit down so rough on her new couch.*

Bucky sat in the old cootie-infested armchair. It was the next piece of furniture scheduled to be replaced when a high-dollar expenditure would not raise suspicion. Tom stared at Bucky and he stared back.

"We've topped five hundred and fifty thousand hits on our website. The next yard sale is gonna be a real killer," Lacy Dawn said.

"Yeah, but how many of those hits were the FBI or IRS?" Tom asked.

He continued to stare at Bucky.

"I will analyze," Bucky said.

Lacy Dawn looked at them. *They're both a mess.*

Tom was shaken by exposure to more of a universe than he could handle. Bucky had an identity crisis with an obvious erection. She looked at her agenda with its ambitious listings, heard her mother giggle from the bedroom, and said, "Meeting adjourned." *Leon would've chaired it better.*

My Best is Bipolar

The next weekend, Dwayne showed Lacy Dawn how to change oil in one of Tom's tractors. Since their trip around Earth, Tom had made himself scarce. On her own initiative, she plowed to ready the fields for planting. A weekend later, Bucky pulled out three tree trunks on Tom's upper meadow. They had been in the way for years. The following weekend, Dwayne spent the entire Saturday hauling manure in Tom's dump truck. There was one more partial week of school left. It was a good time to resume the staff meeting, but Tom was still not ready. He had cut off all communications with the team.

Lacy Dawn had come up with a game to pass time while she plowed the fields and waited for Tom. It was triggered by the human philosophy plug-in she'd studied weeks before. *I am because the Worker at the Welfare Office approved me for food stamps and they are trained to spot fakes—therefore, I must be. I am because Bucky gets an erection every time he so much as looks at that tree.*

"I am because I live inside a tree," Faith called from a dogwood.

"Eat shit. My man would never look at another girl." Lacy Dawn said.

"I am because Brownie likes to lick my face, therefore, at least my face exists," Lacy Dawn said to Faith.

"I wish I had a face," Faith said.

"Me too, me too, me too," echoed throughout the Woods.

Lacy Dawn pulled the tractor into Tom's yard and steered toward his barn.

"Hey, Tom!" she yelled at a slumped figure in a lawn chair, parked the tractor inside the barn, and locked the door. Its key symbolized her status to the world. Tom sat under an apple tree behind his house. He had watched Lacy Dawn from when she had come into view. She walked toward him. *Something terrible is wrong. He never does nothing in the middle of the day.* She sat down in a lawn chair beside him and waited. *I'm determined to break the barrier, and not just because I need him. He needs me too.*

After ten minutes, Tom got up, stepped in his back door, and came out with a beer and a glass of lemonade. He handed her the Miller, took it back, and gave her the lemonade.

"I never did go to church much," he said. "I kinda looked down on most church goers like they weren't as smart as me. But, deep down inside, I always counted on Jesus. It stopped me from taking advantage of people. My father took advantage of everybody. That's how he got rich but I tried to always do the right thing. Jesus would be there to help me out in a pinch."

"More sugar?" Lacy Dawn asked.

"Sorry," he went into the house and returned with a cup full and another beer. Since he didn't bring a spoon, she shook a little in her glass and stirred with her finger.

"Now that I've seen how big everything is — other planets with people, a spaceship that can go around the world in minutes, and a man that can pull out tree trunks with his bare hands — yeah, I saw him — I just can't believe in Jesus anymore. It makes me feel like a fool in the first place. I might as well have acted like an asshole all my life like my dad."

"You are a good person, Tom."

"Nothing matters. I never believed in Heaven. But, I kinda hoped that it existed because I always thought—ever since I was a little boy—that good things would happen to good people in the end. I haven't been able to sleep for days thinking about all this shit."

"I've been worried. You ain't been around and I thought you might be sick."

"I tried to pray. I've never told anyone before that I did it. This time it felt silly. I called my wife and we talked last night on the phone. She didn't listen. Instead, she told me about all the good buys in New York City. We've never talked about Jesus or praying or anything like that before, but I thought she might listen. And, I thought that if I got it off my chest, maybe it would help me out enough so I could sleep."

"Give me a hit. I'm almost sixteen."

"Eat shit. You ain't." He inhaled.

"Sorry," she said.

Tom exhaled in her direction as a courtesy.

"Anyway, last Sunday I flipped through the channels to look for a preacher that sounded real. After the ride in your spaceship, they all look like rip-offs. I can't talk to your dad about this. Sure, sometimes we talk about personal stuff. He's my best friend and all that, but we don't talk about this kind of stuff. It's way too personal."

"He's worried about you too," Lacy Dawn said.

"I like Bucky okay and everything. But, every time I look at your man I get more depressed. I used to get a thrill from looking at your mom if she wasn't wearing a bra, not that I'd ever do anything to piss off your dad, but I can't even get off on that now. It wouldn't help if she leaned over with a loose top right in front of me."

"Want me to bring over some Paxil?"

"The more I smoke, the more I think. Beer makes me sleepy but I can't sleep. Maybe I need to go see a doctor and get some hardcore drugs. I'm sorry to unload. You're only ten years old."

"Thirteen. I mean sixteen."

"See what I mean? I can't think straight. Nothing matters. I can't get off, not on music, stuff, sex, not that I've had any, sorry. Success doesn't matter. Money is a joke. I used to get off when I beat your dad in horseshoes. Now, I can't even walk over to play. He must've put new sand in the pits by now."

"He'd kick your ass."

"I pulled out my Fender and tried to play 'If Six Was Nine,' my favorite Jimi. I couldn't finish. I tried to play 'Stairway to Heaven' but it felt so bad that I put my guitar in the attic for the next maniac who lives here to find."

"I need some more lemonade."

"I downloaded porn but deleted it after I watched a few seconds because it was so irrelevant. I tried to call my mother for the first time in a decade. She didn't answer. Thank God, I mean goodness. I feel so alone. I'm stoned and can't find my way home."

"I heard you play guitar. It echoed off of the hills and sounded great."

"It was shit. I am shit. What's the point anyway? I should've stayed in the band. But no, I listened to my dad. Now look where it's got me. There's no reason to go on and there's nothing I can do about it."

"Let's pray," Lacy Dawn said. "The Lord is my Shepherd, I shall not want...."

Tom threw in a couple of Amen's. After finishing the psalm that she had learned in church, she looked into his eyes. "There was nothing that you saw that should have shaken your belief in Jesus. What you saw and what you will see on our mission will make him look stronger and bigger. Jesus is much more than human-kind. He existed for the salvation of all—not just humans. All means all. His sacrifice was never meant to have been discriminatory or selective to just one kind of people on one planet. Right is right and wrong is wrong. It's just like you know in your heart. Good and evil have always been and will always be the balance on which survival of the universe depends."

Lacy Dawn didn't use a single concept that she had learned from her philosophy plug-in lesson. It was ad lib from the heart—plus a little grandma.

Tom took another sip of beer.

"The manager I told you about has a picture of Jesus on his office wall," she closed. *I hope Bucky can negotiate a picture.*

Lacy Dawn handed Tom a folded picture of Leon Sullivan that she had downloaded from the internet and carried in her shirt pocket while she plowed. It was faded, wrinkled, and a little moist from her sweat.

"That's Leon Sullivan, you dip shit," he said.

"Same difference," she corrected.

They giggled. She finished her lemonade and got up. *He'll be back to normal crazy soon.*

Lacy Dawn gave Tom a sideways hug good-bye. She avoided forward hugs so her breasts could remain off limits.

"I love you, Lacy Dawn," he said.

"There's a staff meeting on Monday. Be there or be square," she said and turned to leave.

"Okay. Tell your dad I'll call him."

Fifteen steps later, she turned around and walked back to Tom's house. He had already gone inside. She knocked, walked

197

in, and said, "It's me."

There were noises but he didn't answer. She waited in the kitchen. Two minutes later, he appeared with his guitar case and amplifier.

"I thought you went home," he said.

"Got your guitar down from the attic, huh?"

"I'm in the mood. I shouldn't have put it up there in the first place—all by its lonesome. Do you wanna jam? I heard you do a mean Janis and I know all of Big Brother."

"I couldn't do Janis if my life depended on it. Nobody can or ever will. I came back to see if you'd be interested in something to help balance out your bipolar cycles. I know something that just might work."

"I've already tried medication. It made me feel half alive. For a little while, on the up side it's a rush, but it's not worth the down side. Pot does more good than medication. I think I'm over it now, thanks to you. I owe you one. Don't forget to tell your dad that I'm gonna call him."

"You remember how angry and mean Daddy used to be? Well, guess who helped him?"

"I thought that maybe it was when your mom started to look so good that fixed him up. I hoped I helped by giving him a job. You tell me. I know it wasn't no VA doctor."

"Bucky," she said.

"No shit?"

"I bet he can help you too. It's just a few minor tweaks of this or that chemical production in your biological systems."

"That's what all the doctors said." *Bullshit.*

"Bucky is smarter than all the doctors in the world combined and he don't believe in medication to fix something that can be fixed without it."

"How would he help me then?"

"When you come over to beat Daddy in horseshoes tonight, I'll have Bucky talk to you. He's the doctor. His machines can diagnose and fix all kinds of stuff."

"It can't hurt to talk. I'd given up on getting any help."

"I love you, Tom." She left for a second time.

Before she had gotten home, Tom played "The Wind Cried

198

Mary." It was followed by a Cream song that she couldn't remember the name of and that Dwayne used to have on eight-track tape until it had been eaten by the player. That evening, Tom beat everybody in horseshoes. They wouldn't let Bucky play because he always got ringers. As arranged, Bucky talked to Tom while Dwayne flipped burgers. Jenny made potato salad and Lacy Dawn took care of the condiments, including solid rock music at all times. After eating, she cornered Bucky.

"How did it go?" she pointed a finger at Tom.

"Patient confidentiality," he said.

"More HIPAA bullshit?" she accused. *Tom and Bucky must have hooked up, cool.*

Later, before the staff meeting resumed, they acted like they'd been best friends forever. Lacy called the meeting to order.

"I believe we've already covered agenda item number one," she deadpanned. "We have told Tom the truth and he has been converted. Agenda item number two. Please pay attention," Lacy Dawn commanded. They did. *I'd better say something good, profound, and motivational.*

"We need a strategy, a plan, a strategic plan. That's what we need. Please start by taking turns describing your view of the situation. I'll go last."

"Since we're celebrities, we can't do undercover investigation," Dwayne said.

"My role is limited. First define the problem and then motivate the most affected into self-help or the project will fail," Bucky said.

"I would do anything for Cher's autograph. The shoppers are willing to risk talking to us," Jenny said.

"I've never seen Shptiludrp. I make it a practice to never buy a piece of real estate unless I've seen it first. I don't see any difference with this project," Tom said.

"Good job," Lacy Dawn said to her team and made eye contact with each member.

"Tom needs to see the real estate. Bucky, can you arrange for a tour at his convenience?"

"No problemmo."

"Good," she said. *I wish he'd hurry up and grow up.*

"I'll schedule a resumption of our staff meeting when Tom returns with his report. This meeting is adjourned."

"Cool beans," the other four shouted in unison.

"Sorry for the formalities. It's practice for when I chair future meetings," Lacy said.

Tom and Bucky left the next day and were gone the better part of a month. In consultation with the Department of Agriculture's extension agent and on her own initiative, Lacy Dawn decided to rotate and plant Tom's crops. She hired Harold's boys, paid cash as usual, and charged the rest on Tom's account at Black's Feed and Seed.

"Harold told me last fall that you were running the show over at Tom's farm. Congratulations. I'm sure you'll do a good job," Mr. Black said.

"Thanks for the free delivery. Mommy ain't learned to drive the truck yet."

Jenny decided to try out the commercial viability of garlic from the hollow and set aside a corner of Tom's bottom. She also bought mushroom spores on-line and drilled holes into hardwood logs that she placed in Bucky's cave. Tom and Dwayne hated cauliflower and asparagus, so they planted some. They fenced off a section and planted herbs. They also planted the regular stuff. Lacy Dawn called her father.

"Daddy, Tom's been gone for a long time and everything is planted except the you-know-what. I don't know where his seed is stored. Can you help?"

"I don't like talking on cell," Dwayne said. "Tell your mom to look for mine where I hid her engagement ring just before we got married."

"Thanks."

They talked a little more and hung up.

"Oh shit, really?" Jenny asked when Lacy Dawn repeated her father's instructions.

Lacy Dawn and Jenny went to the left side of the barn and pulled up a tarp that was held down with cinder blocks. It covered a pile of manure. Jenny pointed to a log sitting in an upper corner of the pile.

"There. We have to move the log first. Then we have to dig up a metal box. Put on your gloves and hold your nose."

"Oh," Lacy Dawn said. *I ain't got a free hand to hold my nose.*

They found the box, retrieved a large Zip'n Seal plastic bag of seed, put back the tarp, and went home to bathe, not shower. It was early evening and perfect for planting. Rain was in the forecast.

"Maybe we should wait until Daddy gets home to do this."

"No way, Jose. We've handled everything else. It's just seed like all other seed. When Tom gets home, I want him to know that the women took care of the entire operation," Jenny said.

"Me too."

Lacy Dawn first checked her email to see if Bucky had sent her another love letter and they went to work. Two hours later, it was done—four seeds in each finger-hole two feet apart to allow it to be thinned by sex. Only the females would be grown. Lacy Dawn went to the barn and plugged in the trip wires. Jenny tested it. The horns on the abandoned cars in Tom's front yard blew so loud that it could have awakened folks in town. Then, Lacy Dawn turned on the valve for the sprinklers, set the timer to three times a day, and pushed the test button. Jenny got wet. She laughed. *I don't care. We've infringed on male dominance.*

Tom showed up the next day and Jenny gave him a full report. Lacy Dawn stayed in her bedroom to listen with her ear against the door.

"Awesome," Tom said, so Lacy Dawn came out of her bedroom.

"What a trip. It's the best little whorehouse in Texas," Tom said about his experiences on Shptiludrp.

"Oh?" Lacy Dawn glared. *If DotCom touched another girl, I'll kill him. Even if he has to go to the bathroom two hundred times a day, I've got to wait and so does he.*

"That's just a movie title. Your man did nothing except miss you. He tried to get me to come home before I wanted to."

"I'll find out right now. He's never lied to me before and for your sake he'd better not start now. I hope you told me the truth, Tom, or you'll be sorry," she said, stomped across the back porch. and glided up the path.

"I need to have a talk with her about men and whores," Jenny said after Lacy Dawn was out of range. The surveillance system picked it up.

"There's no problem. I was having too much fun and didn't want to come home. We didn't buy nothing wrong during the shopping trip."

"Do you want some bacon?" Jenny asked.

"I'd love some bacon. I haven't eaten anything that I liked since we left to go to Shitlip or whatever it's called." Tom sat down.

Jenny went into her bedroom, put on a bra, changed her mind, and took it off. *There's no reason to mess up his recreational interest. He's a trustworthy friend.*

"Thanks," Tom said when she came back into the kitchen with hard nipples showing through her shirt. He knew that Dwayne wouldn't mind.

The aroma of bacon apparently triggered broad response. First, Dwayne pulled into the yard with another home improvement project in a box tied to the top of the company car. Moments after he came into the kitchen, Lacy Dawn and Bucky came through the back door holding hands. Jenny smiled at them all. Dwayne grabbed Jenny's butt and squeezed just right. Then with the same hand, he shook hands with Tom. The kitchen was crowded.

"Lacy Dawn, please go into the cellar and see if any of the tomatoes we wrapped in newspaper last fall are ripe," Jenny said. Bucky accompanied.

"We're having BLTs tonight," Bucky said three minutes later.

"The staff meeting is resumed." Lacy Dawn ate first.

Moaning, they occupied their former positions. Brownie curled up beside Bucky's feet for a belly rub.

"We need a strategic plan and quick. I know that summer's just begun, but I don't want to drag this thing out so it interferes with my school," Lacy Dawn said. "Whatever it involves, I want to save the universe quick."

Brownie stood, barked and growled. Lacy Dawn stepped down as Chair of the meeting. Dwayne stopped fondling Jenny and went to the window.

Somebody pulled into the yard. *It ain't a friend.*

Dwayne got his shotgun. Tom asked for and received a revolver. Lacy Dawn took her post under the living room window to peer out of an intentional crack in the wall. Jenny went to the kitchen window to look out back. Bucky didn't move because he did not have a preliminary analysis of the threat. *I can handle anything that the hollow presents.*

Brownie scouted the inside perimeter of the house in silence, one window to the next. There was a knock on the door. Lacy Dawn nodded yes and Dwayne answered it with his shotgun behind his back.

"I was wondering if you still have some bustles for sale?" the stranger asked.

Dwayne leaned his shotgun on the inside wall and walked onto the porch. The stranger had long blue hair, a nose ring, was dressed in black, and wore winter boots although summer was near. He wiped his nose with a forearm. Dwayne studied him. *There's white powder mixed with snot on his sleeve. If he's an agent of any authority on Earth, I deserve to get busted.*

"Sorry, sold out," Dwayne said after he glanced at Jenny.

She nodded. The last bustle had yet to be played with. *I ain't about to give it up to a stranger who don't even hold a gun.*

Jenny grabbed her own butt to practice in private. *A bustle might be fun once I figure out how.*

"Okay," the stranger returned to his SUV, pulled out of the yard, and drove up the hill. The Cure's "Labyrinth" echoed off the hillsides. Dwayne waved goodbye from the yard. *We won't see him again unless he shows up for the next yard sale. Then, he'll blend in so well that we won't know it's the same guy.*

"Strategic planning!" Lacy Dawn yelled to resume the staff meeting. *I don't want a false emergency to stall progress on saving the universe.*

Dwayne returned to the house and put up the guns. Brownie lay back down next to Bucky's feet and asked for a belly rub that he didn't get considering his last response. The others sat down and everybody looked to Lacy Dawn.

Lacy pushed her hair in place with fingers. *Remember leadership, the value of building teams who take ownership because they've been involved in defining and developing strategies. But, I'm tired of screwing around. Lay it on the line.*

"Alright, you guys, it's time to get it together," she said. *Dr. Sullivan is flat out wrong this time even if he is my cousin.*

"Next trip to Shptiludrp, we're all going. I'll decide when to make the trip in consultation with each of you. It'll be soon. Once there, Daddy and I will ride the slow beltway to interview shoppers until we get the information needed to define and analyze the problem. Bucky and Tom, your jobs are to whisper to shoppers that we will sign free autographs. Mommy, your job is to greet and to remind them that everything said on the beltway is protected by the Privacy Act. Tell them that we can be trusted and will protect their anonymity. Brownie, your job is to ride the beltway with us, look friendly, and warn us if you see someone who doesn't look like an autograph seeker. Do you guys have any questions?"

A minute lapsed.

"Meeting adjourned." She went to bed. *I'm exhausted. I started work in the fields before daybreak and it's after midnight.*

Bucky followed her into the bedroom, kissed her goodnight on the forehead, and walked out with an erection noticeable by the others. They smiled.

"We've finally got us a plan," Dwayne said.

"How long do you think Bucky will make it before he explodes?" Jenny asked.

Shopping in Style

Two weeks later, they were on Shptiludrp. "I was fired as the organizer of daily activities during last night's staff meeting," Bucky said to begin the morning's informal agenda. Everyone else faked a yawn.

Brownie ran around the hotel room looking for a good place to poop. Bucky had negotiated a room with two bathrooms. Morning preparations for the day's activities were faster than with one bathroom, but that didn't help Brownie. He farted. *Help, there's no time to go to outside.*

Lacy Dawn tried to put a different attachment on the commode.

"Bark," Brownie farted again to urge an urge.

"I'm trying to connect it. I don't want you to fall off." She placed him on the commode and closed the door. *He'll try, but I'll end up with a mess.*

The one bathroom left for humans was occupied by Dwayne.

"It'll be a while until the other bathroom clears. Brownie's poop is strong and the vent fan ain't," Jenny said.

"You weren't fired from anything, Bucky," Lacy Dawn said. "Tom wants more fun activities. Mommy wants to shop since she don't need to be so careful like doing it at home. And, Daddy wants to find the smoke shop that he staggered out of trip before last so he can show Tom."

"I'm doing my best," Bucky said.

"Right now, we want our presence known, as much exposure as possible to facilitate our investigation. You have a hard job. No matter what you do, you will not satisfy a majority of the Team. But, a majority will never exist to fire you either. It's a typical upper management situation: uncomfortable, long-term, and no easy way out. Don't let it get to your health," Lacy Dawn said.

"I've never considered health," he said.

"Bucky's role is something that needs to be discussed and voted on," Dwayne said. "For me, I'm tired of being reminded about how much time is left to define the scope of work before Tom's garden is too obvious to neglect and how short the time until we need to return home to your school and our jobs. He's reminded us a hundred times a day since we've been here and it's only been two days. We haven't built in any fun on this trip. All we do is study lessons, ride the beltways, and wave at fans."

"Next," Tom said.

"Go ahead. Speak your piece," Dwayne encouraged.

"I meant next on the bathroom."

"See," Lacy Dawn said to Bucky. "It's all cool."

Three minutes later, Brownie barked. Lacy Dawn opened the bathroom door. *This will be nasty.*

"Good dog!"

Everyone went into the bathroom to look. They joined in with pats and kudos. Lacy Dawn flushed. Brownie whined. *It's sad to see my good work go down the drain.*

Bucky gave him an extra pat. *I know exactly how he feels.*

"Next," Lacy Dawn said and before anybody else could speak up, she shut the bathroom door. She put on a different commode adapter. Last to go was Bucky. He didn't eat much and didn't need to use the bathroom often, not for excretion. He still masturbated several times a day. After using the toilet, Bucky cracked the door and washed his hands so it could be heard. Brownie pushed open the door and looked at the deposit before it was flushed. *It's not much but significant.*

Bucky flushed. Brownie rubbed his snout on Bucky's pant leg.

"What if we skip the tutorials, Bucky?" Lacy Dawn asked. "In the fourth grade, the teacher told us she would grade us on a curve. I still got an A on my report card. Can we go with a curve on this project to make it less boring?"

Bucky nodded. "Yes ma'am, I can curve around the tutorials," he said.

"Convince me," she insisted.

"I can manufacture undetectable communication devices for each to wear, such as a blemish or appendage. This will enable me to provide information applicable to specific situations as needed. Team Members will not have background or contextual data on which to base independent decisions, but we can curve around the general education stage by using technology."

"He's looking better, but still talks like shit," Dwayne said. "I got the stuff he tried to teach us about this and that culture on this and that planet all mixed up anyway."

"Eat shit," Bucky said.

The other team members smiled. Bucky was becoming more human by the Earth minute.

"Don't be so scared of the big words, Daddy. Anyway, I don't want a blemish. I'm sick of pimples. Otherwise, I approve of your plan."

"Why didn't you tell us before that we could skip the training?" Tom asked.

"I want bigger breasts," Lacy Dawn said.

"I've had a headache for two days," Dwayne said.

"I'll take an extra penis," Tom said.

"Some of the information, I appreciate," Dwayne said. "Don't get me wrong. It's just too much. You have organized and structured every minute to improve the odds of success. Your daily percentage reports are driving me crazy."

"I think a pimple would be cool," Jenny said. "I haven't had one since junior high school. It might take me back a few years."

"Bark," Brownie asserted. *Don't forget about me.*

"A diamond nose ring and collar would be pretty on Brownie," Lacy said.

"All this work — it's child abuse like when I used to hurt her," Dwayne said. *Crap, I shouldn't have said that.*

"Wait a damn minute," Lacy Dawn said. "I'm the Leader of this Team and will direct its actions, including your actions. You've crossed the line, Mister. I appreciate your views, but I won't let my love for you interfere with logic in pursuit of our objectives. Either get it together or take a day off."

"I'll reprogram," Bucky said.

"I'll stop complaining," Dwayne said.

"I'll roll up some inspiration," Tom said. *It'll help.*

"Do you need some special attention, Honey?" Jenny asked Dwayne.

Brownie rubbed Dwayne's crotch with his snout and then moved to the other crotches one at a time. Everybody pushed him away except for Bucky.

"I'll lighten up. I'm sorry," Dwayne told the group.

Lacy walked out of their hotel room door. The others followed. *The significance of the mission to the survival of Earth has not yet integrated. What would Cousin Leon do?*

The Team went into the hotel's dining room for breakfast. Except that they were the only humans present, it could have been an IHOP. The waitress had six arms with hands. She juggled plates and jiggled her breasts when she delivered the meals. Tom licked his lips. The waitress noticed and smiled back.

"This bacon is good, but it's not as good as mine," Jenny looked around the table. Nobody gave her a nod of confirmation. Brownie farted and continued to lick his plate. Until then, Brownie had been treated by the hotel staff as a guest of equal stature to the rest of the Team. Lacy Dawn put his plate on the floor where he stayed for the rest of the meal. He licked his lips but nobody smiled. *Bacon is bacon on or under the table.*

"Today will be fun," Bucky said. *I'll overcompensate for my all work and no play approach to management.*

"That was cool," Tom said at the end of the day when they were back in the hotel room.

"Yeah," Dwayne agreed.

Jenny nodded. Lacy Dawn smiled. They all took off their socks and tossed them in the air at the same time in celebration. Jenny unhooked her bra under her tee shirt, but stopped short of continuing the ritual, and laid it beside her on the bed. Tom stared at it until Jenny put it under a pillow.

"You have an email from your wife, Tom," Bucky said and gathered the dirty socks to put in the laundry bag.

"You're kidding. She never contacts me. It's always the other way around. I call her on the cell and she's always shopping somewhere. It's been years since she's contacted me. It must be a big deal."

Tom read the e-mail, frowned, and turned to Jenny.

"I'm glad I wrote this address down for her to use in case of emergency. The welfare woman came by your house this morning. When you weren't home, she came to my house and talked to Barb. Barb thinks she's a real bitch who wants to cause problems."

"I should've had those food stamps cut off, but I wanted to keep up the poverty front at Kroger's. We'll have to pay back whatever," Jenny said.

"She ain't got no shit on your old man. He's been paid in cash from day one," Tom said.

"Yeah, but with my job at Head Start and the VA check, I'm sure that kicked us off food stamps big time."

"They won't try to put me in a foster home will they?" Lacy asked.

"Just don't tell the Welfare Woman about getting engaged and we should be all right. I'd better go home and straighten this out."

"How much gas or whatever do you have in that ship anyway, Bucky?" Tom asked.

Everybody looked at Bucky.

"I have enough fuel for a few more Earth centuries. It has been refueled by Earth's mother lode. But the ship is due for maintenance next Earth year."

"I'll make sure it's in the contract," Lacy Dawn said. "Let me think for a minute."

They sat on the edges of their respective beds for ten minutes.

"DotCom, err, Bucky, you and Mommy go home and straighten out the Welfare problem. We'll stay here and continue to entice autograph seekers into a frenzy by not signing. It will drive up trade value. Mommy, you two get back as soon as possible."

After hugs and kisses, Jenny and Bucky were on their way back to Earth. Ten minutes later, an Earth-like meal, new clothing and clean towels were delivered to the hotel room. Lacy Dawn clicked the remote control to find cartoons on the special TV. Tom lifted the cover on a platter to find green buds. Dwayne opened a cooler that came with the meal to find the complement—six cans of real Bud from Earth.

"Maybe we shouldn't rush this job," Tom said.

"You might be right," Dwayne popped a top.

"Cool it, you two. I'm going to run for Class President. We need to knock this off so I can get home and go to work. Preparation for the election is my summer project. I don't want to lose the first of a long string of elections because you two like to get high too much. Besides, if we screw up, Earth has had it."

"No such thing as too much," Tom giggled when the hotel staff removed dishes and platters.

"Jacuzzi time," Dwayne said and picked up the cooler.

They left through a cloud of smoke. Lacy Dawn watched *The Wild Thornberrys.*

Welfare Fraud

"Like I said before, Lacy Dawn and Dwayne have been gone a couple of days to visit with his relatives," Jenny said to the Welfare Woman. She fidgeted first with the new ashtray on the orange-crate end table and then with last night's empty cigarette pack. It was a prop that she'd placed to crumple, smooth out, and crumple again. *Don't look into the Welfare Woman's eyes.*

Ms. Simon sat on the edge of the stuffed chair that Jenny's mother had gotten Dwayne to haul off for her. Jenny crumpled, smoothed, and crumpled.*I don't want that hard-ass sitting on my new couch.*

The Welfare Woman's attempted eye contact was direct and firm. It captured Jenny every now and then against her will. She was a well-trained and experienced specialist who had been involved in most fraud investigations within the county. Ms. Simon frowned. *I bet this chair has cooties.*

"Your neighbor said that Dwayne helped pull a transmission two weeks ago and refused pay. It's hard to believe."

"They're friends."

"Lacy Dawn's teacher told me that she'd missed some school."

"She had pink eye."

"Reverend Hammond said that he hadn't seen you at church for quite a while. It would be a lot easier if you'd just tell me the exact date that your husband left so I can adjust your food stamps to a one-person household. I know about your job at the Head Start."

"Welfare to Work program," Jenny said.

"If you verify my findings, I'll work up monthly pay-backs that you can afford. Have you signed your husband's name and cashed his VA checks?"

"No."

With her index finger, Jenny drew a smiley face in the cigarette ashes.

"Your answers to my eligibility questionnaire will require further verification."

"You can talk to anybody you like. I don't care. That's all

there is to it. I called your office and left a message to tell my worker that I found a job. I can't help it if you guys messed up."

"Do your husband's relatives have telephones?"

"No."

The face in the ashtray had a frown but Jenny smiled. *I've still got an ace in the hole.*

"I'm sorry. I'll have to report tentative findings to my supervisor. He'll recommend that your family's stamps be cut off. When your husband and daughter return, call me and I will conduct another home visit. You will receive a notice with appeal rights outlined. If I don't hear from you in one week, I'll have no choice but to refer the case to Child Protective Services for investigation. The whereabouts and health of your daughter, ah, Stacy, must be verified."

"Lacy Dawn," Jenny corrected.

"Yes, Lacy Dawn — we need to have her examined and interviewed so that an Attendance Officer can help you prepare for her return to school." Ms. Simon stood and looked down at Jenny. "Take care. Oh, before I forget, I need your pay stubs. Just mail them in. We've already contacted the VA."

For the first time during the home visit, Jenny intentionally looked into Ms. Simon's eyes, extended her hand to shake goodbye, and planted her index finger in Ms. Simon's palm. Ms. Simon walked to the car with the state license plate. On the way, she rubbed her hands together to try to remove the dark smudge on her palm.

Jenny's smile grew bigger. *What a bull shitter. She knows I'll sue her fat ass if she messes with my kid.* Jenny followed and watched the state car attempt to turn around in a driveway that was meant to be backed out. She leaned an elbow on the hood of Dwayne's pick-up, an inconsistency that Ms. Simon had missed, and wiped the mud off a fog light with her hand. *Hope she gets stuck in the ditch.*

Tires spun mud five feet. After fifteen minutes, she was still stuck. A sweaty welfare worker with messed up hair accompanied Jenny back into the living room. Ms. Simon plopped down and leaned back on the living room chair. Since everybody in the hollow knew about the home visit, as usual,

Harold showed up with his four wheel drive and a chain. Jenny's smile grew even bigger.

"Please tell your supervisor that after I called your office about my job, I didn't use the card much. I called your office again but nobody called me back. So, I called the state office on the toll-free number to tell them about it and asked for help. I told them that you were my worker because I couldn't remember my real Economic Services Worker's name. The woman I talked to had me spell your last name twice. She told me to wait until you had the time to figure it out and said you'd send me a letter to tell me what to do."

"Why didn't you tell me this before?" Ms. Simon asked.

"Can you figure out if I owe anything back right now? How many stamps should I return? I have a calculator if you need it. I'd like to get this settled right here and now since you have a few minutes to help me out. You always seem so busy. Would you like a glass of water? Would that help you figure it out? Do you want me to get the stamps? They're in my dresser."

"Got it out," Harold yelled into the living room from the ditch. "When is Dwayne supposed to come home from the visit with his brother?"

"How much do I owe you?" Ms. Simon yelled back at Harold from the front porch and reopened her notepad but closed it without recording. She put it under her arm. Sweat from her armpit flowed and glistened onto its black cover in little streams. Jenny noticed and smiled even bigger again.

"Nothing. I'm just glad I was hauling manure and noticed that you were stuck up. Sorry about the mess on your car," Harold winked at Jenny and reached out to shake Ms. Simon's hand. She ended up with more than a cigarette ash stain, but Ms. Simon didn't pay any attention this time.

"Tell Dwayne he owes me," Harold whispered to Jenny.

"So what do I owe back to Welfare?" Jenny asked Ms. Simon.

"Just forget it. I'll close your case, document that you owe nothing, and recommend that it requires no further investigation if you promise to never call the State Office again and use my name."

"Okay," Jenny smiled the biggest.

Ms. Simon backed out of the driveway a few feet, stopped, got out, and wiped the rear windshield with her bare hand. The car went up the hollow road, stopped again, and Ms. Simon wiped the front windshield. Harold watched her car with his intentional manure smears climb the hollow road. After she had been gone long enough, he took off his gloves, threw them on the porch, reached into his shirt pocket, and found a joint.

"Don't sit in that chair, Harold. It's got cooties," Jenny said.

All Unauthorized Vehicles

"You know what I like about mucus?" Lacy Dawn asked. The team had been in their hotel room on Shptiludrp for forty-eight straight Earth hours waiting for DotCom and Jenny to return. Tom lay on his bed. He re-read a Vonnegut and rolled to change from his right to left elbow. On his bed, Dwayne played one game of solitaire with cards and a second game on the laptop. Brownie slept beside Lacy Dawn on her bed. She had flipped from one TV channel to the next for hours.

"When it's thick enough to ball up so tight that you can spit for a mile."

"That's cool," Dwayne looked up from the laptop.

"I remember in the second grade I lost to Jeff. He took a bunch of his mom's pills and spit almost fourteen feet. I came in second," she flipped to another channel.

"I hope your mom handled that welfare woman okay."

"At least the pot plants are still little," Tom said. "I've heard about welfare workers. They look for any unreported income."

"Incoming," Dwayne lay down his cards and repositioned the laptop. "It's for me," he said. "Do you want me to read it out loud?"

"Hell, yes," Tom answered. "Anything's better than this boredom."

Dwayne read, "…after she got stuck up in the ditch, she came back into the house totally freaked out. I tried to give her the food stamps that I'd saved up but she was so rattled that she said to just forget it…."

Lacy Dawn and Tom moved to read over Dwayne's shoulder.

"Another incoming," Dwayne said.

"During the last scan of DotCom's ship, a human virus was found. To ensure that members of your party are not contagious, despite your VIP status, you are required to go through decontamination procedure. On their return, Jenny and DotCom will be required to dock through normal procedures, including decontamination."

"I wonder why it took them so long to find that out." Tom said.

"With so many ships in and out of the docks, I guess they just now got to it," Dwayne said. "Ask Bucky when he gets back. I don't know shit about decontamination."

Two minutes later, a human-looking escort arrived. It took them to a private, unnumbered room at the end of the hallway on their floor of the hotel. The escort unlocked and opened the door. Inside was a decontamination center for their floor and was similar to what they had seen on their inspection of the planet's docks during the last shopping trip. Last in line, Lacy Dawn entered the room, took off her clothes, and stepped into a chamber. *It ain't as bad as taking a shower in gym class.*

"Please stand still," a computer voice said.She inhaled. Parts moved, lights strobed, she exited the chamber when instructed, and got dressed. *I'm virus free. That was kinda fun.*

Four Earth days and sixteen minutes later, Jenny and Bucky walked into their hotel room. Since the ship was no longer authorized for expedited VIP docking, they had circled the planet until it was their turn to dock, ten hours. Then, they'd spent another four-hour wait to go through the decontamination procedure at the dock.

"They may not be human but they sure liked my boobs," Jenny whispered in Lacy Dawn's ear but loud enough for the men to hear. "Plus, back at home they say there ain't a cure for the common cold. My sniffles are gone after all that."

"It's all your husband's fault," Tom smiled.

"What do you mean?" Jenny asked.

"Your sniffles could be fatal to a person from another planet," Bucky said.

"Let's get to work. After beating up on that Welfare Woman, I feel like I could conquer the world. I mean the universe."

An hour later, they were in their respective positions and roles on the slow beltway. By general email to all shops, Bucky had spread the word that Lacy Dawn and Dwayne would be available to sign autographs—a short-term temporary waiver of the Privacy Act. On the beltway, Brownie took the lead to sniff and control the designated front approach. Dwayne and Lacy Dawn practiced for the aggressive questioning of autograph seekers. Tom covered the back route. He would stop and redirect autograph seekers to the line past Brownie. Jenny would greet, smile, and keep the next in line from getting close enough to hear the interviews. To avoid contamination, each interview required discretion. Team members were wearing their communication devices so that Bucky could advise them during the process. Everything would be recorded for further consideration. They waited for the first autograph seeker.

It arrived and was the same height as Lacy Dawn but that's where the similarity ended. The person's body was a clear gray mass continuously readjusting into lumps. Shapes floated under the skin's surface. There was no face or head, but at least three body parts under the skin looked like bloodshot human eyeballs. Two appendages served as legs and one appeared to be an arm that held out a picture of Lacy Dawn.

"That's one big goober," Lacy Dawn whispered to Dwayne. *It looks like fruit in Jell-O.*

She signed the picture with the pen that DotCom had programmed to ensure that all of her signatures were the same and difficult to forge. The gray person left at the next beltway stop without asking Dwayne for his autograph. It quivered much more on its exit than when it had approached.

"That wasn't part of the plan — free autographs," Dwayne said.

"I'm sorry, my bad. I just couldn't interview it."

"Was it too much culture shock? Bucky warned us that it'd been fatal to a few shoppers over the years. You know what I like about mucous?" Dwayne teased.

"Thank God for 'Star Wars'," Lacy Dawn said.

"That's so true. Get past it. Here they come," he said. A long line of autograph seekers had formed and was lengthening by the minute.

"I'm ready. Sorry about the Jell-O comment," she said.

The autograph line grew even longer. Brownie stopped and sniffed their second interviewee. It was a light blue cloud with a face that floated above the beltway and didn't seem to object to intrusion, but Brownie looked to the team for further instruction.

"I've been thinking about the penis enlargement pills that I shouldn't have mentioned to you. I was drunk. Now, I feel guilty," Dwayne said. "But, I do talk to my penis all the time. I always have. I put it down for no real reason."

"What the heck does that have to do with this circumstance?" Lacy Dawn asked and nodded for Brownie to permit the next interviewee to approach.

"Nothing, except I thought maybe you could give me a little therapy between our interviews of shoppers. You have the magic to …."

The blue cloud floated away with an autographed picture of Dwayne after stealing a kiss that he didn't notice.

"There's nothing creepy crawly at my place," it yelled back to Dwayne on the way to the exit. "Come home with me, Honey, and I'll show you how I can make you feel it better than she can."

Dwayne shrugged at his team members.

The next interviewee bounced past Brownie. It had four arms, no legs, a mouse-like face, and was covered with cherry red fuzz. It also provided no insight that was helpful to the mission, but nuzzled Lacy Dawn's thigh after getting the autograph. Lacy Dawn shrugged at her team members. *What did it mean about no need to spray in the corners of its bedroom?*

One by one, for three Earth hours, the team exchanged autographs for interviews. Eighty-four shoppers had been interviewed when Lacy Dawn called for a break.

"Good. I need to buy some underwear," Dwayne said.

"What?" his daughter asked.

"They confiscated his underwear during Decontamination," Tom said.

The others, except Brownie, broke out into laughter. Brownie sniffed Dwayne's crotch, put both paws over his snout, and rolled onto his back to play dead.

"Why did they do that?" Jenny got serious.

Tears streamed down Lacy Dawn's cheeks from laughing so hard. Tom fell onto the floor of the beltway and howled. Brownie got excited, licked Tom's face, and lifted his leg to pee on the beltway rail. The puddle glistened on the rubber-like surface and flowed toward the next autograph seeker. With no room to back up, the he/she/it straddled the spreading urine.

"Recess! Come back later," Lacy Dawn said to the line and pushed the beltway's stop button.

Autograph seekers did an about face and left the beltway without protest. The Privacy Act had been reauthorized. Maintenance staff arrived to mop up and disinfect the pee. The Team got on the fast beltway.

"Why did they confiscate your underwear, Dwayne?" Jenny asked on their way back to their hotel room.

"I don't know."

"Hum." Bucky mimicked a human reaction.

"Okay, okay," Dwayne said. "The official report: my underwear was so contaminated that no sterilization process short of destruction would protect shoppers from the creatures that inhabited them."

Tom howled again so loudly that it drew the attention of pedestrians on the other side of the beltway rail. Brownie licked his face a second time. However, Lacy Dawn and Jenny didn't crack a smile. Bucky assessed the situation, saw the looks that the women gave Dwayne, and turned away to escape involvement.

"They can cure the common cold but they can't clean your underwear?" Jenny asked. "Haven't they heard of new improved Blue Cheer, a cup of bleach, and three hours of sunshine on the clothes line?" Jenny asked.

"New Improved Blue Cheer was a fabulous L.P. from the early 70s," Tom changed the subject.

"Yes, it was," Bucky went along. "Would you like to hear it again at the hotel?"

"Yes!" Dwayne and Tom yelled.

"I'd rather hear Cher," Jenny allowed the change of subject. *No album that sounds like laundry detergent could be romantic. His underwear was clean when I took them off the line.*

"The shops need de-bugged," Lacy Dawn said ten minutes later, back in their hotel room.

"My programs have more protections against bugs than any planet has for its people," Bucky said. "It's an ancient and very successful approach that protects programming above carbon-based life forms."

219

"I mean real live bugs, not computer bugs," Lacy Dawn said.

After the guys smoked a bud, Blue Oyster Cult blared in the hotel room. The Shptiludrp Library turned out not to be exhaustive. It did not include Blue Cheer. Nevertheless, Dwayne and Tom played air guitar and sang along with lyrics that neither remembered. Jenny went into the bathroom, shut the door, and started reading a romance novel brought from home. Brownie crawled under a bed. *I'm so embarrassed about farting at the table and peeing on the beltway.*

"Mr. Prump has just instructed that we report our tentative findings," Bucky yelled to Lacy Dawn from his seat in front of his computer screen.

"Tell him we'll be there in a couple of Earth hours," she yelled back over the music.

"He expects immediate compliance."

"Too bad," Lacy Dawn lay down with a pillow over her head. The guys noticed and turned down the music. Jenny came out of the bathroom and lay on the bed beside her daughter.

"A nap does look good," Tom agreed and headed to bed. Brownie came out, curled up beside Lacy, farted, and crawled back under the bed. Bucky sat down in an over-stuffed arm chair and waited for permission to comply with a direct order from the most powerful being in the universe. *I hope she doesn't get me fired with her obstinacy.*

Three hours later, the Team was in an elevator that eventually led to the Office of the Manager of the Mall. It was a suite in the only high-rise office building on Shptiludrp. The security officer on the elevator looked like a small, leafless Earth tree. "Nice ass," it whispered in Lacy Dawn's ear as they exited onto the top floor.

Bucky had heard the tree but didn't react. The Team stood in a small enclosed area. They opened the only door and went into a reception area ten times larger than Bucky's ship. It was decorated with flowering plants and had clear plastic-like walls behind which scenes of waves, falls, bubbles, lakes, streams, rapids, and rivers faded in and out. Purple leather-like couches and chairs of different sitting heights and contours were arranged in a semicircle. A dark blue table as big as a one-ton pick-up truck sat in the middle of a white deep-pile carpet in the middle of the floor. They were alone. Above the ocean sounds piped into the ceiling speakers, there was a loud argument.

"You know the regulation, Ms. Thompson. First-offense parking is a fine equal to one-half of the offender's annual earnings. The penalty for a second offense is confiscation of the vehicle and three-quarters of the violator's annual earnings. And, for third-offense parking, the penalty is death with, of course, confiscation of all assets."

"But it was my mom with our lunches," a voice that sounded like a female from Earth said through her language conversion device. "You forgot to sign her parking permit, again."

"If the system makes an exception for one, others will expect the same," a voice that sounded like a male from Earth said.

"If you terminate Mom, I'll quit this job."

"I don't believe you."

There were two minutes of silence. Lacy Dawn's team stood in the reception area. They took up positions in front of a counter that had sections of different heights, behind which were a wooden desk and cabinets. They looked at each other and waited. Jenny put her index finger over her lips for silence.

"What's for lunch, anyway?" the male asked.

"My resignation if you don't fix this right now," the female answered.

"I give. Sign my name to an Authorized Vehicles Only Permit and send it to your mother's personal transport. Tell her to have the Parking Attendant scan her vehicle's I.D. He will apologize. Good enough?"

"Yes." A person who looked like a twenty-year-old Sophia Loren stomped out of the inner office. She had three breasts.

"Application for an Authorized Vehicles Only Permit?" she asked from behind the counter with a professional smile.

The First Sexual Harassment Complaint on Shptiludrp

Lacy Dawn led her team into the Inner Office. She looked to see if Leon Sullivan's picture was hung on the wall. His portrait was there among several other non-humanoids. She gave Bucky a thumbs up. Jesus' picture wasn't there but Tom didn't complain. She threw Bucky a kiss. *I knew he would never lie to me.*

Lacy Dawn scanned across a desk larger than her bedroom and lowered her gaze until just above the desk top. In an oversized swivel chair behind the desk sat a humanoid with a third eye in the middle of a forehead. Mr. Prump stood up. He raised his gaze level a few inches and his entire face could be seen. He extended a hand with six fingers, each of which had at least two overly large golden rings.

"It's very nice to meet you, Lacy Dawn," he ignored the others.

Bucky tried to get her attention with a touch on the other hand. *Remember, my name is DotCom and not Bucky.*

"He looks almost just like that short guy on those taxi cab reruns," Dwayne whispered. "What's that actor's name?"

"Shhhh," Lacy Dawn glared.

"I have a complaint to make," Lacy Dawn said to Mr. Prump.

"Oh?" Mr. Prump sat down, opened a drawer, and shoved a form across his desk in her direction. "Please call me Mr. Prump." *Hospitality has been extended to her entourage.*

The form ran out of momentum half-way across the desk. Lacy Dawn extended and retracted because it stopped well short of her reach. *That's too far regardless of obligatory respect.*

"I was not aware of any dissatisfaction of any type, sir," Bucky reverted to his role as DotCom in the presence of his long-term authority figure. Lacy Dawn gave him The Look and trumped.

"Your elevator operator just told me that I have a nice ass," she said.

Dwayne started for the office exit to get the offender. Lacy Dawn pushed him toward one of the chairs in front of the desk. Tom grabbed Dwayne's arm. Then, Tom and Lacy Dawn had to restrain Bucky's attempt to leave. Lacy Dawn and Jenny stood alone in front of the desk while the males sat. Jenny moved to her daughter's side. Brownie growled. So did Bucky. *Delete human jealousy. I am The DotCom.*

Mr. Prump shoved another form in her direction with the same result. The complaint forms were the only papers on the desk. *DotCom's acting weird. Maybe I should call Security.*

"Tree says that to me all the time," the receptionist said from the doorway. "Would anybody like something to drink or a snack?"

Nobody responded except Mr. Prump. He extended a cup that had been on his desk, but the gesture was ignored.

"That's different, you..." Tom started but Lacy Dawn's look cut him short.

"The females of those people got no figures at all—straight up and down," the receptionist said. "I wouldn't take it personally, Lacy Dawn. All males from that planet become infatuated with any curve on anybody that they think is female. He's a nice person once you get to know him."

"Regardless, it was inappropriate for him to tell me that I have a nice ass."

"Yeah," her team said in unison. DotCom was the loudest except for Brownie's bark followed by another growl.

"I ought to kick his ass for talking trash to my little girl," Dwayne said. *I'm such a juvenile.*

Lacy Dawn glared again.

"Sorry," Dwayne hung his head.

"Further," Lacy Dawn continued. "I'm not about to do business with any planet that permits the sexual harassment of its visitors or employees to go undisciplined."

Jenny sat down.

"Yeah," the receptionist said.

Mr. Prump sank deeper into his seat. The top of the eye in his forehead was just above the surface of the desk top.

"I'm never going to sit on your lap again unless I want to," the receptionist said. "And, as for anything else, you can just forget it from now on unless you take care of this. Take care of the whole problem on the whole planet—equal respect for all

223

people—within their financial means, of course."

"Take a memo to Division Managers with a copy to All Staff."

Lacy Dawn stood alone before the desk. He dictated the memo and she listened. *It's pretty good. There's procedure for making sexual harassment complaints, investigation, due process, and penalty.*

"That's all for now. I'll contact you tomorrow to begin negotiation of terms," she said.

Mr. Prump asked her what time but she didn't answer. Lacy Dawn had concluded her first meeting with the most powerful being in the universe. They left.

Mandatory Staff Training

In the hotel room, Lacy Dawn put a halt to the males' plan to get high. They didn't protest. It would have been insubordinate.

"Staff training time, it's mandatory," she ordered.

"I think I've got a nice ass too," Jenny said as she looked in the dresser mirror.

Bucky logged onto his ship's computer, called the front desk and ordered a projection screen. It was delivered in two minutes. The agenda, a PowerPoint-like presentation, had been put together the night before. He tested it with the screen in place. *Nobody messes with Lacy Dawn.*

Brownie nosed Tom to get him to set the correct adapter on the commode. After installation, Tom turned on the vent fan and closed the bathroom door. It was a necessary delay to staff training. They waited.

"You think my ass is fat, don't you?" Jenny asked Dwayne.

"I love your ass and you know it."

They kissed. Bucky got up, walked within a foot of them, and watched. Afterward, he made notes about the kiss on his laptop.

"I call this staff meeting to order," Lacy Dawn said when Brownie got out of the bathroom. There was no need to inspect it since he was now so well trained.

The first topic was an overview of the general history of Shptiludrp. Lacy Dawn's teammates stifled their yawns. A survey of the mineral content of planets, carbon-based intelligent life forms, and planetary taxation practices followed. They still didn't yawn.

"Break," Tom went to the bathroom. There was no mess by Brownie there, but the commode did need to be flushed. When he got back, the slide show summarized the unionization of the first miners of Shptiludrp, then known as Ammonite. It covered a computerized mining program so efficient that it revolutionized the practice of exploiting planets by robbing them of essential minerals.

"Dwayne and I are both related to Mother Jones," Jenny told Tom.

"Break," Dwayne went to the bathroom.

When he got back, the slide show summarized the exploitation of oxygen and other gases on planets by early Managers of Ammonite. It was a practice that exterminated life forms. Brownie howled and Jenny covered her eyes at the depiction of beings that gasped for air and failed to survive. With Lacy Dawn's permission, since she had not had time to preview the actual slides, Bucky skipped over several sets of the most graphic scenes.

"Break," Jenny went to the bathroom. Her sobs were heard above the sound of the vent fan. She returned with a wad of toilet paper clutched in her hand and a swollen, red face.

The next scene was taken at the office of the Manager of the Mall. The audio had been converted to English by Bucky for the staff training session. The video showed the current Manager's initial job interview. He looked exactly the same as yesterday, short and ugly, even though the video was shot thousands of years before.

"What does 'diminishing returns' mean?" Jenny asked. It was a recurring theme in the video's dialogue.

Bucky stopped the presentation.

"It means that the more you do the same thing, the less you get back until it gets to the point that you put more into something than it's worth," Dwayne answered. He had learned the concept from a counselor employed by the Veterans Administration and, at the time, it referred to his lack of progress in mental health treatment.

"Yeah," Tom agreed. "It's like when you work on a truck and get to a bolt that's stuck. The best thing to do is to spray it down with penetrating oil and wait. Don't try to force it or you might break off the head and be in bigger trouble. Just wait—even if you have to wait overnight. Then, take it slow. Don't force it. I learned that from your husband, Jenny."

"That ain't the same thing, dude, but thanks," Dwayne said.

"It's sort of the same," Tom countered. "The more effort you put into a stuck bolt, the less you get until it's broke off. Besides, I had to say it someplace and now's my best shot."

Bucky restarted the staff training video.

"If the current practice does not stop, there will be no

226

marketplace and no profit," Mr. Prump said during his recorded job interview. "It's not a matter of ethics and has nothing to do with killing intelligent life forms by exploitation of planetary resources. I propose that we cultivate the marketplace by helping it grow—by assisting the evolution to consumer status on every possible planet. For example, consider planet Earth. My research found that all it needs for a boost to consumer status is three or four role models to accelerate its religious movement. I recommend that we accommodate the planet's need. Let's send it a couple more and see what happens. My bet is that with a Jesus and Mohammed—I made up the names—we can assist this population achieve consumer status. A more intelligent strategy of exploitation will maximize our profits. That's just one example of a planet's potential."

The next scene was the construction of buildings. The buildings turned into stores bigger than any Wal-Mart Super Center they'd ever seen on TV. Shoppers were everywhere and looked more or less humanoid. The scene faded and the team members viewed a significant difference in the shops and customers. The shops were much smaller and specialized. The shoppers were much more diverse instead of humanoid.

"Expansion of the marketplace," Bucky said.

"But, the bigger the shop size, the better the prices," Tom said.

Bucky stopped the video again.

"Shptiludrp is one big shop with consolidated purchases and sales. There is no actual competition between proprietors on Shptiludrp. Any appearance of competition between shops is contrived to motivate spending by customers."

He restarted the presentation.

"I thought it was over," Dwayne said.

As if it had rewound to a prior scene, people close enough to be called humanoid gasped for air and fell. The view panned back. Like a balloon with its air escaping, the planet on the screen shrank and dimmed.

"We've already seen this part," Jenny said with her hands over her eyes but with fingers spread.

"By Earth time, this was recorded yesterday," Bucky said.

The training program moved to a scene of another planet that experienced the same destruction. Jenny watched between her fingers. Children of people who didn't look a bit humanoid gasped for breath. Jenny's tears ran down her arm and dripped off her elbow. Just as in previous scenes, the planet shrank to a circumference half of its former size.

"Shptiludrp has competition," Lacy Dawn said. "The exploitive and now illegal practices that helped establish Shptiludrp as the center of the economic universe are being repeated. Millions of intelligent beings will be killed if we don't diagnose and fix the problem here. The competitor intends to construct a new shopping mall for the universe and is willing to do anything it takes."

"Why doesn't somebody just stop it?" Jenny watched another scene through spread fingers.

"Call the police," Dwayne said. *That's stupid. It never works in the Hollow and sure won't way out here.*

Bucky shut down the computer and stared at the blank screen. Brownie placed both paws over his snout. Jenny curled up into a ball on the bed and whimpered. Dwayne's face turned beet red. He clenched and unclenched his fists the way he used to do before Bucky had healed him. *Too many holes in too many walls.*

"This is not so different than selling pizzas," Tom said. "To stop the massacres we need to ensure that our product is so good that it discourages the competition."

"Why would another pizza shop think it could succeed in the same town as one of my shops?" Dwayne threw a pillow at the wall.

"Because your shop has bugs, stupid," Jenny said. "Everybody found out about it and they're afraid to order your pizza."

Tom rolled a fatty that he, Dwayne and Bucky began to smoke. Lacy Dawn curled up beside Brownie and went to sleep on the floor. Brownie opened his eyes. She crawled under the bed. Brownie howled.

What's wrong with humans? Since it's only bugs, I'll eat them all and save the universe—whatever that is. No big deal.

Jenny went into the bathroom, got naked and slipped on a nightshirt. She came out and modeled for the men.

Maybe, it'll take their minds off this mess. They deserve it.

That night, everybody dreamt about different ways to kill bugs.

To Pesticide is to Specialize

The next morning, Lacy Dawn stayed in the bathroom an extra-long time. Thinking while on the pot is common but her analyses required more time than usual. Others knew that she was making decisions about the important matters that the team faced. Nobody interrupted. *We don't know what we're dealing with. There are millions of different kinds of bugs on Earth. There must be zillions and zillions in the universe. I wish I had a better bug background.*

"Let's go shopping incognito," she said when she came out of the bathroom.

Thank you, Mr. Commode. You were a good consultant.

"Go shopping where?" Dwayne smiled.

"Isn't there a topless beach a little south of Cancun?" Tom asked.

"Bucky, you're in charge of the costumes. Order something for each of us that won't be too uncomfortable to wear all day. I don't want it to be like the Trick or Treat when I wore that stupid Princess Leia costume. It had a mouth hole so small that I couldn't breathe and it stayed on top of my head all evening. Everybody could see I wasn't a princess. I want costumes that are functional."

"Brownie will be the most difficult. He may try to tug his off," Bucky said.

"He won't if I tell him not to." *Don't piss me off, young man.*

"Have you ever seen the movie *Ghostbusters?*" Tom asked.

"No," Lacy Dawn answered. *Don't piss me off, Tom.*

"I think it's the perfect time," he said.

Tom sat down, got out his stash, and started to roll. Lacy Dawn sat beside him and held out her hand for the seeds. "I like to crunch and spit them out. They're sterile from the decontamination procedure anyway." She crunched and spat. *Why not watch a movie? It'll take a while to obtain costumes.*

"I trust you, Tom. That's why I wanted you as a consultant." *Everything he does and says has hidden agendas.*

She took a slow, deep breath, crunched and spat some more toward the garbage can, but sometimes the marijuana seeds went anyplace they wanted. She picked a shell from between her teeth. *I've made everybody crazy this trip with all work and no play. Maybe that's why Tom wants us to watch a movie.*

Bucky downloaded the requested movie. Lacy Dawn used the bathroom before she let him start it – her grandmother's instruction about using it before going to the movies. An hour into the video, the costumes arrived. Bucky stopped it, pressed his thumb on the hotel staff's laptop to pay for the merchandise, and put the boxes on a bed. Lacy Dawn looked through the contents and gave Bucky the nod to restart the movie. *It's a deductible business expense in the contract. Stop! I've made myself crazy, too.*

After the movie, Tom screamed, "Who you gonna call?"

"Lacy Dawn!" Tom, Jenny, and Dwayne hollered and giggled. It drowned out Lacy Dawn's "*Ghostbusters!*" They tried on their disguises.

Lacy Dawn and Jenny ended up with three breasts each, no head hair, mustaches, and tails that moved like a cat's in irregular sequences. A spray came with the costumes to make the nipples harden. Jenny's breast matched her own size. Lacy Dawn's breasts were so big that they would have caused back problems if real.

"It's excellent," Jenny squeezed her fake breast.

"Let me try it," Dwayne said.

Bucky and Tom got behind him in line. Jenny shooed them all away.

Tom got a clear skin that exposed internal organs. It made him look naked. The costume came with a rubber-like penis bigger than the ones sold in the head shop closest to the hollow. The shop had added adult novelties to increase revenue. It did.

Dwayne put on a metallic skin with tiny lightning bolts constantly flickering between dozens of knots that glowed blue when hit by a bolt. He had long hair like in high school, except it was pink. Plus, he put on a nose ring and special gloves with extra thumbs that worked.

They modeled.

"Tom's costume is cool," Jenny stared at the extra-large penis.

"I'll buy you one when we get home," Dwayne said.

231

Brownie turned into a person that looked like an Earth pig with a very large cranium. It had a digital display where numbers flashed on the forehead. He bit a leg and pulled.

"Stop!" Lacy Dawn told him and he did.

"Don't forget your ID cards," Bucky reminded the group.

The Team left to shop in anonymity. Nobody in the hotel lobby gave them a second look. Bucky tipped the hotel manager on duty per the Standard Confidentiality Agreement on Disguises. It was a large tip that would ensure hush-hush.

"Everything's cool," Dwayne whispered to Jenny after looking around the lobby. Lacy Dawn stopped them a few yards from the hotel.

"Remember, this is serious business. Our job is to find the bugs so Bucky can identify them and tell us which pesticides to use. Keep your zip lock baggies handy and don't be squeamish. Daddy, try not to talk with other people because they might recognize your voice. It's famous."

"Sir, yes sir," Dwayne said.

Five minutes later, she noted uncharacteristic behaviors by her team members. *Why are they acting so weird? We ain't at Myrtle Beach. They're going to get us busted like Harold did last summer.*

"My ding a ling, my ding a ling…," Tom sang and played with his fake penis when people he presumed were females approached.

"Take a chance. Pick the right bump to light up next and win a prize," Dwayne said to passer-bys and poked the knots on his costume with his fake thumbs.

Jenny alternately made one nipple and then the other hard with the spray that came with the costume. She giggled at each occurrence. Whatever they were made of, the nipples responded naturally to the cold and turned into protrusions over an Earth-inch long. Tom noticed them and stroked his fake penis and his real one. Brownie pooped in public and ate it. Lacy Dawn stopped the Team. *This is embarrassing.*

"Back to the hotel!" she yelled.

In their room, they took off their costumes and Lacy Dawn called for a huddle.

"My bad," she said. "Complete anonymity is a frequent catalyst of flight-of-idea cognition which manifests in stress reduction behaviors in environments that provide freedom from the consequences. I should've warned you."

"What?" Bucky asked.

"Let's take a short break and try again," Tom said.

Jenny tossed the almost empty can of refrigerant into the trash can. Brownie crawled under a bed. Dwayne and Tom lay down with pillows over their heads. Bucky plugged himself into a human psychology course. Lacy Dawn turned on the TV to watch cartoons and waited.

An hour later, she put on her knapsack with the firewood inside that Faith occupied. It balanced the weight of her large fake breasts. Bucky got Brownie into his costume and the others put on theirs. The Team was ready to give it a second try, so they left the hotel.

"Let's look," Lacy Dawn pointed to a shop. *This is a test, only a test.*

Dwayne acted the same as when he shopped on Earth—he was tugged into the shop. Inside, Jenny bought a golden chain necklace. Dwayne complimented it and copped a feel of her fake breast. Lacy Dawn laughed. *Daddy's on track. Mommy and Tom are cool too. At least I don't have to carry these huge boobs around for nothing.*

After two hours of shopping, nobody had seen any bugs. Team members had looked in corners, underneath shelves, behind displays, and had made a diligent effort without drawing attention to their objective. They went into what appeared to be a pet shop. Lacy Dawn touched the outside of a glass-like case with pretty animals inside.

Maybe the people we interviewed lied about Shptiludrp being infested with bugs. "Be careful. You might get bit," Faith said from the knapsack. She was inside a piece of firewood that Lacy Dawn had brought from Roundabend.

"I will, but the animals all look friendly."

"I mean by a bug."

Within the shop, small living things of various appearances were in cases and cages with removable covers. The creatures ran, slept, played, ate, and nuzzled the extended fingers of shoppers. Brownie left the shop and waited outside by the front door.

"He's worried that I might buy a new pet," Lacy Dawn said.

"Me too—I need all the attention I can get," Faith said.

Lacy Dawn walked to a cage that contained animals with bodies similar to Earth gerbils. They had six legs, long blue hair, squashed faces like Pekingese dogs, and stubby tails that wagged nonstop. She consulted with Bucky. *Oleins—that's a weird name for a pet.*

"Look, Mommy. This one's too cute to pass up."

Jenny ignored her and browsed elsewhere. Lacy Dawn got a specialized language converter from the shop's front counter, watched the monitor above the cage, and pushed Select when the price dropped to the Earth equivalent of twenty dollars. *High price for a gerbil, but it's soooo cute.*

"Just don't put it in here with me," Faith said. *I shouldn't have said nothing. Lacy Dawn told me not to unless it was real important. Roundabend I have friends to talk to. Now, I'm stuck in this backpack.*

"You could snuggle with something cuddly. Wait until you see it." Lacy Dawn said to her.

The shop's proprietor watched where Lacy Dawn pointed her finger and reached into the cage. He picked up the Olein she had selected. A bug scurried back under the cage's bedding. Lacy Dawn motioned for Bucky to join her.

"Tell the others that we hit pay dirt. I'll tell the proprietor that I want to consider another purchase before we finalize this one. Go get us some pencils or something like that."

As instructed, the proprietor left, put the Olein in a box, and attended to other customers. Bucky returned with pencil-like objects. Team members stirred up cage bedding with their sticks.

"There're bugs everywhere," Jenny whispered to Dwayne and Tom.

"Bucky, tell the shopkeeper that I want to take my pet with me instead of having it shipped. Have him put it in a sealed box with as much bedding as will fit. The box it's in now is perforated and our bugs might get out. And, I want enough food to last for a week in a separate sealed package. There might be bugs in it too. Make sure he gets the bedding and food out of the cage and not off the shelf. Give him a big tip for his work before he starts so he does a good job."

"I love you, Lacy Dawn," Bucky said.

He opened his arms for a hug that he didn't get.

"Then, I want to get back to the hotel quick before there's any risk of suffocation. It's so cute. I'll tell everybody else about the plan and make sure Brownie's awake. You take care of the transaction. We'll be outside."

Bucky nodded. Brownie whimpered. *I bet she gives the Olein a hug.*

"Good job," Faith said.

"Thanks."

Only Bucky could purchase anything on their incognito shopping spree without disclosure of their true identities. While each team member now had credit, its use would have given them away. Any shopkeeper would take advantage of a purchase by a celebrity to flood the store. Bucky had no customer draw. Everybody knew that there were many identical DotComs that helped manage the universe and one that wore pants was inconsequential. The form was pictured in all the history text books about the Mall. His purchase did not raise an interest. He came out of the shop with two plastic bags. The team got on the fast beltway.

"Thank you, Bucky," Lacy Dawn hugged him. "I love you, too."

Brownie's head drooped. After they got off the beltway, he was the last to enter the hotel. Jenny pushed the stop button for an Earth minute while they waited for him to get in the elevator. On their floor, he lay in the hall and refused to get up until coaxed to go in their hotel room. *Why did she want another pet? I'm a good dog. I didn't even pull off that stupid costume.*

"I've been an insensitive asshole," Lacy Dawn said to the group.

She called Brownie to her bed where they curled up in love. Next, she went to her mother and father with hugs and kisses. Then, she wrapped her arms around Tom's neck and kissed him on the cheek. She kissed Bucky last.

"I need a hug," Faith said.

"As soon as we get back home, inhabit Walnut and I'll give you a big one."

Then Bucky went to the bathroom. *I can't control this thing!*

Then Dwayne went to the bathroom *I want to go home. I'm so horny.*

Jenny went into the other bathroom. *I want to go home. I've got a new vibrator waiting for me there.*

It was Tom's turn to use it. *I'm so lonely. Maybe Jenny knows somebody nice that I can hook up with.*

Brownie moved in front of the table on which the pet box sat and assumed an on-guard stance. Team members took turns rubbing his head. On duty, he didn't roll over to ask for a belly rub.

"Good dog," Lacy Dawn said. *It's time to be a domineering bitch again — back to business.*

"I need to explain something," Bucky said. "That shop was not a pet store. I didn't have a chance to tell you before."

"What was it selling?" Jenny asked first.

"Hand lotion, body wash, wrinkle remover, hair remover, hair restorer, perfumed lotion, deodorant, skin softener, hair colors, and those types of items. It was a cosmetics shop that targeted consumer interests from a selected number of planets."

"But, I bought a pet," Lacy Dawn said.

"No, but you did buy an animal," Bucky corrected. *I have to tell her the truth. There is no other option.*

Brownie wagged his tail.

"You bought an organic, fresh, and very popular hair lotion. In its current form, it looks like a pet. However, the Olein's life span is very short. A few Earth days after its puberty, the Olein will begin to run in a tight circle. It will not stop until it is dead—the time of its harvest. It is a creature that has mystified scholars for thousands of years."

"But, it's so cute," Lacy Dawn said.

"If purchased as a short-term pet, an Olein will die eight Earth weeks after birth. Scholars have theorized that the entire species would have been extinct if not for the discovery of its medicinal value. Profitable gardening of Oleins was the only thing that saved the species. It is a suicidal anomaly to survival of the fittest. Shopkeepers guarantee that an Olein will live within ten minutes of a specified time or money back. A purchaser's harvest must be timed or the investment will be wasted."

"Were all the other animals in those cages the same?"

"No. Each species was there by individual attribute. The thing that all the animals in that shop had in common was that they would not have existed without intervention because they had some value to a higher order," Bucky said.

"Why does it die?" Jenny asked.

"As the Olein runs, it generates intense body heat that cooks itself. Its life can be extended for a brief period with chilled sprays. However, the Olein samples tested in captivity tried to avoid the sprays and appeared discomforted. Numerous other techniques have been attempted during clinical trials."

"What's it good for? Why do people buy them?" Tom asked. *It's going to die anyway.*

"It is purchased by people who want to grow hair on almost any carbon-based surface. Typically, purchasers of Oliens have lost hair that had been on a body part in their younger days. When the Olein dies, as its body cools a split opens in its belly. The lotion is extracted, for example, with a human finger. The cage is returnable. I would have paid a refundable deposit if we had not bought this one in a disposable box."

"That's gross!" Lacy Dawn said. "Can we somehow keep it alive?"

"I know of no way to extend its life for more than two Earth minutes," Bucky said.

Lacy Dawn patted Brownie. *Cute from a distance is better than a cuddly false hope.*

"We could make a lot of money from these things," Tom said. "Have you seen the Hair Club for Men commercials?

"Don't be disgusting," Jenny said.

"Not a bad idea, Mommy. It could be a product at the next yard sale in the hollow." *Never fall in love with a harvest animal. It ain't no pet. Cows have beautiful eyes too, but their fates are sealed even if they are cute.*

"After this one dies, smear a little on that big bald spot you've got, Tom. If it works, we'll talk about it some more," Lacy Dawn said.

"I will."

"Enough talk about cosmetics," Lacy Dawn said. "Get ready to see if we have a bug or two to capture. Let's catch them alive if we can. Brownie, if you see a bug, please don't eat it unless necessary. We want the bugs to study and not for supper."

"Give him a rawhide chew," Jenny recommended. Dwayne did but Brownie ignored it.

"First, let's look in the box with the food," Lacy Dawn said. If it has bugs we can just punch a couple of real small air holes and then reseal it. The holes are risky, but I don't want our samples to suffocate. If the box with the Olein has bugs, we will need to put them in the other box and reseal it again. I hope they don't bite."

Tom and Dwayne cleared the table to use as a work station. Jenny got three pens out of her purse. Without instruction, everyone took positions around the table so that an escaping bug would be caught. Brownie waited under the table. He was ready to capture and not eat. Lacy Dawn opened the first box and stirred the food with a pen.

"Roaches! Shptiludrp has roaches and can't get rid of them!" Lacy Dawn said and resealed the box top.

"I hate roaches," Jenny said. "Do you remember when my cousin moved into that housing project in the city and we went to visit?"

"I'll never forget," Lacy Dawn answered. "I didn't eat anything the whole weekend. I was afraid that the food had roaches in it. They were everyplace."

"Everyplace," Jenny agreed. "So why didn't we see roaches on Shptiludrp until we looked real hard? I ain't seen none in our hotel room."

"The roaches here must be smarter," Lacy Dawn said. "In the project, that girl about my age picked them up with her fingers and threw them in the commode. What was that girl's name? Anyway, she told me that they used to step on them or squash them with a piece of paper towel, but it made too big a mess. So they decided to pick them up with their fingers and flush them. The guts didn't squish out that way. I bet the roaches here know all the tricks."

"Those things are not coming into my house to be studied," Jenny said.

"We can conduct our research on the ship after we return to Earth. I must prepare a special compartment," Bucky said. "It will be a biohazard box that presents no risk of escape. Ships have been placed out of commission because of roach infestation."

"You knew about the roaches all along," Jenny accused.

"Lacy Dawn's prerequisite for the job was the Problem Statement," he said.

"Some boyfriend you are. You could have cheated a little," Jenny said.

"My man don't cheat."

"At this point, I recommend that we move the boxes into the bathtub," Bucky said. "The current situation is not secure. The roaches will eventually eat through the box material. If an escape occurs, it will be more visible in the bathtub than anyplace else."

"Sounds like a plan," Lacy Dawn said. *I'm too grossed out to chair this meeting.*

Brownie crunched his rawhide chew. *Roaches taste awful. But, I'll eat one if I have to.*

"I anticipated the team's success and have already ordered the fabrication of a metal box from which the roaches will be unable to escape. Its design includes an internal air circulation system charged by replaceable external screw-on atmospheric canisters. They will have sufficient food and water until we transfer them to the biohazard box on the ship for research. The container should be delivered shortly."

"I've never screwed on canisters before," Dwayne said.

"However, I did not anticipate the purchase of the Olein. I will have a cage delivered. When the Olein is removed from the box, it will need to be washed to ensure that it is not carrying any roach eggs before we place it in the cage. I will also order new bedding and food for the cage—sanitized and guaranteed bug-free."

The laptop booted up, the order was placed, and both the cage and the special roach container arrived ten minutes later. The team took positions beside the bathtub. Lacy Dawn was on her knees. The others stooped and crouched in various postures. They were ready to contain escapees. Brownie placed his front paws on the rim of the tub and waited. Bucky held the cage and kept its door open. Lacy Dawn leaned into the bathtub and removed the Olein from the box. A roach gripped onto its hair, let go, and ran around the bathtub. All hands slapped at the escapee.

"Yuck!" they exclaimed in unison when Brownie lapped up the roach just before it went over the side of the tub. *I've tasted worse.*

Lacy Dawn washed the Olein with human shampoo and put it in the cage. Bucky handed her the special container for the roaches. She put the boxes inside and after applying a silicone-like substance from a tube, he screwed down the lid.

"I must leave to construct a biohazard compartment on my ship. While my ship has the most sophisticated internal defenses against infestation available and always receives high priority attention while docked on Shptiludrp, I'm not taking any chances with roaches on-board. This box is guaranteed to be escape proof. However, baby roaches have unimaginable means. Brownie, would you mind standing guard until I get back?"

"I'll email Mr. Prump to set up a private meeting," Lacy Dawn said to her team. "It will be a general terms negotiation and I won't need any help."

"I need a nap," Jenny said.

"Let's party," Tom said to Dwayne and they left before Bucky.

Five minutes later they were in the hotel bar. Autograph seekers didn't bother them. Over a can of beer, Tom said, "it'll take a specialized insecticide to kill those mothers. They've evolved. Raid ain't gonna get it."

"Got to specialize to insecticide," Dwayne said.

Fitting into the Boss's Schedule

"The boss had to leave early to take his youngest son to soccer practice. His youngest wife has a headache and said she couldn't take it any longer. Hope this information is helpful," the receptionist for Mr. Prump replied to Lacy Dawn's email.

"Thank you," Lacy Dawn replied. *She's liberal with his personal information. It's to my advantage, but I'd never hire her.*

Jenny was asleep. Nobody else was in the hotel room except Brownie. Dwayne and Tom were still at the bar. Bucky was building a biohazard compartment on his ship. Brownie had an important assignment to watch the roach container and to eat anything that escaped. He was too busy to cuddle.

"I'm going window shopping, Brownie," she whispered, put on her backpack, and picked up her laptop. *Mr. Prump might have an opportunity to respond to my request for a meeting while I'm out.*

"Be back in a few." *Feels like when I used to sneak out of the house to go Roundabend.*

With disguise intact, Lacy Dawn walked to the closest shop of interest. It contained tables and shelves full of various fabrics. She took the piece of firewood that Faith inhabited out of the knapsack and they browsed.

"This is like the shop in town that me and Mommy went to. She'll shit if she wakes up and finds out I'm gone."

"I wish I could shit," the log said.

Lacy Dawn had helped her mother pick out material to make a wedding dress for her grandmother. Grandma on her father's side decided to get married for a fourth time after she killed off the three previous husbands. She was sixty. Grandma on her mother's side had attended the wedding. She'd stayed with the man she married when she was thirteen because he was good on the inside. He finally proved that he wasn't by not buying her heart pills. She was seventy. It was a nice ceremony. White fabric didn't seem right for Grandma—not to her or anybody else.

"Only the lowest class of people buys pets from stores," Faith said.

"I saw the store, too and I ain't going back in there. I should've listened when Daddy told me the same thing. But, the Olein was so cute. At least we've got roaches to study."

"Nobody can get rid of roaches," Faith said. "Earth has had it. I just hope I die like everyone else when it happens. I don't want to be stuck in something with nobody to talk to."

"It's worth a death or two, a few, a million or billion to save priority life," Lacy Dawn said. *DotCom was right about war.*

"I died and look what happened to me. I guess I wasn't no priority," Faith said.

"Of course, priority is a matter of perspective. My perspective is that Earth life is top priority. I'm sure that there are a lot of folks who would disagree. The roaches, for example. Do you like this?" Lacy Dawn held up a bright paisley print fabric. Unlike some others in the shop, it remained a fixed design. She dug on the bottom shelf to reach another roll.

"Roaches," she said out loud and whacked with her palms. Before she had smashed more than a couple, a soft padded pole extended from the shelf frame and scooted her aside. A hose sprang from the shop's floor and misted a substance on, under, behind, and between the shelves on which the paisley printed fabric rested. Lacy Dawn inhaled.

I know that smell.

She left the shop, sat on a bench, plugged the laptop into a port, put Faith beside her, and checked her email. "Please confirm your availability for a meeting," Mr. Prump had written. It was scheduled in fifteen minutes. The time counted down on the screen by Earth seconds. She put Faith back in the knapsack. Lacy Dawn responded that she would attend the meeting, and went to the Office of the Manager of the Mall.

Once there, she began unequivocal negotiation. "I have defined the problem and I accept the assignment to develop a solution. Your problem has evolved for many thousands of years. The future of Shptiludrp depends on my success. The competitor is closing in. But, I work cheap."

"I pay the market," he said.

"From this point forward, DotCom is my man. He's not your

man or any part of your management. He will have no constraints from you or by any historical tradition on how he helps me solve the problem. He will have immediate, unlimited, and uncensored access to everything and every resource that he believes would be relevant to facilitation of the mission. Your rules have delayed progress, sorry, Leon. Either you agree to this first and very basic term or I will go home."

"I agree."

"Put it in writing," Lacy Dawn said.

Mr. Prump did so in triplicate and affixed his official seal.

The Welfare Department Supervisor's Decision

A week after the team returned to Earth with their roaches, Jenny answered the door to a young man who gave her a subpoena to appear in Magistrate's Court for welfare fraud. She watched him back out of the driveway and climb the hill, hid the papers in her shirt, and went into the bathroom to read them. *I played the home visit by the Welfare Woman so cool. I'll keep this a secret.*

Ten days later, Jenny sat in the waiting room at the courthouse. The case had been docketed for 11:30 a.m. It was 11:45 and she'd been there since 10:00. Except for a Deputy Sheriff in uniform and a boy handcuffed to him, she was alone. The boy, who had fallen asleep, lay on two adjacent chairs. Four women in dark suits arrived. Jenny nodded hello. *No big deal. Just say it like you practiced.*

A minute later on public announcement of her case name, she and the four Suits went into the courtroom. The hearing was called to order. Before either side said anything, the magistrate proclaimed: "I have reviewed this matter. I hereby refer the case back to the administrative level for a hearing before an Administrative Law Judge of the Department of Human Resources. It was misfiled. If resolution is not reached at that level, or upon appeal of either party, the case may be re-filed in Magistrate's Court. Does either party have any questions?" The Magistrate left the courtroom. One of the four Suits approached Jenny.

"You'll receive a notice of the charges against you with the time and place to appear. We want to work with you to resolve this matter. If the hearing is set at an inconvenient time, please so indicate on the bottom of the form and fill in when you would like to have your administrative hearing re-scheduled."

"I'd like to get this taken care of today," Jenny said.

"The ALJ, that's short for Administrative Law Judge, has a very busy schedule. But since we're all here, I'll call him to see if he can work us in."

Jenny smiled. *I should've brought a roach egg to slip in that woman's pocket.*

"Good news. The ALJ can squeeze us in between hearings in fifteen minutes. They are conducted at the local office of the Department of Human Resources. Do you need transportation?"

"Do you mean the welfare office? I drove my SUV," Jenny said.

"Yes," the Suit answered.

Ten minutes later, she walked into the conference room also used for hearings. Jenny nodded to the judge. He sat at a table in the front of the room that faced two other tables—one for the petitioner separated by several feet from the other for the defendant. *I've seen him at church. His fingernails are always clean, but I never thought he'd turn out to be a judge for Welfare. I'm going to tell on him.*

"It's nice to see you again, Jenny," the judge said.

She smiled. *Oh my God, it's Roger from junior high. I let him kiss me beside the fire exit to make Dwayne jealous.*

"Nice to see you too, Roger." *There's no way he'd put me in jail.*

She sat down, crossed her legs, and slid her hem three inches above her knee. The petitioner entered, sat at the opposite table, and laid down a thick file.

"Can I be excused to go to the restroom?" Jenny asked the Main Suit.

"Judge?" the Main Suit redirected.

"Of course, I want everyone to be comfortable. I've postponed my next hearing for an hour. Unless there's an objection, we can work through lunch to hear this case."

In the public restroom, a place that she knew well, Jenny used the cracked mirror decorated with lipstick obscenities to double-check her own. After a touch up and an extra shot of hair spray, she stepped over the turd that had been placed in the middle of the floor and left. *I look good enough for Court TV.*

"Jenny!" a woman yelled from an office on the way back to the conference room.

Out of the office staggered John Davis. Everyone in town knew John. He was famous for his military exploits. They had been verified and acknowledged by the closest detachment of the National Guard and the local Veterans of Foreign Wars. He was always eligible for one free beer at the only joint allowed in city limits. Jenny reached out to shake his hand. *He ain't sobered up since coming back from Vietnam fifty years ago.*

Behind him came his wife, Denise. She was the biggest gossip at church and an office assistant for Welfare. Denise directed her husband to a side exit. He leaned on the wall and didn't budge.

"Third offense DUI," she smiled. "Now he'll get the help he needs, long-term lock-up."

Out of the same office came Ms. Hedges. Denise introduced her as John's court appointed lawyer. Next, the other Ms. Hedges, the Assistant Prosecuting Attorney, came out of the office. They were sisters. Jenny was introduced to her also. Everyone smiled except John. The two Ms. Hedges followed him out of the Welfare Department's side exit.

"What brings you around these parts?" Denise asked.

"I've got a meeting to close out my food stamps," Jenny said.

"How's the family?"

"It's fine. Dwayne works out-of-town. Lacy Dawn works for Tom until school starts. I'm so proud. She made straight As. When Head Start begins, I'll get back to work too."

"Well, it's nice seeing you," Denise frowned and went back into her office. Jenny returned to the conference room.

"Miss Jenny Skeen?" the ALJ asked as if he didn't know that she was now Mrs. Hickman. It was her maiden name.

Jenny slinked to her chair, flashed her pearly white teeth, sat and crossed her legs, adjusted the chair to give Roger a more direct view, re-crossed her legs, and adjusted her hem line. The ALJ alternated stares from breasts to legs.

"We might be in trouble," the Main Suit whispered to the other Suits.

Jenny licked her lips. *He spent the first semester of ninth grade algebra trying to look up my skirt.*

"It's my understanding that the public defender, Ms. Simpson, called into work sick this morning," the ALJ said. "Do you have an attorney?"

"No, your Majesty," she smiled.

"She's slick. We are in trouble," the Main Suit whispered.

"Rather than a hearing, since you've not had an opportunity to secure counsel, let's try to resolve this matter through mediation. Nothing will be admissible in any subsequent proceeding, if necessary. Are there any objections?"

The Suits looked at each other, flipped through legal pads, and shrugged.

"Having heard no objections, I dismiss the transcriptionist," said the ALJ. The court transcribe left for lunch.

The ALJ spread out pages from a file and glanced at Jenny every few seconds. The Four Suits adjusted their postures and hem lines. They didn't achieve the attention of the ALJ.

"In a nutshell, the Department's allegation is that you applied for and received food stamps for a family of three, but your husband has left you and you didn't report it. What do you have to say about the Department's allegation?"

"I kept calling Welfare and got that stupid answering machine. It said if my last name started with A through F, or G through whatever, to push the star on the telephone. I pushed it and got another machine. I left messages, but nobody ever called me back."

"How many people live in your household?" the Main Suit asked.

"Three, but Dwayne only comes home on the weekends."

"I was hoping, ah, I thought that he was out of the picture." the ALJ said.

"Look, this whole thing is too stupid. I hardly even used that food stamp card. Just tell me how much I owe back and I'll pay it."

The four Suits consulted. One got out a calculator.

"You owe $302.00."

"Can I pay it back in food stamps?"

"Judge?" the Main Suit asked. "I do want to call to your attention that the Department now uses a card rather than stamps."

Jenny crossed her legs again.

"Repayment in food stamps is acceptable," the judge said.

Jenny reached under the table and got the plastic Kroger bag that she'd had with her all morning, dumped it on the table, and counted stamps. With every hundred-dollar value, she dumped a pile on the Petitioner's table in front of the Main Suit. She reached $302.00, and scooped the much larger remaining pile back into the plastic Kroger bag.

"Please verify," the ALJ said to the Main Suit.

"It is payment in full."

"I will sign a dismissal order in the morning. Is there anything further?"

The four Suits got up and left. The ALJ moved to the chair beside Jenny.

"What's the real deal?" the ALJ asked.

Jenny re-crossed her legs. *I need to help save the universe and you're annoying. That's the real deal.*

"Everything's cool," she said.

"Do you need any money?" he asked.

"I'm okay. Dad's helping. I just need some time." *That line always works on assholes.*

"Call me if you need anything."

The ALJ wrote his home phone number on a notepad that had his name on top in fancy letters. He extended his hand as if to shake hers, but instead—fondled it.

She smiled. *Creepy.*

"I've not been on a date since my wife left me four years ago. There's nothing like junior high memories to rekindle romance."

"I know someone I might be able to fix you up with. She's real nice and pretty."

"Anybody I know?" he asked.

"No. She ain't from the hollow. Her man came back from the Gulf in a box. Do you remember him, Jack Clendenin? He was the boy in the eighth that lived on top of the Good Shepherd Funeral Home?"

"No, I don't remember him."

"If you think I'm pretty, wait until you see her. She's got one heck of a figure and a stomach as flat as a pancake. She ain't had no kids."

"Okay."

"When her husband didn't come back, Barbie started drinking. She didn't run around—stayed home and courted Old Crow. Her family put her in the state hospital and she ain't touched a drop for three years, ain't dated nobody, and I see her every Sunday at church. Maybe you've noticed her. She has blond hair and long legs and sits with the preacher's wife. Anyway, last Sunday she told me that she was so horny that she was about to explode. She said that her husband never could get it up before he got killed and there's nobody in her AA group that can still get an erection. Except for a finger or three, she's a virgin."

"I can quit drinking," Roger said.

"Call me tonight about eight o'clock. I'll have it set up. Just don't tell her what I said about her being horny. And remember that nothing should happen on the first date. After that, it all depends on you."

"I don't act like no asshole," he said.

"I remember," she acknowledged.

Just before she left, Jenny turned around to verify that his eyes were focused on the spot where her ass had just been. They were.

"Have them send me one more month of stamps. Then I'll send you a letter to have them cut off," she closed.

"A deal's a deal," the Administrative Law Judge said.

Getting High on Roach Spray

After the administrative hearing, Jenny returned home to find a house that smelled like bug spray. On investigation, she found that the smell was coming from a pair of jeans in the middle of Lacy Dawn's bedroom floor. *That girl.*

Then, she found both the washer and dryer full of Dwayne's clothes that he had not finished before he went out-of-town to work. *That man.*

She started the washer. It was a brand new automatic that had replaced the wringer. But, it had no wheels to roll onto the back porch, so it sat in the living room, connected to new water lines that Dwayne had run and discharged soap subs into the creek. She added a fabric softener sheet and restarted the dryer. It matched the washer beside it and was plugged into an outlet that had been wired into a new circuit breaker box. *It's quicker but don't feel as wholesome as sunshine.*

Lacy Dawn came home with Bucky.

"I don't know, Mommy, those roaches are strong. We've put all kinds of pesticides inside the decontamination container on the ship and it don't work. Sometimes they roll over on their backs, but if you watch—after a few minutes they get up and act like they're fine. Plus, there are more of them than we brought home—a lot more. They're having babies in the middle of all that roach spray. Maybe we can't pull off this job after all. Maybe, Shptiludrp is doomed. I need to take a shower."

"I do too. I mean after her," Bucky said.

"I'll take your dad's clothes to him," Jenny folded. "It will take a few hours so don't worry. There's a pile of food stamps on the table in the kitchen if you want to go buy some other kind of roach spray."

"They won't sell me roach spray with food stamps," Lacy Dawn leaned out of the new bathroom door. *I love teasing him.*

"Dora is cashier tonight," Jenny said. "Just make sure you get in her line and please don't tell her we got roaches. It'll be all over the hollow by tomorrow."

"Okay, but I don't think any bug spray in the store will work."

Lacy Dawn leaned further out the bathroom door. Steam

billowed. Bucky stared.

"Where were you today?" Lacy Dawn asked her mother.

"Protecting the family name," Jenny answered.

"Did somebody call you a hick?"

"Something sort of like that."

An hour later, Bucky and Lacy Dawn returned from the store with more roach spray that didn't work. Lacy Dawn had driven. Afterward, they put the empty cans and bottles in a garbage bag and threw it in the back of Dwayne's pickup. The bed was full and ready to be unloaded at the dump down the road where it would be covered with dirt to hide it. Lacy Dawn called Tom.

"I'm not an expert on insecticide. What've you tried?" he asked.

She listed brand names and read from a journal that Bucky had insisted be kept as acceptable protocol—every ingredient of every over-the-counter poison recorded by date of application. She had objected to the detail at the time. *We can always read labels later if we find something that kills these mothers.*

"I'm kinda busy now," Tom said. "You know the Olein? I put some on my bald spot? It worked great, but the hair's blue. I look like a punk rocker," Lacy Dawn told Bucky while Tom waited on the other end of the line.

"Bucky said we bought the wrong breed. We needed one for an Earth-like color. My bad. It was soooo cute."

"Great. After I dye my hair, I'll come over. Is your mom home?"

"She's gone to visit Daddy," Lacy Dawn said. *I'm not wearing a bra but you wouldn't even notice.*

Tom arrived a half hour later.

"Like I said before, I'm not an expert. I think you ought to go to the Feed and Seed and talk with someone. Tell them our barn is infested with roaches."

"Sounds like a plan to me. Except, let's say it's one of your out-of-town apartments. Mommy don't want her good name associated with roaches."

Bucky squirmed. *She has not consulted. No insecticide in the universe will kill the roaches unless it also kills everything else.*

Tom left. Nobody else was home.

"Let's snuggle," she said to Bucky.

"You still stink. It's the roach spray," he declined.

"I know. I'm going to take another shower. This time I'm gonna use Daddy's Permatex hand cleaner as a body wash. If that don't work, I'll use Greased Lightning."

"I'll try the decontamination process on my ship and see you in the morning. The alarms are set so you don't have to worry about intruders since you are home alone."

"I feel kinda drunk or high or something," she said.

"I don't think it is a matter of you being high as much as poisoned," Bucky said.

"Still feels good," Lacy Dawn giggled.

She gave him a side-ways hug and went into the bathroom to take another shower.

Fine Points of an Impossible to Perform Contract

The insecticides failed to exterminate the roaches in the ship's contamination chamber and were a waste of food stamps, except to continue to get Lacy Dawn high. Their attempts took two weeks. Despite exhaust fans that ran constantly, the ship smelled like the inside of a Raid spray can. DotCom didn't tell her it was pointless because she wasn't asking for his consultation.

"What else can we do to kill them, Bucky?" she finally gave in.

He frowned. *Why didn't you consult with me before we wasted all this time on insecticide?*

"The following is a general listing of what's been tried to kill the roaches: spray poisons of all known types in the universe, poison baits, poison powders, targeted explosives, selective demolitions, floods, electrocutions, freeze sprays, and very small arms used by skilled specialists. I can provide detail if requested," Bucky said. "There have been millions of roach casualties over the years as a result of every strategy. However, afterward the roaches came back stronger than before. Every attempt inconvenienced shoppers and drew attention to the problem. Entire sections of the Mall were closed during some of the efforts."

"Do you have a recommended course of action?" she asked.

"I wish that I did. You are the one and only Lacy Dawn."

"It's time for the Team to brainstorm." She went home.

The next weekend, the Team sat in the living room with a poster-board-sized pad that listed prior strategies that had been used to try to kill the roaches. Bucky described each and she drew a red marker through every one listed. After she sniffed it, she put the lid on the marker and sat down.

"Let's smoke one," Tom said.

Brownie followed to get secondary smoke. Another was rolled just for him. Without inhaling, the guys blew in his direction until it was gone. A few minutes later, he barked nonstop at Lacy Dawn. It was like old times when he used to bark as an early warning system. It could have been dismissed as cute, but Brownie was persistent.

"It's something about the roaches," Bucky said about Brownie's input. "I don't know what he is talking about. It sounds like the roaches have at least a level of intelligence capable of communication."

"I thought they were too busy with sex to talk," Tom said.

"Talking always messes everything up," Dwayne said.

"If you can't talk, you can't have sex," Jenny said to both.

Tom nodded his understanding. Dwayne didn't. *Talking to women ain't easy, but if I keep nodding my head at the right time when she talks maybe she'll keep giving it up. Tom messed up—it was the wrong time to nod.*

"Can you learn how to understand Brownie?" Lacy Dawn asked Bucky. *Now that you're through adolescence, you're a genius again.*

"I think so. It will take a few days. He has never demonstrated the capability to communicate content verbally until now."

"Meeting adjourned absent objection. We have an avenue. I will negotiate terms for the contract. Bucky, please work on whatever it takes to understand what Brownie tried to tell us."

By email to Mr. Prump (prump@youruniverse), Lacy Dawn outlined the minimum proposed terms of her contract to rid Shptiludrp of roaches:

(1) DotCom will remain a permanent consultant and friend to Lacy Dawn in this generation and all subsequent generations if her line continues.

(2) DotCom's ship will be maintained and refueled at no cost to DotCom or any Earth resident, or replaced as determined by DotCom.

(3) There will never be any inquiry into anything that DotCom says or does for the entire length of his existence.

(4) DotCom will have full access to any and all information available from any source available to Management.

(5) Brownie will be memorialized as a statue in front of the office building of the Manager of the Mall after he dies.

(6) An invisible shield will be placed over Tom's secret garden that will protect it from any and all unwanted intrusion for as long as Tom lives and has a garden on Earth or any other location.

(7) Jenny will have free access to all shops on Shptiludrp and can charge all purchases to the Manager of the Mall's personal account for as long as she lives without any limitation or qualifier.

(8) Dwayne will have the same access to shopping on Shptiludrp as Jenny, but will also receive free shipping for all auto or similar parts or accessories that he might order by e-mail for the rest of his life.

(9) Lacy Dawn will receive free tuition, books, and housing at any educational institution in the universe that she decides to attend.

(10) Any and all available medical coverage will be made available to everyone who lives in the hollow on the effective date of the contract - to cure or treat any medical condition diagnosed by Earth physicians, except as otherwise instructed by an individual's Living Will and subject to full consideration and explanation from loved ones to the patient about the advanced opportunities that medical science presents because of the hollow residency status pursuant to the terms of this contract.

She inserted text to the effect that negotiations of the terms of the contract were confidential and not subject to consideration by any competitors. It was a clause that sealed the deal, and added,

(11) Any Earth resident who wants can compete for eligibility to shop on Shptiludrp.

(12) And, if they want, team members can shop on Shptiludrp to buy items for resale on Earth at a yard sale or any other retail venue.

"Agreed," Mr. Prump replied in his emailed response. "However, this agreement is limited to my term of office except as otherwise binding on subsequent terms by contract." He had been in office for thousands of years and would occupy the post for as long as the planet survived. Lacy Dawn smiled. *He's such a pussy. I hope Bucky figures out how to understand Brownie and that he can really communicate with the roaches. Otherwise, this contract ain't worth the paper that it ain't written on yet.*

"All terms which do not directly benefit me or my family or

255

Tom, including terms that benefit DotCom, should be bound to subsequent administrations of Shptiludrp." *I'm not stupid.*

"So noted," Mr. Prump agreed and added, "Good luck. Your contract ain't worth shit if you don't rid Shptiludrp of its roach infestation. I don't pay for lack of performance."

"I'll send DotCom to get my original signed copy and return him with my original signature to your office."

"Fine."

"It's not just eligibility for payment based on the terms of this contract. If I don't pull this one off, my planet ain't worth shit and neither is your planet. The exploitation has started. Our days are numbered. We don't have time to wait for the next generation of me to solve the problem," she clicked.

Most Meaningful Communication

For the next month, Bucky plugged Brownie into human communication studies and himself into Earth canine studies. Like the humans, Brownie now had a port at the top of his spine. It was covered by thick dog hair when not in use.

After starting Brownie's next lesson plan, Bucky flipped open the tip of his right index finger and put it into a socket on his console. It immediately achieved high speed educational input. He frowned about the information available from Earth's Internet about canines. *Canine trainings presume too great a superiority of humans.*

"There are no educational resources in Shptiludrp's Universal Library to tap into on the topic of roach communications," he told Lacy Dawn after she arrived at the ship that evening. "There's nothing available on roach psychology or sociology. There is information about roach biology and extermination. It requires constant update because roaches become immune and evolve new survival skills."

Brownie licked his penis. Lacy Dawn didn't scold. *He must be at the part of the plug-in lesson about human sexuality.*

"Outdated research is typical," Lacy Dawn said and left the ship.

"I've got a good team," she said to an oak tree. "Bucky's about grown up. He thinks with the correct head again. Brownie's better educated than most people. Mommy's got great intuitive deduction. Daddy can figure out stuff real good. And, Tom can make anything that's possible happen."

"Don't forget about me," Faith tagged along from one inanimate inhabitation to the next.

"Never," Lacy Dawn agreed.

"Goodbye, oak tree. I'm sorry for the brag about my team. You're an important part of it too."

"It was better than when I try to listen to softwoods," the tree said. "Please keep me in the loop. Don't ever tell the other trees, but I agree to consult with you into adulthood—for as long as I am needed and standing. So will Rocker if you put a naked butt on him every once in a while. Boys are so easy and your acorns are ripe."

"Sometimes boys ain't that easy to put up with," Lacy Dawn said. She walked part of the way home, stopped behind Maple, and sat down with her back on it.

For the next month, Team members waited to see if there would be any progress on Brownie learning to talk to the roaches. Lacy Dawn checked in at the ship at least once a day after her work in the gardens.

"I don't want to push them too hard," she directed bean vines around their poles.

"You can push me as hard as you want. I'm on the team too," Faith said. *I need a good reason to live. Now that your daddy ain't so mean anymore, I ain't got much to do.*

"All I ever wanted out of life was to help save parents from themselves," Faith continued. "I guess I'll have to settle for helping you save the universe. At least it's not dodge ball."

"Do you think I would ever leave you out?" Lacy Dawn asked.

"Everybody else did."

"Never—you are my best friend. What do you think will kill the roaches?"

"It gets cold sometimes."

"Cold? I'm ready to start up the company car and hit A/C."

"Don't leave me."

"See you tomorrow, you big baby."

"Eat shit," Faith snuggled inside the maple tree. *Maple has had the warmest heart.*

"No problem," Lacy Dawn went beyond Faith's unassisted domain. *Almost in the eighth grade: chess club, swimming team, debate team, school dances....*

"I'm going to run for class president. Then, I'm going to be president of the U.S. And then, I'll get elected to be in charge of the Earth for a while. After that, I'll get a management job on Shptiludrp with good retirement benefits," she said to a walnut tree on her way home.

"Not unless you save the universe," the tree said. "With straight As and no disciplinary write-ups, you should receive the school's administrative support," the walnut tree said when she got that far down the hill. "What's an administrative?"

"You're so pretty. Why don't you just be a star instead of running for class president?" the walnut tree continued. "I'd look at you. What's a president?"

Lacy processed: *Yeah, the hormonal idiot vote at school is in the bag. With Bucky for my boyfriend, the females won't run against me because of jealousy. They know I ain't interested in their boyfriends.*

"I need to start on an acceptance speech."

"Do not count your acorns before they germinate," the oak tree said.

From dawn to dusk for the next month, Lacy Dawn worked daily. She plowed, hauled, and managed Tom's farm. With new specializations—mushrooms and frozen vegetables and a new marketing strategy that linked websites—her responsibilities expanded into nontraditional duties. More neighbors were hired. Tom purchased another abandoned farm and bud sales at the Farmers' Market tripled.

"I'll give you a big juicy kiss for some good news," Lacy Dawn said to Bucky. It was two weeks before school was scheduled to start.

"Pucker up, sweetheart," Bucky said.

"Tell me first."

"No way, Jose," he countered.

She pecked him on the cheek. He stumbled back and stood quiet for ten seconds.

"It is not much," Bucky began. "Three words from Brownie— it's a start that shows the possibilities. Thanks for the juicy— not! It was appropriate for my very limited findings."

"Just tell me. I hate being strung along like I'm in the second grade," Lacy Dawn said. "By the way, do you like maple syrup?"

"Spermatophore was the first word," he said.

Brownie wagged his tail.

"What the heck does that mean?"

"It is a sack of sperm that roaches use to impregnate females."

"They don't have hot sex?"

"Yes, in a manner of conception."

"A lot of human women would prefer that," Lacy Dawn said. "What were the other words?"

"My and Manager," he said. "I think they go together, but we're still working on it."

"Good dog," Lacy Dawn patted head.

Brownie showed his belly. She ignored it.

Lacy reprocessed: *I have to be results-oriented. Outcome measures must be adopted to move the project forward. A real kiss or a good belly rub will have to wait for more progress. Mere efforts don't count.*

"How can he do it? How can he communicate with roaches, anyway?" she asked.

"It appears to be telepathy," Bucky said. "Roaches have many survival skills. For example, they have compound eyes with over two thousand lenses. They can process visual images from many directions at the same time. The ability to communicate with telepathy must have evolved after their introduction on Shptiludrp. Perhaps it was stimulated by the thousands of targeted mass-destruction campaigns. It may be a means to warn comrades to leave targeted areas. That's a guess. While I was well aware of their survival skills, I never suspected that roaches had an advanced ability to communicate until Brownie told me." *I will publish my work to update the Universal Library.*

"That's another thing," she said. "How in the universe did Brownie learn to tell you anything? Brownie and I are close and I can usually understand what he means—like if he wants bacon—but Spermatophore? That's too much."

"I used the same established technology that converts your language to any other person's language and vice versa when shopping on Shptiludrp. It has been available for thousands of years. I started the input of Brownie's verbal and nonverbal behavior for analyses several years ago with no expectation that he would learn how to communicate with humans. Input is the time-consuming part of language conversion."

"If I plug in a language conversion device, can I talk to my dog?"

"Yes, but do not get too excited. After all of his plug-in trainings, he is still a dog. He mainly communicates about food and smell—unless you want me to turn him into something other than a dog."

"Could you?" she asked.

"No. That was a joke. A dog is a dog is a dog."

"Good. I don't want to marry Dr. Frankenstein," she said.

"The roaches are confined behind a glass. There is a barrier between them and Brownie. Therefore, we do not maximize our opportunity to promote communications. Unless you order me to, I refuse to let them out. It's too risky. There are several thousands of species of roaches already on Earth. The introduction of another and more evolved species is not advisable."

"Could you learn how to communicate with them?"

"Not within your natural lifetime," he answered. *I won't let you leave me within such a short span.*

He puckered. She didn't.

"Why can't someone as smart as you learn how to talk with roaches that a dog learned how to talk to?"

"I love you," he answered.

"Don't get mushy now. Why can't you talk to them?"

"First, while I may have humanness, I am a long way from intuition. I am much farther from its first cousin—telepathy. You may be in a position to learn to talk with the roaches faster than me. Brownie is in the best position because Earth dogs have powerful natural emapathy skills. He always licked your face when you hurt, and no sentient being in the universe has been victimized more so than cockroaches. Everyone on our team except Brownie hates them, especially your mom—everybody has hated them forever. Only God understands the critical role that cockroaches have played in the survival of all species on every habitable planet. She also knew that you were destined to save the universe."

"God?" she asked. *He said that word again.*

"Everybody has a boss," he answered.

I Breathe Through My Sides and Fart Out My Asshole

After going home that night, Lacy Dawn went to bed and started her "Now I Lay Me Down to Sleep" prayer. It was the first time in a long time. *If Bucky believes that everybody has a boss, I'm not taking any chances.*

"God Bless Brownie," she prayed twice for emphasis. *The mission depends on him. He needs all the help he can get.*

The next morning, she returned to the ship for an update. Bucky was on duty and not in the bathroom when she arrived. Lacy Dawn sat down at her monitor. *I hope my boy ain't sick.*

"I think we're closer to communication with Brownie," he said.

She bent forward. He still didn't notice.

"Daddy will be home tonight," she sat up. "I'll see if Tom is available tomorrow after I let the farm crew off work. Mommy and Brownie will be home. Have language converters available and put together a training session. I want them to learn how to communicate with Brownie," Lacy Dawn gave him a kiss goodbye on the cheek. He embraced air because she had stepped back.

On the path home she stopped, turned, and stuck her tongue out at the cave. Back home, she entered the date in Outlook for a staff meeting—now. She borrowed the sheer skirt that Jenny had bought for four dollars, looked at her skinny legs in the mirror, and put on jeans underneath.

"Sure, but remember it's almost harvest time. I hate to leave town for very long." Tom said by cell a few minutes later.

"This trip should take two or three days at the most. School starts for me and Mommy in a few days, too. I just hope Daddy can take off work."

"I recommend that you or I call him now so he can set it up with his staff."

"Would you mind?" she asked. *I hate to ask him for another interruption in his career.*

"No problemmo."

"Thanks."

Lacy Dawn looked at herself in the mirror and left to get Faith. "Get packed," she said to a boulder.

"There ain't no good logs here. They're all rotten and moldy," Faith said.

"Practice on smaller pieces. See that piece over there? Get inside it. See the little one next to it? Get inside that one."

"I'm too fat."

"No you're not. You don't even have a body. Just practice."

"I've got bigger boobies than you."

"It's baby fat. I want you in the smallest object you can inhabit for this trip. You were too heavy last time. Later," she said before she returned to the house. *Now that I need it the most, DotCom seems to be losing interest. I'm almost fourteen, almost an old maid.*

At the staff meeting the next day, Bucky made a progress report. It concluded with the six distinct roach words that Brownie had translated. The presentation started with Spermatophore and its definition. *Ain't nothing wrong with my man except he's been working too hard.*

"Brownie needs face to face interviews with roaches on Shptiludrp in order to proceed," Bucky finalized his report.

"Bullshit," Tom said.

Jenny nodded agreement. *The boy's lost his mind.*

Team members fidgeted and looked at each other but stayed seated.

"Move to the second agenda item, Bucky."

He dropped a language conversion device, leaned over to pick it up, and handed the devices out to team members.

"Bullshit," Tom said again.

Experienced, they plugged in. Tom winced. *Man, the skin around my port is still sore.*

Lacy Dawn woke up Brownie. He walked over to Jenny.

"Watch," Lacy Dawn instructed.

Jenny patted Brownie on the head. *Just sounds like wake-up noises. Wait. I hear words.*

"Hey," Brownie said to Jenny. "Is it bacon time?"

"Not now, Brownie," Jenny answered as she always did

without language conversion. Her eyes widened, mouth opened, and she looked at Dwayne. The others had heard Brownie talk also.

"Shit," Brownie said.

"Not in the house," Dwayne said.

Brownie turned to face Dwayne.

"Of course not, do you think I'm stupid? Is it time to talk to the roaches again?" Brownie asked and turned his head to Lacy Dawn. *They woke me up for some reason.*

"Why don't you go check on my upper garden?" Tom asked.

"Oh, okay. I have to pee anyway." Brownie said.

Brownie trotted from the living room toward the back door. The three got up, went to the kitchen, and watched through the window. After he peed, Brownie went Roundabend and out of sight.

"I'm amazed," Tom said.

"I'm not after everything else we've seen," Dwayne said.

"I'll fry that boy some bacon," Jenny said. "And, when he comes back, I'll ask him how many pieces he wants just to see what he says."

Ten minutes later, Brownie squeezed through the still-torn bottom half of the back door screen. The bacon fried. Dwayne mixed eggs for omelets and Tom cleaned green onions to go in them.

"Everything's fine up there," Brownie said. "The buds are so big that they smell fruity. I hope nobody gets too close or it could attract attention."

Tom slapped the table top and looked at Dwayne. *He understands the concept of concealment.*

Dwayne smiled at Tom and grabbed a handful of onions for the eggs. Jenny smiled at Dwayne and turned the bacon. Bucky stared at Lacy Dawn's crotch, so she moved it into a more enticing position.

"Let the demonstration speak for itself," Lacy Dawn whispered to Bucky. She pulled him into the living room and gave him a peck on the cheek.

"How many pieces of bacon do you want, Brownie?" Jenny asked.

"I'm trying to watch my cholesterol, just four."

"Watch out. The skillet's still hot," Jenny said.

"Please, let it cool down before you put it on the floor. Or, put some cold water in first. I keep burning the crap out of my tongue. I'm just a dog."

"What did that roach taste like?" Tom asked. *I'll see if he's got a sense of humor.*

"Like raw hamburger sprayed with Raid. Roaches have this bad tasting place inside. If roaches decide to eat a dead roach, they eat around the bad place. They told me it's like a human liver where bad stuff is stored. That's why it tastes awful. They said that dead humans taste worse because they eat crap, but I've never tried one."

"I'm convinced. Let's go to Shptiludrp," Tom said.

Lacy Dawn went into the kitchen and reached down to unplug Brownie's language conversion device. He looked up from the skillet and avoided her contact by a move toward the bathroom.

"Last winter, Tom told me that he'd like to make bacon with your mommy, Lacy Dawn," Brownie scurried around the kitchen.

"Brownie! It's not nice to repeat everything you hear—especially not something like that."

"What?" Brownie asked before she caught him and he was unplugged. He finished licking the skillet clean. *I've always understood most everything.*

Nobody reacted. Lacy Dawn patted him on the head. *I hope he don't tell Mommy about me getting high on roach spray.*

Jenny gave him more bacon grease mixed with water. *I hope he don't tell Dwayne about me trying to watch Tom pee.*

Dwayne blew a hit in Brownie's direction. *I hope he don't tell Tom about the vibrator I bought Jenny for Christmas.*

Bucky faced the back door. *I wonder what else I can do with my penis.*

They all looked down at Brownie, who had curled up on the kitchen floor, then at each other, and nodded agreement: *I ain't saying nothing personal to that dog ever again. He's such a blabbermouth.*

Two days later, they were on their way back to Shptiludrp.

Jenny used the trip as an opportunity to begin knitting another new cover for the new couch. *Space travel ain't exciting like it used to be. It used to be fun, helped us build drive and feel like a team. Now, we're just addicted to shopping and have to save the universe in order to keep it up.*

"If there're so many different species of roaches, Bucky, why do the ones we got look almost the same as those in my cousin's apartment in the housing project?"

"Everybody, please remember to call me DotCom once we land," he said.

"That's a stupid name," Tom said.

"Roaches look similar," Bucky answered. "This includes what you call water bugs. But, there is a wide variety of appearances and sizes if examined closely. Some are more popular among pet owners than others."

"Pet owners! Yuck!" Jenny said.

"Sure. Every civilized planet in the universe, including Earth, has a small population of people who buy, sell, collect, and trade roaches for pets—as well as most other insects."

The ship circled toward a decontamination dock that had been cleared for them. Expedited decontamination was a fine point of their contract that had been agreed to by Mr. Prump.

"Bug collecting is not so strange," Tom said. "When I was in college, my roommate and I put a loaf of bread in an empty aquarium. Mold changed colors all through the semester. It was the centerpiece of an orange crate table. Even though we put plastic wrap on the top, the roaches still got in and added a little action to the show. People would sit for hours and stare at it."

After the ship landed, the decontamination procedure went smoothly. Nobody made any type of suggestive comment or did anything close to sexual harassment.

Lacy smiled: *Being naked is easy now that I've got something to show. Gym class here I come. It'll be a great place to campaign for class president.*

"I'm getting pretty," Lacy said to her backpack.

"You ain't got anything that I don't," Faith said. "I just needed to find it."

Dwayne put on a brand new pair of underwear before they had

left Earth. His boxers were folded, on the tray, and ready for him to put back on after the decontamination procedure. Tom—wearing his jeans—had his underwear on his head when he came out of the decontamination chamber. He went back in and put them on after nobody laughed.

Brownie was required by the Shptiludrp decontamination screeners to have a flea shampoo. It was an alternative that Lacy Dawn selected since she was more familiar with the technique compared to any other option. Since it was part of a free service, she also had his hair styled. Brownie whined during and after the procedure. *This is bullshit and I'm going to tell her so once I'm plugged in again.*

Their roaches in the escape-proof container were confiscated and sterilized. Of course, none of them died during the process. There were more roaches than when they had first started the trip to Shptiludrp, but Bucky was prepared and brought them in a larger container.

"Mr. Prump knows that our roaches will function as aides during the mission," DotCom said. "He waived the policy that required their destruction. However, the container must be inspected. I expect no negative findings and it should be delivered to our hotel room later this evening."

"I'll miss you," Brownie said to his roach friends when they were hauled off by security officers.

"Get over lost relationships. I did," Faith said to Brownie.

At the hotel room, Brownie went to sleep and wouldn't eat or play when prompted until his roach friends showed up. Once they had arrived, his tail wagged nonstop.

"Why didn't you hook him up with a communication device and tell him that the roaches were on their way?" Tom asked Bucky before the staff meeting began.

"It wouldn't have helped. The technology can't communicate the emotional content that was needed. A dog is a dog is a dog."

"A log is a log is a log," Faith said.

"Stop interrupting," Lacy Dawn whispered to her backpack.

Brownie barked and sniffed the backpack. He wouldn't quit until Lacy Dawn put it on a high shelf in their hotel room closet. The others watched but didn't question.

"Here's the plan," Lacy Dawn said. "After we rest up a little, Bucky—I mean DotCom—please think of a way to disguise the roach container so we can take it with us shopping. I don't want anybody to see that we have roaches. I'll get fired for sure."

"Don't let the roaches get in here with me!" Faith yelled from the closet shelf. "I should've stayed at home Roundabend!"

"And been cold?" Lacy Dawn asked the closet.

"It's better than roach shit," Faith said. "Besides, I'm hot in love with Maple."

"I expect you to do your job. If you're going to whine the whole time you're here, maybe I should've left you."

"Sorry, Boss," Faith said.

Jenny looked at her daughter talking to the backpack on the shelf but didn't question it. Instead, she walked behind her and placed a hand on Lacy Dawn's forehead to check for fever. Dwayne and Tom straightened their postures, ready to take orders. Having felt no temperature, Jenny did the same. *Why is Lacy Dawn talking to her backpack? I'm just going to do what I'm told.*

A group hug later, Lacy instructed, "Brownie, you're not allowed to talk to anybody except one of us and the roaches. I'd trust you with my life but you don't know when not to say something. You're a big blabbermouth. Please don't say "roach" or "roaches" when you talk. Someone might overhear. This is like Tom's garden—a secret mission. Do you understand?"

"Of course, but please remind me again before we leave the hotel and a few times while we're shopping too," Brownie said through his language conversion device. *I think I understand.*

"Like I said before, our job is to pay close attention to Brownie. He's already told me last night that we're looking for Mr. Rump, the Roach Manager of the Mall—the big roach boss. You guys were asleep. I hope Brownie can talk with any roaches we find. Look for them real close. Since our roaches are back home on Shptiludrp, it's possible that they will be able to help more than when they were on Earth—it's their natural environment... Remember not to make fast moves or threaten if we get close to one or more roaches. They're paranoid and have experienced thousands of years of attempted destruction."

"I'm getting high for this trip," Tom said.

An hour later, they were on the slow beltway in their disguises. Tom had forgotten and left his super-sized penis—now very used—on Earth for Barb. A new roach container had been placed on a dolly. It had translucent perforated plastic walls so the roaches could see light, smell, and could peer through the small holes in the container. Brownie stayed beside the container and occasionally nuzzled it.

"They're still mad about getting sterilized and won't talk," Brownie said.

"We're too obvious. Let's buy something," Lacy Dawn said.

The team entered the closest shop.

"This shop sells perfumed disinfectants for septic tanks and sewage treatment systems," Bucky said. "Deliveries are made in mass quantity to planet addresses. You can buy a sample to take home."

"This one smells like Chanel No. 5," Jenny bought the sample on Bucky's debit card and the team left the shop.

"Not one roach in there," Brownie said. "Let's find a candy or a meat shop."

"There's a candy shop two doors down," Tom said. *I've got the munchies.*

"Now we're cooking with free gas from the well," Brownie quoted Jenny after they entered the store. Jenny patted him and browsed.

Jenny remembered: *Brownie was just a puppy when they drilled that well on our property.*

"Put the r—I mean the dolly—over here. Then, leave me alone," Brownie said.

The others shopped for candy. It was displayed behind glass-like cases on platters that revolved under changing white light hues. The cases had buttons that could be pushed to deliver a bite-sized sample.

"Not that platter," Brownie whispered to Jenny. "They shit on that one in protest. The shopkeeper murdered one of their relatives near there."

"Do you have any candy that is still hot and fresh off the press?" Lacy Dawn asked the shopkeeper.

"In ten minutes," it answered. *She must have known about the roaches in my shop.*

"We'll take five pounds when it's ready. Please put it in a sealed package that we can take with us."

Team members walked around the shop and looked at the displays. They didn't try any free samples. Brownie barked every now and then, wagged his tail, but didn't involve the humans in his research. Lacy Dawn sporadically rubbed his back. *I hope he's not so excited about meeting new friends that he forgets about the mission.*

"Hrrruff," Brownie said to the display case and walked out of the shop. The others followed. Jenny carried the candy.

"Well?" Dwayne asked.

"His office is in the sewer somewhere," Brownie said. "They've never been there. They recommended that we find the stink roaches and ask for help, but said not to piss them off or we'll be sorry."

Jenny gave Lacy Dawn the package of lime green fudge wrapped in clear plastic. The team got back on the slow beltway to talk. It made sense that Shptiludrp had sewers, but the team members had never considered their existence. The sewers were not a part of their employee-only inspection of the planet.

"I apologize," Bucky hung his head.

"Give me a piece of candy," Tom said.

"Me too," Dwayne followed.

"Me three, and four, and five," Bucky said, but didn't put out a hand for a piece of fudge. *They will have to wait for an explanation about Shptiludrp's sewage systems. I must follow instructions from the Manager.*

"Did the roaches in the shop say anything else?" Lacy broke off a hunk of candy for each including herself.

"Yes," Brownie continued. "First, they said that their boss lost his head during an extermination explosion in his youth. Second, the stink roaches may try to trick us with a fake manager. They will want us to get lost in the sewers. Even though most roaches only eat humans as a last resort, human-like flesh is a delicacy for the stink roaches. But, they won't attack. They will only eat human flesh that is rotten because it smells so irresistible. Once we get lost and you guys rot for a week or so, it's happy meal time."

"I want a piece of candy too," Faith said.

"You're already too fat," Lacy Dawn said to the backpack. It was lying on the beltway. The others looked at Lacy Dawn but still didn't ask why she talked to it. Jenny felt her forehead again. Lacy Dawn wrapped up the rest of the candy and put it in the backpack with Faith.

"I'm disgusted. All the talk about rotten flesh," Jenny said.

"Oh, I don't know," Brownie said. "Sometimes I like to nibble and roll in a fallen deer that has lain long enough to be stinky."

"Too much information," Tom said.

"Tell Bucky about it. He put this thing on me so you can understand. I was fine before. But no—now I have to save the universe. Not to complain, except you guys didn't even bring me a rawhide chew. How about some consideration? Okay, give me a piece of that ugly green candy. I need something before we go into the sewers. I held off on correcting you humans for as long as I could, but now it's time to either save or not save the universe. Please, get it together you guys."

Team members had not given the respect due to Brownie's contributions to the mission. Lacy Dawn reached down and opened her backpack to get the candy. Her team members gathered around and jockeyed for the best position to look into the backpack. Dwayne leaned the most. Still, nobody gave Brownie his due respect, so he asserted even more.

"Why did you bring a piece of firewood to Shptiludrp?" Dwayne asked.

"I'm not firewood!" Faith objected.

"The firewood said it ain't firewood," Brownie sniffed it to demonstrate intelligence.

"It's a long story. Let's concentrate to get this job done. I'll explain and introduce you when we get back home. She's a team member you can trust."

"Sir, yes sir," Dwayne said.

"I'm not prepared to go into the sewers," Bucky said. "I recommend that we return to the hotel room. I need time to download and analyze schematics of the sewage systems."

"Okay, everybody's getting grouchy anyway," Lacy Dawn said.

"I want some equipment—like a mask to filter the stink," Tom said.

Everybody except Brownie nodded agreement. They got on the fast beltway to return to the hotel room. Lacy Dawn put on the backpack to balance the weight of her fake breasts.

"We're privileged to have the opportunity to meet the real Manager of the Mall," the lead roach in the container told Brownie after they got back to the hotel.

"Cool beans," Brownie responded.

"We don't want you humans to mess up. We'll help in any way we can."

Brownie reported what the lead roach had said. The others listened without comment. They all looked at the backpack on the closet shelf. It stayed put. Dwayne approached the closet.

"Our roach friends promised to tell on the stink roaches if they try to trick us," Brownie continued.

Lacy Dawn nodded her acceptance of the report from Brownie and blocked her father in route to the closet. Nobody else tried to get the backpack. They just stared.

"Anything else?" she asked.

"Not of any significance," Brownie scratched an imaginary flea. *You promised to return to the container if we allow you out long enough to kiss the ass of the Supreme Being. I said I'd tell her but I can't do it. Sorry.*

A half-hour later, team members were suited to go into the sewers. A schematic of the systems was in Bucky's head. They left the hotel. Once at the right place, Bucky opened a floor-port into regions beneath the Mall. The team walked down a stairway that became a maze of sewer lines that led to the Cosmic Blaster—a big sphincter that blew waste products into the planet's atmosphere.

"Atmospheric decontamination will be accomplished if and when convenient and economical," Bucky continued the explanation of the sewage system.

Two steps down, roaches of different colors and sizes scurried. Team members held onto a handrail. Step by step, they descended.

"Tell your team members to stop for a minute so their eyes can adjust," Faith said. "Don't let them step on anybody." The firewood wiggled in the backpack.

"Hold up for a minute and be careful," Lacy Dawn said to the Team.

"You finally said something sensible, Faith." Lacy Dawn had leaned over her shoulder to whisper.

"Asshole," Faith accused.

"You wish you had one."

"Why didn't Mr. Prump have the sewage systems filled with a poison that worked?" Tom asked Bucky. "With all this technology on Shptiludrp, it seems like his scientists could have come up with something to kill roaches."

"I could provide numerous environmentally based answers. However, I am now permitted to tell you the truth. Before now, I was prohibited from full disclosure and it hurt me—as a human. The answer is that it would have been a violation of a treaty between cousins."

"I don't understand," Lacy Dawn made a step adjustment to avoid squishing roaches.

"The two Managers of the Mall are first cousins—they're both roaches. It is the most secret of all secrets in the universe. After you defined the problem statement, Lacy Dawn, I was provided additional information. Nobody else has ever been privy to this piece of history. I was instructed to withhold the information until you stepped foot in the sewage systems. Please use the information with extreme discretion."

"My first cousin was a Roach before she changed back to her maiden name and she has roaches in her apartment," Jenny said. *That was too stupid.*

"One manager manipulated his genetics to evolve into a human likeness and became Mr. Prump. It was similar to my manipulating my carbon base to become human-like. The other manager didn't. A little mechanics, cosmetics, and several thousand years later, Mr. Prump obtained a form best suited to his purpose. The Roach Manager, Mr. Rump, did the same except by maintaining roach attributes."

"Why did one want a human likeness?" Jenny asked. "I'd rather have three breasts."

"You are universally regarded as most pretty—stupid but pretty," Bucky explained.

"Thanks," Jenny said. "I'm so pretty, oh so pretty…."

"The two managers signed a treaty to respect each other's domains and agreed not to communicate so they would not expose their covers. Over the years, Mr. Rump may have lost control of his subjects—growth in population and their natural sexual tendencies. Mr. Prump believes that Mr. Rump's roaches invaded the surface of the planet in violation of the treaty. Whatever caused the infestation, nothing could stop it despite the killing of millions by every conceivable means. Both managers likely realize that Shptiludrp is doomed unless a solution is found."

"Why didn't you tell me all of this before?" Lacy Dawn asked.

"I was prohibited by Leon Sullivan's Principles. Mr. Prump decided that I could not tell you unless and until you made it into the sewers. He believes that you will solve this problem—one shitty step at a time."

"Instead of Leon Sullivan, you've been working the Leon Russell Principle," Tom said. "Whine until you dine."

"Yeah," Dwayne said.

"This ain't the time or place for team members to argue. Please get it together," Lacy Dawn stepped over a convergence of roaches.

They reached the bottom of the stairs and stood on a concrete-like walkway. Brownie did not estimate casualties during the descent. At the bottom, he snuggled his face on their roach container. Both the roach and human teams awaited his instruction.

"May I help you?" Said a twenty-four-inch high roach who stood upright.

"We would like to speak with Mr. Rump," Lacy answered. *That's one huge cockroach. I don't know if I'm ready for this.*

"Take a left."

"Liar," Brownie said.

"Be careful. He's a stinker," Faith said.

"You will be demoted or worse if we do not arrive," Lacy Dawn said.

"I'll lead you."

She nodded. *I trust Brownie, his roach team, and Faith. We'll be informed if there's one false move by Stinker. Otherwise, we're lost in the sewers and the universe will crumble.*

"One screw-up and you're dessert," Brownie warned the roach.

"I breathe out my sides but I fart out my asshole," Stinker said.

Feelings are So Much More than Seeing

The concrete passages accommodated roaches more so than humans. They were dim with an occasional wall light, but most were burned out. The air was thick, moist, and warm. The humans had to walk stooped over because the ceilings were low. The sewage flowed through what looked like plastic pipes that dripped at most joints.

"Do these air filters have a dial to turn them up?" Jenny asked. "I've never smelled anything as awful." *Maybe I should tell them the story about when the Revenuers almost busted Grandpa for making moonshine and he was saved when a smelly breeze stopped them from looking in the outhouse where he kept his stash. Naw, there ain't no breeze down here.*

The team followed Stinker. Brownie gave corrected directions based on input from his roach friends. The population became dense—everywhere: on the walls, ceiling, and catwalk. Like the Red Sea when Moses parted it, a path opened and closed behind as the team walked toward Mr. Rump's office. The metal handrail was not usable. It was a roach highway with two lanes going in opposite directions. Lacy Dawn concentrated. *Don't rush.*

Nobody touched the handrail. Lacy led. *I trust Brownie.*

"The left side of the catwalk is caved in six feet ahead," Faith warned. "Roaches on each side have clung to each other to mimic a solid surface. The handrail is gone. They've also clung together so that the handrail appears intact."

"Stop," Lacy Dawn said.

"Fart," Stinker said. *If they'd fallen off the walkway, we could have had humans for dessert next week.*

"How did you know?" Lacy Dawn asked her backpack.

"It felt like waiting to be switched. I checked out Stinker's intentions. He's meaner than my daddy and wants to eat you. Not the way the boys at school want. I mean really eat you. He's easy to read."

"The Manager is near," Brownie said to the team.

"How do you know?" Tom asked. "I can't see a damn thing."

"My friends told me. They can feel his power and are excited about the opportunity to be in his presence. See the light in the distance? They told me that he lives on a farm just beyond."

"Hug the wall to the right. Let's go," Lacy ordered.

The team proceeded and made a right turn in the passageway. They saw the source of the smell—a lake. Stuff floated on a thick liquid fed by open PVC-like pipes. Occasionally, things would break the surface like fish, except they did not look like fish. They looked like giant green turds with fins—giant green turds with fins—giant green turds with fins—more than were countable.

"There's a good pet," Dwayne said.

Vegetation grew under artificial lighting on the banks of the lake. Roaches a foot long walked on the banks. Single lines of ten or more roaches pulled ropes that were attached to different sections of plants. Smaller roaches walked to the edges of plant leaves and dropped their poop at bases. Other roaches mixed it into the soil.

"They're farming," Brownie said.

"No shit, Sherlock," Dwayne said. "I've spread enough manure in my day to know what they are doing."

"Be nice," Lacy Dawn said.

The team moved on the catwalk—one carefully considered step at a time. Jenny held Dwayne's hand—then Tom's hand too. Tom bumped Jenny's butt. *At last, it's the right opportunity.*

He did it again and again. *It's cool as long as Dwayne don't notice. Jenny won't mind. She understands.*

"Dwayne!" Tom shouted, stopped bumping and pointed. "Look there! If I'm not mistaken, that's a cash crop if I've ever seen one."

"Sure enough," Dwayne evaluated and reached over the handrail for a bud that he couldn't quite reach. He squished a few roaches with his movement. All stopped. The farmers stopped. The commuters on the handrail created a giant traffic jam. Stinky halted. Brownie's roach friends stopped running around inside of their container. What had been a constant motion of walls and ceilings became fixed. Only the turds in the lake moved. They continued to jump out of the goop.

A minute later, three very large roaches approached the team.

They walked upright and carried switches. Roach heads of various sizes bowed as they passed. The three climbed the concrete-like wall out of the vegetation toward the Team.

"Shit," Dwayne said for the group. "I haven't been switched since I was fourteen."

"It's about time," Faith said. *I see the justice.*

"Read them," Lacy Dawn said to her backpack.

"An eye for an eye," Faith said. *That should shake her up.*

"No, they're just Morgue Technicians here to do their jobs," Faith corrected.

"Be cool," Lacy Dawn said to her team.

The path closed in front and behind. One baby step by anybody would've resulted in more squished roaches and placed the team and its mission at greater risk. The humans bowed their heads, though Lacy Dawn and Brownie kept their eyes peeled.

"Crap!" Dwayne muffled a yell.

The roaches switched him again on the right ankle. Beads of blood stained his pant cuff. The other team members inhaled, held it, and stood still. Twenty seconds passed and they exhaled. Nobody else got switched.

"The Lead Mortician is sorry, Dwayne. He said that you couldn't avoid your murders and that he couldn't stop his switches," Brownie said.

The three large roaches paused above the remains that lay on the catwalk. They picked up the dead in their mouths and walked away. The largest roach pooped on Dwayne's left tennis shoe—twice.

"He said you are forgiven," Brownie said. "He understands how difficult it must be for a person to have been born into such an inadequate body—no antennae or feelers, an underdeveloped sense of smell, and dependent on eyesight that only uses one pair of eyes with one lens each. He asked that you please be careful."

"So you can communicate with them? Did it say anything else?" Lacy Dawn asked.

"He said that your mother has a nice ass."

"I think he's kinda cute too," Jenny responded.

Life Space Crisis Intervention

Stinky stopped at a doorway that had a tapestry hung over it and left. The paisley print was in constant motion like most of the ones at the fabric shop on the surface, but slower as if it was worn. They surveyed. The catwalk curved around the end of the lake and headed back in the direction that they'd just come from, but on the far bank. On the wall high above the ground at the end of the lake, a fan with twenty-foot blades turned slowly. A console with a flashing light was connected by what looked like electrical wires to the ends of dozens of sewage pipes.

Lacy Dawn pointed to the room. *We're at the anus. I don't want to be anywhere close when that fan comes on. There's no escape except to meet Mr. Rump.*

"Take off your masks," Lacy Dawn said. Team members took a deep breath, held it, and complied.

"Tell them to get rid of their masks—not just take them off. They should put all equipment on the catwalk before they enter. A very proud person is inside that room. Filtration of the environment will be seen as an insult," Faith advised.

Lacy Dawn so instructed per Faith's input. She had to yell above the increasing noise. The lights on the console were blinking faster.

"If we need them to leave the sewers, they'll be here!" Lacy Dawn yelled.

They held breaths that didn't last long enough. Jenny and Tom began coughing nonstop. Dwayne puked and Brownie took a quick lick of it. Lacy Dawn rushed through the doorway. The others followed. They faced a large wooden desk. The air was fresher. On a swivel chair behind the desk sat the largest roach that any human had ever seen—four feet tall and two feet wide. Mr. Rump faced away and typed. Data flashed on a large monitor hung on the concrete-like wall above the keyboard. As if yawning, wings emerged from the manager's back and retracted-- a six foot wing span. He farted for forty seconds— loud and blubbering. Lacy gave her team a thumbs up. *If that's his most significant comment, this is in the bag.*

"Please shut the door. It's time to expel," Brownie interpreted for the team.

After looking behind them, Tom helped Dwayne push a foot-thick metal-like door closed. Expulsion started like a jet taking off from the runway but a lot louder and ended two minutes later.

"Mr. Rump said to hold on for a minute until he's finished," Brownie reported. "He also said something that I couldn't hear."

"Be like you were when Dwayne wanted to kill your mom over the Playboys," Faith instructed Lacy Dawn. "I've been in these situations a million times after I died. It's just a big show to impress. Actual greatness is much less dramatic."

"I'll try," Lacy Dawn said.

"You'd better or we're all tacos."

Five minutes later, Mr. Rump swiveled around. On top of his roach body sat a human-like head that was identical to the head on Mr. Prump. Their mouths gaped.

"It's a black joke," Mr. Rump said in a voice that could be understood by all. "I lost my head during an explosion on the surface. I needed a replacement. My cousin had this one made for me. It's functional but not very pretty. Roach faces are beautiful. Don't you think so?"

"How did you survive such an accident?" Dwayne asked

Lacy Dawn gave him The Look.

"Roaches carry their most important brains in their bellies instead of their heads. I could've lived a couple of weeks without my head. I would've starved to death if my cousin hadn't saved my life with this replacement."

"Sometimes, you don't think with the head on your shoulders either, Dwayne," Jenny said.

"Why can we understand each other without Brownie?" Lacy Dawn asked.

"My cousin put all kinds of stuff in this head. There are almost as many brains in my new head now as in my belly. That's enough small talk. Have a seat and we can get down to business. I have an operation to run. I can't afford to waste time."

The team members looked around the room. There were no chairs. They sat in a circle on the concrete-like floor. Brownie lay down and appeared to fall asleep. Mr. Rump disappeared for a moment and reappeared as he squeezed under the bottom of his desk. He joined the circle, sat on his belly, and folded each of his six legs at three joints each. Lacy Dawn took off her backpack.

"First, I want to tell you that I know we're in a crisis," Mr. Rump said. "But, it is all my cousin's fault. He's a capitalist pig. If Shptiludrp loses its business and zillions of people are killed, I performed my job. He was the one who screwed up. He doesn't realize how hard it is to schedule workers down here. They sleep seventy-five percent of the time and eat half of the rest of the time. Think about it. Even though he gave me a computer and it's networked to the sleep areas, I still spend almost all my time just on work schedules. And, that doesn't count time off for Spermatophore or raising babies. He doesn't realize what a chunk of time maternity leave eats up. Now, he blames me for surface visits that he calls infestation. They aren't even my roaches. Those roaches on the surface came here from someplace else. He's done a bad job with his decontamination procedures."

"You sound frustrated and concerned about the situation," Lacy Dawn said. *I've gotten good at my active listening skills.*

"Sure, I'm concerned. We're all in this together. If Shptiludrp goes down, I go down with it. I don't want us all to die so someone else can construct another Mall. Without trade, Shptiludrp will not have energy. Everybody will freeze. That's the only way left to kill us. We've evolved to the point that we can detoxify all poisons. We're too smart to be tricked with bait. And, there's way too many of us to take out any other way. We'd come back. I may be paranoid, but maybe he does want Shptiludrp destroyed so he can say to everybody up there that he got rid of the roaches—as if he wasn't a roach himself."

"Let me get this straight," Lacy began. "Thousands of years ago, your cousin started to alter the genetics of my ancestors so I could be born to come here and freeze to death with you and your families?" Lacy Dawn rubbed the Manager's reality.

"When you put it like that, it does sound silly. But this situation is still all his fault."

"Good job. Nail him and he'll break," Faith whispered to Lacy

Dawn.

"Brownie!" A small, solitary voice screamed from the roach container the team had brought from Earth. Brownie's ears perked up. He nuzzled the box to get in a position for better reception. *Maybe I'm getting too big for my britches, if dogs wore britches, but I feel important again. I'm going to help to save the universe.*

"Is that my daddy?" the small voice asked Brownie, who blurted it to the humans like a good dog shouldn't. Lacy Dawn nodded. Mr. Rump stopped his presentation on who to blame for their threatened existences. With her pocket knife, Lacy Dawn unscrewed the eight Phillip heads and cut the silicone seal to remove the fine mesh lid off the roach container. *With roaches everywhere, it's pointless to have a few dozen incarcerated.*

Mr. Rump looked inside.

"I stand corrected. Some of my roaches must be on the surface," Mr. Rump said. "That one is my son," he pointed with a front leg hair. "What happened to his brothers and sisters?"

"The other roaches ate them," Brownie said.

"Please remove my son from that container."

Lacy Dawn nodded to Jenny. *Cool—a daddy that don't demand DNA testing. That's rare.*

Jenny peered into the container. After consulting with Brownie, she extended an index finger and the roach climbed on board. The other roaches in the container stopped movement. Jenny held the son out to the Manager.*This one is larger and has four orange spots on its back like Mr. Rump.*

"Put him on my desk," Mr. Rump put his face over the container and inhaled the entire contents into his mouth, bedding and all.

"Yuck!" Lacy said.

Brownie whimpered and pretended to go back to sleep in the corner.

"Good dog," Mr. Rump said. "Any dog that can make friends with roaches is someone very special. I had no choice but to destroy them. They're an inferior species that would have contaminated years of family-planning efforts. The females of that particular species put off such a strong odor that my males

282

can't resist—they abandon their work sites at times they are needed most. I'm sorry, Brownie."

"How can we save Shptiludrp?" Lacy Dawn asked.

"I'll get a nanny for my boy and then we'll talk. I could smell your body odors from when you first came into my domain. It got stronger with every step. I'd planned on giving you a lot harder time, but I didn't expect the return of a son that I had never met; a dog that makes friends with roaches; a leader who at fourteen human years is an expert in roach psychology; a maternal instinct from a human toward a roach nymph; a father who knows how to keep his mouth shut and to stay out of his daughter's affairs when she is doing well; an adviser who inhabits a piece of firewood; and a consultant who said nothing during a meeting. You are a well-put-together team. I'll be happy to work with you any way I can."

"Good job. Don't relax. It's far from over," Faith said once Mr. Rump had left the room.

Co-Dependency of Primary Missions

"The deal was that you'd get rid of waste products?" Tom interrupted Mr. Rump. *Let's figure out how to save the universe.*

The meeting had started with otherwise uninterrupted narration by the roach manager of the mall. The team was still sitting on the floor before the desk. However, Brownie was still in the corner, and Faith, who had been taken out of the backpack, lay on the desk. The firewood she occupied was the only decoration in the room.

"Why didn't you tell your team the history of Shptiludrp, DotCom? I'll have to start from the very beginning. You won't learn this in school," he leaned back and stretched his wings.

"Apparently, my databases have gaps," Bucky said.

"And your cousin would build and maintain a shopping mall on the surface?" Tom again attempted to redirect the meeting.

"Why did you enter into such a partnership?" Jenny asked. *I hate waste products.*

"At the time," Mr. Rump began and paused. "For thousands of Earth years prior to the establishment of Shptiludrp, ongoing war among planets had killed life forms indiscriminately. While motivated by the desire to exploit, war had also become a game."

Tom got off the floor and sat on a corner of the desk.

"Unless something could put an end to it, roaches were sure to eventually inherit the universe. However, on every habitable planet, we had evolved into mere defensive existences. There was no such thing as arts appreciation, interpersonal ethics, family values, recorded history, meaningful contributions, or anything else except survival instinct. Such higher values don't come easily to roaches anyway. It took millions of Earth years to cultivate them. The situation threatened the permanent extinction of meaning. In short, life would become very boring."

Dwayne sat on the other corner of the desk. *I wish you would shorten this boring story. My bad knee is killing me.*

"My cousin and I agreed that we wanted more out of life than mere survival. So, we decided to do something about it. We stowed away on a pirate ship that we knew would be launched to exploit anything left on otherwise dead planets. After it landed here, we incapacitated the ship by chewing through essential networks. Shortly, the crew members killed each other for fun. The ship was ours and that was the beginning of Shptiludrp. Here comes the good part."

"I'm sorry, but we don't have time to go through the entire history lesson," Lacy Dawn said. "My school starts in a few days and I plan to be home for it—regardless. I don't mean to sound insensitive, but human life is very short. Please get to your recommendations on how to save Shptiludrp in its current situation."

"Sorry. Nobody ever visits me and it's fun to have someone to talk to for a change. I guess I got carried away."

Mr. Rump got up, went to the corner of the room, and patted Brownie on the head. Brownie didn't open his eyes.

"How long since you've talked with your cousin?" Jenny asked. *Maury Povich.*

"I will need to check my back-up tapes."

"Guess," Dwayne insisted.

"It's been a few thousand years." He tried another pat.

"Ain't no time like the present," Brownie opened his eyes.

Team members stood up in front of the desk and stared at Mr. Rump.

"Do it now," Faith said. "If I'd told when I should have, I'd still be alive."

Mr. Rump crawled under his desk and into his swivel chair. The humans gathered around and watched the monitor. He opened his wings and his e-mail. *I'm not getting out of this.*

Brownie walked to the opposite corner of the room to talk to his last roach friend. It had grown up a lot since the beginning of the trip, but Nanny still wouldn't let him out of her sight. She was about the same size and color as Brownie's paw. He lay on the concrete floor beside her. "Hello," she said. Brownie wagged his tail. *I can't read email anyway.*

"Daddy's a good guy," Brownie's buddy said.

"Yes, but he ate my friends."

"The mean roaches ate my brothers and sisters," the little roach countered.

"Let's talk about something else…" Brownie pooped for his friend to play in. Nanny let him.

"It's been a while since I last talked to you," Mr. Rump wrote. "I decided to touch base." The Team read the English on the monitor until the email was sent. Lacy Dawn patted Mr. Rump's back. *He is trying to be a good host. He's just inexperienced.*

"How have you been?" Mr. Prump replied.

Lacy Dawn scratched her head, smelled her underarms for excessive body odor, and pulled her panties out of her butt crack. Exiting the scene was not an actual emergency. But, given increasing nausea, and that they had all become hot, sweaty, and had been on their butts or feet on concrete floors for hours, departure had become pressing, especially for Lacy Dawn. *I need to shit too and I ain't going to do it in a corner. It's going to take a while for the two managers to re-establish a positive relationship. We should come back later.*

She placed both of her hands over the keyboard to prevent him from typing and asked, "Is there a shorter way to the surface than the way we came in?"

"Sure. Straight up that stairway," Mr. Rump pointed. "When you get to the top, punch in 1, 2, 3, and 4 on the keyboard. The cover will open and you'll be in front of your hotel. Please move your hands."

"I don't remember why we had such a falling out," Mr. Prump had written. "I apologize for calling you a socialist."

"How do we get back in?" Lacy Dawn removed her hands.

"Knock three times on the cover if you want me," Mr. Rump said.

"Twice on the pipes if the answer is no," Jenny whispered to Dwayne. *If Tom uses one bathroom and Lacy Dawn uses the other, we can get in a quickie unless DotCom jumps in front.*

Lacy Dawn put Faith in the backpack and motioned her team to leave. Brownie said goodbye to his friend, who was still playing in dog poop under the strict supervision of his nanny. Mr. Rump typed on.

"Have Bucky intercept their email," Faith said as they walked up a spiral staircase to the surface. "And use the bathroom first when we get to the hotel because one of them will be occupied for a long time."

"Thanks," Lacy Dawn said. "I'm sure he has the passwords in his head. If not, I do."

Gushy-Gushy Don't Get Nothing Done

At the hotel, Lacy Dawn monitored the communications between the two managers, consulted with each team member, and called for a staff meeting five hours later.

"I know how to save the universe," she announced to open the meeting.

"You're a genius," Bucky said.

The others nodded.

"Now, it's just a matter of convincing the two managers to commit to the plan. C'mon, let's head back to Mr. Rump's office. I'll explain on the way."

"How did you figure it out, honey?" Jenny asked.

"I've had excellent advice," Lacy Dawn pointed first to the piece of firewood on the table, then to each member of the team in turn. She rubbed Brownie's belly. They left the hotel without gas masks or disguises and were immediately swamped by autograph seekers. Through the crowd, Bucky led the team back to the same place that they had exited the sewers several hours before. He tapped three times with his foot. There was no response. The crowd got thicker. He tapped again. Lacy Dawn and Dwayne signed autographs.

"Back to the hotel!" she said. *I hope my plan to save the universe works better than this one did. Some genius I am. I forgot all about us being celebrities.*

It took two hours to get back to their hotel. Twenty minutes later, they left the hotel again in their disguises. Once again, Mr. Rump didn't answer. They went shopping for a while and tried again later. This time when they tapped, the life form cover opened and the team descended into Shptiludrp's sewage system.

"Dude, what took you so long?" Dwayne asked on their way down the spiral staircase.

"I was communicating with my brother." Mr. Rump returned to his swivel chair in front of the monitor.

"I thought that Mr. Prump was your cousin?"

Lacy Dawn gave Dwayne the Look. *Daddy, you promised not to open your mouth.*

"We've become so close in the last few hours. We decided that the term cousin described too distant a relationship. Now, we are brothers for life," Mr. Rump responded.

Lacy Dawn gave her team The Look. They sat on the floor. Despite the hectic approach to Mr. Rump's office, they had been prepped and knew to sit.

"We have an idea that we would like your opinion about," she said.

"Okay. But, if it involves killing, I don't like it before you start."

"What about moving your over-population to a new planet—your own roach world. It has lots of food and fun things to do. It's a place where your people wouldn't have to work all the time. They could go there and come back to visit every now and then if they wanted."

"No such place exists," Mr. Rump said.

"Yes it does," Bucky got up and walked to the computer to demonstrate. He minimized the email and inserted a disk. "This was once an exploited planet. All of the roaches were killed. But, vegetation has grown back. With the export of a few animals of your choice, roaches will prosper on it. The atmosphere is compatible. The entire planet is temperate. The water tests cleaner than here. Drought has been demonstrated as an unlikely phenomenon during the next century." Bucky clicked the mouse here and there.

"It would soon become overpopulated as it is here. My people would resort to cannibalistic behaviors that would defeat the reason for existence." *I have no optimism left.*

"Due to lingering radiation from the exploitation, Spermatophore would not survive. As you know, they are much more fragile than roaches. The radiation is not strong enough to affect your migrating peoples. It is powerful enough to serve as a type of birth control—the population would remain constant for at least the next thousand years."

"Would they mutate into roaches even more ugly than my face?" Mr. Rump asked. *Is this possible?*

"I think you're cute," Jenny said.

"My research has found little support for the possibility of mutation," Bucky said. "I, of course, cannot guarantee anything. The radiation level appears likely to serve as birth control but insignificant to health. Because of your heavily built bodies, I believe that it will not affect a single roach's life or enjoyment of it. Without intervention, there will be fish in the seas of the planet within the next century."

Jenny smiled and winked at Mr. Rump. *Bucky could sell used cars like Dwayne.*

"Will you please stop flirting with every man you meet," Dwayne whispered to her during a lull in the presentation.

"I wish she'd flirt a little with me," Tom whispered to Brownie.

Brownie wagged his tail. *I hope I remember to tell this one to Lacy Dawn in front of everyone else.*

"Why is this planet still available for development? Who owns it?"

"At this point in time, no intelligent life form other than the roach can safely inhabit the planet," Bucky answered. "The lingering radiation would significantly shorten the life span of all others. It will also affect procedures for the harvesting of food animals, but not to an extent that would diminish supply."

"How much will it cost? Nothing is free on Shptiludrp."

"You already own the planet, Mr. Rump," Dwayne closed the sell as rehearsed. "It was where you used to live before you moved here. There's nobody else left to make a claim except your brother."

Jenny got up from the floor and gave Mr. Rump a kiss on what passed for a check. Tom approached and extended his right hand. It was grasped by three claws. Brownie went and nuzzled a leg. A tear hit the keyboard. *I became so involved in my work....*

"Email your brother to see what he thinks about the plan," Lacy Dawn said. "DotCom will provide the planet's coordinates and additional information as required. We need to bring your brother on board now. He needs to commit before it goes too far. Otherwise, he will reject the possibility just because he was not involved in the plan's development."

Mr. Rump typed. Tom gave him the handkerchief he'd been

told to bring. The email took fifteen minutes to write. After sopping tears and blowing snot, he clicked send, and laid his head on the desk to await a reply. *It's the only option. Lacy Dawn's brilliant. All my trials, Lord....*

"You nailed it," Faith whispered.

Mr. Rump paraphrased the business portion of the emailed reply. "My brother said that he trusted your judgment more than that of his own staff. He said that his staff has failed to deal with the matter for thousands of years and that you have evolved for this sole purpose—saving the universe. Please send the logistics so he can make preparations."

"Great! The proof is in the pudding," Lacy Dawn quoted her grandmother.

Mr. Rump got up and Bucky took his place at the keyboard. He first sent the planet's coordinates and then the other details by attachments. *This plan will work. The Manager of the Mall and his staff will be impressed.*

Mr. Rump snuggled up with Brownie on the floor.

"A protocol to minimize resistance to the proposal is still needed," Bucky said and typed. Based on consultation provided by Tom and approved by Lacy Dawn, he had already researched the Shptiludrp Personnel Department's structures, functions, and personalities. With the approval of his former boss, Bucky sent copies of the general email with specialized attachments for formal approvals through all of the chains of command on the surface of Shptiludrp. *Mr. Prump prefers to respect procedure. Proper distribution will ensure that this project is perceived as routine instead of extraordinary.*

"That's a smart boyfriend you've got," Faith said. "I wish I had a boyfriend."

"One thing at a time," Lacy Dawn picked her up and laid the firewood on the floor in front of Mr. Rump. "Besides, you've got the maple tree and she's probably better than any boyfriend."

"I know someone with a special talent for helping others," Faith said to Mr. Rump. He was curled up into a fetal position with six hairy legs around Brownie, but with protruding stiff wings.

"Who you gonna call?" Dwayne and Tom whispered to Jenny

at almost the same time.

Lacy knelt on the floor and faced the Roach Manager's back. "Guilt is like a series of powerful ocean waves that subside toward low tide—each a little less intense as time heals the innocent," she read his feelings.

"I know that I've got to do something about it. My neglect is already responsible for the destruction of one planet—my home planet with all the ones I loved. I don't want to be responsible for the destruction of the entire universe," he unhooked from Brownie.

"Lay on your abdomen. Take slow, deep breaths," she said. "Close your eyes...." His sides expanded and contracted. She placed her hand on his carapace and chanted, "All you need is love...All you need is love...."

"Where'd you get those good words?" Faith whispered.

"The Beatles, 1967, shh," Lacy Dawn continued. "Imagine that you're lying on a beach with your butt toward the ocean. It's a beautiful day with no pressing issues. A wave flows over you and back out into the ocean. It takes all your guilt with it into a body too large to notice, leaves you limp, and retreats. The next wave flows less powerfully, looks for leftover shame, and...."

Mr. Rump began to snore. Lacy Dawn shook him.

"Now, let's face irrational thinking. You were so busy saving the entire universe from total devastation. How can you blame yourself for loss of life...?" These treatments lasted for twenty minutes until Mr. Rump again sat before his monitor.

"So how do we get the roaches to want to leave Shptiludrp?" Jenny asked.

"Poison-free traps," Lacy Dawn said.

"You won't trick them," Mr. Rump said. "I'll try anything you advise, Lacy Dawn, but I know my kind."

"It will involve a lot of labor to move the traps to the ships, too," Tom said.

"Yes," she agreed with both. "And, there can't be another roach killed on the surface or they won't trust the traps. That kind of thing gets around—like in the hollow."

"I can order roaches under my control to load up. I have no control over the roaches on the surface. When I said that I thought that surface roaches were imported from other planets, I meant it. I admit that some of my roaches may have gone upside for a fling. I apologize for the breach in treaty, but I can't control them after they've been exposed to pornography."

"I've got it! I've got it!" Jenny said.

Brownie woke up.

"Sex—that's it. That's the only bait that works on your dad. It's the only bait that will get the male roaches in the traps."

"Mommy..." Lacy Dawn shut up when Dwayne and Tom nodded. *Adolescence is permanent and not just for males. I'm glad.*

"You've got a smart mommy," Faith said. "I wish I had a mommy."

"You do," Lacy Dawn said.

"She wasn't no mommy. She watched me get switched to death and didn't say a word to stop it."

Lacy Dawn pointed at Jenny and said, "There's your new mommy and she's a good one."

"What about all the other kids who need good mothers and fathers? They keep asking me to help and sometimes I can't turn off their screams," Faith said.

"If we save the universe, let's work on helping them together."

"Okay, just don't forget."

Bucky interrupted. "I can simulate the female roach smell that would attract all males."

"If anybody in the universe could do that, I just knew it would have to be you." Lacy Dawn smiled and gave DotCom his first hug in a month.

"My males wouldn't be capable of resisting. I can't address the sexual needs of the surface roaches. I shouldn't have eaten the ones that you brought in your container. I do have a few similar female roaches in captivity that would be appropriate to use for samples to simulate super strong sexual attraction."

"You pervert!" Brownie said. *You ate my friends.*

"I was developing the young whore roaches just in case my brother ever visited," Mr. Rump looked to Lacy Dawn for more guilt relief exercises.

You Don't Need No Red Light, but a Strong Back Would Be Helpful

"I don't have time for all this," Lacy Dawn carried another poison-free trap filled to the brim with male roaches to a ship's cargo bay. Dozens of other ships waited in port to be loaded and to transport the roaches to the new planet—temporarily called Plymouth Rock until its governing body could be established and come up with a permanent name. "School starts next week."

They had been moving the traps for three days. Muscles were sore, but the relocation of the male roaches to the receiving planet was progressing well. As analyzed by Bucky, there had been no negative impact on the immigrants caused by Plymouth Rock's leftover radiation. But, absent the female option, the male roaches were apparently so horny that homosexual activity had become commonplace.

"I don't have much time left either," Tom said. "It's harvest and you know how short the window of opportunity is in order to get premium bud. But, if we involve the locals to help, we'll blow this gig," He carried two traps in each hand. Bucky carried six. *I hope his garden is okay.*

The Team worked on a concrete-like surface bigger than that of the airport closest to the hollow. Lacy Dawn, Jenny, and Bucky carried the specialty roach traps from trailers driven by Tom and Dwayne—in disguise as garbage collectors so as to avoid attention, especially by autograph seekers. Most ships were about the same size as Bucky's ship—a small Earth school bus. Their lights blinked constantly. Pilots of various descriptions, who had been sworn to secrecy, leaned on their cargo bay attachments until time to help stack the traps. Ships came and went.

"Enough is enough. I'm going to email Mr. Prump," Lacy Dawn looked for a laptop. "This is ridiculous. We can't possibly relocate all the roaches in time for me to get home for school."

The managers arrived. She gave them The Look.

"Why didn't you direct more assistance?" Mr. Prump asked his brother.

"Why didn't you factor the logistics?" Mr. Rump asked back.

"They can't move all these cases themselves before we have a homosexuality crisis on the new planet. You know what they say about tight holes."

"That's why I'm here, Bro," one manager said to the other manager, who said the same thing right back.

"I'm not that tight anymore. I just can't find much that I enjoy spending money on." The two look-a-likes faced each other off. It was the first time that they had done so in millennia— formerly it had been a common occurrence. Tom stopped work. Bucky kept going and awaited a compliment for his dedication.

"The ship's full!" Brownie said. "I've reassured all passengers that they will arrive in a new place with lots of food and fun and no exterminations. The ship's ready to leave."

The pilot acknowledged Bownie's assessment and the ship departed. Personnel instructions had been clear. Brownie was the only one authorized to order the departure of a ship carrying roaches to their new home.

"I'm about ready to depart myself if you don't get it together," Mr. Rump said to his new brother / old cousin.

"This is it, girl," Dwayne said. Jenny huffed by his side. "I don't know how many more male roaches there are to capture and load, but I can't hang. We need some help."

"Yeah," Jenny sweated. "There could be even more female than male roaches. Everybody knows that it takes a lot more than sex appeal to attract females."

"It does?" Tom rolled up some inspiration for the break. Consistent with work ethic, all of the males, including the managers, took a hit or two. When the joint became a roach, Mr. Rump ate it.

"Here's the deal, dudes," Lacy Dawn said to the managers. "I've almost fulfilled my contract with the removal of the male roaches. My team's exhausted and we have pressing business on Earth. At this point, I'll take partial payment and let you two argue over the detail for the rest of the job."

"Wait a minute, sugar," Dwayne whispered. "You're tired. Remember when we bought your mom's new couch. Play it the same way."

"Relocation of the female roaches to Plymouth Rock will be

easy," she modified her negotiation strategy. "The females will come to you. You won't bait the traps with the same sleaze that attracts males into sexual interludes. The female roaches will board the ships without trickery or coercion if given the proper motivation and respect."

The managers nodded. Each considered: *I think I can respect females.*

Tom hung his head. *I've got some stuff to work on when I get home. No wonder I haven't had sex for ten years.*

"Tell us what to do. If it works, you've saved the universe, Lacy Dawn," Mr. Prump said. "I didn't expect all of the manual labor. Your team came through because you told them to. I certainly respect that."

"It sure did," Mr. Rump said.

"Bucky saved the universe. That's DotCom's name now," Lacy Dawn said. "Without him, we'd all still be sick, undereducated, and stuck in the hollow. He made us well, capable of love, and I'm going to marry him as soon as I graduate from college. He's got a penis. We're going to have a family as soon as I'm ready."

"Cool beans," Mr. Rump said.

"The last thing I need in order to authorize payment in full is your plan on female cooperation," Mr. Prump said. "Of course, payment will be prorated by outcome. My brother will take care of the relocation of his crews. It's the female roaches on the surface that now present the most difficult problem. A minimal number of roaches in the sewers will remain on Shptiludrp. A population is necessary to operate the planet's anus. I'm sure he will direct the rest to relocate to Plymouth Rock."

"What's it worth?" Dwayne said.

Lacy gave him The Look.

"If you're holding out for a bonus, it's okay. I've played that card lots of times and with lots of contracts. Before your involvement, the only options that I considered were extermination. It was a failed strategy that insulted my true background and killed millions of evolved life forms. You have shown me the light—to remain true to myself and my biology," Mr. Prump said.

"What a crock of shit," Tom said. *He's trying to personalize payment. It won't work on her. She's too smart.*

"Shit that will fertilize Plymouth Rock," Mr. Prump said. "Without roach shit, your planet wouldn't exist. My roach shit made your planet. Earth evolved into a place that produced Lacy Dawn to save the universe. It all started with roach shit and will be the same on the new planet."

"Sure does seem to grow great looking bud," Dwayne said. *He's trying to apply past payment to a contract that has a more recent effective date. It won't work on her either. She's too smart.*

"My cousin has a handsome face when philosophical, doesn't he?" Mr. Prump said, enjoying the self-compliment.

"I think he's kinda cute," Jenny said. *I'm getting in shape to keep up with the kids at Head Start.*

"This isn't rocket science," Lacy Dawn said. "Think about it. We captured almost all of the male roaches with sexual attraction. What do you think will capture all of the females?"

"Two hundred and seventy-three loaded ships of male roaches have left Shptiludrp for Plymouth Rock," Brownie reported.

Actually, two hundred seventy-seven ships had departed. Brownie didn't count that well and management information is always an email behind. Lacy Dawn gave him the play dead sign with her hand although it never worked until now. A minute later, he went back to work. The next ship launched.

"Two hundred and seventy-four," the managers incorrectly corrected at the next take-off. Final negotiations were being processed.

"My staff has removed and shipped over five thousand vegetable starters and one thousand fish turds for transplant on the receiving planet," Mr. Rump said. "And, we have a newly established government according to the most recent transmission," he pointed to the earphones he wore. *Don't look at me. I don't know how to attract females. I've never been any good at it.*

"So?" Dwayne objected to the diversions from negotiations.

"We have outlawed homosexuality until the female roaches arrive. Public masturbation is permissible and the new government has come up with a permanent name for the planet. The sex laws won't work, never have and never will, but they may keep sexual behaviors in the closet until the planet is fully populated and free choice becomes possible. After that, all private sex acts will be encouraged, except those which demonstrate an increase in health care costs, of course."

"Sounds like a place that I need to visit, badly," Tom said. "Did I ever tell you about...."

"What did you name the planet?" Lacy Dawn asked.

Dwayne gave Lacy Dawn The Look.

"Earth," Mr. Rump said.

Tom and Jenny placed their palms on their chests over their hearts. Dwayne saluted. Bucky entered the name into the universal database. When an error message indicated that "Earth" was a duplicate entry, he overrode the programming. Brownie said goodbye to more roaches. Jenny smirked.

"You guys sure are stupid," she said to the Managers.

"The planet's new government thought the name would be regarded as a tribute," Mr. Rump said. "You are famous."

"Not that," she took a hit from Tom's next joint. It was the first time in a long time and she regretted it immediately. "I meant you're stupid about how to get the female roaches to cooperate." *I always get paranoid when I smoke that shit.*

"Maternal instincts," Lacy Dawn said and Jenny nodded. *Males are ignorant.*

"Sorry. We have never and will never meet our mothers," the managers of the mall explained their conceptual deficiency.

"All you have to do is collect a few spermatophores and place them in the same poison-free traps on the ships. The female roaches will follow in hopes of fertilization. You won't have a single female roach that can resist maternal instinct if there is a possibility of a single birth," Lacy Dawn said. *I've completed my contract.*

"Brilliant," both Managers agreed.

"It's better to have a good mommy than just a boyfriend," Faith said.

"So true," Lacy Dawn agreed.

"I wish I could take a hit," Faith said.

"One thing at a time," Lacy Dawn reminded.

"What about our bonus?" Dwayne asked.

"When we get home, you'll get a bonus like you've never felt before," Jenny said. "I've learned a lot from the roaches."

Tom overheard and got aroused. *If that's what respect of women gets, I hope to learn it quick.*

"I'll let Brownie stay on the job until the females are loaded," Lacy Dawn said. "He can tell them about the trip to the new planet and can reassure the spermatophores. Sperm cells are much more sentient and aware of their circumstances than anybody will ever acknowledge on this or any other planet."

"I brought you a going-away present," Mr. Rump handed Dwayne a cigar-sized box of bud that had red fluorescent tips. The men decided to wait until they were home to try it out. Jenny looked in the box and backed away. Bucky continued to load roach-filled containers. He was beckoned to stop and to appreciate the gesture, but declined to accept immediate gratification. *I'm the designated driver.*

Lacy Dawn shook her head at the box. She had vowed abstinence. *Not until I've graduated from college.*

"There's a lot more work to be done in the universe, Lacy Dawn," the managers of the mall said at the same time.

"It's a kid's job to help save her universe and any kid who don't ain't much of a kid and maybe don't even deserve to live," Faith said.

The Team left the roach-loading area and walked to Bucky's ship. After hugs, Brownie bounded out. He had a roach on his back. The managers tried to capture it but the roach ended up a squish because two heads, especially artificial, are never better than one.

"Goodbye, P & R," Lacy Dawn yelled from the ship.

"I need some bacon if you expect me to continue to work on saving the universe," Brownie told the managers and continued to supervise operations. DotCom would come and get him when the job was done.

"One planet at a time, we'll rebuild the marketplace," Mr. Prump said.

"Not without some really rich roach shit—it's the catalyst of

299

abstract reasoning—spawns the evolutionary process...." Mr. Rump farted.

"You think I don't remember last eon?" Mr. Prump said. *This was a good session. Next time I'm going to listen to my heart and not just to the rumbling of logic. Thank you, Lacy Dawn.*

"Good job, Bucky," the Managers of the Mall yelled to the ship. It left to return to the primitive planet Earth, which had moved up several notches in universal standings.

Onboard, Dwayne begged, "Will you ever forgive me, Lacy Dawn? I used to be so mean."

"No, but I will always love you."

The End of This Adventure

Made in the USA
Middletown, DE
22 September 2018